Through the Red Door

Book Nirvana One

Sadira Stone

Through the Red Door

♥

Two good men vie to heal a widow's heart—but it only holds room for one.

Clara

Unless I find a lifeline, my bookstore will close its doors forever. My best shot at saving Book Nirvana is my late husband's collection of rare, racy books, but I'm not ready to open that red door and face the flood of memories. And I'm not ready to open my heart again, even if the two new men in my life tempt me to try.

Nick

I came to Book Nirvana in search of antique bawdy books and fell hard for lovely, lonely Clara. As a widower, I understand her skittishness, but the spark between us is undeniable. My academic connections could rebuild her clientele, but if she discovers my secret scandal, her fragile trust will shatter.

Dalton

I'm over the moon for beautiful, bookish Clara, but how can a teacher like me compete with a suave professor like Nick? Clara and I have so much in common, and our sweet friendship could bloom into something deeper if it weren't for my rival's grip on the vulnerable widow. I don't trust him, and neither should she.

Come to Book Nirvana for chosen family, laughter and tears, sizzling passion, and a love triangle for the ages.

Through theRed Door was previously published and has been revised and updated with new chapters.

A Note to Readers:

First of all, I do not use generative artificial intelligence in any part of my writing process. All my books were written by me, with feedback from my human editor and human beta readers. Different "authors" may make different choices, but I believe the best art comes from human minds, spirits, and hearts. Take that, robot overlords!

Through the Red Door was previously published under the same title by The Wild Rose Press in 2018 and has been substantially revised and updated.

Back then, I wasn't as knowledgeable as I am today about the usual structure of a romance novel. Thus, you'll see that most of the story is told from Clara's point of view, with only a handful of scenes from the hero's POV. In my later romance books, the POV distribution is more equal.

And it's a love triangle! I didn't know at the time that love triangles are one of the most hated romance tropes. Ah well, it is what it is.

Let me assure you, the guy who doesn't win Clara's heart gets his HEA in Book Two of the *Book Nirvana* series. I hope that helps you enjoy the story as it unfolds.

But despite its flaws, *Through the Red Door* is the book of my heart, filled with so much passion, humor, found family and tasty angst. This is the story that inspired my author tagline: *Pacific Northwest Romance with Heart & Heat.*

Clara, Nick, and Dalton's story has undergone some significant changes, including a switch to first-person point of view. I think it works well here and look forward to your feedback. As always, thanks for reading!

Contents

Chapter One

♥

Clara

The dream is fading fast. I snuggle into the warm sheets and cling to the last wispy echoes of Jared's touch. His hand slides up my thigh and traces the curve of my hip, igniting a silvery shiver of pleasure. He whispers against my throat and gently cups my breast...

The merciless phone alarm shatters my bliss.

With a groan, I roll over to his side of the bed.

Empty. Cold. Jared still visits my dreams, but the break of dawn carries him away like drifting smoke.

I reach for the framed photo on my nightstand. Astride his racing bike, my husband grins as if forever stretches out before him and the ride is all downhill. His triathlon T-shirt molds his muscular chest, and shiny spandex shorts hug his powerful thighs. He told me once that on his bike, he felt invincible.

He was wrong.

And so I begin another day of widowhood, aching for the soul mate a careless teen driver killed while checking her phone. All that remains are memories, echoes, and dreams.

I kiss his image, then wipe the smudge off the glass and sit for a long time on the edge of my too-large bed, gazing at nothing. A pair of little black-headed juncos hop on the linden branch outside my window. Jared loved that tree's perfume when it blossomed in early summer. He'd leave the window open, so we could wake to its fresh scent.

No flowery scent invades my bedroom this morning, but the tree will bloom soon, another sharp, stabby reminder of what I've lost.

Just two more weeks until the anniversary of Jared's death, and I still don't know how I'm going to make it through that day. At least I have work to occupy my thoughts.

I trudge to the bathroom, let my nightgown drop to the floor, and stand under the massaging showerhead Jared installed. Near-scalding water pummels my shoulders and trickles down my cheeks, making it easier to pretend I'm not crying.

A few months before he died, Jared finished this bathroom remodel, adding grab bars for the hot, slippery moments we shared beneath the steamy spray. I remember his muscular body pressed against mine, warm water flowing over and between us while his soapy hands slide over my skin, clutch my hips, lift my thigh...

—A jet of cold water breaks the spell. Once again, I've stood here dreaming until the hot water tank is exhausted.

I climb out and wipe steam from the mirror. Dripping wet and still flushed from the hot shower and hotter memories, I examine the dark circles beneath my eyes and pull out a tube of concealer. Damn, I'm almost out.

I yank a comb through my snarled hair, long overdue for a trim—but why bother? My customers at the bookstore don't care about my wild mane or my pale, unadorned face. I pick up a lipstick, then drop it back into the drawer. It'll take more than a swipe of color to revive my looks, especially after a year of the grief diet. Nothing tastes good anymore.

Squinting at my reflection, I trace my jutting collar bones, then the curve of my breasts, still reasonably perky for my age because I've never nursed a child. And now, I never will.

We'd been trying when Jared died, and for a few weeks afterward, I clung to hope. But no, it was just grief knocking my body's rhythm out of whack. There will be no baby with Jared's lake-blue eyes, his shiny chocolate-brown hair, his warm laugh. Yet another layer of regret weighs me down.

I quickly dress in a worn satin blouse and jeans, plus Jared's vintage tweed vest, then gulp down scalding coffee and gather my things for work. Our Eugene, Oregon bookshop opens at ten, but I like to arrive at least an hour beforehand to deal with paperwork, deliveries, and special orders.

Jared and I bought Book Nirvana from an old hippie couple the year after we married and devoted the next seventeen years to lovingly building up the business. Even though I sense his presence strongly there, the memories are gentler, easier to take than at home—maybe because I'm seldom alone at the shop.

There's Harry, our silver-haired part-time salesclerk whose crooked smile always lifts my spirits. And there's Margot, our twenty-year-old tattooed, spiky-haired pixie who works around her classes at the University of Oregon. Customers too, of course, though not enough. They come in to browse, sell used books, and pet Lulu, our aggressively friendly orange tabby. Besides soothing my gloomy moods with purrs and head-butts, she also keeps the mice at bay.

I can't afford to lose inventory to mice. In fact, I can barely afford to keep the shop running with just two employees. Since a major chain bookstore opened a few miles away, my stream of customers has thinned to a trickle. Jared would've known what to do. He was the one with business training and networking skills. My specialty is arranging the shop floor and organizing the books. Now, all the responsibility rests on my shoulders—hard work, endless worries and decisions—but

I'm determined to hang onto what Jared I started together. Book Nirvana is all I have left.

The brass doorway bell jingles as I let myself in and pause for a moment to breathe in the sweet, musty scent of books, old and new. If I could bottle that perfume, I'd make a fortune. Who can resist the warm woody bouquet of paper and lingering vanilla top notes?

An hour before opening, the shop is an oasis of tranquility. I set my bag on the glass counter, then check the round oak table where we display books by local authors. As usual, Lulu tumbled the books during the night. The yellow vase of daisies will last for another few days, and Margot did a good job of neatening up the kids' corner, though I'll probably find building blocks and plastic dinosaurs stashed in unexpected places. Those littles are wily.

Relishing the stillness, I scan the aisles for loose or mis-shelved books. When I reach the rear wall, I trail my fingertips over the red door, its shiny lacquer smooth and cool.

Jared's low, sexy chuckle echoes in my memory.

I lean my forehead against the painted wood and close my eyes. My hand drifts to the doorknob, then drops.

It's too soon. I can't.

Purring like a motorboat, Lulu hurries over to twine around my ankles.

"Good morning, puss-face." I scoop her up and bury my nose in her silky, book-scented fur. She indulges me for a moment, then twists out of my grip and trots to her food dish with a demanding yowl.

After serving her majesty's breakfast, I turn my attention to the wheeled cart of books waiting to be shelved. I enjoy tucking new acquisitions into their proper place, setting everything to rights. Today's cartload includes a half-dozen copies of a local writer's latest mystery, several cookbooks, and a stack of slender graphic novels: anime, horror tales, and urban fantasies.

With all these nestled into their spaces, I return for the last book on the cart. My breath catches when I spy the bright pink Post-It on the cover. This volume is bound for our special collection.

Even though I'm alone, I glance over my shoulder before opening the big coffee-table book of African erotic art. The first full-color page depicts a gleaming wooden sculpture—a stern male figure with an elaborate headdress and a huge, erect phallus. Heart hammering, I slam the cover shut with a bang.

The special collection was Jared's baby. He lovingly curated hundreds of erotica books and arranged them in the cozy room behind the red door. Visitors who cross its portal can browse beautiful volumes of artwork, photography, Victorian erotic stories, and more. Truly, it boggles my mind how many ways people have dreamed up to celebrate sexuality.

I keep the back room locked, of course. Can't have kids wandering into the adult collection. I only unlock it for non-creepy-looking adults. Over the years, I've learned to detect a certain vibe that signals potential sticky spots left behind.

After losing Jared, I'd just as soon forget about the walls of sexy books. Let people think the red door leads to a storage closet. But even without advertising, our special collection continues to draw a steady stream of collectors and connoisseurs.

A smart business owner would build on that advantage, but since Jared's death, I haven't set foot inside the red room, too intimidated by the tumble of memories, the echoes of passion. Images of beautiful people sharing ecstasy still ignite tingling warmth between my thighs, a reminder that my body is very much alive. But those books, those feelings also fill me with aching sorrow for what I've lost.

Jared used to bring home volumes from our adult collection, and we'd page through them together, curled up on the couch. Literary foreplay.

I close my eyes and drift back to Jared's deep voice narrating an erotic story by Anaïs Nin while his free hand delves inside my top, teasing my nipple with feathery strokes...

The doorway bell tinkles, jolting me from my reverie. Harry backs into the shop, his long arms wrapped around a plastic storage bin. I blow out a shaky breath, set down the book, and trot over to help.

"Good morning, Boss Lady. Glorious weather, eh?" He beams, then peers closely into my face. "You okay? Your cheeks are flushed."

"I'm fine. I, uh, overslept. Had to rush. What's in the bin?"

"Why, we talked about this yesterday. Don't you remember? Margot and I are redoing the front window display." He pries off the plastic lid to reveal a collection of seashells. "She's making a sign: *Your Perfect Beach Read.*"

"Oh, right." I start toward the counter, then swivel back to Harry. "There's no beach in Eugene."

He chuckles. "Actually, there is, along the river. Anyway, the idea's what's important. The beginning of summer break is a great time to grab new customers."

God knows we need them. Spring has been slow at the bookshop, with barely enough profit to keep the lights on and make payroll. And our lease expires soon. Our landlord hasn't raised the rent in years. If he does...I try not to think about that.

"I'm sure it'll be beautiful, Harry."

"Damn skippy!" He deposits the bin behind the counter and rubs his bony hands together.

Before he came to work for Jared and me, Harry was a postman, which accounts for his trim, wiry build and deep tan, now maintained by a daily run. If I were thirty years older, I could fall hard for handsome Harry. His dazzling white hair gleams in the sunlight streaming through the plate-glass window. He sheds his denim jacket and pulls on his Book Nirvana apron.

The aprons were Jared's idea, deep red, emblazoned with '*Serving up delicious reads since 1973*,' technically true because we bought the shop from an old hippie couple who settled in Eugene after the Summer of Love.

Harry gets to work on the window display, leaving me to concentrate on paperwork and the few customers who wander in. When Margot arrives a little after two, I retreat to my office, really just a small desk behind a carved wooden screen. I'm ready for a coffee refill when she knocks on the screen and peeks around the corner, her eyes twinkling.

"Hey Clara, there's a dude here who wants to look in the back room." She waggles her thrice-pierced eyebrows. "You wanna check him out, or should I just give him the key?"

"What's he like?"

Margot rolls her eyes heavenward. "He's gorgeous!"

"Well then, guess I'd better have a look." I'm curious to see what sort of guy merits that label in Margot's world.

I stride around the screen and skid to a stop.

She's right. He's gorgeous.

The man leans over the counter, examining the fliers posted there, so my first view is the firm curve of his behind, cupped by soft wool slacks. His crisp white dress shirt stretches across broad, muscular shoulders, and his rolled-up sleeves reveal powerful forearms dusted with sleek, sable hair. At my approach, he straightens to greet me, a half-smile on his full lips.

I gulp, and my hand strays to the locket nestled between my breasts.

Dark eyebrows arch over his espresso brown eyes. His nose is straight and sharp with flaring nostrils, and his olive complexion whispers of strong sunlight. Mediterranean, or maybe Caribbean? A shadowy beard dusts his jaw, and when he inclines his head to smile down at me, one perfect black curl flops onto his forehead. The hand he extends is broad and warm and surprisingly gentle.

I gaze into his sparkling eyes, step in closer—then jolt backward, startled by my own reaction. Not since Jared have I felt so compelled to touch a man.

"You must be Clara. I'm Nick." His voice is deep and velvety, like rich dark chocolate. Weird—I'm suddenly hungry.

He reaches into his breast pocket and hands me his card: *Nicolas Papadopoulos, Ph.D., Professor of Cultural Anthropology, University of California, Berkeley.*

I fan myself with the card, then tuck it into my pocket. My hand lingers over my heart, toying with my locket, a nervous habit since childhood.

The professor's eyes home in on my fiddly fingers. "That's a lovely piece you have."

A hot flush races from my belly to the roots of my hair. "What can I do for you, Professor Papa...um?"

"Just Nick." His slow smile is mesmerizing.

"You're certainly the tallest Greek I've ever met." I wince, mortified. In nervous moments like this, I tend to blurt whatever stupid thought comes to mind.

"My dad was Greek," he explains. "The height comes from my mom's family."

Something about the professor's elegant posture reminds me of the sculpture from this morning's new book, gazing imperiously into the distance, its oversized phallus at attention. A shiver dances down my spine.

"Sorry, I just...what can I do for you, Nick?"

"Ah. Yes." He takes a step backward and clears his throat.

Is he flustered as well? A smile tugs my lips upward. Who'd have thought I still have the power to fluster a man—especially one so jaw-droppingly handsome?

"I'm researching for a book project" His gaze flicks toward the back wall. "Your collection is well spoken of in my circles. I hope to find some new material."

"Anthropology books?"

He clears his throat and rocks back on the heels of his expensive-looking Oxfords. "My specialty is cross-cultural sexual practices and mores." He flashes a bashful smile, his eyes cast downward.

Is he for real? He certainly looks the part of a professor, and his business card seems legit.

"Well, since you're an expert..." As I reach behind the counter for the red room's key, the motion tugs my blouse loose from my jeans. When I turn to hand it over, I catch his gaze flicking upward from my butt.

I tug my blouse back down and hope he doesn't notice the blush staining my cheeks. "Pull cord for the lights is on your left. Please let me know if I can be of any further assistance."

"Or me!" Margot pipes up from the children's section.

She's been listening, then. Well, who could blame her? We both watch him stroll languidly down the cooking aisle toward the back room, turn the key, and step inside, pulling the door closed behind him.

Margot fans herself with a Doctor Seuss book. "What a hot-tay! Mama like!" She waggles her eyebrows. "Why don't you give him a tour of the special collection?"

I aim for a nonchalant laugh, but my jaw clamps so tight that it comes out a choked squeak.

Margot hurries over and drapes her skinny arm across my shoulders. "God, how stupid am I? I'm so sorry, Clara." She squeezes me in a side hug. "It's too soon, right? Sometimes I forget. I mean, I don't forget about Jared, of course not. I just don't think..." Poor girl looks like she wants to crawl under a bookshelf.

I return her hug. "Hey, kiddo, you meant nothing by it. All the same, I think I'll leave the back room to you and Harry a while longer."

With the distressingly handsome visitor safely out of sight, I force my attention back to my work. I file invoices, clean fingerprints from the glass counter, and restock paper bags, but again and again, my gaze is drawn to the red door.

Chapter Two

♥

Nick

Book Nirvana is aptly named, that's for damned sure.

There are places in this world where a person feels instantly at home, and Ms. Clara's shop is one of them. The sweet, almost edible scent of books hangs in the air. Early-summer sunlight bathes the space in a welcoming glow and highlights the colorful posters on the walls—Peter Max's psychedelic sunset pointing toward the art books, the Beatles' Yellow Submarine above the music section, and a lush still life of fruit, bread, and wine for the cookbooks. Farther down, I spot comic superheroes, a futuristic spacescape, an armored knight charging into battle. Above the famous red door, Ingres's *La Grande Odalisque* throws a languid glance over her bare shoulder—at once an invitation and a dare.

But the jewel of the collection is Clara herself. My buddy at the University of Oregon told me about the pretty shop owner, but "pretty" hardly does her justice. A hint of fire glimmers in her unruly dark hair. Like the Pacific on a stormy day, her eyes shift between green and gray—eyes a man could get lost in. Something about this woman revs my pulse.

So what do I do to impress the lady? I ogle like a horny teenager as her delicate fingers fiddle with the locket between her breasts. And of course she noticed.

At least she let me enter her erotica collection. Leo, a cultural anthro prof like me, warned me I'd have to pass Clara's inspection before she'd unlock her red door. And what I've found on the other side is breathtaking.

This snug, richly decorated room is the perfect metaphor for my book project, an invitation to discover sensuous secrets. Red tones bathe every inch of this jewel box, from the worn Persian carpet to the reddish-brown bookshelves that fill the walls floor to ceiling. In the corner, there's an ornate wooden stepstool to help visitors reach the top shelves. In the center of the room, a plush antique love seat with an S-curved back so that two people can sit side by side facing opposite directions. I run my hand over the scarlet velvet, worn bald in places. What kinds of spicy conversations have played out on this odd little sofa?

I picture myself seated here, opposite Clara, a large, illustrated book balanced between us—maybe a Japanese pillow book? Ancient Indian temple carvings? Bewigged Baroque lovers cavorting in manicured gardens? Clara's pretty mouth falls into an O of surprise, her hand grasping mine as an erotic image makes her breath catch and then quicken...

I shake off the inappropriate fantasy. I'm here for work, not seduction, no matter how lovely the bookshop owner is. I've got too much riding on this project to permit any distractions. Besides, carrying a torch for a woman who lives so far away is pointless.

I fire up my tablet and get to work.

Two hours later, my rumbling stomach reminds me how long it's been since lunch. I stand and stretch my shoulders, stiff from hunching over books. Exploring this treasure trove in just one session is impossible. I've got two weeks in Eugene before I have to return to Berkley for my summer graduate seminar. Hopefully, the lovely Clara won't mind me hanging around her secret chamber.

Since I'll be spending so much time here, I really should take her out for coffee. Strictly a professional courtesy.

Right. Would I ask her out if she weren't so stunning?

Of course I would. We share a common interest. And it's just coffee, right?

My conscience harrumphs. "Hands off," the pesky little fucker grumbles. "Don't mess up a valuable connection."

He's annoying, my inner chirpy cricket, but he's right. I've learned the hard way that mixing business and pleasure can be disastrous.

Nevertheless, this kind of work requires caffeine, so I smooth my shirt, square my shoulders, and open the red door.

"Be right with you," a female voice calls. While I wait at the counter, a sleek orange tabby cat trots over, sniffs my pants leg, and meows. I crouch to stroke its silky fur, and the cat answers with the loudest purr I've ever heard and twines around my ankles in a figure eight.

"Wow, she really likes you." Clara's spiky-haired young assistant rounds the corner, pushing a book cart. "Lulu, don't trip the customers."

Clara steps out from behind a carved wooden screen—Balinese, if I'm not mistaken. Just for a split second, her eyes widen and her lips part. Then the moment passes, and her startled expression relaxes into a cool smile. It happens so fast I almost doubt my perception. But no, that spark was real. It echoes behind my sternum, a powerful magnetic tug.

"Did you find something interesting?" she asks.

I hold out the old-fashioned key, but it sways on its velvet cord and slips from her grasp. Don't want her to think I'm toying with her, so I take her hand in mine and place the key in her palm, a simple touch that shoots a thrill of warmth up my arm. "Interesting is not a strong enough word for what I found here."

From behind the cookbooks, the young assistant titters like a demented sparrow.

I clear my throat and tap the cover of the book I'm holding. "I've never seen a finer volume of Japanese Shunga. I'll take this one today, please."

"Would you like me to wrap it for you?"

"In plain brown paper, you mean?" I suppress a teasing grin, noting the rosy wash tinting her cheeks. "No wrapper needed, thanks. I want to read it right away. I'll be back for more volumes soon." I hold up my phone. "I hope you don't mind. I took some photos to present to my department chair in hopes of enlarging our collection."

"Oh. Er, yes. Of course." Clara rings up my purchase.

I glance over my shoulder at the assistant, who makes a show of arranging comic books. Yeah, she's definitely eavesdropping. I lean onto the counter and lower my voice. Clara's rose perfume wafts between us, rich, simple, ripe.

"I noticed the little coffee shop next door. Can you spare me a few minutes to discuss your collection?"

Clara seizes her lower lip between her teeth. Her gaze flicks toward the front door and back. Seems I'm the only customer at the moment.

The beauty squares her shoulders. "Margot, I'll be next door for a few minutes. Can I bring you anything?"

The girl grins. "Oh no, I'm fine. You go ahead, Boss Lady. Get off your feet."

As Clara steps around the counter, Margot shoots me a merry wink.

I duck my head to hide my grin. Looks like I have an ally. Now, to disarm her skittish boss.

·❤ · ❤ · ❤ · ❤ · ❤·

Clara

When Nick holds the door of Coffee Dreams for me, I pass close enough to inhale his cologne: fragrant wood, a touch of moss, and a hint of old books. When his warm breath brushes the back of my neck, my knees wobble just a tiny bit.

What's wrong with me? Handsome men come into my shop all the time. Why is this one making me so dizzy?

Relax, you goof, I tell myself. It's just a coffee break. We're in public and fully dressed. If the conversation lags, I have the perfect excuse to flee back to my desk.

The tempting odor of fresh coffee and sweet baked treats reminds me I haven't eaten in several hours. Since losing Jared, I often feel disconnected from my body, as if sensations like hunger or fatigue are happening to someone else, not to me. But my stomach picks this moment to rumble loudly as I approach the glass case laden with muffins and fat cookies.

"I'll have a large cappuccino and one of those blueberry scones," Nick tells the server. "And the lady will have..." He smiles over his shoulder.

"I'll have the same, thanks." My greedy stomach clamors for more, but I restrain myself, not wanting to abuse his hospitality.

"Let's sit over here by the window." Nick indicates a low armchair for me and lowers himself gracefully into its neighbor. He takes a bite of his scone, then carefully wipes his fingers before opening the book he bought. The endpaper inside is swirled with cloud-like designs in delicate blues and grays. When he turns the page, my eyes bug out.

The drawing fills two pages: a Japanese courtier, his silk kimono open, presents a kneeling geisha with his huge, engorged penis, dark purple and ridged with bulging veins.

My fingers clench around my scone, crushing it to smithereens.

"Oh crap, I'm sorry." I drop the mess onto my plate and brush crumbs from the page, which sends them tumbling onto Nick's lap. I reach for his leg, realize what I'm doing, and snatch my hand back, mortified.

My hands fly to my glowing cheeks—probably just as flushed as that enormous painted penis.

"Here, let me get you another scone." Nick rises and moves to the counter, giving me a minute to swallow my humiliation and clear away the evidence.

While his attention is diverted, I can't resist taking a peek. The next two-page spread displays an orgy scene: an elaborately coiffed woman astride the huge cock of an elegant, balding man who reaches out to diddle another woman between her splayed thighs. Surrounding them are six more women, each rubbing a companion's foot against her own clitoris, all of them entwined in an intricate human knot.

Jared and I were adventurous lovers, but this is beyond anything we ever tried or even imagined. Turning the book sideways, I peer closer at the drawing. Something touches my shoulder. Startled, I squeak like a little girl and slam the book shut.

Beside me stands Nick, the smutty professor, holding a plate with two scones. Is that a blush coloring his chiseled cheeks? With his dark olive complexion, it's hard to tell. I lower my gaze and find myself staring right at his crotch.

Damn it!

With no safe place to direct my eyes, I close them and take a deep breath.

Nick chuckles, a low, rumbly sound. "Sorry, Clara. Beautiful women bring out my devilish side. Please forgive me." He slides a new scone onto my empty plate, then sits beside me. "I guess Shunga isn't everyone's cup of tea."

"Shunga?"

He opens the book and points. "This type of painting or woodblock print. There's usually a funny text to go with it."

He balances the volume between us, resting on the arms of our chairs, then glances at me, one eyebrow raised.

Okay, Clara, pull up your big girl panties. You can handle this.

I nod.

Nick flips to a new page. "These beautiful costumes and hair arrangements date from the Edo era, roughly the 1600s through the mid-1800s. And here's the text." He points to columns of delicate characters.

"Can you read it?" I ask.

"Not very well. I have a friend here at the university who can help with the translations. This really is an extraordinary book." He sips his coffee and flips the page.

"Are their, um, private parts always so large?"

He flashes another wicked grin. "Always. You know, it's funny. In European artwork, male genitals are often unusually small, compared to..." He glances at his own lap.

I follow his gaze, then jerk my eyes away. My voice cracks like a twelve-year-old boy's. "Yes, I've noticed."

"But in Shunga, all the genitals are outsized."

"Doesn't that scare women away?"

"On the contrary—these drawings were presented in 'Pillow Books' designed to instruct young couples in the art of love."

He flips another page. A lovely woman gazes serenely into the distance, combing her flowing black hair, while her open kimono displays her large, fuzzy bush. A man crouching to watch her from behind an urn appears to be salivating.

Nick flips the page again and points to an image of a couple going at it fiercely. "Notice how the woman's toes are curled?"

I giggle. "I thought that was just an expression. You know, he made my toes curl."

Nick closes the book. Something mesmerizing and a little bit dangerous glimmers in his dark eyes. The corners of his full lips twitch upward. "Everyone deserves to have their toes curled, don't you think?"

My ribs seize, halting my breath. Discussing sexy artwork with this gorgeous professor is a weird combination of awkward and titillating, but this is tipping into flat-out flirtation. Nick's warmth, his husky voice, the erotic images laid out before us—it's all too much. I'm hot and tingly, squirmy with embarrassment, and heavy with guilt. I'm not ready to feel this way again, despite my body's undeniable reaction.

Time to be honest with this kind man, before he takes this any further.

I clear my throat and sit up straighter. "I'm a widow, Mr. Papa—Nick. My husband passed away a year ago."

His teasing smile melts, and his dark eyes shine with emotion. "I'm sorry, Clara. I hope I haven't made you uncomfortable." He lays his hand over mine, his touch warm and gentle. "I lost my wife two years ago. Cancer."

The tension drains from my body like water through a sieve. He understands.

"My husband is the one who took care of our..." I gesture to the open book. "...our special collection. I haven't set foot through that door since he died. But we still get a lot of visitors wanting to see those books. They used to talk to Jared, but now I have to screen them."

"How do you decide who's allowed inside?"

"Gut instinct. People have a certain oily vibe when they just want to leer at dirty books. And they'd usually be disappointed. I mean, it's mostly older stories and artwork, and most of the books are quite expensive, which keeps the perverts away. They're hoping for cheap porn, not art."

The corners of his mouth quirk up. "So, why did I pass the test?" Deep within his dark irises, flecks of gold catch the light.

"Well, you are a professor and all."

"I am indeed. And you know what they say about us academics—'Publish or perish.' I heard about you from a colleague at the university here. I've been under pressure to publish something new, so..." He pulls out his phone and taps the screen. "I made a list of titles I'd like to buy for my department. It might take a few days to get an okay from our chairwoman. If I send you the titles, will you hold them for me?"

That means he'll be back, giving me time to reflect on my reaction to this deliciously disturbing man.

As if reading my mind, he adds, "I'd really appreciate your help. And if I can't get funding, I'll buy them myself. These books are nearly as fascinating as their owner."

I gape like a goldfish, then fold my hands in my lap and paste on a pseudo-calm smile. "I'd be glad to hold the books for you, Nick."

I'd be glad to hold anything he wants me to hold.

For a terrifying moment, I'm sure I said those words aloud. I take a deep, trembling breath.

So does Nick. He gives my hand a final squeeze. When we stand up, I notice the top of my head only comes to his chin. I've always had a weakness for tall men, especially ones with deep, velvety voices, sparkling dark eyes, devilish smiles—

I squash those dangerous thoughts into an iron-clad box and slam the lid. This is a business connection we're forging, a potentially valuable one. "Right. I look forward to seeing you soon."

"Not as much as I look forward to seeing you, Clara." My name slides off his tongue like a caress.

As I walk toward my shop, the heavy warmth of his gaze heats my back. Just to be sure, when I reach the sidewalk, I turn for one last glimpse. He's still watching, a mysterious half-smile on his lips.

Chapter Three

♥

Clara

What the hell was I thinking?

Back behind the safety of the wooden screen delineating my office area, I collapse into my chair and hide my roasting-hot face in my hands. If I didn't know better, I'd suspect Arnie, my barista buddy next door, slipped something into my coffee. Is it possible to get drunk off a man's smoldering gaze? And is that yearning simmering in Nick's dark eyes, or am I just flattering myself?

He's probably just one of those guys who flirts with everyone. Thinking of him that way makes it easier to face the prospect of seeing him again when he comes for the rest of the books on his list.

Guilt pinches me hard, right in the gut, because lusting after someone new feels like a betrayal to Jared. He's only been gone a year, for cripes' sake. There's no way I'm ready for a—what, a fling? A flirtation? A hot tumble among the naughty books?

But the thought of running my hands over Nick's tawny skin warms me in places that have been too cold for too long.

Gripped by frustration and shame, I scan my desk for a distraction. The bills overflowing my inbox clamor for my attention, but I need to move my restless body. Since customers have the annoying habit of re-shelving books any old where, there's always work to be done.

I find a cookbook in the mystery section, children's picture books in the history aisle, and gardening tomes planted among the memoirs. As closing time nears, I'm rearranging art books back near the special collections room. I jiggle the antique glass doorknob, just to be sure. Shut tight. My fingers slide over the door's shiny red lacquer, cool and smooth.

"Good night, Boss Lady." Up front, Margot shrugs into her leather biker jacket. "I'll see you tomorrow afternoon."

"Thanks, kiddo. Please lock up. I'm going to stay here a bit."

She pauses in the doorway and regards me, head cocked to the side like a curious bird.

"Was there something else?"

"No. Well, yeah. I mean..." She fiddles with one of her jacket's many zippers.

"Out with it, then."

Since the day she came to work at Book Nirvana, I've held a special fondness for Margot. If Jared and I had a daughter, she'd probably resemble this lively little bohemian.

Margot's sigh puffs out her cheeks. "I just worry about you. You should be out having fun. You spend too much time here at the shop." She twirls a hand as she searches for the right words. "Before Jared, you know, you used to have this light about you, and now it's so dim." She wrinkles her pointy nose. "I'm not explaining this well."

Eyes prickling with tears summoned by her sweet concern, I push up from my crouched position at the bottom shelf, cross the distance to Margot, and enfold her in a tight hug. "Thanks for caring, kiddo, but I'm fine, really. In fact, I have a date to meet with my girlfriends tonight and guzzle some wine."

Which is a bald-faced lie. The only girlfriends I'll be communing with are characters on a reality TV show. The wine is real enough, though.

Margot's grin lights up her pretty pixie face. "Okay then. Good for you."

She has a point, damn it. Since Jared's death, I've spent far too much time alone. Many of our friends have trickled away, uncomfortable with the singleton in their smugly married midst. A few steadfast friends from college still squeeze me into their busy schedules, but not as often as I'd like. And I'm partly to blame. I've turned down too many invitations with the excuse of needing to work. After a while, people gave up trying. And so, once again, I find myself alone on a Friday night.

At seven, the sky is still light, but a summer storm is brewing. Dark clouds roil overhead, and a brisk wind blows trash into little sidewalk cyclones. The humidity pulls my hair into curls which escape my chignon. Surrendering to the inevitable, I remove the pins and let it fall.

How have I become such a shaggy beast? My reflection in the window gazes back, a wild Celtic warrior-woman from a romance novel cover, battle-weary and scarred. But instead of a tightly laced bodice, I'm wearing one of Jared's old tweed vests over a black satin blouse. Since his death, I never leave the house without something of his—sometimes his favorite pendant, a silver Celtic knot on a leather cord, sometimes the scarf his mother knitted for him. His scent faded long ago, but burying my face in the soft wool still comforts me.

I rub the worn tweed between my fingers and summon the memory of his face. "What shall I do, my love? Something's got to change. I can't live the rest of my life in this shop."

No answer, but somehow, Jared's presence surrounds me. In this bookstore we built together, his love, his warmth, his pride in what we made still linger.

It was Jared who refinished the round oak table holding our display of recommended books. It was him who installed the ornate crown molding overhead and stenciled the gold lettering on the front window. His vision polished what had been a dingy, dusty space into this warm, welcoming shop. Stepping through its door always buoys my spirits.

But if I don't find a way to draw in more customers, I'll soon lose this refuge. Then what?

A soft knock on the window startles me from my reverie. Harry stands under the awning, sheltering from the rain. He grins and waves.

I hurry to let him in.

"Harry! What brings you here so late? Don't you have a date tonight?"

Beneath his standard-issue Pacific Northwest rain jacket, he's dressed to impress in charcoal slacks, a crisp Oxford cloth button-down with natty yellow stripes, and a tie printed with Van Gogh's sunflowers. A broad grin creases his weathered face.

"Yup. This one's special, so I want to look nice." He pulls a comb from his pocket and tames his wiry white hair. "I'm meeting her up the street at Pomodoro. Saw the lights on in here." He pivots to show me his outfit. "So, do I pass inspection?"

"Very snazzy. If you weren't already booked, I'd ask you out myself."

He drops the grin and takes my hands in his. "Clara, I want you to think about something."

Uh oh. Harry knows about the ever-growing pile of bills and the ever-shrinking profit margin. He's come up with dozens of ideas to bring in more customers: a slam poetry competition, a drink-and-paint night. He's even suggested a yoga class among the exercise books.

His wiry eyebrows draw together. "You know I love you like a daughter, and I want you to be happy. Don't you think it's time to meet some new fellas? You can't live the rest of your life alone."

My shoulders sink under the weight of his kind but insistent gaze.

"It's too soon, Harry. I just—I'm not ready."

"Look, kiddo." He leans an elbow on the counter, bringing his gaze level to mine. "I knew Jared for years before I met you, and I know he'd want you to live a full life."

The force of my sigh lifts a stray curl from my forehead. "You're right. I just can't deal with dating yet."

"I'm not saying you have to get serious about anyone, but don't you think it's time to dip your toes in the pool?" When I don't answer, he continues. "It was really hard when I started going out with ladies again, after Eleanor..."

A few years back, Harry bought his wife a laptop for her birthday. She became a social media addict, reconnected with her high school boyfriend, and ran off with him, leaving Harry devastated.

"The thing is, Clara, I'm happy again. I have friends, and I have a new love. You could have that too. It's what Jared would want for you."

I don't answer, too choked up to speak, but he lifts my chin until I meet his gaze. "You won't find love hiding out among your books."

The kindness of Harry's words and the weight of their truth make my eyes mist over. Seeing my reaction, because my wise old friend notices everything, Harry pulls me into a warm, bony hug. After a moment, he clears his throat and grasps my shoulders gently.

"What, Harry?"

"So, there's a nice young guy in my running group." His eyes twinkle.

"How young?"

"Around forty. He's divorced, a high school teacher, good-looking fellow. Thought I might bring him by the shop, show him our running books."

I give a little snort. "Show him me, you mean?"

"Why not? I can vouch for his character, at least. He's a nice guy, and funny too."

I cock my head, taking in Harry's hopeful smile. Like Margot, his gentle prodding comes from a place of love. And why not? I've already had coffee with a handsome stranger. One more won't hurt.

"Sure, I'd like to meet him."

"Good." He strides to the front door, leans out, and whistles.

"Wait, you mean now?" I rake my fingers through my humidity-snarled mane. "Harry, I'm not—"

"No time like the present." He grins, the sneaky devil.

Panicked, I duck behind the screen and fumble in my purse for my hairbrush and lipstick.

A moment later, the doorway bell tinkles again. With a gulp, I force my hunched shoulders down and step out to face my surprise blind date.

Harry stands grinning beside a tall, lanky man who gazes bashfully at the floor. He raises blue eyes to meet mine, flashes a wry grin, and shrugs. I chuckle in sympathy. This poor guy seems just as embarrassed as I am. And I have to admit he's kind of cute.

He's wearing a dark windbreaker over jeans and expensive-looking running shoes. He removes his knit cap to reveal a shiny shaved head, but his bony face is unlined, and an attractive blond scruff covers his sharp jaw. When Harry pokes his shoulder, the visitor ambles over and extends his broad hand. His touch is light and cool—comfortable, even.

My shoulders unclench. He's a local and an athlete. Familiar territory.

"Hi, Clara. I'm Dalton Garvey, from Harry's running club. Sorry to come by so late. I got caught up in a parent conference..." His voice is deep and gravelly.

"No problem, Dalton. I'm always glad to meet Harry's friends." A giggle escapes. "Dalton. Sounds like the hero of a cowboy romance."

He gives a one-shoulder shrug and a sheepish grin. "My dad's a huge fan of westerns. I'm more of a history guy. Harry tells me you have an impressive collection."

My gaze flicks to the red door, then to Harry, whose smile is the picture of innocence.

"Were you, uh, looking for anything in particular?"

"As a matter of fact, yeah. *Born to Run*, by McDougall."

My relief escapes in a giggle. Two red room visitors in one day would push my limits to the breaking point. Sports books? Piece of cake. "I think we have a copy. Right down this aisle, second shelf on the left."

Harry makes a theatrical gesture of checking his watch. "Oh my, look at the time. I'd better hurry or I'll be late. See you tomorrow morning, Dalton?"

"Wouldn't miss it," Dalton calls over his shoulder.

I grasp Harry's elbow and whisper, "Give me a little notice next time."

"If I had, you'd have chickened out."

He's right. I probably would have. When the door closes behind Harry, I go back to help Dalton find his running book. He's waiting for me in the sports aisle, book in hand, and smiles at my approach. Nice smile. Open, unguarded.

"Harry was right." He inclines his head toward the bookshelves. "Your collection is better than the big chain store across town."

"Tell your friends. That store's been sucking our customers away."

"Well, you've got something they don't."

I glance at the red door behind him. If he only knew.

"Personality," he continues. "That other place feels like the mall. Your shop is more..." He trails off under the weight of this awkwardness.

"Thanks. We try." I gaze down at my feet.

Dalton clears his throat. "So, Clara, do you run?"

"Depends on who's chasing me." Oops. I didn't mean to sound so flirtatious. "Sorry. I'm sure you've heard that dozens of times."

"More like hundreds." But his kind smile reappears.

"I've done some running—not much in the past few years, though. I've been pretty busy with the shop."

"Right. Harry told me about your husband." His voice softens. "It must be so hard, continuing after someone you love is just—just gone."

This time, I don't tear up. Interesting. Usually, my eyes mist over when anyone offers words of sympathy. Could Margot and Harry be right? Maybe I'm finally ready to begin the process of moving on.

That thought sends guilt worming through my gut.

"You should come meet our group," Dalton says, seemingly oblivious to my inner battle. "Lots of good people."

"Oh, I'd be lagging behind you, I'm sure."

"There are plenty of beginners. And Harry's not breaking any speed records, but he always finishes the race. I admire that."

"Harry's a good man."

"He is." He glances down at the book in his hand. The overhead lights gleam off his shiny bald scalp. How would that bare skin feel under my fingers?

"So, um, Clara..."

Here it comes. He's going to ask me out. Do I want him to?

"Could I interest you in a cup of coffee?"

"Now? It's pretty late."

He taps his watch, a sleek model that probably monitors his mileage, his pulse, and God knows what else. "Oh, Jeez, sorry. How about a beer, then?

When I hesitate, he adds, "I won't keep you long. Just one drink?"

It's a beer, for goodness' sake, not a big wining and dining deal. And once upon a time, I was brave. I miss that Clara, the one I lost in a fog of grief.

I raise my chin and look him in the eyes. "Why not?"

He blows out a long breath, then grins. It's comforting to realize he's as nervous about this as I am. Maybe Harry gave him a push as well.

We spend a pleasant hour perched on bar stools in the noisy tavern up the street, sipping Ninkasi IPAs, sharing a plate of tater tots, and talking about our town. How did I miss meeting Dalton before now? He grew up in Eugene, plays darts at a pub near my house, competed in the same triathlon as Jared two years ago, has even visited Book Nirvana a half-dozen times, yet I've never noticed him.

I answer his questions about the shop, steering the conversation away from Jared.

He tells me about the social studies classes he teaches at North Eugene High School and about caring for his ailing mother. "A little more of her slips away every day, you know? It's hard."

When I squeeze his hand, he holds on for a long moment. His grip is gentle, smooth and dry, but no sparks of electricity zing up my arm, nothing like the full-body flush Nick's touch ignited. Just a pleasant warmth. In the long run, isn't that better? No man could ever replace the passion I shared with Jared, so why even try?

"So, our runners' group meets at Blackbeard Coffee, Saturdays at eight. You know the place?"

"I do."

"Why don't you come by tomorrow? Harry will be there. You don't have to run the first day, just say hi."

"But if I want to run?"

A broad smile lights up his bony face. "That'd be great. I'll introduce you to Mona. She's always glad for someone to bring up the rear with her." His gaze slides down my body, and he quickly corrects himself. "Not that you'd be slow. You look pretty fit."

Skinny and fit are not the same thing, but I don't spoil the moment by explaining how grief zaps my appetite. "Okay then, I'll think about it. And thanks for the beer. I'd better get back home."

He walks me to my car, parked in front of the bookshop. While I fish in my bag for my keys, he shuffles his feet on the pavement, reminding me of a cute, gawky adolescent.

"I hope I see you soon, Clara."

"Me too." The orangey light of the streetlamp gilds the pale scruff on his jaw. How would he react if I stood on tiptoe and kissed his cheek? Would his skin be scratchy beneath my lips? Would he kiss me back? Would I like it if he did?

I give my head a little shake. What's wrong with me today? Since meeting Nick, I'm not myself.

I climb into my old Subaru and roll down the window to wave goodnight.

"Drive safe," he calls as I pull away.

The misty rain patters softly on the windshield, blurring the familiar route toward home.

What a nice guy. Maybe this is the right path for me—just a nice, ordinary guy to share occasional evenings with. Someone to ease the loneliness, someone who doesn't make me nervous and jumpy, like Nick does. Dalton's touch is gentle, comfortable, while Nick's is too electric, too magnetic.

Too dangerous.

Chapter Four

♥

Clara

Jared comes to me again in a dream so vivid, I'd swear he's haunting me—if a haunting could be so sensual. He lifts the sheets and slides into bed beside me. The pale moonlight reflects in his midnight-blue eyes as he presses his warm, muscular body against mine. Holding my gaze, he skims his hand up my side, his fingertips tracing little whorls on my belly. He breathes my name, then buries his face in my hair and kisses the sensitive skin behind my ear. I wait, afraid to move, almost afraid to breathe lest I break the spell. Even asleep, I know this encounter is fleeting, and yet I'm so grateful to feel his touch again, to hear his voice, to taste his skin.

"Clara." He sighs, shifting his weight over me. The box springs creak as his body drives me deeper into the mattress. "My lovely girl."

He's called me that since our college days. I'd been with a few boys before Jared, but he was the first one who really loved me, who knew how to melt my reserve and open me, body and soul, like a full-blown rose. I always felt beautiful in Jared's arms.

And now his hand slides down to caress my inner thighs, tracing a silvery line of pleasure up one leg and down the other, barely brushing the soft, yielding flesh between, until I clutch the sheets and throw my head back in frustration. Every cell in my body cries out for him.

In the moonlight, Jared's roguish smile gleams. This is no misty, insubstantial vision. He's right here with me, as heavy and warm as in life. He leans in to nibble my lower lip. "You want?"

In a voice hoarse with need, I groan out, "I want. Oh God, I want."

His lips brush slowly, teasing as they feather down my throat, between my breasts, over my belly, down, down, down. When he finally reaches my tingling clit, I lift my hips to reach for his kiss. With exquisite slowness, he parts my slick folds with the tip of his tongue and licks me once, twice, and then slides back upward, his skin warm against mine, the length of him filling me in one delicious rush. His hot mouth clamps onto my shoulder as he thrusts hard and fast, banging the headboard against the wall.

I grasp his back and raise my legs to take him deeper, my heels digging into his muscular backside. He bucks against me, sending waves of electric pleasure up and down and in and everywhere, sparkling like stars beneath my skin until I cry out and clutch...

The long body pillow Jared gave me the last Christmas before he died. Just some cloth and stuffing, damp and warm but not alive, not a man, not my love. As the pulsing between my thighs subsides, I sob into the pillow, whispering his name again and again.

"Come back to me, Jared, come back..."

The sight of my tear-swollen eyes and blotchy face is almost horrifying enough to keep me from joining Dalton and Harry's running group before work. Then again, don't most runners have blotchy faces by the end of a run?

"Just go," I tell my reflection while adjusting my headband. Since Jared's death, I've let the physical side of my life fall away until—well, here I stand, pale, flabby, and pathetic.

At my husband's side, I spent whole days biking on rough trails, hiked Mount Hood, and swam in the sea. Now, my only exercise is toting books. Though I'll probably come in dead last, running outdoors with a bunch of strangers will at least get me out of my sluggish rut. Jared would approve.

And so I pull on my running tights, lace up my long-neglected Nikes, and drive across town to Blackbeard Coffee. Soft spring air caresses my cheek through the open window.

At this early hour, most of the Market District is still dark, but cars pack both sides of the street near the café. Walking from the public lot two blocks away, I count a dozen *26.2* bumper stickers. Great, Harry's running club is full of marathoners—as if this isn't already intimidating enough.

Through the glass front, I see runners from early teens to eighties jammed into the narrow coffee shop. Fighting the urge to flee, I square my shoulders, whisper, "Fake it till you make it," and step inside.

Happy voices echo off the café's cement floor and walls, a roar of greetings and conversation punctuated by hisses from the espresso machines. I spot Dalton's shiny, shaved head above the others. Catching my eye, he waves and slides through the crowd, then takes my hands like it's the most natural thing in the world, as if we've been friends for a long time. The corners of his blue eyes crinkle into smile lines.

"Clara. I was hoping you'd come."

"Yeah, well, I could use the exercise. And I felt like trying something new."

I wince, realizing how flirtatious my words might sound, but Dalton's relaxed smile doesn't flicker.

"Here, let me introduce you."

I follow him, watching the easy movement of his long, graceful body as he makes his way back to the counter. Dalton is taller than Jared, with a runner's wiry muscularity. His shoulders are broad beneath his reflective windbreaker, and his legs are sculpted like a superhero's. I bite back a giggle at the thought: Super-Dalton, swooping in to save me from isolation and indecision.

"Clara, this is Mona." He grins and slings his arm around the shoulders of a plump woman about my age with sturdy legs encased in hot pink, tiger-striped leggings. A neon-orange sports bra corrals her enormous boobs beneath her unzipped Oregon Ducks hoodie, and a turquoise headband restrains her corkscrew curls. She's a running rainbow! And the bright colors she wears don't come close to outshining her smile as she grabs my hand and squeezes.

"Hey, glad to meet you, Clara. Dalton says you haven't run in a while."

I give her a sheepish grin. "Yeah, I hope my knees don't give out."

She pats my hand. "Well, you just take it easy today. Stick to the back of the pack with me. You've got long legs like Dalton. I'll bet you'll be chasing after him before long."

Does she mean...? I glance up at Dalton, whose cheeks are bright pink beneath his blond scruff.

"Clara!" A pair of strong arms wraps around my shoulders from behind and squeezes. "You came! Good girl." Harry presses his scratchy cheek against mine.

"Oof. Easy, Harry." I rotate to greet my old friend—and matchmaker, it seems. Caught in the act of winking at Dalton, Harry grins and shrugs.

"Will we be back in time to open the shop at ten?" I ask Harry.

"I'll open today. You take your time, Boss Lady. Enjoy yourself." He pats my arm and moves off toward a pair of sleek, gray-haired women.

Dalton rolls his eyes. "Harry's kinda..."

I nod. "He's a good soul. And he likes you. That counts for a lot with me."

He grins down at his shoes. "Thanks."

His shyness is dangerously endearing. Or maybe it's just the unaccustomed early start that's got me feeling a little off-balance and giddy.

After everyone arrives, an older man briefs us on the day's route, and we set off, heading toward the river. Huffing and puffing, I chug past shuttered art galleries, antique shops, and bars, struggling to keep pace with the pack. I'd forgotten how hard the first minutes of a run can be. My leaden legs protest every step. Rosy memories clash with painful reality—how did I ever think running was fun?

But after ten minutes of hell, my endorphins finally kick in, my gait smooths out, and I settle into an easy, fluid rhythm. I grin at the road stretched out before us and the bobbing backs in front of me. Look at me—running again! For the first time in ages, I'm fully in my body and in the moment, and it's freakin' exhilarating.

The pack of runners stretches out as the speedier ones take the lead, Dalton among them, Harry not far behind. Soon, we leave the busy downtown streets and turn onto the South Bank path along the Willamette. The broad river slides smoothly past, its surface glittering green. The sun warms my back, and a cool breeze refreshes my sticky brow. Despite the effort required to keep up, I'm loving the camaraderie of all these people running together. I'm actually having fun! How long has it been since I could honestly say that?

Mona keeps up a steady patter of conversation, testimony to her superior lung power. "So, bookstore owner, huh? Must be fun."

"It is," I gasp, "but the record keeping is a lot of work."

"Man, I'd love that. I'm a CPA." Puff, puff. "For city water and electric." Huff, puff. "Not exactly thrilling, but it pays the bills, ya know?" Puff, huff. "Only books I see are the ones I bring in." Huff, huff. "Love me some romance books. You know, the spicy ones. Muy caliente."

Thus begins a breathless exchange about favorite books and authors, and before I know it, we're rounding the corner back onto Pearl Street. Blackbeard Coffee is just a few blocks ahead. Buzzing with the thrill of victory, I pick up speed.

"Come on, Mona. I'll buy you a coffee."

Red-faced and panting, Mona matches my burst of speed and grabs my hand as we cross the imaginary finish line, applauded by the others gathered in front of the coffee shop.

"Tah dah!" Mona pumps our clasped hands overhead. "You did it! Four miles, baby!" She pulls me into a squishy, sweaty hug.

My grin stretches ear to ear. "Great run. Thanks, Mona."

"Any time. You come back next week, you hear?" She peers into the crowd and waves overhead like an excited kindergartener. "Here she is, Dalton."

Dalton pushes his way toward us. He's shed his windbreaker, and his faded marathon T-shirt is plastered damply to his chest, revealing chiseled pecs and a tight belly.

I yank my gaze back up to his flushed, grinning face. "You finished! Really good, Clara. How do you feel?"

"Marvelous!" A hundred percent truth—my blood is singing, my cheeks are hot, and my legs tingle. I know I'll pay for this workout later, but right now, I feel like I could fly.

"Two days. Epsom salts." Mona gives my back a hearty pat.

"Huh?" I turn to ask for clarification, but she's already moved back into the café.

"She means you'll be sorest two days after the run," Dalton says. "A hot bath will help relax your muscles."

"With Epsom salts. Right." I grin up at him, feeling a little giddy. From the run, no doubt.

"Do you have to leave right away?" he asks, his eyes lingering on my face, not my sweaty bod.

Bonus points for class, Dalton.

"Pretty soon. Saturday afternoons are a busy time at the shop. But I promised Mona a coffee."

"Good. Can I join you?" His smile is lopsided, a bit bashful, and very charming. No wonder Harry thought I'd like him. He's easy to talk to, and I could use a little easy.

Over foamy cappuccinos, Dalton and Mona introduce me to several members of the running group, a friendly bunch from widely different backgrounds, united by their love of running outdoors. Even though they're all way ahead of me in terms of endurance and speed, every single one of them makes me feel welcome and at ease.

Afterward, my hips protest when I hop down from my bar stool. Mona chuckles knowingly. "Take a few Ibuprofens, hon, and just keep showing up. That's the important thing. Running is wonderful for clearing your mind, even if it hurts sometimes."

Dalton walks me back to my car and waits while I unlock the door and peel off my clammy windbreaker. Sweat has glued my workout top to my skin., and when I look up, I find him gawking, pale eyes wide and lips parted.

He chuckles and gives his head a shake.

"Sorry, Clara. You're, um, very pretty. I hope you don't mind my saying so."

"Not at all." In fact, his compliment brings a smile to my lips, though I certainly don't feel attractive in my wind-blown, sticky state. "See you next week, then?"

"Count on it." He flashes a broad grin, takes a few steps away, then turns back. "Say, do you like musicals?"

"Sorry?"

"You know, *Sound of Music, Cats, Les Miz.*"

"Oh, um...sure. I mean, I'm not a singer or anything, but I like to watch musicals."

"Our school's drama club won a state-wide competition, so they're putting on an encore performance at the park's amphitheater on Tuesday night. It's *Little Shop of Horrors*. Lots of my students are in the play, so I pretty much have to go." He twists his knit cap in his hands. "Maybe you'd like to come?"

A high school musical? Of all the dating scenarios I imagined, this has to be one of the most unexpected. On the other hand, he's hardly likely to make a move in front of his students, so really, it's just a friendly night out, a symbolic toe-dip back into the kinda-sorta dating pool. If it doesn't feel right, we can go back to being running buddies—no harm, no foul.

Plus, Dalton's hopeful expression is kind of adorable.

"Okay, why not? I'd love to."

He pulls his cap back on and grins broadly. "Cool. I'll pick you up at six. At your shop? We can do dinner first if that's okay. You like Thai?"

"I do. I'll see you then."

I shake my head and chuckle. A new hobby, a new friend, and a new date, all in one morning.

Driving home, a jarring realization hits me—I haven't thought of Jared since I left the house. Neither have I worried about the bookshop or Nick, the too-handsome-for-my-mental-health professor who jolted me with his smoldering gaze and his flirtatious ways. Huh. I feel...relaxed, I guess. Maybe even a little bit like my old self?

The memory of Dalton's friendly, lopsided grin follows me back home. When I emerge from my post-run shower, I point my toe and flex my quads. Maybe I could become a real runner, even train for a race. As Mona said, running is a great way to clear the mind, and mine certainly needs clearing.

I towel off and, humming, let my imagination wander. I picture Dalton's tall, lanky form behind mine, his shiny, shaved head gleaming, his pale eyes darkening as I stroke lotion onto my legs, smooth it across my belly and hips. How would his long fingers feel on my body? Would they glide across my skin like this? Would they cup my breasts with whisper softness, or grip me urgently?

A stiletto of guilt shatters my steamy daydream. What the hell is wrong with me? What kind of wretch desecrates the home she shared with her dead husband by fantasizing about a new man?

Dizzy and nauseated, I clutch the bathroom counter and gulp deep breaths.

This can't be healthy, this sickening fear that grips me whenever I think about moving on. My lonely home has become a shrine to lost love, a cave where I hide from the outside world, my broken heart wrapped up in memories.

But you can't live in a shrine.

I meet my own gaze in the mirror, my vision misted by tears.

"What should I do, Jared? I ache with missing you, and I'm so damn lonely."

A soft breeze lifts the bathroom curtains. With a whispering sound, they settle back against the wall. I grip the towel tightly over my thundering heart. Is that Jared's answer? He visits me in my dreams, but can he reach me during my waking hours?

Through the open window, a fat black fly buzzes into the room, zooms in frantic loops, then pings off my forehead.

"Oh, God." I collapse in a fit of giggles. Here I stand, naked and dripping, searching for messages from the great beyond, and what do I find? A fly. With tears of laughter streaming down my cheeks, I roll up a magazine and chase the little pest back through the open window.

I skid to a stop. Poised on the windowpane, a butterfly gleams like moonstone, a gossamer creature of silvery blue. I hold my breath. The tiny flier slowly closes its wings, then opens them.

"Are you…" I don't finish the thought because that possibility is too eerie to say aloud.

The butterfly slowly folds its wings again, opens once more, then flutters away, dancing on the wind.

I stare after it, hand to my heart, my mouth open in wonder.

Chapter Five

♥

Clara

"Hey Clara," Harry calls in passing, "some guy from the U of O was here asking for you. He left a note. It's on your desk."

Nick. My mouth silently forms his name. He said he'd be back soon for more books. Is today the day I must face him again?

At the counter, Harry chats with a sixty-something couple wearing motorcycle leathers.

"Here's our boss lady." His grin etches deep parentheses in his tan cheeks. "Molly and Dave brought us some good stuff."

On my way to them, I nearly trip over Lulu, who twines around my ankles in greeting.

I nudge her aside. "Move it, kitty. I'll feed you in a moment."

I extend my hand to the couple, first her, then him, both pink-cheeked and beaming as if they'd started their morning with a bracing bike ride. Or perhaps something even more fun.

Dave slides his arm around his wife's waist. "We're cleaning out the attic. Going to move to a smaller place, spend more time on the road. Hope you can use some of these books."

"I'm sure we can. Do you prefer store credit or cash?"

"Cash, please. We need the gas money." He slaps his wife on her leather-clad behind. "Got places to go with my sweetie. Maybe Baja."

I quickly flip through the books, mostly hardbacks, including several coffee table books with gorgeous travel photos, and one for the special collection: a beautiful volume titled *Paris Brothels of the Belle Époque*.

Molly grins and winks. "This one's an old favorite. Lots of good memories there." She pats my hand. "Enjoy, darling."

Maybe someday I will, when I can work up the nerve to pass through the red door. Until then, I'll leave that realm to Harry—and perhaps Nick. I whip out my calculator, figure a fair markup, and make them an offer, which they accept. Smiling wistfully, I watch them through the window as they fire up their huge Honda Gold Wing and drive away. Seeing an adventurous older couple so much in love gives me a whisper of hope for my own future.

I retire to my desk behind the wooden screen to tackle paperwork: bills, orders, bills, advertisements from publishers, more bills and, on top, a folded piece of notepaper. I open it carefully.

Even Nick's handwriting is beautiful—bold, slanted script.

Clara,

I'd like to come by this afternoon with my assistant Darcy to get started.

About one? If that doesn't suit, please give me a call.

I look forward to seeing you again.

Nick

One o'clock. That leaves me—I check my watch—three hours. I take a few deep breaths to steady my jangly nerves. Three hours to brace myself before Nick strides through my door. Before his low, husky voice vibrates my bones. Before his dark eyes incinerate my defenses. Before the warmth of his body heats my skin...

Enough!

I fold the note, slide it into my desk drawer, and set to work. The deep pile of paperwork awaiting my attention almost keeps my mind off Nick's impending visit. Almost.

All morning, I find myself glancing at the clock. Just two more hours, just one...

This is dumb. I'm getting all worked up over nothing.

I open my desk drawer and sweep the remaining paperwork inside. There's no reason to let Nick see how flustered he's made me.

Sunlight streaming through the big picture window makes the bookshop warm and stuffy. I unfasten the top buttons of my blouse and check my reflection in the mirror on the wall, then re-button both buttons, then unbutton one, all the while giving myself a stern, silent talking-to.

Stop dithering, you dolt. So the man makes you thirsty, so what? This kind of reaction is to be expected. You're a healthy-ish woman with a perfectly normal libido. Your body doesn't understand how much it'd cost your heart to jump into Nick's arms. Or Dalton's. Or anyone's...

"Argh!" Disgusted with myself, I glare at my reflection. Before losing Jared, I was a strong, sane, level-headed person who handled life's little catastrophes with poise and calm. Will I ever see that self again?

"Help me, love," I whisper. "This is so hard without you."

My hand strays to my throat, and a shiver prickles my skin. Where's Jared's necklace? I clearly recall laying it on the bathroom counter before my shower—a silver Celtic knot on a black leather thong. Has it fallen somewhere? Or did I just forget to put it on? Nick will arrive in less than an hour, and for the first time since losing him, I'm not wearing anything of Jared's.

I'm defenseless.

My stomach lurches.

"Memories do not live in things," I remind myself with a whisper. "Memories live in our hearts."

The affirmation from my grief support group helps a little, but my nerves still crackle with tension. I need to move. I'll go shelve some books.

When I come out from behind the screen, the fringe on my scarf snags on a book cover from the self-help section and tumbles the volume to the floor. Bending to pick it up, I read the title: *Learning to Love Again after Loss.*

Blinking hard, I peer up and down the aisle. No one in sight, just voices up front, Harry and a customer discussing classic comic books. But somehow, the air around me crackles, as if a lightning strike were imminent. The brass doorway bell tinkles, and the little hairs on my nape rise in response.

I hear a woman's voice, then Harry's. "She's in the back. Clara?"

I straighten my spine and turn to face the customer.

She's stunning. Taller than me and a good fifteen years younger at least, the visitor strides forward with the assured carriage of a comic-book super-heroine, maybe one of Wonder Woman's Amazon clan. Swirling tattoos cover her bare arms. Long, gleaming blue-black hair falls over her shoulders and down to her narrow waist. Slashes in her tight jeans reveal smooth, ivory skin, and her heavy leather biker boots clomp nearer and nearer. Pale blue eyes lock onto mine and narrow, appraising me without mercy.

"Clara?"

I nod, clutching the book to my chest like a shield.

She extends her hand. Soft and smooth, it holds no promise of my imminent demise.

"I'm Darcy Lee, Dr. Papadopoulos's grad assistant. He told me to meet him here. We're going to look at the sexy books, right?" She squeezes my hand and flashes a saucy grin. "Nice way to spend an afternoon. So, where they at?"

"I, um, the erotica section is back there. I'll get the key." Flushing like a radioactive raspberry, I slide behind the counter.

The key to the red door dangles from Harry's bony finger. "You want me to handle this?"

I take a deep breath and give him a tight smile. "No thanks. I've been avoiding that room long enough. I'll let her in. Her boss should be along soon. Tall guy, curly hair, Greek name. Please show him back when he arrives."

Harry arches his wiry eyebrows but relinquishes the key.

I unlock the red door and wave Darcy into the small room. She pulls a tablet from her leather messenger bag. Its reflected light lends her pale eyes a slightly sinister gleam. Fingers flicking across the screen, she sashays slowly around the perimeter, her hips sliding from side to side like a 1920s movie vamp. She pauses here and there to check her tablet, pull out a book, and add it to the growing pile on the antique settee.

"This okay?" She inclines her head toward the pile of books. "He gave me a pretty long list."

"Sure, of course. Can I, um, be of assistance?"

She rakes her gaze down my body, her scarlet lips stretching in a slow smile. "Oh, I'll bet you could."

Spluttering, I step back, not certain whether Darcy's tone is flirtatious or mocking.

She trails her hand over the book spines until she reaches the volume she's looking for. She caresses the cover and lifts an elegantly arched eyebrow. "I especially like this one. *Tales from a Dressing Table*."

She leafs through the pages, her vivid lips forming silent Oh's as she reads.

"Look." She shows me an art nouveau drawing of two maidens cavorting naked on a bed, surrounded by piles of frothy discarded skirts and a little pug dog who licks his mistress's ankle while she writhes under her friend's caresses.

Darcy moves in closer, lowers her voice, and turns the page. "It gets better. See?" She reveals an image of two women with elaborate upswept hair, naked but for stockings and delicate high-heeled shoes, each rubbing her crotch atop a severed male head. My stomach lurches as I back slowly toward the door, fumbling behind me. But instead of the hard, wooden door frame, my hand encounters something more pliable. And warm.

"Hello, Clara."

I jump so violently. I nearly knock us both to the floor.

Nick's hand closes over my arm and pulls me around to face him, close enough to see the golden flecks glimmering in his dark irises and to inhale his woodsy cologne.

"Steady, now." He chuckles. "I see you've met my assistant."

Keeping his hand on my shoulder, Nick reaches for the book, which Darcy obediently surrenders, her eyes downcast.

"You'll have to forgive Darcy. She takes delight in shocking people." He releases his grip on me and flips through the pages. "You're not the first to be startled by Franz von Bayros. His work got him exiled from more than one city."

I peek over his shoulder and see a woman reclining on a couch, enjoying the attentions of her dog's tongue between her legs.

"He drew many forbidden fetishes: bestiality, necrophilia. Like our Darcy, he liked to shock."

"I had no idea we had something so creepy back here." I shudder.

Nick closes the book and places it atop the pile on the settee. "I'll be glad to take it off your hands."

"Please do." The startling images make this rosy little room too hot and stuffy. Closing my eyes, I take a deep breath.

Again, his warm, heavy hand falls on my shoulder. He leans in closer, his dark eyes twinkling. "Don't worry, dear lady. My interest in such kinky material is purely academic. You're safe with me." Nick slides his hand down my arm and softly clasps my fingers. His touch leaves a trail of tingles and, in my imagination, his hand continues to glide over the silky fabric of my blouse, then inside, skimming over my bare skin...

He holds my gaze for a long moment, a hint of a smile on his full lips.

Darcy's voice breaks the spell. "Here's another one from your list, Professor."

Leaning closer, he whispers in my ear, "Back to work." His breath brushes against my skin like a kiss.

I'm jolted by a sudden urge to flee—away from the confining little room full of disturbing, titillating images—away from the press of Darcy's teasing pale eyes and Nick's inviting dark ones. Back to the safety of cookbooks and hobby books and mysteries.

"Right. Well then, I'll leave you to it." I back toward the red door, close it behind me, then lean against the wall to catch my breath.

Clearly, I was wrong. I'm not ready to face the red room. It's too intoxicating, too unsettling. And so is Nick.

Chapter Six

♥

Clara

"You okay with being alone until Margot gets here?" Blue eyes crinkled with concern, Harry tilts his head toward the red door. Nick and his intimidating assistant still haven't emerged. What's keeping them back there so long?

I force a reassuring smile. "Oh, I'll be fine."

Harry nods but doesn't move toward the exit.

Surely my trusty assistant has better things to do than babysit me. I squeeze his arm. "Really, it's okay. And hey, thanks for this morning. I haven't run in a long time. It was fun. Helped clear the cobwebs from my mind."

Up goes one wiry eyebrow. "And Dalton?"

I shrug, but a grin tugs at the corners of my mouth. "Dalton's nice. He asked me out."

"Good." He beams. "It's about time. For both of you. So, big plans?"

"He invited me to a drama performance by his students."

"Really?" He huffs a laugh. "I'll have to talk to Dalton. I know schoolteachers don't make much money, but he can do better than that."

"You'll do no such thing, Harry. Please. I don't need the pressure of a fancy date right now." I stare him down until he raises his hands in surrender. "Besides, it'll be fun. I used to act in plays back in high school, you know."

"Well, I'm glad to see you getting out. And Dalton's a good guy. You could use someone stable like him in your life." Glancing at the red door, he lowers his voice. "I'm glad you said yes to Dalton before that slick professor snatches you up."

My cheeks heat. "No one's snatching me up, Harry."

"Pretty sure he wants to ask you out, though."

My heart gives an emphatic thump. "Did he say that?"

"No, but..." He squints at the red door. "I've been around the block a time or twelve, and that guy looks at you like you're his favorite dessert."

I pat his shoulder and push him toward the door. "I'm a big girl. I can handle the professor. Now go. Enjoy your day."

He pecks my cheek on his way out.

Harry's not wrong about Dalton. A sweet guy, he made his interest obvious without jangling my nerves the way Nick did. Nick's flirtatious banter is thrilling, but when he's near, my mind races too quickly to places I'm not ready to go. Too scary, too much, too soon. Better stick with Dalton. I close my eyes and recall his bashful smile, his cool touch. Safe, easy—that's what I need.

The hours tick by. Margot arrives shortly after Harry leaves, and together we field a steady stream of customers shopping for gifts, cookbooks, comics, mysteries, local authors—everything but erotica, thank goodness. The red door remains firmly closed. What are Nick and his assistant doing back there? In a quiet moment nearly two hours after their arrival, I hear a loud feminine squeal, then masculine laughter, followed by soft murmurs.

I move closer to rearrange the messy cookbook aisle—which just happens to be conveniently located opposite the red door.

Again and again, Darcy giggles. Passing by with an armful of books, Margot rolls her eyes. I take care to keep my expression neutral, as if I haven't heard anything, but my imagination is naughtier than the books behind the red door.

I picture Darcy and Nick on one side of the twisted little settee, somehow managing to balance both their gorgeous bodies while peering over the divider at a large picture book laid out on the other seat. Darcy leans over to turn the page, her river of glossy black hair fanning over the book while Nick's hand slides beneath her tight T-shirt. He cups her pointy little breast and squeezes. She squeals again and pushes her hips back, grinding her perky ass against his crotch. He moans—softly, because he's a classy guy—and whispers a suggestion in her ear, his other hand lifting her silky hair to kiss the back of her neck, inhale her scent...

The red door flies open with a bang, startling me into dropping the heavy cookbook I'm holding—right onto my toe. "Motherfudger," I hiss and crouch to pick it up, then glance up to find Darcy framed in the doorway, her spooky pale eyes narrowed.

"You scare too easily." She strides over and widens her stance, boxing me in with those black motorcycle boots. I can't straighten up without bonking into her, so I peer up at her like the nervous dolt I am.

Her expression is not unkind, merely curious. "Don't give in to the fear, love. Try something that scares you." She shifts her pile of books to her hip, reaches out a hand, and pulls me to my feet. Her eyes half-close into a feline gaze as she brushes a lock of hair from my forehead.

"Red hair. Pretty. Hey, do you want to take a ride on my Harley sometime? It'd do you good, I bet. Shake things up." With a low, earthy laugh, she sashays to the counter and sets down her pile of books, then turns to wink over her shoulder.

My pulse picks up speed, and I remind myself to breathe. She's only teasing me, trying to get a reaction.

Margot hops down from her stool behind the counter and reaches for the books, eyes wide. "Is this all for you?"

"Oh no, I want more. Lots more." Darcy leans onto her elbows, rests her chin on her interlaced fingers, and bats her lashes at Margot, who blushes like a fuchsia.

From behind them, Nick calls, "Darcy, when you're quite finished flirting with the ladies, let's carry out the rest."

He stands in the doorway, his crisp dress shirt unbuttoned at the collar, revealing a dusting of silky black hair. The tall pile of books in his arms threatens to slip sideways. When I hurry to relieve him of half his stack, and he murmurs in my ear, "Darcy can be hard to take, but she's an excellent assistant. She'll try to get under your skin. Just ignore her."

But Darcy's intense gaze now focuses on Margot, who's pulled up her Betty Boop T-shirt to display the swarm of tattooed bees dancing across her hips. Darcy traces their progress with a long, black-lacquered fingernail. Margot giggles and twists away, but not too far away.

"What a sweet little honey you are," Darcy purrs.

With a thunk, Nick sets down his pile of books.

Darcy straightens up. "Right. Off I go."

"I'll help you." Margot trots after her new friend.

Nick pushes an errant dark curl back into place above his forehead. "Kids."

I clear my throat. "So, it looks like you found plenty of, er, materials for your project."

"Oh, we did." He nods. "You've created quite a collection there. I hope I'm not causing trouble by taking so many books."

"No, no, it's fine. Like I said, I really don't have much to do with the back room."

He cocks his head, smiling gently. "I'll bet you don't realize what you have here. Your husband had an extraordinary eye for beauty, both words and images. After all, he chose you, the brightest gem in his collection."

Nick's kind words about Jared stab me right in the conscience. What a traitor I am, spinning lustful fantasies while these two explore the erotica wonderland my dead husband created. I clutch a book and close my eyes against the tears threatening to drop onto its leather cover.

Nick steps back, both hands raised. "Oh, crap, I'm sorry. I've upset you. It's still too fresh, isn't it?"

I nod, swipe at my eyes, and ring up the first book. When I reach for the next one, he gently grasps my hand.

"Clara, would you rather not part with these?" His warm, dark eyes focus on me with such kindness. Knowing he's been through a similar loss helps me articulate thoughts too painful to say aloud—until now.

"In some ways, I'm glad to see those books go. They stir up feelings I'm not ready to confront."

He nods and glances toward the open red door. Inside, Margot and Darcy giggle as they gather more volumes. Darcy scolds, "Don't drop it again, or Mama will spank you."

Nick rolls his eyes and leans on the counter, his long, graceful fingers tented inches from my face while I bend to check the price stickers.

"Clara."

"Yes?" I glance up to find him searching my face.

"I was hoping you might have a glass of wine with me tonight. We could...discuss my project?"

My breath catches. "Oh! Well, I...uh..."

He straightens up. "Do you already have plans?"

"Not really, but I'm—" Nick's been so kind to me, and he deserves an honest answer. "I'm sort of seeing someone."

"Oh." He purses his lips. "Is it serious?"

I shrug, hoping to appear cool and collected—which I definitely am not with Nick watching me closely, as if my face holds some secret code. "Not yet."

"Well then, what's the harm in a friendly drink between fellow book lovers?" He raises one dark eyebrow, and a friendly challenge twinkles in his gold-flecked eyes.

I remember Darcy's words: *Try something that scares you.*

"Sure. Okay. Why not?" I straighten my shoulders, relishing the rush of my own daring. "I close up at seven tonight."

Take that, Darcy.

"Excellent. I'll see you then." The warmth of his smile dampens my inner warning bells. I even allow myself to meet his gaze for a long moment. Such lovely eyes, dark and mysterious and inviting...

Just then, Darcy and Margot come giggling up the aisle, weaving back and forth under the weight of the books they carry. Margot helps ring up the total, which comes in at over six hundred dollars.

Darcy whistles. "Did you go over budget, Prof?"

"A little." Nick signs the slip and tosses his car keys to Darcy. "Bring her around, will you?"

Darcy flashes a grin at me, then at her boss. "I tried, but it looks like you got to her first." She hefts an armful of books and hip-bumps Margot. "Give us a hand, my little chickadee?"

Margot gathers as many as she can hold and trots after Darcy like an eager puppy following its master.

Nick leans one elbow on the counter and chuckles. "Puppy love."

"In Darcy's case, it's more like wolf lust." My bold words startle me. It's as if he's jarring something loose, prying away a few bricks in my wall of reserve.

"Oh, her bark's worse than her bite, if you'll forgive the cliché." He stacks up the last of the books. "So, I notice the café next door is having a wine tasting tonight."

Next door. Familiar people, familiar territory. "Sounds great."

I watch him go, sighing softly as I drink in the curve of his muscular ass beneath his soft dress slacks, the span of his shoulders, the graceful way he hefts the heavy stack of books. Lulu hops up on the counter and mews her approval.

"Right, puss?" I sigh. "That man is stunning."

She gives me an affectionate head-butt before leaping down to continue her rounds.

A moment later, the bell over the shop door tinkles and Margot comes tripping back, a goofy grin on her elfin face. She pauses in the doorway, rubs her arms, and hugs herself.

"I like them," she declares.

"Them, or her?"

She shrugs. "Both, but mostly her. We have a date tonight."

I giggle. "Almost makes me wonder if the two of them came here on false pretenses, just trawling for chicks."

Margot's eyes widen. "You too?"

When I nod, she skips over and squeezes me tight. "Clara, that's so cool! It's about time." She clears her throat. "I mean, I'm glad you're going out with someone."

"Just a glass of wine, nothing to get excited about." But the quaver in my voice belies my brave words.

"You nervous?"

"A little. I mean, I've been alone for a year, and now I have two dates in one day."

"Whoa!" Margot fans herself. "You're hot stuff, Clara."

"It's no big deal, just a run this morning with Harry's friend, and now—"

"Hey, there's no rule against dating more than one person at a time, especially if you're not serious yet." Margot grasps my shoulders. "Are you serious about either of these guys?"

I dismiss her ridiculous suggestion with a wave of my hand. "No, of course not."

She slaps the counter with her palm. "Tell you what, why don't I close up tonight? I don't have to be ready until ten. You old folks will probably be in bed by then."

My jaw drops. "Margot!"

"Oh, jeez, no. I just meant you don't stay up so late. I didn't mean...Sorry. Never mind." Her expression is so contrite, I immediately forgive her and accept her offer to close up.

"And you be careful, Miss Margot," I say on my way out the door. "I don't trust that Darcy. She's a predator."

Margot grins. "Hey, sometimes it's fun to play with fire."

Chapter Seven

♥

Nick

I park my Karmann Ghia in front of Clara's bookshop just before seven and give my reflection a final check in the rearview mirror. No spinach in my teeth, no visible boogers, no stray fuzz in my hair. I check my fly, pop a mint, and take a few deep breaths before climbing out of my low-slung car. Here we go.

It's been a long time since I've cared this much about making a good impression. Charming and disarming women usually comes easy to me—a skill I learned from the ultimate schmoozer, my Greek father. I swear, the man could charm his way into any woman's good graces. The trick, according to Baba, is to notice that special something that makes a woman unique—and above all, be sincere. Women can smell phoniness a mile away.

Dad knew what he was talking about. After all, the cocky little Greek charmed my proud, statuesque mother right off her feet. God, I miss him. Baba would know what to do about this fascinating, alluring widow who lives too damn far away.

Why her, why now? It's one of those questions you can't answer with logic. The answer lies somewhere deep inside my primitive animal brain. Something about her voice, her scent, the tilt of her head when she gazes up at me. We've only spent a few hours together, but in her presence, I feel a bone-deep sense of rightness. Trouble is, I can't quite trust my perceptions, especially after last year's huge lapse in judgment nearly cost my career.

It blows my mind how perfect she is for me—owner of an amazing bookshop, and a widow too. She understands what it costs to open up your heart after such a deep loss. At least, I hope she does.

Right, enough stalling. I square my shoulders and stride to the entrance of Book Nirvana. Behind the counter, Clara's spikey-haired assistant bends over a ledger. I try the door. Already locked. When I knock on the glass, she looks up, flashes a merry grin, and points toward the coffee shop next door.

Through the café's window, I note the long, narrow space is already packed with customers. I spot Clara perched on a stool. God, she's lovely. I pause a moment to drink in the sight of her. She's let her hair down to fall in soft, russet waves over her slim shoulders. Her satin blouse has come untucked in the back, baring a crescent moon of smooth, pale skin above her dark jeans. Her fingers toy with a coffee stirrer, her gaze far away, as if daydreaming. She shifts in her seat and leans her cheek onto her hand.

A shiver vibrates deep in my belly at the memory of my own awkwardness when I first ventured out after Diana's death. This is a huge deal for Clara, even if some not-yet-serious rival has taken her out. And it's a huge deal for me.

The last time I felt this gut-level certainty about a woman was when I met Diana, back in our undergrad days. Sure, I'm attracted to Clara—what straight man wouldn't be? But beyond that, she's a sweet, fascinating contradiction—lonely and sad, brave and hopeful, uncertain but reaching out anyway. Even if she doesn't choose me, I want to help her step through the door and build a new life for herself.

When I push the door open, Clara glances up. Her wide-eyed gaze locks onto mine. Her lips part, and she grips the counter's edge. Beside, her, the barista, a slim guy with a lacquered pompadour and huge doe eyes, looks me up and down.

"This him?" he asks Clara, his Southern drawl booming above the rumble of conversation.

She nods.

"Nice." He pats her hand, straightens up, and addresses me. "Welcome to Coffee Dreams. The wine guy is set up in the back." He hollers over his shoulder, "Two more, darling!"

From the back of the café, a man with a perfectly groomed rectangular beard flashes a thumbs-up.

Clara makes the introductions. "Nick Papadopoulos, this is Arnie Stewart, barista extraordinaire."

"For now, dear lady, for now." Arnie heaves a theatrical sigh and wipes a wine glass with his bar towel. "Wish I had a crowd like this every night. The competition is getting fierce, especially since the chain that shall not be named opened up the street. If the new landlord raises the rent, I'm screwed." He calls to the tattooed young woman at the other end of the counter, "Lana, would you find these good people a nice seat?"

Lana leads us to a tall café table and returns a moment later with a plate of olives, cheese cubes, salami slices, and nuts. "Compliments of the chef." She grins and thumps her chest. "Which is me. Hey Clara, you met the new landlord yet?"

Clara shakes her head and reaches for an olive.

The server purses her lips. "I hear he's a real prick. Anyway, enjoy."

The din of conversation and laughter make it difficult to talk without shouting, so I scoot my stool closer to Clara's. She doesn't pull away when my knee presses against hers beneath the table. Does she feel it too, that sharp zing of pleasure where our bodies touch?

"So, what brings you to Eugene, besides erotica?" She pops a cheese cube into her mouth, then slides the plate to me.

I munch a few almonds before answering. "One of my anthropology students gave me the idea. I'd assigned some readings on shifting notions of sexual attractiveness—you know, what was considered 'hot' in different places and times."

She nods, her gaze on the slice of salami she's trying to spear with a toothpick. "Sounds like a fun class."

"This kid didn't think so. Told me the homework was boring. He said I should write a book about it, one with lots of pictures, like the slides I show in class. And it got me thinking—why not? I pitched the idea to my department chair, and she agreed a scholarly book with broad appeal would reflect well on the department, and maybe help my career too."

"Your career needs help?" Clara spears me with those ocean-green eyes, and I nearly lose the thread of our conversation. Imprisoned by her gaze, I reach for an olive at the same moment she does, and my hand closes over hers instead. Her skin is soft, warm, silky.

Jolted, I release her. "Yes, unfortunately. There are three of us up for tenure next year. Let's just say certain of my colleagues don't approve of my area of specialty."

"At Berkeley?" She raises an eyebrow. "I'd think you'd be rolling in sex out there."

"Wouldn't you? Fortunately for me, our department chair likes my work, but she's not the only one who decides whether I get tenure."

"Ah. Office politics."

"Can't escape that." I nab a few more almonds and watch Clara fiddle with her toothpick, like a nervous undergrad facing an oral exam.

The bearded vintner slides between the tables and pours our first sample. "We're starting with a crisp Pinot Grigio..." He natters on about nose and legs and bouquet and lingering afternotes. Clara flashes a shy grin and takes a sip, then closes her eyes and exhales through her nose.

"Well?" I ask.

"It's—surprising." She takes another sip.

"Do you like surprises, Clara?" I didn't mean it to sound like a challenge but realize too late she might take it as one.

Don't scare her off, numbnuts.

She meets my gaze, her eyes soft and thoughtful. "I used to. I think maybe a few surprises would do me good." But before I can pick up that promising thread, she swallows the last of her wine and laces her fingers together. "You've travelled a long way just to find some sexy pictures."

"Actually, I come up here several times a year. There aren't many people working in my area of concentration, but there are three at the U of O." I arch one eyebrow. "Must be something in the water up here."

"Oh yeah, we're a very sexy state." A sudden flush lights up Clara's cheeks. Is it the wine or something more interesting?

"Plus, my sister and her family live up in Corvallis, and my parents retired to Portland."

Clara tilts her head, her expression hard to read.

"So," she continues as the vintner pours our next sample, a fruity Chardonnay, "you get together with these sex professors and, what, write about historical sex?"

"Cultural anthropologists. And yes, that pretty much sums it up."

"And they pay you for that?"

I chuckle. "Not as well as I'd like, but yes."

"Nice gig."

"So is running a bookshop. That must be fun."

"It mostly is." She tastes the wine, closes her eyes, and moans softly. "Oh, my."

I take a sip, purse my lips, and snuffle comically. "Lovely top notes of apple and pear, with muscular legs and a firm behind."

Clara giggles. "Spoken like a sex professor."

When I raise my forefinger, she interjects, "Sorry, cultural anthropologist."

Our third sample arrives. The pours are getting more generous, our host's voice more musical. Must be sampling his own wares. "This is a German-style Riesling. Notice the pleasant balance of acid and sweet, with notes of wet stone."

I stick my nose into my glass and sniff. "Wunderschön."

Clara sips and smacks her lips. "Ach du lieber."

Laughing, I parry, "Wiener Schnitzel."

"Oktoberfest."

"Weltschmerz."

She taps her pursed lips. "Umm...Dachshund?"

I bark out a laugh, rocking on my wobbly bar stool. She joins in, her laughter ringing like silver bells. I can't recall the last time I had this much fun being silly with a woman—except for Diana. A thread of bittersweet weaves through this happy moment.

Diana would've liked Clara. My take-life-by-the-horns wife had a knack for spotting people with kind hearts, and she would've appreciated Clara's brave honesty.

I wipe my eyes. "You have a wonderful laugh, Clara." I reach for her hand. She lets me take it, but the moment has passed. Her smile flattens, and her gaze turns inward.

"It's hard, isn't it?" I ask.

She nods and sighs.

Let me in, Clara.

I take her other hand, holding them both lightly. "After Diana died, I used to feel guilty whenever I found myself having fun. Crazy, right? I mean, the last thing she'd want is for me to sit alone, all wrapped up in a blanket of grief. But it was hard to enjoy the lighter moments because I felt like I was..."

"Betraying her?" Clara's eyes shine bright with unshed tears.

An almost irresistible urge wells up in my chest. I want nothing more than to enfold her in my arms, to cushion her against this hard, hard moment. But rather than risk our tenuous connection, I content myself with gently cradling her hands.

I clear my throat, my voice thick with emotion. "Listen, I've been through what you're going through now. Of course, your experience is different, but I can tell you loved your husband very much, and you're having a hard time letting go of your pain. Am I right?"

She takes a shuddering breath and nods.

"The pain will always be there. Sometimes it's like an ocean wave, knocking you down when you least expect it. But here's the thing." I shift in my seat, searching for the right words. "You can't stop the tide, but you can ride the waves when they come, then get up again and keep walking."

She raises her gaze to mine. I hold the connection for a quiet moment before continuing.

"I know it's hard to believe, but you will know joy again. At first, just little moments of lightness, like sun breaking through the clouds. And someday, not too far from now, you'll find yourself happy for whole days at a time. I promise. Accept those moments when they come, Clara. Don't push them away."

I squeeze her hands. She drops her gaze but holds onto my fingers. Thank God. Otherwise, I wouldn't be able to resist brushing a stray curl from her cheek, stroking her heavy auburn hair, and then...

"Ahem." The vintner stands beside our table, holding a bottle. "Pinot noir?"

I blink hard and release her hands. "Sure, please."

I watch her sip the wine, my gaze never leaving her face until she finally looks up. The corners of her mouth twitch upward. "It's good."

I nod.

"The wine, I mean."

"Oh, right." I shake off my fog of infatuation and take a taste. "It's very—what, silky?"

"Yes, and a bit...velvety."

"With just a hint of..."

"Denim?"

"I'm thinking burlap."

Laughing, we resume our wordplay over the wines, light and easy and fun. Finally, as we drain our glasses, I steer the conversation back to Clara, treading carefully. "So, has Eugene always been your home?"

"No, just since college." She stretches her arms overhead and yawns. "Sorry, it's been a long day. I went running this morning, and I'm starting to feel it."

"You're a runner?"

"I was once, but it's been ages. You?"

I note her habit of deflecting questions about herself. "I'm a rower."

"In the San Francisco Bay? Isn't that dangerous?"

"There's a lagoon where we practice. It's peaceful out there, especially early in the morning."

She nods, eyelids half-closed. "I'd like to try that someday, just gliding along on like a—what do you call it—a water strider?"

"Oh no, you're much too lovely to be a water strider. You're more of a dragonfly, I think. Bright, like a jewel, and hard to pin down."

That pierces her armor. Her lashes flutter, and her mouth relaxes into a soft smile. "Thank you, Nick. I've always liked dragonflies."

"I'm afraid I've been more of a bumble bee tonight, buzzing on about myself. I'd like to know more about you, Clara."

"Oh." She glances at the delicate silver watch on her wrist. "Well, it's getting late."

"There you go, flitting away again."

Please stay, Clara.

"Mea culpa." She raises both hands in surrender. "So, how long are you in town?"

"Let's see..." I check my phone. "I have to head back to Berkeley no later than...so...twelve more days."

"Well then, maybe we can continue our discussion later."

I bite back the grin that threatens to blow my cool cover. "Your boyfriend won't mind?"

She blushes again, and damn, she's so pretty in pink.

"He's not really my...I mean..." She clears her throat. "Anyway, I'd like to hear more about your project. But I do need to get back home." She wobbles a bit as she steps down from her stool.

I rush to steady her, wrapping my arm around her shoulders and inhaling her scent. She smells of roses, simple, sweet, and intoxicating.

"Can I drive you home?"

She raises her eyes to mine, and for a dizzying moment it seems she might say yes. But she slides out of my grip. "No, thank you. My car's right outside. I'm just a bit stiff from my run. I'll be fine."

"Let me walk you to your car, at least."

She sighs. "Okay. Thanks."

As we walk to her parking space, a fine drizzle pats our cheeks like a caress. We stroll side by side to Clara's Subaru, its windows fogged with dew. Illuminated by the streetlamps, the mist sparkles and dances down like a swarm of tiny fireflies. I want to linger here until the rain drenches us to the skin.

As she inserts her key, I sense the tension radiating from her body. She squares her shoulders, then turns to face me, her jaw tight. "I had a good time, Nick. Thank you."

I hold the door while she slides behind the wheel. Perhaps the barrier between us makes her more secure because she rolls down the window and reaches for my hand. "It's such a relief to talk to someone who understands."

My heart gallops. She's getting away, and we haven't set a date to meet again. She starts to roll up the window, but I hook my fingers over the glass. "Clara, wait."

She pauses, eyebrows raised.

Don't push too hard. Don't scare her away.

I crouch, bringing my face level with hers. "Whatever happens, if you need someone who understands this journey, I hope you'll think of me. I'm always ready to listen."

And then, much to my astonishment, she slides her warm, delicate hand behind my neck, pulls me closer, and presses her angel-soft lips to my cheek.

"Thank you, Nick. Good night."

Rooted to the pavement, I watch her drive away. When she disappears around the corner, I spread my arms wide, turn my face to the sky, and whisper, "Yessss!"

Clara

I run my tongue over my tingling lips.

Why did I kiss him?

The hiss of my tires on the wet asphalt echoes the buzzing in my brain. Once again, the strong tug of Nick's physical magnetism drew a startling reaction from me.

So what? It's a cheek kiss, for cripes' sake. Just a friendly gesture. No big deal.

But the butterflies in my stomach disagree, and so does the heat between my thighs.

Still, how lucky to find someone who understands what I'm going through, especially with the first anniversary of Jared's death so near. Of course, I'll have Harry by my side, and

Margot. My younger sister will check in, my stepsister too. Dad will try to persuade me to come stay for a few days. But the thought of enduring such pain under the scrutiny of my brassy, bossy stepmother...I shudder. Better to ride it out in familiar surroundings, to find comfort in routine up until the wave of grief washes through me.

Maybe Nick could tell me how to weather the anniversary of my terrible loss. He's already been through it. Twice, in fact. And he promised I'd one day know joy again. He was right, too. For those few hours in his company, I felt—what? Lighter. Warmer. Tickled by the possibility of something better.

I pull into the driveway of the upstairs flat I shared with Jared, now dark and still, full of echoes and memories. What would he say about Nick?

I glance at my reflection in the rearview mirror and whisper, "I need your help, babe."

An answering gust of wind blows across the windshield, carrying damp petals from the linden tree beside the driveway. They stick, plastered to the glass by the rain. I reach out and stroke the window with my fingertips.

Jared's favorite blossoms, a gift of remembrance and love.

Tears blur my eyes as I whisper, "Thank you."

Chapter Eight

♥

Clara

"Nooooo." I reach out from beneath the covers and swat my alarm clock. "Five more minutes."

I yelp in the middle of my wake-up stretch. Everything below my waist protests: my lower back aches, my hips are stiff, my calves throb, and my feet cramp. Those four miles have left their mark all over my body.

"Effin' Epsom salts," I groan. I forgot to buy some. In fact, my spontaneous evening with Nick precluded the hot bath Dalton recommended, so last night I simply tumbled into bed.

"Stupid, stupid, stupid." I slowly heave myself upright and penguin-waddle into the bathroom. I'd love to take the day off, but Sunday is one of our busiest days, with just me and Harry on duty from noon till five. Time off will have to wait until I can afford to hire another assistant.

Ibuprofen dulls the pain by the time Harry backs into the shop, his wiry arms wrapped around a folded wooden contraption.

"What you got there, Harry?"

"Check it out." He sets down his burden and shrugs off his jacket. "Found this in my garden shed. A bit faded, but..." Grunting, he wrestles the thing into position.

"There." With a wide grin, he gestures to an old-fashioned deck chair, its well-worn striped blue and white canvas now stretched taut.

"Another seat for customers?"

"No, silly. For the window display. You'll see."

Ten minutes later, he's filled the chair with paperbacks, with more peeking out of a child's beach bucket, and still more scattered among the seashells on the display floor.

I clap my hand, tickled by his clever arrangement. "That's marvelous, Harry."

"Wait, it gets better." From his jacket pocket, he pulls a thick plastic packet, turns his back, and blows into a valve. Puff by puff, a shiny inflatable palm tree takes shape. "It's too flimsy for real books, but I'll tape some dust covers to it." Harry steps back and grins at his creation: a perfect summer tableau filled with tempting beach reads.

"Brilliant. What would I do without you, Harry?"

With Harry's help, I field a thin but steady stream of customers. Sundays draw lots of browsers to our shop-lined street, and Harry's window display seems to lure a few more shoppers than usual into Book Nirvana. The comforting routine keeps my mind off conflicting thoughts and emotions stirred up by the new men in my life.

Shortly before closing time, a young mother comes in trailing twin preschoolers who make a beeline for the children's section, a sunny corner filled with beanbag chairs in primary colors and a low table whose legs are painted like crayons. One of the boys heads straight for the toy box and carries an armload of plastic blocks to the table, his cupid's bow mouth set in a determined line. His brother stands on tiptoe to whisper in his crouching mom's ear.

"Well, go ask the lady," she says. "Mama's going to look at grownup books. I'll be right there, see?" She points to the mystery aisle, then gives me a weary smile. "Jared has a question for you."

My hand flies to my throat.

The dark-haired tot reaches up his soft, sticky little hand. Blinking back tears, I let him tug me to the picture books.

I kneel beside him. "What kind of books do you like, Jared?"

With the heartbreaking trust only small children possess, he leans his curly head against my shoulder and whispers, "Dinosaurs."

"Well then, let's see what we can find." I sit cross-legged on the floor, and the little guy climbs into my lap. His soft, baby shampoo-scented hair tickles beneath my chin. I close my eyes and inhale, and a pang of longing pierces me to the bone.

Our child would have resembled this cutie.

I battle to keep my voice steady and gentle as I pull books from the shelves. "How about this one? *Dino Danny Goes to the Beach.*" I open the cover, and immediately Jared's twin scoots over and leans against my ribs.

"I like dinosaurs too," he declares. "'Specially the T-Rex. Rawr!" He claws the air and grins.

When the boys' mother returns, little Jared sticks out his lower lip. "I wanna finish the stoooory."

His mom collapses into a beanbag chair. "Go ahead. Mama will read her book until you're finished." She mouths a silent "Thank you."

I read on, my two squirmy little customers punctuating my narrative with comments and laughter.

"Look," Jared says, "he has sand on his butt!"

"In his butt crack!" his brother chimes in, and they both fall over in a fit of adorable giggles.

"And so, with his bucket full of seashells and his shorts full of sand, Dino Danny climbed back into his mommy's dino car. 'Goodbye, ocean,' he called out. And swoosh, whoosh, the ocean waved goodbye." I close the book. "The end."

The kids jump up, and Jared's brother snatches the book.

"Ah, ah, ah!" their mother interjects. "What do you say, boys?"

Both brothers speed back to give me a hug, their sweaty little bodies colliding against mine with a solid thunk. Jared plants a sticky kiss on my cheek. "Thank you, Book Lady."

"You have kids?" the boys' mother asks as I ring up their purchases.

Keeping my gaze on the cash register, I shake my head.

"You should. You're a natural. Thanks again for the break." She stuffs their books into her backpack, takes each boy by the hand, and leads them outside.

I stare after them, lost in reverie and regret. A memory floats up: hot tears streaming down my face, yet another plastic stick clutched in my hand. "Negative again. I was so sure this time."

Jared's deep blue eyes glisten with unshed tears as he enfolds me in his warm, strong arms. "It's okay, babe. If it's meant to be, it'll be. If not, we can adopt. There are lots of kids out there who need families. Just have faith."

But we waited too long to begin trying, devoting the early years of our marriage to building the business. And now, my chance at motherhood is gone.

Harry approaches from behind and gently grips my shoulder.

"Having a hard time, eh?" His voice is raspy with emotion. "I miss him too."

I take a deep, shaky breath. "I know you do, Harry." Battling for control, I step out of his embrace. Too much sympathy and I'll dissolve into a quivering mess.

But Harry isn't so easily dissuaded. He grasps my hand. "Clara, I know this is hard to talk about, but listen." He holds on, his grip warm and firm, until I meet his gaze. "The anniversary is coming up. If you need some time off, I'll cover for you. Or we could close the shop for a few days."

"We can't afford to close. Besides," I swipe at my eyes with the back of my hand, "I'd rather keep busy. Here, at least I'm doing something useful. Crying alone at home doesn't help me heal."

He releases me. "I know it's not the same, but Eleanor left just a few weeks before our wedding anniversary. Our twenti-eth." His smile is misty, his gaze far away. "I had a big surprise planned, a trip to the coast, a fancy hotel, spa day, the works." He sighs. "Anyway, I went for a long run on that anniversary. Ran till my feet were bloody. Kept the crazy thoughts at bay."

I squeeze his arm. "Well, I'm not in great shape like you are, but I might give it a try. And thanks, Harry. You're my rock."

He kisses my cheek, his bristly whiskers scratching pleas-antly. "You're not alone, Clara. I'll be here for you."

But he's seventy-four. How much longer will he want to work in the bookshop? Surely, he has other adventures planned, dreams that will take him far away and leave me to manage things on my own.

The shop closes on Mondays, my one day to get away. Maybe I'll follow Harry's example and take a run in the park to clear my head. If nothing else, the exercise will build my strength. Between my floundering business and my broken heart, I'm going to need every bit of strength I can summon.

Chapter Nine

♥

Nick

"It's not the same, Leo."

"Bullshit. Canoe, scull, kayak, they're all rowboats, right?"

I grumble as I climb into the two-man inflatable kayak my friend brought for the afternoon of rowing he promised me. I envision the two of us gliding along the Willamette River in a sleek double scull, not this plastic toy. I feel like an utter fool, dressed for a serious workout in my skin-tight competition rowing trou and snug Cal T-shirt, while all around us families in baggy shorts and life vests paddle placidly on the park's narrow canoe canal.

"I thought you said the U of O rowing team practiced here?"

"Nope, I got that wrong. They're out at Dexter Lake. Too far to make it out there and back in time for this afternoon's session."

A cultural anthropology professor at the University of Oregon, Leo invited me up to Eugene for a "professional conference" with a few of his U of O colleagues and another anthropologist from Washington State. Turns out, Leo's "conference" is really just a casual, boozy get-together and bitch fest, and his idea of a workout won't even break a sweat.

And God knows I need to work off some of this tension. The memory of Clara's graceful body, her shy smile, her sad, ocean-green eyes, her soft lips against my cheek—the reaction they stir makes tight athletic shorts a perilous wardrobe choice. At least she won't see me dressed like a freakin' sausage.

I'd have blended right in among the competitive rowers I was expecting. But out here, amidst the kids and the ducks, I look ridiculous.

"Careful there, it's tilty as shit," Leo warns me as I settle into my mesh seat.

"This thing's a bath toy compared to my scull back home."

"How does a big guy like you not sink in that floating sliver?"

"A little thing called balance, my friend. Want lessons?"

"Nope. I got this." The kayak wobbles ominously as Leo lowers himself into the front seat.

He's a bulky bear of a man, tall and wide and ungainly, but a great teacher and a good friend since our undergrad days. His recent split from his longtime girlfriend shook him badly, and I know Leo's craving company more than a real workout.

Leo pushes off, and we glide out into the canal, now crowded with canoes, kayaks, and stand-up paddle boards. The watery playground echoes with the splashes of amateur rowers, the laughter of children, and the ducks' noisy commentary. I much prefer the near-silent, rapid backward slide of rowing, but this will have to do. And anyway, my friend needs me.

I, of all people, know how hard it is to put on a happy face and start again after the loss of a great love.

"So, what did you think of the bookshop?" Leo asks. "Find some good smut?"

I smack the water with my paddle, splashing my rude friend. "The lady does not peddle smut. And yes, I found some high-quality erotic art books."

"Oho!" Leo twists to grin back at me. "The lady, eh?"

"Isn't that why you sent me?"

"I sent you for the books. Never met the lady, just the old guy and the younger dude with dark hair."

"That was her husband."

Leo lifts one shoulder. "Too bad. If she were single, maybe she'd tempt you to stay up here."

Oh, she's tempting, all right.

"She's a widow. Bike accident."

"Wow. That's rough." He points with his paddle toward an overhanging willow tree. "This way."

We pivot smoothly, finding an easy rhythm as we dip our paddles into the jade-green water. Soon we glide beneath the trailing branches to a spot hidden from other boaters.

From the pocket of his cargo shorts, Leo pulls a slim flask. "Wee drappie?"

I check my smart watch. "It's not even noon yet."

"Ach, ye spoilsport. Yer harshin' me buzz."

"Away with ye, Redbeard." My pirate accent is even worse than Leo's. "I'll save me grog fer later."

Leo strokes his bushy copper whiskers. "Suit yerself." He takes a healthy glug. "So, pirates of the high seas we be, lurking in the shadows, scoutin' out booty."

"How's your pirate novel coming, anyway?"

He sighs. "No further, alas. But speaking of booty, tell me about the bookseller's widow."

Jealousy prickles like a belly full of burrs. Leo may be a big, fuzzy lummox, but he's smart and funny. And here. Clara might soon hook up with him, or with someone like him. In a town this size, there must be hundreds of men ready to charm her out of her sorrow and into their beds. Why did I have to meet such an interesting woman so far from home?

"Well, she's..." I search for words adequate to the task of describing her.

"Pretty, I'll bet."

"Very."

"And young?"

"About our age."

"And hot for my Greek friend?"

I shake my head. "I don't think she's ready for romance."

But the memory of Clara's kiss raises goosebumps on my skin.

"Well then, it's your job to persuade her otherwise!" Leo slaps the water with his paddle, splashing me and startling a mother mallard and her string of fuzzy ducklings from their hiding place along the bank. Quacking and peeping, they jet across the kayak's bow.

Leo resumes his pirate's brogue. "All righty then, shore leave be over. Back out to sea."

We spend a pleasant two hours paddling back and forth on the canal, talking about our work and our fellow boaters. A canoe full of giggly college-age girls turns up beside us again and again. Finally, a tall, slim girl with rich brown skin and elaborate braids calls out, "Doctor Jones, is that you?"

Leo shields his eyes and squints. "Depends. Who's asking?"

The girls paddle closer. "It's me, silly." Seeing Leo's awkward half-smile, she adds, "Lenora Addison, from your anthro seminar."

"Oh, right, of course. Lenora with the stories about hiking in Peru. Didn't recognize you in your, erm..." He flaps his broad hand in her direction.

This is one of the hazards of being a college instructor. Lenora and her friends all wear tiny shorts and bikini tops. And this girl's smile is dangerous, spiced with the brash confidence of a skilled huntress. Leo had better watch out. Such temptations could cost him dearly, especially when he's in such a vulnerable state.

The girl's sharp gaze lasers in on me. Her long, elegant fingers toy with her braids. "Who's your friend, Prof?"

Her boatmates giggle.

"Ah. This fellow here is a colleague of mine."

"Really? What do you teach?" the blonde girl in the middle asks.

"Cultural anthropology." I clear my throat. "In Berkeley."

"Too bad," the huntress says with an exaggerated sigh. "California is so crowded. Wouldn't you rather be a Duck?"

"Sorry?"

"Come teach here!" the cute Asian girl up front squeals. And then, in a peal of giggles, the trio dig in their oars and splash away.

"Well, damn," Leo complains, "you've been up here, what, two days? Already you've seduced a pretty bookseller and three students."

"What did I do?" I protest. "I'm just minding my business and rowing your heavy ass around this duck pond."

"I've gotta get me some ugly friends," he mutters. "Can't get any women with you around." He dips his paddle, and I match his rhythm as we move back toward the boathouse.

"I thought we came out here to get some exercise, some sun, not some women. Speaking of, you're getting pretty pink there, my friend." I tap Leo's neck, now roasted to a deep magenta. "You forget your sunscreen?"

He wrinkles his ruddy nose. "Sunscreen is for sissies, not for pirates."

"I wear sunscreen."

"Why? Women swoon for your swarthy skin." Leaning on his paddle, he noses the kayak onto shore.

"Having dark skin doesn't protect me from skin cancer," I tell him, echoing Mom's admonition. In summer she'd slather my sister and me with sunscreen from head to toe, despite our squirmy protests.

"You want to stay pretty?" she asked us, though it wasn't really a question. "Then take care of your skin. You think your father would have fallen in love with me if I didn't take care of myself?"

"Bella, I would love you if you had warts," Papa crooned. "I'd love you if you had whiskers. I'd even love you if you were short. You are my goddess."

I smile at the memory of my stocky little dad standing on tiptoe to kiss my Amazonian mom.

"Help me with this, lover boy." Leo's voice breaks through my fog of nostalgia.

Together, we hoist the dripping boat and fasten it to the roof of his Rav4.

"Be right back." Leo trots toward the restroom while I stretch my back and shoulders. Despite my grumbling, those two hours of paddling gave me a decent workout. I interlace my fingers, raise my palms to the sky, and close my eyes, letting the sun warm my stiff muscles.

At the sound of approaching footsteps, I move back to make way for a woman jogger. Red-faced and puffing, jaw set in grim determination, long auburn ponytail swinging in rhythm with her steps, she's a stunner.

My senses prick up to high alert. My pulse revs.

"Clara?"

She spins to face me, frozen like the proverbial deer in headlights, and nearly gets sideswiped by a speeding cyclist. She stumbles backward just in time, then claps a hand to her chest while staring bug-eyed at me.

Thank the gods she's wearing more than those college girls. Nevertheless, the way her sleeveless top and running tights hug her slim curves stirs a reaction I'd rather not display in public. I quickly untie the windbreaker knotted around my waist and clutch it in front of my crotch, trying to strike a casual pose.

I like to think of myself as a sophisticated, mature guy, but I can't help drinking in the sight of her, from her glistening forehead to her heaving breasts to the curve of her hips and her slender, strong legs. My gaze rises just in time to catch her giving me the same lingering up and down glance. Beneath my crumpled jacket, my dick strains against my tight shorts.

I move closer, checking both ways first to make sure another biker doesn't mow us down. "Dangerous here, isn't it?"

Still breathing hard, she nods.

"Shall we?" I gesture to a bench a few steps away. She sits, and I sink down beside her, draping the jacket across my lap.

Clara unknots a bandana from her wrist and uses it to wipe her damp face and throat.

"I'm a mess." Her shy smile tugs at my heart—and other parts. Hey, I'm only human.

"Me too. Hot today." I'm not usually this tongue-tied, but with her so close to her lovely body in that revealing outfit, I find it hard to think of anything beyond how much I want to run my hands over her, press against her, feel the slippery slide of her sweaty skin on mine...

"You come here often?" Chuckling, I swipe a hand down my face. "Yeah, I'm a smooth talker."

She chuckles, a low, earthy sound that gives me happy chills. "I don't, actually. It's been ages. You were rowing?"

"More like chasing the ducks. My friend—"

"Well, now, who have we here?" Leo strides toward us, a broad smile on his red, fuzzy face. He nudges me aside and plops down beside me, forcing me to slide against Clara, our shoulder pressed together, our damp thighs touching.

He grins expectantly.

"Clara, meet my friend Leo Jones. He's a professor at the U of O."

"Let me guess, cultural anthropology?"

He beams. "Oh, she's a smart one. Is this the fair bookseller?"

I nod and shoot him a warning glare.

She extends her hand to Leo. "Clara Martelli. So, Nick, you told him about my shop?"

"Right." He nods, then actually winks at me—who does that? "Did my buddy clean out your erotica collection? He's going to need a lot of reference material for his new book."

Clara shoots me a wary glance. "Oh, we still have plenty of books left."

"Good news!" Leo brays and smacks my shoulder. "Means he'll have to come back for another look." He pushes himself up with an exaggerated groan. "My, I'm sore. Not like Nick here. He can go all day. Right, buddy?"

I glare daggers at my smart-ass friend, now sidling toward the parking lot.

"I'll just go fasten down the boat." He says with a little bow. "A pleasure to meet you, Clara."

When he's safely out of hearing range, she leans against my shoulder and giggles softly. I fight the urge to slide my arm around her.

"He's quite a character." She pushes up from the bench. "Ouch. Sitting was a mistake." Placing both hands at the small of her back, she arches into a stretch, pushing her pelvis forward.

My cock throbs painfully.

With a gulp, I rise to my feet. "It was good to see you again, Clara."

"You too, Nick." She takes a step backward but keeps her gaze on mine. "Um, I was wondering..." Another step backward. "I know you're busy at the college, but could we have a coffee sometime before you go? There's something I want to ask you."

My heart dances a happy samba in my chest.

Keep cool, Mr. Horny-Pants.

"Well, I'm busy today. How about if I stop by your shop tomorrow?"

"Okay, then." She smiles like a woman who's drunk too much wine, too fast. "I'll see you soon."

She takes a step toward me. Will she give me another kiss like the one replaying in my head on loop? No, alas, just a tentative finger-wave and a crooked grin before she jogs off down the path.

I watch her disappear behind a grove of pines. And then my wistful smile evaporates in a cold wash of horror. My hands are empty. My jacket lies crumpled on the bench. I've been standing here in front of God and everybody in my stupid stretchy shorts, my erection on full display.

Shit. Did she notice? Shit shit shit.

Clara

Oh. My. God. Oh. My. God.

The words echo in my head, pounding to the beat of my footsteps on the riverside trail. Some things, once seen, can never be forgotten. The image of Nick's huge erection straining against his shiny black shorts will remain etched in my mind's eye until the day I die.

Even the unaccustomed strain of running doesn't come close to explaining my thundering heartbeat. I don't know whether to giggle or moan or scream, so I obey my body's most pressing command: flee.

I weave between the other runners on the path, letting my vision blur, focusing all my attention onto the jolt of my feet hitting the ground, the rush of breath through my lungs, the ache in my quads.

Finally, out of breath, I plod to a stop and rest my back against a tree, head down, gulping air.

Okay, let's not get carried away. He's a guy. Our legs were pressed together. His body reacted. No big deal.

Except it is a big deal, a huge deal, because since Saturday night I've been rehearsing how I might broach the subject I so desperately want to discuss with Nick. The anniversary of Jared's death looms over me like a thunderous black cloud, and I need him to give me perspective, maybe even hope.

But now, the idea of opening up the tenderest corner of my heart to a man whose lust is so evident—well, it's just, just...

Impossible.

And he's coming by tomorrow.

I lean my head against the rough bark and whisper, "Help me, Jared. There's no one I can talk to but you."

His answer comes in a sharp bonk on the head. An immature pinecone, tight and hard, drops beside my feet.

"What the..." From a branch ten feet above, a fat gray squirrel swishes its bushy tail, laughter in its bright, beady eyes. As if lecturing me, it barks and chatters, then scampers up the trunk. A few seconds later, another pinecone tumbles down and hits my shoulder.

"Okay, okay." I rub the spot and back away, surprised by my own laughter. "Maybe a little stiffy isn't such a big deal. Is that what you're telling me?"

I set off at a slower pace, heading toward the parking lot. "It was a pretty big stiffy, though."

A crow swoops low overhead, cawing as it passed.

"I got the message!" I call and shield my head with crossed arms. "Don't drop anything else on me."

Now that laughter has calmed my jingly nerves, I notice the loveliness of the summer sunlight through the trees, dappling the path as if someone had sprinkled golden confetti. A light breeze off the river cools my flushed face, and other runners greet me with waves and smiles, as if I belong among them. I'll have to come out here more often. Nick said he's only in town for a few weeks, so soon I'll be able to run in the park without danger. No more distressingly handsome Greek gods in tight shorts.

Chapter Ten

♥

Clara

I stand in the sports books aisle, befuddled. In my left hand, a big, shiny paperback titled *Training for Your First 5K*; in my right, the memoir of an Olympic rower turned rowing coach. "This is so weird," I say aloud. Lulu agrees, giving the box a sniff before twining around my ankles.

When I cut open this carton of new releases, I found these two volumes on top. Clearly, the book gods are sending me a message.

"What's weird, Clara?" Margot calls from the other side of the bookshelf.

"Oh, just an odd coincidence." I lift each book in turn. Both are eye-catching, with glossy photos of handsome athletes on the covers. The paperback about running is flexible, lightweight, and less expensive. The hardback memoir costs more but offers more substance. I flip through the pages and stop at a photo of a muscular rower, his body arched backward, straining against the oars, eyes shut, face turned to the sky, as if caught in a moment of passion.

"Someone's trying to tell me something." I slide both books onto the shelf.

She peeps around the end cap. "My psychic grandmother says there's no such thing as coincidence." She waggles her pierced eyebrows.

Well then, what kind of read do I want? Quick and easy, or long and deep?

A moment later, the doorway bell tinkles.

"Got it," Margot scoots toward the front counter. A moment later she calls out, "Clara, visitor."

I close my eyes and puff out a breath, like a track athlete about to sprint. This morning, I dressed with care, knowing Nick might stop by. I tug the hem of my blouse, then change my mind and tuck it into my jeans, fluff my hair, roll my shoulders, and finally step out of the aisle.

"Hey there." Dalton springs up from the worn armchair near the front window. I relax at the sight of his crooked smile—so like a bashful teenager's. But his broad shoulders and the golden beard across his strong jaw are very grown up indeed. Today he's dressed for work in crisp chinos, a striped Oxford-cloth shirt with the sleeves rolled up, and a tie printed with running shoes. Cute, and a little sexy. I'll bet at least one student in his class has a crush on him.

"Hi, Dalton. Good to see you again." I check my watch. "Weren't we meeting at six?"

Looking sheepish, he examines his gigantic loafers. "I'm playing hooky."

He's so freakin' cute. My heart gives a little squeeze. "I've never heard of a teacher cutting class."

"It's my planning period, so...Anyway, I just got my teaching assignment for next year: world history. The textbook is pretty dry, so I'm looking for inspiration. We start with the Ancient Sumerians."

"Weren't they the ones with the curly beards and the winged lions?"

"Yup. They even put curly beards on the winged lions. Big fans of the curly beards."

While leading him back to the history aisle, I scan my memory. Do we have any books on Ancient Sumerian art behind the red door? The thought arouses a tingle between my thighs, but it's Nick, not Dalton, who I imagine helping me search for erotic images from long, long ago. I blow out a deep breath and force my focus back to the present moment.

"I like the way you use posters to label the different sections of your shop," Dalton points to the reclining nude above the red door. "What's in that room, art books?"

With my heart leaping in my throat, I fight hard to keep my voice steady, my tone casual. "That's our erotica collection. It's mostly art books, plus some literature and history."

Dalton whistles. His facial expression remains a mystery, though, because I can't force myself to look at him until we're safely past the red door. Fortunately, he doesn't ask for a peek inside.

"Let's see, lots of photos in this one." I stand on tip-toe, reaching for a heavy volume titled *Art Treasures of the Fertile Crescent*. It nearly slips from my fingers, but Dalton lunges and catches it gracefully, though he lands with his chest against my face. He smells nice, like Irish Spring soap, my father's favorite. For a fraught moment, we freeze in this position, and I realize how easy it would be to reach up, wrap my arms around his neck, and kiss him.

Clearly, too much time without sex has warped my brain. Pull yourself together, Martelli!

"Dangerous work environment." Dalton grins and steps back. "Maybe you should wear a helmet."

"Probably no more dangerous than teaching high school."

"Naw, our kids are good. It's the parents I'm scared of." He carries the book to a low table beside the window and gracefully lowers his long body into an armchair. "Do you have a minute?"

I glance around. Margot's at the counter, chatting with the only other customer in the shop.

"Why not? Leafing through the books is the best perk of working here." I scoot a stool next to him and lean my elbow on the arm of his chair. How cozy, sitting there together, warmed by the afternoon sun. Dalton's a cozy kind of man, easy to talk to—soothing, even, with his gravelly voice and crooked smile.

He turns the pages slowly, pointing to the photos. "Curly beard." Flip. "More curly beards." Flip. "Bull with a curly beard."

"Maybe your students can make curly beards out of construction paper?"

"Cute idea. That'd make a great yearbook photo." Dalton closes the book, peers at the price tag on the back, and whistles.

"Yeah, sorry. These big coffee table books are expensive."

"Ah well. Guess I can write it off as a work expense, right?" He leans closer, and his warm blue eyes crinkle at the outer corners. "So, how are your legs after Saturday's run?"

"Not as bad as I expected, but a little sore. The Epsom salts helped."

"Stretching helps, too, and getting back on the horse."

"The horse?"

"Going for another run."

"Oh, I did. Yesterday morning, in the park."

"Lucky you," he says with a wry grin. "I was leading a unit review, not that anyone paid attention."

"Just one more week of classes, right? Anyway, I'd better get back to it. But I'm looking forward to tonight."

"Me too." He unfolds his lanky frame, reaches down for my hand, and tugs me to my feet. After he pays for his book, I walk him to the door. "See you at six?"

"Can't wait." There it is again, that boyish, bashful grin. "You're a good sport to join me for a school play, Clara. I promise you'll enjoy it."

"I'm sure I will." I give his arm a squeeze, and he surprises me by drawing me into a brief hug. His lanky body is hard and warm against mine, and he's so tall, my head tucks neatly under his chin. The contact feels...nice, I decide. Not electric, like Nick's touch, but definitely pleasant.

He releases me just as the doorbell tinkles, signaling the arrival of a new customer. Dalton turns and lopes out, sidestepping around the dark-haired man who stands in the doorway, his brow furrowed.

Nick.

He squints at Dalton's retreating back, his full lips clamped together. His ribcage expands in a deep breath, then he runs his fingers through his shiny black curls before turning to face me. His tight expression softens into a smile.

Compared to our usual outdoorsy Northwestern customers, Nick is the picture of casual elegance. His dress shirt skims his muscular chest and shoulders, and his soft wool slacks cling to the curve of his powerful thighs. Realizing my gaze has drifted down into the danger zone, I force my eyes upward. His sculpted cheekbones seem ruddier than I remembered. Is he blushing? I definitely am.

"Nick. So good to see you again," I squeak, then clear my throat. "What brings you here?"

He tilts his head, and one perfect curl flops onto his forehead. "You asked me to come by, remember?"

My fingers fly to my mouth. "Oh, right, I did."

"Did I come at a bad time?" He glances over his shoulder in the direction Dalton went.

"Oh, no, no. This is a great time." I call to Margot, "I'm going for coffee. Can I bring you one?"

She flashes a wide grin. "Nope. I'm good. You go on. No hurry. I'll just—" She picks up a rag from beneath the counter. "I'll dust the books."

"Right." I bite back a giggle. No doubt about it, Nick has a talent for flustering women.

"Do you have time for a coffee?" I ask him.

"I'm at your disposal, dear lady." He crooks his arm and waits, his lips tilted in a flirtatious smile. I slide my hand into the crook of his elbow, enjoying the feel of his solid muscles beneath my palm, and let him lead me to the café next door.

"My, my, you two are becoming regulars," Arnie sings out as we pass the counter. "What's this, the third date?"

Nick gracefully ignores Arnie's comment and orders our coffees. I sit in one of the squishy armchairs by the fireplace. Nick joins me, carrying a tray with three muffins.

"In case you care to crumble one again." He helps himself, takes a bite, and moans. "So good."

Startled by the rawness of his voice, I very nearly do crumble my muffin.

Nick wipes his mouth with the back of his hand. "So. Was that your new boyfriend?"

I blink at him, my mind momentarily blank.

"The guy who hugged you?"

"Oh! Oh, that's Dalton. He's just...I sort of joined his running club, his and Harry's."

"Mmm hmm." Nick raises one eyebrow.

"Harry's my clerk. And my friend."

"Mmm hmm." The corner of his mouth twitches upward.

Itchy under his scrutiny, I babble on, "You could come run with us if you like. On Saturday morning. It's fun..."

"That's okay." He lays his warm, heavy hand over mine. "I'll stick to the water. Anyway, you wanted to ask me something?"

"Yeah, uh..."

Now that the moment has arrived, my courage flags. But he holds onto my hand, his gentle gaze inviting me to continue.

I gulp around the boulder in my throat. "I want to ask you, because you've been there..."

He nods, waiting.

"It's almost here, the anniversary, and I don't know how to get through it."

"Your wedding anniversary?"

"No, the day Jared..."

"Oh." He releases my hand, fists his napkin, and stares into the distance.

"Nick, if you don't want to talk about this—"

"No, it's fine. I wish I had someone to talk to when the first anniversary of Diana's death rolled around. You won't believe me, but it caught me by surprise. I kept myself so busy with work and rowing and I...I guess I was in denial about the date." He leans forward, elbows on knees, his shirt stretched tight over his broad back.

I'm hurting him, forcing him to discuss his own hardest moments. I reach out a tentative hand, pull it back, then swallow hard and lay my palm on his shoulder. "Nick, I'm sorry. I didn't mean to cause you pain."

"No, no, it's fine." He straightens and takes both my hands in his. "I said you can always talk to me, and I meant it."

"Thank you, truly." My voice wobbles. "So, any advice? Because frankly, I'm terrified. I'm sure it'll get better eventually, someday, but how do I handle June twentieth?"

His narrow gaze holds mine for a long moment before answering. "Okay, here's what I suggest. Have a picnic."

My whole face screws up into a scowl of confusion. Is this his idea of a joke?

"The park where we met is a pretty place. Did you and Jared go there?"

"Sometimes."

"What did he like to eat?"

"Umm...fried chicken." To my astonishment, I feel a smile stretching my lips. "He rode so many hours on his bike, he could pretty much eat anything he wanted."

"All right, get some fried chicken, the best in town. Pack a blanket, maybe a journal. You have one of those?"

I nod. I tried writing out my churning emotions in the first weeks after Jared's death, but journaling only magnified my shock and pain. Instead, I've kept myself busy in the bookshop in an effort to keep my mind off my grief.

"So, I should go have a picnic...alone?"

"No, with Jared."

Stung, I jerk my hands free. "Nick, that's not funny."

He leans in, forcing me to gaze right into his eyes—his dark, liquid eyes with their shimmering flecks of gold. "Clara, I'm serious. Look, you talk to him, right?"

"Right..." I haven't admitted that to anyone. "Do you talk to your wife?"

"Diana? Yes. Often." He sips his now-cold coffee and grimaces. "Some might find it odd, but I know she hears me, somehow."

"Does she answer you?"

A slow smile spreads across his lips. "In her way, yes, she answers me." He huffs a laugh. "You know, Clara, you're the first person I've ever admitted that to. I talk to my dead wife. Does that make me crazy?"

"I don't think so." I take his hand and lace my fingers through his. We sit together in silence, breathing through the pain only someone like us can know, someone who's lost the love of their life.

Finally, Arnie the barista saunters over with a steaming carafe. "Really, y'all, I appreciate the business, but don't come over here to mope and let your coffee get cold. You're depressing the other customers." After refilling our cups, he sashays back to the counter, clucking his tongue.

I take a sip. "So, you think I should, what, spend the day with Jared?"

"Exactly. Talk to him, sing to him, write him a letter, draw his picture, take a walk with him." He grips my hand again and presses a kiss to my fingers before continuing. "If Jared could have one wish, it would be for another day with you."

My breath catches, and a ragged cry bursts from my chest, as sharp as broken glass. I hide my face in my napkin and curl forward, quaking with sobs. Nick's hand traces gentle circles on my back. Even through my shuddering moans, I relish that warm, human contact.

He understands.

I'm not one of those stoic widows who reins in her tears. I've cried gallons since losing Jared, but this wash of tears feels cleansing, even healing.

Wordlessly, Nick hands me more napkins. When I've caught my breath and mopped up the worst of the damage, I slowly straighten up.

Nick's voice lowers to a soft rumble. "My experience was different from yours. Diana died from cancer, so we had those final months to talk through our goodbyes. We said..." He trails off, turning away. "We said so many things to each other. You never got that chance. You still have a lot to say to Jared."

His message slowly sinks in. I've been so focused on the pain of talking about Jared, about what could have been, should have been. Talking *to* him would be so much easier.

Sniffling, I squeeze his hand. "Thank you, Nick."

"My pleasure, dear lady." He releases me and sips his coffee. "And now, I want to ask a favor of you."

"Of course."

"I'm hosting a little get-together on Wednesday at my place."

"In Berkeley?"

"No, the house where I'm staying, near the campus. It'll be low-key, just a handful of colleagues and their significant others. Wine, snacks, small talk."

"A professor party?"

He chuckles. "Sounds dull, right? But Leo will be there, and the other cultural anthropologists who came down for our 'professional conference.'" His fingers hook into air quotes. "Anyway, I'd love it if you'd join us. Leo told his department about your special collection."

I reflect for a moment. It does sound dull—except for the part where I get to spend more time with Nick. "Sure, I'd love to come."

He beams. "Marvelous! Here's the address." He pulls a pen from his pocket and scribbles on the back of another business card. "It's two blocks from the campus library. Any time after seven."

"Can I bring anything?"

"Just your lovely self. The woman I'm staying with is a marvelous cook."

He's staying with a woman? For a moment, I wonder if I've misread his intentions. I was so sure he was flirting with me, but perhaps that's just his way—one of those charming guys who flirts with little girls and old ladies and every female in between. Then again, his reaction in the park suggests otherwise.

I tuck the card in my pocket. "Anyway, thanks so much for listening, Nick. It's so good to talk to someone who gets what I'm going through. But now, I'd better get back to work. I have—"

"A date with the skinny bald guy?"

My jaw drops.

I thought Dalton's crooked smile was cute, but Nick's is heart-melting. "Hey, if he didn't ask you out, he's a fool." He pushes up from his chair. "Have fun tonight, lovely Clara. If you change your mind about tomorrow, you have my number."

I nod.

"I hope you won't change your mind, though." One last lingering glance, then he strides through the door.

I watch the smooth motion of his muscular body until he disappears from view. Suddenly, a dull cocktail party never sounded so good.

Nick

I sit behind the wheel of my Karmann Ghia and watch Clara stroll back to her shop, hips swaying deliciously. The wind lifting her hair is balmy, but she keeps her arms crossed over her chest, as if she were cold. Or perhaps she's just protecting her heart.

I answered her summons in hopes of a bit of flirtation, another date if I got extraordinarily lucky. But I hadn't expected this. After that gut-wrenching discussion, I feel…

I swipe a hand down my face.

Wrung out, that's how I feel. Two years after losing Diana, it still costs me dearly to talk about the horrible months after her death. And so I seldom do, not even with those closest to me.

But opening up to Clara leaves me feeling lighter, too, as if I've set down a heavy burden I'd gotten used to carrying. Because she understands—or at least she's on her way to understanding—the process of grieving a great love. We're walking the same path, though she lags several steps behind. And what I want now, more than anything, is her company on the journey.

I massage my hand, remembering the soft warmth of her palm against mine. Sure, I'm attracted to her—very much so. Any hetero man would be. What surprises me is my need to comfort her, and how much I'm dreading my return to Berkeley. Only eleven more days until my summer seminar begins.

But Berkeley isn't the far side of the moon, and my family lives in Oregon. I'll be back soon.

Careful, I caution my over-eager self. Go slow. Don't scare her off.

The magnetism between us is undeniable. It shines in her eyes, sizzles in her gentle kiss on my cheek—but another show of lust like in the park might send her skittering away, never to return. Clara's heart is still fragile. I know well just how fragile.

In the months after Diana's death, friends and family urged me to talk through my grief, but after watching my wife waste away to a silent, gaunt shadow, I simply didn't have the energy.

My sister Calista came down from Oregon to drag me to a grief group. She held my hand as we perched on hard folding chairs in a church basement, listening to sobs and moans and yells and whispers about the cosmic unfairness of it all. And when everyone in the circle had spoken, when it was my turn to bare my aching soul to those strangers, I just couldn't. Even with Cali by my side, I couldn't say a word.

So my brave, beautiful older sister unburdened her heart while I sat there stoically, listening to her regrets about how she'd never be an aunt now, never hold my child in her arms.

"It is what it is," I tell my reflection. Diana is gone until we meet again someday in the great whatever-comes-next.

But Clara is here. Clara with her sea-green eyes, her blushing freckled cheeks, her shy but knowing smile, with her collection of erotic books locked away, like her locked-away heart. If she gives me a chance, I'll stand beside her while she opens the door.

Chapter Eleven

♥

Clara

Cleaning up after a crying jag is no easy feat in the bookshop's tiny restroom. I splash water on my face—and my blouse, and my jeans, and my shoes. I check my reflection. Mascara gone. Hair dripping. Eyes puffy. Nose red. And just two more hours until my date with Dalton.

I went to the café with Nick hoping for some practical advice, or so I told myself. But who am I fooling? I am far too attracted to Nick Papadopoulos for my own good. With his gentle gaze and probing words, he has an uncanny knack for peeling back my defensive layers and uncovering pain that...well, I can't put off dealing with this question forever. Maybe Harry and Margot are right, and I should look for a new partner, not that anyone could ever match the love I shared with Jared, but perhaps someone to share fun times and...yikes, sex?

It's not easy going through daily life with my heart at war with my lady bits. A little meaningless sex might calm my inner strife. Or it might throw me into a tailspin of guilt and regret.

"One baby step at a time, Clara girl," I mutter as I blot water from my face and throat. Dalton asked me to a high school play, not a romantic evening. In fact, watching kids cavort onstage will be fun. I remember well that uplifting, giddy energy from my own teen performances.

Tonight, Harry volunteered to help Margot close the shop. He arrives at four, wearing a University of Oregon T-shirt and a smug grin. After tying on his Book Nirvana apron, he drops his knuckly hand onto my shoulder.

"So, big night tonight, eh?" His grin etches his whole face with laugh lines.

Hmm. He seems awfully invested in my evening with his running buddy.

I pick up the price gun and start labeling new books for shelving. Keeping my voice casual, I ask, "Harry, what's your connection to Dalton?"

He rubs his lower lip with his thumb. "Just the running club, mostly."

"Mostly?"

He throws up his hands. "Okay, you got me. He's my cousin's boy. So I can vouch for his family too. They're a good bunch."

Figures. But that's not necessarily a bad thing. Over the years, Harry has proven a good judge of character.

"Did you know his ex-wife?"

Harry wrinkles his nose. "Kind of a drama queen. Wanted a man with more money."

"Ah. That's too bad."

"When Dalton refused to give up his teaching job, she dumped him."

"Wow." That sounds too cliché to be real. Is Harry sharing the full story? But the more questions I ask about Dalton, the more Harry will think I'm interested in his cousin.

Guess I'll have to ask Dalton directly, if we get that far. Time will tell whether this set-up has potential.

Harry smacks his big hands together. "Anyway, I'll handle close up, so you can go get fancy for your date."

"Right. I'll dust off my pearls and mink stole."

Evening traffic lengthens my usual five-minute commute to ten. I come back to the shop freshly showered and perfumed, hair fluffed, and wearing an outfit I hope is dressy enough for the occasion without suggesting seductive intentions. Since we'll be outside, I've layered a warm cardigan over my blouse, with a scarf tucked into the pocket just in case the wind picks up off the Willamette. I'm behind the screen fiddling with my hair when the doorbell tinkled.

"Ahoy, Dalton!" Harry calls.

I take a deep breath, smooth my sweater, and emerge to greet my date. "Cute" is the first word that springs to mind. Dressed as before in chinos and a button-down shirt, he's ditched the tie and added a tweed sport coat that, by the rumpled look of it, gets very little wear.

"Evening, Harry." He claps his cousin on the shoulder. "How's your knee?"

"Better. The wrap you recommended helped." Harry makes a show of polishing the counter. "You kids run along. Don't want to be late for the show."

I scoot behind the counter and peck his scratchy cheek. "Thanks, Harry. What would I do without you?"

Even at the low wage I can afford to pay him, he's always ready to pull extra hours when I need him.

He smooches my forehead. "Speak nothing of it. Now go have fun."

At the Thai restaurant, a little family-run place with blaring Asian pop music, Dalton and I chat about our work over delicious shrimp in fiery red curry sauce.

"What made you choose this age group to teach?"

He wipes sauce from his lips. "I like teenagers. They can be snotty sometimes, but they're really hungry for attention from adults."

When he talks about his students, Dalton's face lights up in a way that makes him look—well, not quite handsome, with his prominent nose and deep-set eyes, but very attractive. Face to face like this, he radiates warmth and kindness. I bet Jared would have liked him, considering how much they have in common.

He nabs another shrimp with his chopsticks. "Anyway, I want to hear more about you. You've been running the bookstore on your own ever since your husband..."

"Since Jared died, yes." People have a hard time saying the D word around me. I get it—before losing Jared, I found myself tongue-tied around grieving people.

"How long has it been?" he asks.

"Almost a year."

His smile droops.

"It's okay. I don't mind your asking." I squeeze his hand. "And yes, I own the business, but I get a lot of help, especially from your cousin."

"Oh, he told you that, eh? He's more like an uncle, since he's so much older." Dalton rubs the back of his neck. "Harry's a great guy, but I'm afraid he's a bit of a matchmaker."

"I noticed."

"He really likes you, though. Speaks highly of your strength, your kindness." He flashes his shy grin again.

"That's nice to hear."

As we both munch our meal, an idea swims into focus. Is Harry pushing me toward Dalton out of concern for my welfare, or is it the other way around?

"So, Harry tells me you're divorced."

"Yup." Dalton keeps his eyes on his plate and doesn't elaborate, so I drop it. Maybe the wound is too fresh. In any case,

I'm glad he doesn't launch into a diatribe about his evil ex. That speaks well of his character, at least.

He checks his watch. "We'd better book it. Show starts soon."

He insists on paying for dinner, and afterward we climb into his battered VW station wagon. "Not very glamorous," he says with a wry grin, "but it gets me where I need to go."

"That's all that matters, right?" I've never been one to judge a man by his car. Guess his ex didn't agree.

The setting sun gilds the Willamette River as we pull into the parking lot near the Cuthbert Amphitheater. Swallows tumble and swoop among the cars, snatching bugs attracted by the overhead lights. A cool breeze carries the rich, green odor of freshly mowed lawns. At the box office, teens in North Eugene High School Drama Club T-shirts cluster, giggling and swatting each other with rolled up programs.

"Mr. Garvey! You came!" A tiny girl in striped stockings and Doc Martens bounces like an excited puppy.

"I said I would, and I always keep my promises." He accepts the program she hands him, then takes another for me. As we pass through the gate, the girl whispers to her companions, and the whole pack breaks into shrill giggles.

Compared to concerts I've attended at the Cuthbert, this crowd is pretty thin, but the seats closest to the stage are packed with students, parents, and teachers. A stocky boy with multi-pierced ears stands to let us pass.

"Yo, Mr. G, this your lady friend?" he asks with a smirk.

"Shut up, Brock," Dalton says with an indulgent smile.

"Niiice." The kid whispers to his buddies, who chuckle and snort.

"Sorry about that," Dalton sighs as he folds his lanky body into his seat. "Sophomores tend to be, well, sophomoric."

"It's fine." Being surrounded by so many teens triggers my mischievous side. "Shall we make out and give them something to talk about?"

Dalton's blushing face glows even in the waning evening light. "We'd probably end up in the yearbook."

A hefty dad takes the seat next to me, forcing me to lean against Dalton's shoulder. Soon the stage lights flare to life, bathing the scenery in a rosy glow, and the band strikes up the overture's first notes. A little thrill of nerves runs over my skin, an echo of my own opening nights. Right now, the actors are huddling behind the canvas flats, jazzed and terrified as they peek out at the audience.

"Thanks for coming, Clara." Dalton interlaces his fingers with mine. "You're a good sport." The intimate gesture surprises me, and I find myself more focused on his big, cool hand than on the kids singing and dancing on stage. I readjust my position, trying out the sensation of my hand in his, my arm against his. Not thrilling, but still very nice. Comfortable.

The appearance of Audrey Two, the giant, papier mâché, man-eating plant villain of the story, draws me back into the present moment. It looks like something a large dog chewed on, but the kid who voices the plant off-stage is a talented singer and comic. "Feed me, Seymour," his baritone voice rings out.

"You know this kid?" I whisper into Dalton's ear.

He turns to reply faster than I expected, and his lips nearly brush mine. He hovers there a moment, just millimeters away, before pulling back with a small whoosh of breath.

"Sorry, I—"

"No, my fault," I reassure him.

But he's clearly flustered. He fumbles through his program. "Um, let's see. Audrey Two...Freddy Camacho. Soccer team captain. Class clown. You know the type..."

So, Dalton's a nervous blatherer, just like me. I wonder whether taking his hand again will calm him or make him even more nervous. It's worth a try. But before I get the chance, a roar from the audience pulls my focus back to the stage.

Audrey Two is listing hard to starboard. The plant's lower jaw, which bounces along with the offstage actor's every word, has somehow come unhinged, revealing two black-clad puppeteers inside, scrambling to hold the wood and wire structure together before—

Too late. The plant's face crumples like a used Kleenex. The boy and girl leads gape over the wreckage, then the girl flaps her hands and wails.

"Oh no." Dalton moans.

From somewhere behind us, someone chants, "Freddy, Freddy, Freddy." All around, kids pick up the chant, until the voice-over actor steps out from behind the curtains, clutching a microphone. That big, booming voice belongs to a short, muscular boy with slicked-back hair and a macho swagger.

Grinning, he raises his hand and says into his mic, "The show must go on, right?"

When the laughter and applause die down, he stands beside the monster plant's remains and picks up his last line, "Feed me, Seymour." He ogles the ingenue, a lustful leer on his handsome face.

She and her partner exchange a shrug, pick up their lines, and the show does indeed go on. When the moment arrives for the plant to swallow the female lead, the two puppeteers make a ring of their arms. She steps through and crouches behind them while Freddy makes "Nom, nom, nom" noises and rubs his belly.

Dalton and I laugh until tears stream down our faces. What a triumph!

After the final curtain call, Dalton rises. "Want to go meet the kids? I really should say hi."

We inch our way toward the exit, eventually filing past the actors and crew who've lined up outside the theater. All along the way, kids and parents greet him warmly.

I pat his arm. "You're quite the popular teacher. I'm impressed."

His answering grin is less bashful than before.

"Not so popular on quiz days. But yeah, I like the kids."

And to think his ex-wife asked him to give this up. Clearly, Dalton had integrity, generosity too.

"Mr. Garvey!" The tall, busty lead actress throws her arms around his neck and dance him in a circle. He carefully extricates himself with a glance back at me.

"Oh, sorry." She seizes my hand. "You must be his girlfriend. Did you like the show?"

"It was marvelous. Great recovery."

"Thanks!" She hugs me tight, smelling of sweat and cheap makeup.

Her costar tugs at her arm. "Easy, Becca. You're scaring people."

As we make our way down the line, I watch student after student light up for Dalton.

"Mr. G!"

"Yo, Mr. Garvey!"

"Hey, Garvaaay!" This last greeting comes from Freddy, the actor who saved the day. He exchanges an elaborate handshake with Dalton, then turns his high-voltage grin on me, looks me up and down, and nods his approval. "Thanks for coming, Miss. You takin' good care of my favorite teacher?"

"Well, I—"

"Mind your business, Camacho." Dalton's brows rumple in mock sternness. "And good job."

"Wow," I say as we cross the parking lot. "I'm really impressed."

"Yeah, the kids were great."

"No, I mean you. They clearly adore you."

"Oh, well..." He leans against his car door and resumes his aww-shucks routine. "Beautiful night, eh?"

I settle beside him, my hip against his thigh. He slings his long arm over my shoulders and lets it rest there. No pressure, just pleasant warmth.

We gaze up at the stars sparkling in the clear summer sky.

"I really love my work," he says at last. "It's exhausting, and it doesn't pay as well as corporate jobs, but the kids make it worthwhile."

"And your ex didn't appreciate that."

Oops. Dalton never told me about his gold-digger ex. That was Harry.

Dalton frowns at the pavement. "Yeah. That's about right."

"Hey, sorry. It's not my business."

He squeezes my shoulder. "Don't worry about it. I'm sure Harry will make my business your business if he has his way." He slides his hand into mine. "I don't mind, though. Do you?"

The corners of his mouth lift in a hopeful half- smile. His touch is gentle, his size and presence reassuring.

This could be a very good thing for both of us.

"I don't mind at all." I step into his embrace.

He pulls me closer and brushes his lips against mine. Sweet, soft, easy. I lean my cheek against his chest for a moment, surprised by how loudly his heartbeat thunders through bone and muscle. His fingers slide into my hair and gently stroke the back of my neck.

I offer my lips again. This time, he takes them forcefully, mashing them against my teeth. He clutches me tightly. His long body is hard against mine—and so is the swelling pressed into my belly.

My spine stiff with outrage, I plant both my hands on his chest and shove until a good two feet of cool night air blows between us. He blinks for a moment, as if surprised to see me there.

"Oh, hey, I—" His broad shoulders slump, and he passes his hand over his face. "Clara, I am so sorry."

I glare, my eyebrows reaching for my hairline.

Backing away, he raises both hands in a placating gesture. "I was way out of line. I'm not usually so—it's been so long, and you're so beautiful, and you smell so good, and I'm—" He grimaces. "I'm a complete and utter asshole."

I have every right to be outraged, but something about his flustered, sputtered apology melts my anger. So he got an erection. That's hardly worth tossing the whole man into the nearest dumpster.

I cross my arms over my apparently irresistible boobs. "I'll forgive you on one condition."

He nods rapidly. "Anything. Name it."

"Think you can drive me home without mauling me further?"

"Absolutely."

And he does. An awkward silence fills the car as we make the short drive back to Book Nirvana, but he keeps his hands on the wheel and off me.

When we pull up in front of the bookstore, mine is the only car still parked on the deserted street, and I'm glad to have a large male companion watching out for me, even one as horny as Dalton.

He springs up from his seat, holds my car door while I settle inside, then leans onto the roof and gazes down at me like a giant puppy who's been caught shredding the couch, a pretty funny expression on such a tall, gangly man.

"So, uh...I want to apologize again. My behavior was totally uncalled for. And out of character."

I purse my lips to hold back a smile. "Maybe it was all those teenage hormones."

He nods. "Absolutely. And if you'll give me another chance—which I don't deserve, by the way—I'll show you what a gentleman I can be."

I wait, one eyebrow raised.

"Dinner on Friday? At Pomodoro?"

The new Italian bistro downtown is pricy and swanky. Not easy on a teacher's salary.

"I promise to keep my hands to myself," he adds. "I'll even sit on them if you want."

I consider his offer for a long moment, mostly for the fun of watching him squirm.

Finally, I smile and put him out of his misery—because despite his gaffe, I'm coming to like Dalton. "Okay, I accept. But I'm holding you to your promise."

He grins broadly. "Great. It might be hard to eat spaghetti while sitting on my hands, but I'll manage if it means I get the pleasure of your company again."

For a micro-second, I consider rising to kiss him good night, but decide against playing with fire. Friday is soon enough.

"Good night, Dalton. And thanks for a fun evening."

As he backs away, I note the impressive bulge in his jeans, now right at eye level, has not abated in the least.

Oh my.

After he drives off, I sit in my car for a long moment, reflecting on tonight. I ought to feel—what, angry? Disrespected? Violated? I'm not feeling anything like that, though. Dalton was clearly contrite about his lapse in self-control.

Am I hot and bothered? After all, he's an attractive man, graceful and athletic. But even the sight of his enormous stiffy up close doesn't leave me especially tingly. And yet, my growing fondness for Dalton is undeniable, and I look forward to our next date.

Oh, but Nick.

Remembering tomorrow night's meeting with the sexy professor kicks my pulse into overdrive. His sweaty, muscular body in the park, his powerful erection straining his tight rowing shorts—the image jolts me like a live wire, making my breath catch and my stomach clench.

In a week, I've gone from being a lonely recluse to dating two men. Two very amorous men.

Well, as Margot said, there's nothing wrong with dating more than one person, especially in the early, getting-acquainted phase. And anyway, my next meeting with Nick is just a staff party. It's not like I'll fall into his bed after—I do a quick mental calculation. We've already met up three times, if I count our two talks in the coffee shop, plus the wine tasting. Will Nick interpret this next encounter as an invitation to do more than talk?

"Relax," I scold myself aloud, clasping the wheel. "I'm just exploring my options. Baby steps, and all that. Nick's leaving soon, anyway." The long breath I blow out fogs my windshield.

As I wipe it away, I notice a light left on inside the bookshop, a glowing line beneath the red door.

Chapter Twelve

❤

Clara

The tinkle of the doorway bell rings eerily loudly in the empty bookshop. I lock the front door behind me, fetch the red room key, and step slowly toward the glowing light beneath the red door. In the darkness, the bookshelves seem to loom over me. I inch toward the door. Something collides with my ankle. With a loud squeak, I jump backward and bonk into the cookbook shelves.

"Mew?" Lulu butts her furry head against my leg.

I clutch my jacket over my heart and, when I can breathe again, let go a loud laugh.

"Jeezus, you scared me, Puss-face." I stoop to pick her up. Purring like a cement mixer, she cuddles against my chest.

"Harry must've left the light on, eh?" Comforted by the cat's weight and warmth, I insert the key.

The red door swings open at my touch, yet I hesitate on the threshold, gripped by a nagging sense that something's not right. There's a weird heaviness in the air, as if a storm is brewing. Nothing has changed back here—nothing visible, anyway. The Victorian lampshade Jared found at an estate sale sheds a warm pink light, giving the little chamber a womb-like coziness. All I have to do is grasp the silk tassel beside the door and tug to turn off the light. No big deal. Yet I freeze in the doorway, lost in memories.

Lulu mews and rubs her silky head against my ear, then hops down and sashays to the S-curved settee. She springs onto the seat and sprawls, staring as if impatient for me to get on with it.

Get on with what, though?

"Rrrrowrrrmmmrrrrp."

"Okay, fine. But just for a minute." Who can resist an invitation like that? I gingerly step inside, sit opposite Lulu, and reach over the curved seat back to rub her warm, fluffy belly. From the depths of my memory, Jared's raspy chuckle wraps around me.

"This'll prevent couples from getting carried away by the racy books," he said when he installed the distinctive Victorian piece. And he was right. We tried. The antique conversation settee keeps a barrier between readers tempted to act out fantasies inspired by our erotica collection. Still, the worn velvet upholstery is warm and inviting beneath my hand.

In the capricious way of cats, Lulu hops down and strolls out of the room.

"I see how it is," I call after her. "Lure me in and abandon me."

Whispering, I add, "Thank you."

It took my cat's invitation to help me cross this threshold. And really, my fear of this room is silly. Thanks to the erotica collection, the shop's reputation has spread beyond Eugene, beyond Oregon, even. It's high time I pull on my big-girl panties and make the most of it.

I stand and pivot, taking a mental inventory. Despite Nick's recent book splurge, the floor-to-ceiling shelves are still mostly full. Jared cultivated so many connections with collectors and suppliers that new books arrive regularly to replace those we sell.

I walk slowly around the perimeter of the room, trailing my forefinger over the book spines as if tracing a lover's ribs through his flesh.

Letting my sense of touch guide me, I stop at a thick, leather-bound volume.

"Pick me," it whispers.

I ease the heavy book from the shelf. Its textured russet cover has worn smooth at the corners, its title barely legible: *Erotic Art of Ancient Greece*. I slide my fingers inside and admire the swirled end papers, tracing the hypnotic whorls with my fingertips. The page edges, velvety from much handling, still glimmer with gold leaf. Someone crafted this beautiful book with love.

I sit on the settee, kick off my boots, and curl my feet beneath me. As I slowly turn the pages, the strangest sensation dances over my skin—a warmth, a presence, as if Jared is hovering over my shoulder.

The illustrations are mostly photos of ancient Greek frescoes, amphorae, and urns, painted with images of handsome, well-muscled men and graceful women captured in moments of passion. Here, a slim maiden clambers atop a beardless youth seated on a chair, his erection pointing upward in anticipation. In the next image, a muscular, bearded man stoops to penetrate a woman sprawled on a couch, her head thrown back in ecstasy as she holds a dildo complete with a pair of balls. The man penetrates himself from behind with a similar dildo.

I laugh out loud, the sound muffled by the books and the soft Persian rug. It seems the ancient Greeks liked toys. Not surprising, I guess. Humans are always looking for ways to amplify their pleasure.

A bas-relief sculpture on the next page shows a young man reclining on a couch with a woman stretched atop him, while a bearded man penetrates her from behind. Another urn portrays a trio of men stacked one behind the other, having a very good time, judging from their half-closed eyes and gasping mouths. Lucky guy in the middle.

And here's a grinning satyr preparing to mount a gazelle who gazes back at him tenderly. Fascinating and a little disturbing. Does it count as bestiality if the satyr is half goat?

The images swim before my eyes as, entranced, I turn page after page. It seems there wasn't an erotic possibility these long-ago people didn't explore. The air becomes warm and uncomfortably close. I open the top buttons of my blouse and let my hand stray inside, remembering how often Jared would pull me into this room for stolen caresses. My fingers brush feather-light over the furrow between my breasts.

He visits in my dreams, but it's been a year since I've felt Jared's touch on my body. And though guilt gnaws at me, I long for that sensation again. Am I ready to bare my heart, or even just my skin, to a flesh-and-blood man? Will I ever be ready?

I set the book aside and close my eyes, sensing Jared's presence, his breath on my throat, his hand guiding mine over my body, down to my thighs, and back up to brush over my nipples, pebbled hard and exquisitely sensitive. I know this isn't real, but can't resist sliding into a heady mix of fantasy and memory. My skin is electric with want and remembered pleasure.

"You are more beautiful than any work of art in this room." Jared's voice whispers in my ear, and I swear I feel the heat of his breath. My fingertips slide lower, stroking down the tender inside of one thigh, then up the other. I recline against the padded seatback, squirming and sliding under the memory of his touch. It's as if he's right here with me—his warmth, his weight, the whisper of his lips against my throat.

My fingers glide over the seam of my jeans, pressing the rough cloth against my clit. A tingling ache is building there, hot and sweet and urgent.

"Give yourself to me, Clara. Let me take you there." Jared's shadow moves over me, his strong, muscled arm over my belly, guiding my hand. I arch my hips forward, my free hand still clasping the book's cover, the soft leather warm like living skin. I tense my legs, reaching for release, my slick core aching, pulsing...

A hard knock on the shop's front door jerks me upright, but it's too late. My body convulses in a climax so sharp it steals my breath. Electric shivers dance from my center, up and down and everywhere. I have no choice but to ride out the sensation, biting my lips together to stifle my cries.

When my breath finally slows, I listen. The red door stands open just a crack. No one can see me back here, and the knocking has stopped.

Thank God. In no state to face an after-hours visitor, I rebutton my blouse and rise, unsteadily, to my feet.

Is the intruder gone? I peer around the red door and jerk backward on a gasp. The front lights are dark, as I've left them, but the streetlight outside reveals the silhouette of a tall man peering through the glass door. My pulse breaks into a fresh gallop.

Nick.

The lights above the entrance reflect in his glossy dark curls, so like the enticing figures in the book I've just released. Cupping his hand over his eyes, he searches the interior of the bookshop, the long fingers of his free hand splayed against the glass.

I can't let him see me like this, disheveled and flustered and flushed. Can I stay hidden until he gives up and leaves? Too late. He's seen the movement when I opened the red door. He raises his hand to wave.

Caught.

I scrape my tumbled hair back into place and gulp several steadying breaths before striding to the front door in my best imitation of calm confidence. With each step, the seam of my jeans rubs my still-tingling flesh, triggering aftershocks of pleasure.

I paste on a smile and unlock the door. "Hello, Nick. What brings you here so late?"

"I was driving back from Leo's place and saw your lights on." He glances at the slim gold watch on his wrist. "Sorry, Clara. I didn't realize how late it is." He pronounces my name slowly, as if enjoying its texture in his mouth. "Are you all right? I'm surprised to find you working at this hour and—alone?"

His eyes flick to the red door, then to my chest. Glancing down, I notice I've mis-buttoned my blouse. For a long moment I stand like a dolt, blushing hotly, my mouth hanging open.

He reaches for my shoulder and cups it gently, his hand heavy and warm through the thin satin.

"I'm sorry. I should've left you in peace. You must be tired. See you tomorrow?"

I nod, grateful he didn't ask what I was doing back there—not that it's any of his business.

"Tomorrow, yes. I'd better get home."

He glances up and down the street, now nearly deserted. At the corner, three grungy young guys lounge beneath a streetlamp, braying with laughter. One points toward us, and a fresh guffaw breaks out.

Nick executes the most elegant eye roll I've ever seen. "May I walk you to your car?"

My hand flutters to my chest. "Oh. Well, uh, thank you. I'll get my..." I quickstep to the counter and retrieve my purse.

"Aren't you forgetting something?" With a teasing smile, he inclines his head toward the red door. The light is still burning inside.

And so is my face, even though there's no way Nick could know what I was up to in there when he knocked, unless... Can he smell my arousal? Or does that only happen in romance novels?

"Right. I was just, er, shelving books. You know how easy it is to lose track of time when you're working, right?" Pivoting quickly to hide my reddened cheeks, I trot back to turn off the lights and lock the red door.

Nick waits while I shrug into my jacket and secure the shop, then crooks his arm, an invitation to slide my hand into the space he's made for me, just like Jared used to do—a charming, old-fashioned gesture, and a protective one. A twinge of guilt pinches me as I take his arm.

No matter how delicious Jared's dreamy touch might be, it can't match the warm solidity of Nick's flesh.

He walks me the few steps to where my Outback sits, now slick with rain. The drizzly evening mist pats my cheeks with butterfly kisses.

Nick lays his hand over mine, his skin at once silky and a bit rough. Calluses from rowing? My mind zooms back to the image of Nick in tight rowing shorts, his hefty erection seeming to reach toward me. Heat suffuses my face.

Either Nick doesn't notice, or he has the grace to pretend not to. "See you at seven-ish tomorrow?"

My tongue feels too thick. "Um, yes. Sure. I'll see you then." I release his arm and slide behind the wheel.

Before closing my car door, he leans in close, giving me a clear view of those dark, long-lashed eyes, those elegant high cheekbones, those silky curls, now spangled with mist.

"I'm grateful to have met you, Clara. It's not often I meet someone who's so easy to talk to. I hope..." He glances down and flashes a soft smile. "Well, I'm glad you're willing to share your time with me." With his forefinger, he touches my hair above my ear. A drop of water falls onto my jeans.

"Better get home and dry off." Something deliciously wicked glimmers in his dark eyes. "You're wet."

Chapter Thirteen

❤

Clara

"It's all about chemistry." Margot purses her lips and nods, a sage little professor lecturing me about life and love. "Either you feel it, or you don't. If there's no chemistry, all you can ever be is friends."

Biting back a grin because I remember how cocky I was at Margot's age, I slide another cookbook onto the bottom shelf. "And you have chemistry with Darcy?"

"Oh yeah." She fans herself with her hand. "Like, dangerous chemistry. Highly inflammable."

With a muffled groan over my still-sore muscles, I push to my feet. "But she's leaving soon."

Margot lowers her gaze, and her voice flattens. "Yeah, she is. But what am I gonna do, say no to a grand passion just because it's not permanent? I mean, passion is never permanent, right? It fizzles out and you're left with—I dunno, companionship? A nice roommate?"

I pat Margo's skinny shoulder through her vintage Ozzy T-shirt. "Jared and I shared a grand passion for seventeen years."

She claps her hand to her mouth. "Oh God, Clara, I'm sorry. I didn't mean—"

"It's okay. We had a wonderful time together, and..." I let my gaze drift toward the red door. "Maybe someday I'll feel that way about someone else. I mean, look at Harry. He's seventy-four, and he's absolutely smitten."

Her wistful smile is adorable. "Yeah, they're so cute together. I wonder if they..." She raises one pierced eyebrow.

"I'll bet they do. Like bunnies."

I leave my giggling assistant and return to my desk to wrestle with today's pile of bills, my own words echoing in my ears. This is the first time I've ever expressed that possibility aloud—passion with someone other than Jared. Even if it was just a casual comment, saying the words is a huge milestone, and I'm not sure how to feel about it.

And I pictured Nick's face when I said it—his chiseled cheekbones and strong jaw, his tawny skin, his dark eyes with glints of fire, his husky voice, his broad shoulders, his—A pling from my computer signals yet another demand for payment, this time from the department of public utilities.

I moan and slump in my chair. "How can we possibly spend so much on water? All we have is the one bathroom!"

Harry peers around the screen. "It's highway robbery."

"We've gotta find a way to up our profits, Harry."

He smacks his hands together and rubs them vigorously. "Well now, I have lots of ideas for you."

"I know you do, it's just..." Every week, he comes up with a new scheme to bring more customers into the shop, and most of them have been utter flops. The haiku club brought in a grand total of three participants, and the poetry books I ordered for their meeting didn't arrive on time. The indie comics party was scheduled the same weekend as Rose City Comic Con, so only a few broke stragglers showed up. The banned books club idea was a good one, but the big chain bookstore across town beat us to it. Meanwhile, our landlord is handing off the building's management to his son, who's rumored to be planning a brew pub. As if Downtown Eugene isn't already packed with pubs and taverns.

Harry hooks a thumb over his shoulder. "I was talking to Arnie next door. You know he sometimes has wine events, right?"

"Right…" Where on earth is he going with this?

He takes no notice of my skeptical tone. "Well, what we need is a beer night, with books. We'll call it Books and Brews! Arnie can bring in a local brewer or two, and you can set up beer-themed books, maybe bring in local authors." Harry paces back and forth, waving his hands.

"Beer-themed books, Harry?"

"Sure, why not?"

"Such as?"

"I'll find some. And I have lots of beer steins at home. We can fill them with free pencils or bookmarks." He resumes his pacing. Must be the running that gives him so much energy. "Why don't you hit up your local author contacts? I'll go talk to Arnie about the beer."

"I'll see what I can do." Resigned to another probable fiasco, I retreat to my desk and start sending emails.

Harry's still next door when Margot calls for my help with a customer wanting to sell used books. A middle-aged woman in a tailored blazer stands at the counter beside a brimming carton.

"I'm moving to a smaller place," she says, patting the building box. "Time to clear out the superfluous, get down to what really matters. You know what I mean?"

I don't, though, and that's the problem. I've filled my days with the bookshop for so long, I'm not sure what else really matters.

When I hand over her check, the woman tucks it into her breast pocket. "Don't you just love a fresh start? I'll use this to buy curtains for my new place." She winks. "Or maybe I won't.

Let the neighbors get an eyeful. Who knows? I might find a new lover to go with my new apartment. Nothing like a good romp to clear out the cobwebs, eh?"

Her saucy words are such a contrast to her strait-laced appearance, I can't help but laugh. And her playful attitude toward sex might do me good too. A meaningless fling might clear my mental cobwebs and get me started in a new direction.

Could Nick ever be my friend with benefits? God knows my body responds to his, and he's leaving Eugene soon. His imminent departure puts a limit on my expectations.

Or is Dalton the better choice? Clearly still working through his feelings about his ex, he probably isn't interested in love. A little friendly sex could invigorate both of us.

My body is definitely ready to dance again—preferably a passionate horizontal mambo—but my mind and heart remain shy wallflowers.

Frustrated with my own pointless rumination, I get back to work shelving books.

Harry returns fifteen minutes later carrying two large paper cups. "Black coffee for Clara, Hazelnut-Chocolate Latte with extra foam for Margot."

We both smooch his scratchy cheek.

"You're a peach, Harry," Margot chirps.

"And Arnie's going to look into beer vendors. Say, Clara, I had another idea while I was over there: how about we do something with the runners' group? We could get a speaker from the college, maybe offer a class and pile a table high with running books."

"And rowing?" Margot suggests, aiming a cartoonish wink at me.

"Sure, why not?" Harry slings his wiry arm over my shoulders. "Especially since you're a member of the club."

I raise my hands, palms out. "Hold on, I've only been running with you exactly once."

He squeezes me in a side hug. "You'll be back now that you and Dalton are keeping company. Too bad you can't come along on our trip this weekend."

"You're going on a trip?"

"Big race in Tacoma. I'm sitting this one out." He picks up a rag and polishes fingerprints off the glass counter, avoiding my gaze.

Well, shit. Doing without him on the weekend would be tough, but after all he's done for me, I hate to think of Harry missing out on a fun trip just to babysit my mopey, indecisive self.

"You should go with them, Harry."

He sets down his rag and wags his finger like a grandfather gently scolding a favorite grandchild. "Absolutely not. You're coming up on a tough time. There will be lots of other races. Once we get our sales up, you can hire another helper, and then I'll go."

Tears prickle my eyes as I slide my arms around his waist and squeeze. "Thank you, Harry. What would I do without you?"

His warm, callused hand closes over mine. "Don't give it another thought, dear heart."

But how can I not? Harry is spry and fit, but how many more years of running does he have left? I need to get my business healthy enough to spare my dear friend so he can run his races and have some well-earned fun. And if that means trying more kooky events, I'll do whatever it takes.

Chapter Fourteen

♥

Nick

"For goodness' sake, calm down, Nick." Ruth Goldfarb scoops baba ghanoush into a plastic bowl. "Nobody expects an elegant presentation in this place."

Easy for her to say. My temporary roommate is tops in her field, so she's already impressed the hell out of tonight's invitees—except for Clara, who will no doubt be charmed by Ruth's frank, friendly demeanor.

Meanwhile, I'm trying to polish a turd here, and I care a great deal about impressing the beautiful bookseller.

While Ruth washes up, Darcy sashays into the living room. "Nick is worried his new lady friend won't like this dump."

She's not wrong. The university's housing for visiting staff is shabby chic, minus the chic.

Ruth arches one gray eyebrow. "New lady friend? You're a fast mover, Nicolas."

"She's not my..."

Both women eye me with amused expressions.

"Okay, yes, I like her." Doing my best to ignore their teasing, I set out plastic wine glasses on the battered sideboard.

Ruth busies herself lighting candles. A chemistry professor from the University of Washington, she's leaving for home in a few days and suggested we co-host a party to thank our colleagues for their hospitality.

The scent of toasted spices wafts from the oven. "The nuts are ready," Ruth calls out. "Let's see. What can we serve them in?"

"How about this?" Darcy holds up a souvenir ashtray. "Greetings from Fabulous Las Vegas." When I raise an eyebrow, she adds, "It's clean."

"Viva Las Vegas." Ruth dumps the nut mix into the improvised serving bowl, then bustles off to her room, down the hall from mine and across from Darcy's.

"Sooo," Darcy ambles toward me, her hips swaying. "The merry widow's coming tonight?"

Glaring into the mirror above the fireplace, I straighten my tie, re-adjust the knot, then give up and pull the damned thing off.

Darcy gives me a Cheshire Cat smirk. "What's happened to my suave, lady-killer boss?" She leans forward to pick a crumb of mascara from her cheek, then tugs her brocade vest down to display the top of her lacy black bra.

I keep my expression carefully neutral, knowing if I don't give her a reaction, she'll lose interest in needling me. Sharp, insightful, and a tireless worker, Darcy is the best research assistant I've had—even if she sometimes pokes a toe over professional boundaries, like the gray tabby I once had who'd stare me in the face while reaching a paw toward my sandwich. Naughtiness is in Darcy's nature.

I very nearly let her go early in our working relationship, but once I made it clear I won't be one of her many playthings, we came to an understanding that works for both of us—mostly.

She's probably heard about my prior indiscretion, though she's never mentioned it, another point in her favor.

"Mind your own business, Darcy. Don't you have a date tonight?"

"I promised Doctor Goldfarb I'd help set up and serve." Pouting, she slicks dark red gloss over her lips. "Don't worry. I'll be out of your hair soon."

She's on the prowl tonight. That poor girl from Clara's shop won't know what hit her.

"Here, let me." Darcy pulls a comb from the pocket of her low-slung jeans and tackles my messy curls. "See? Much better. You're irresistible."

"Right," I deadpan and check my teeth again. "The next George Clooney."

"George who?" With a smile that drips scorn for her dinosaur boss, she pivots and struts away.

My reflection and I share an eye roll. I mean, sure, I didn't do too badly in the genetic lottery, but Diana never cared. "I fell in love with your heart, Nick, not your pretty face," she'd tease when she caught me at a mirror, "so come to bed and let me mess up those curls."

A familiar pang slides between my ribs. God, I miss her. In a perverse way, I wish I could ask her for advice about tonight. I'm so damn out of practice and nervous about coming on too strong.

Graceful and kind, Clara puts on a good show of being demure, but her languid movements and the heat in her sea-green eyes tell another story.

I unfasten the top two buttons of my shirt, then re-close one. Don't want to look like an oily lounge lizard.

I'm surprised she agreed to come at all, after I made such a spectacle of myself in the park.

My vision slides into soft focus at the memory of her feather-light touch on my hand, her soft lips on my cheek, her rose perfume, her silky hair falling across those fire-bright eyes...

"Come on, Eros. Stop mooning in the mirror and help us find serving platters." Ruth tilts her head toward the little kitchen.

That obvious, eh? With a self-conscious chuckle, I set to work plating Ruth's gourmet party nibbles. When the doorbell clangs, I wipe my damp palms on my pants. Deep breath. Be cool. I start toward the door.

"Got it." Darcy dashes ahead of me and flings open the door. Leo and three of his colleagues burst into the room, filling it with loud laughter and shouted greetings.

"Darcy, you luscious morsel." Leo wraps her in a bear hug and lifts her off her feet. "Is he driving you mad with his lovesick moaning?"

Well, shit. I've only mentioned Clara briefly to Ruth, just to let her know a non-university guest is coming, and I haven't discussed her at all with Darcy. And yet, all three of them are in on the joke.

Might as well wear a flashing neon sign: *Nick's smitten.*

Clara

Pulling my wrap tighter against the chilly evening wind, I totter along the sidewalk on the ridiculously high heels I chose for this not-really-a-date with Nick. I have zero experience with faculty parties, and I feel like a nervous undergrad on her way to an oral exam.

What do professors wear when socializing, anyway? Will the other party guests have Nick's casual elegance, or will they be rumpled and bawdy like his friend Leo? I hope my velvet jeans and silky T-shirt strike the right note.

Nick's temporary quarters turn out to be a stucco cottage near the U of O. Amazing how little the scenery has changed here. Even at this late hour, students lounge on benches, sprawl on the lawns, stroll hand in hand between the residence halls and classroom buildings.

A vivid flash of memory halts my steps. There it is across the street, the enormous red maple where I first met Jared. He was lounging against the trunk, his long, muscular legs stretched out in front of him. I was walking by, my nose buried in a book, and tripped over him, leaving us both scraped and bruised. He insisted on taking me to the health clinic, and the rest, as they say, was kismet.

But Jared is gone, and here I am, trying to rebuild my life one precarious step at a time.

I raise my chin. I can do this. I'm an intelligent, mature woman who is perfectly capable of making small talk with strangers. If nothing else, tonight will be good exercise for my long-neglected social muscles.

Before climbing the low steps to Nick's door, I extract a brush from my purse and run it through my hair, then immediately regret not having pinned it up. Up looks sophisticated. Down looks messy. Damn.

I squeeze my eyes shut and breathe deeply. *Help me, Jared. I'm scared.*

"On your left." A young man on a racing bike zooms past. His slipstream lifts my hair and brushes my nape.

A young woman follows him, her passage wobblier. "Sorry," she calls over her shoulder.

The cottage's door opens, spilling light and laughter onto the narrow walkway.

"Here she is!" Nick's friend Leo booms from the doorway. "Come in, dear lady. We're looking at your dirty books."

For a split-second, I fight the urge to flee. But Nick was so kind to me yesterday. The memory of his sympathetic gaze and soft touch pushes me up the stairs.

Nick's dark head appears over his friend's shoulder. When his eyes meet mine, they widen, and his nostrils flare. Just a lightning-quick reaction, probably unconscious, but my heart flutters like a manic squirrel.

"Clara, I'm so glad you came." He nudges Leo aside, takes my hands, and stands in the doorway, his mouth half-open as if about to say something.

I wait, barely breathing.

With a gentle grip, he eases me across the threshold.

Nothing scary happens. In fact, this gathering looks like a typical grad-student party, but with quieter music. About fifteen people ranging from early thirties to Harry's age sit on the saggy couch, perch on wooden stools, or stand in clusters, chatting and laughing. Candles in jars flicker from the mantelpiece, the scarred sideboard, and various other pieces of scuffed-up furniture. On the dining room table, half-empty dishes remind me I haven't eaten in hours.

A motherly, sixty-something woman strides over, her beaded earrings jingling.

"You must be Clara. I'm Ruth Goldfarb, Nick's roommate." Laugh crinkles frame her friendly gray eyes. "Don't worry, dear, I'll be leaving in a few days, so Nick will have this palace all to himself. Come, let me introduce you to my colleagues."

Ruth links her plump arm through mine and introduces me to several chemistry professors munching and conversing over the coffee table. This bunch is more or less what I expected: older academics wearing rumpled sport coats or plain knit dresses. In her embroidered tunic and leggings, Ruth is by far the most colorful.

The anthropologists, on the other hand, are more boisterous. Reclaiming me from Ruth, Nick leads me to where Leo holds court at the dining room table, roaring with laughter and dishing out teasing comments along with plates of food.

"Here's the lady now," he bellows as we approach.

From a tall stool at the kitchen counter, Darcy glances up from her phone and raises one corner of her scarlet mouth, then slides down and ambles toward us, hips swaying like a pendulum.

"If you're all set, Nick, I'll take off now." She fixes me with a heavy-lidded stare. "You two have fun." She saunters away.

A tall woman with thick blonde-gray braids chuckles. "Well, someone doesn't like sharing the spotlight." She holds out her hand. "I'm Greta. Nice to meet you, Clara. I want to hear more about your bookshop. Get the lady some wine, Nick. Where are your manners?"

Nick shoots me an apologetic look and moves off to do her bidding.

Greta turns out to be another anthropologist at the U of O, specializing in archeology. She tows me to a wooden desk holding Nick's book purchases and opens a hefty volume: *Erotic Temple Art of Ancient India*.

Oh Lord, this is embarrassing. I'm no prude, but examining sexy art with strangers, even professional experts, makes my cheeks flush hot. I scan the room for an escape route, but Nick has disappeared.

"This is one of the best books I've seen about the Khajuraho temples." Greta points to a carving of a man and woman coupling in a particularly acrobatic way. "I've taken a lot of yoga classes, but I've never tried this pose. Imagine if you fell." She giggles like a girl half her age.

"I like this one better," a heavyset guy interjects, pointing over Greta's shoulder to a stone frieze of couples in erotic poses: lying down, standing up, upside-down, front to back, a woman sandwiched between two men, oral sex for her, for him, for both...

"Something for everyone." Grinning, he extends his hand. "Louie Stern, U Dub, bio anthro."

"I beg your pardon?"

Nick steps up behind us, holding two glasses of wine. "Clara's a civilian. You'll have to speak English to her."

I barely resist the urge to lean back against him and drink in his warmth and his woodsy scent.

Louie elaborates, "University of Washington, biological anthropology. Mostly bones of ancient humans. Not as sexy as Nick's work, I'm afraid."

"Nick's a sexy guy," Leo claps his friend on the back. "Even his bones are sexy."

Nick rolls his eyes. "Leo's always busting my ba—er—chops." He hands me a glass. "I hope red's okay. The chemists already drank up all the white."

"Red is fine." I take a sip. "Very good."

Mega understatement—the wine is rich, spicy, heady, like the man who poured it.

While the anthropologists examine Nick's books, their conversation punctuated with chuckles and guffaws, I follow him to the little kitchenette, where we perch on stools at the counter.

He nudges me softly with his shoulder. "Thanks for coming, Clara. I'm sorry they're such doofuses tonight."

"Your friends are not what I expected. They're..." I lose my train of thought under the spell of his heavy-lashed, dark eyes. Holding Nick's gaze is the bravest thing I've done in a long, long time.

Finally, he looks away and sips his wine, freeing me to breathe again. His rumbling laugh sets a hundred fireflies dancing deep in my belly.

"If you never leave college, you sometimes forget how grownups act. These guys swoop in, gobble up all the food, drink all the booze, then take off." Leaning closer, he whispers, "That's the good news. They'll be gone soon."

Those fireflies zoom in dizzy circles, crashing into each other and setting off sparks. I gulp my wine, just as Leo rushes over waving another book. "Get a load of the rump on this one!"

My ill-timed giggle makes me snort wine, leading to a coughing fit. By the time I catch my breath, I've got wine dribbling down my chin and tears streaming down my cheeks.

"Leo, for God's sake!" Nick glares at his friend and pulls a linen handkerchief from his pocket.

"Oh, sorry. Proceed." Looking not one bit contrite, Leo retreats.

I clutch Nick's handkerchief in my clean hand, unwilling to stain it.

"It's okay," he reassures me. "I have lots. My grandmother sends a box every year at Christmas."

"Well, thank you." Feeling like a clumsy dork, I mop up the mess. "So, how's your project going?"

"Excellent, thanks to you."

"Oh? I'm, uh, glad to help."

Nick spins his stool to face me, his elbow on the counter. "You know, I've found several mentions of your shop in book collectors' forums, but nothing on any academic site. You're missing a big market."

"You mean, all the professors with sexy bones?"

He chuckles. "Well, anthro people like Leo and me, plus art historians, sociologists, students... If I were closer, I'd help you catalogue your collection and design a better website."

"It's a shame you're not closer, Nick." Already, the wine is loosening my inhibitions. "I mean, I could use the help."

"Nicolas." Ruth steps into the kitchen, her voice stern. "You're a terrible host. Have you offered this young lady something to eat? The shrimp toasts are almost gone, and the dates are getting cold."

"Sorry, sorry. Shall we, Clara? Too much wine on an empty stomach makes me talkative."

Nick and I finish off the bacon-wrapped dates, along with the last of the silky eggplant dip, some crisp sliced fennel, several marinated olives, and garlicky shrimp in olive oil.

"So good," I mumble around my last bite.

Nick swipes his sauce-smeared plate with a hunk of bread. "Once Ruth leaves, we'll be limited to takeout, I'm afraid. That is, if you come back. I hope you will." He wipes his mouth, and I watch the napkin's path across his lips, riveted.

"I can cook," I blurt, then kick myself mentally because a boast like that requires a follow-up dinner invitation.

"Oh, can you now?" Nick cocks one glossy black eyebrow.

Retreat! "I seldom bother anymore since it's just me."

Another outbreak of braying laughter makes me jolt.

Nick rolls his eyes. "Come on, let's sit over here."

We settle onto a pair of cushions on the hearth and chat about our favorite dishes, an easy, safe topic. Nick's eyes turn dreamy as he describes his mother's moussaka. "Better than anything you'll find in a Greek restaurant. Her béchamel is so fluffy."

"Wait, isn't your father the Greek one?"

"He is. Mom's father was Nigerian, but she grew up in Portland. When she and Dad traveled to Greece, she learned Greek cooking from my grandmother."

While Nick rhapsodizes about his mother's cooking, the guests begin to take their leave, and when Leo comes over to say goodbye, I realize the room has mostly cleared.

Nick and Leo exchange a back-slapping hug, then Leo crooks his arm. "Miss Clara, it was a delight to see you again. Walk me to the door, won't you?"

Nick's eyes narrow. "Leo, you can find the door on your own."

"I'll give her back, Nick. Just chill." Leo takes my arm and steers me toward the exit.

Outside, we stand side by side on the porch. The cool evening air is refreshing after the stuffiness of the cottage. Crickets thrum their night song from junipers lining the path.

"So, you like my friend?" Leo's expression is friendly enough, but his blue eyes scrutinize me closely.

"I, uh...yes. I like Nick."

A subtle shift in his posture prickles my skin with goosebumps. He folds his arms over his chest. "It's hard to believe, but our Nick has had some bad luck with the ladies."

"You mean Diana?"

His expression softens. "She was one of a kind. Losing her nearly broke him. But he's had other problems." His eyes narrow. "And the way he's looking at you worries me. It's unlike him to ignore his friends the way he did tonight."

A flush rises from my chest to my hairline. "What are you saying, Leo?"

He clamps his big hands onto my shoulders and squeezes, not painfully, but firmly enough to pin me in place. "You're not toying with my friend's heart, are you, Clara? Because I don't want to see him go through that again."

Emotions roll through me, knocking me off balance: anger, defensiveness, confusion. Fortunately, Nick steps into the doorway, putting an end to Leo's interrogation.

Leo clicks his heels and executes a crisp bow. "Good night then, lovely lady. Nick." He strolls away, his gait loose and easy, as if he hasn't just accused me of...what, exactly?

Nick gently grips my arm, his forehead rumpled, his eyes sharp. "Was Leo putting the moves on you?"

"No, I...We were just talking." I suck in a deep breath and give him a smile I hope rings true. Until I understand what Leo's getting at with his pointed comments, I won't insert myself between two old friends.

"Just talking?" Nick's eyebrows shoot up, but when I don't elaborate, he lets it go. "Ruth's going to bed. Do you have time for one more drink?" He grins down at his shoes. "Maybe we could check out some of your books?"

I'm still not sure what Leo meant by "the way Nick was looking at me," but the look he's giving me now is adorably playful. A glossy black curl tumbles onto his forehead, and his dark eyes sparkle. The smart part of my brain waves a warning flag. But other parts? Lulled by wine and the nearness of this beautiful man, those parts flush with courage.

"Why not? Let's."

Chapter Fifteen

♥

Clara

"You looked so serious just now. I know Leo can be a little tactless. Did he upset you?" Nick's forehead rumples with concern as he holds up a wine glass and a bottle of Malbec.

"Just a taste. I have to drive home."

He pours me a half-glass of garnet wine. I sniff the plummy aroma, then sip. "Wow. Powerful."

He sticks his nose into his glass and snuffles like a bloodhound. "Suave," he croons, "with notes of blackberry and pencil shavings."

"And the faintest hint of gym socks."

"A fine wine for looking at dirty pictures." He turns down the volume on the Brazilian jazz playing from a speaker on the mantelpiece, then gathers an armful of books. "You haven't answered my question, though. What was up with Leo?"

Panic flutters in my throat. "You don't trust your friend?"

"With my life. And I recognize that look he gets when he's up to something." He raises one perfect eyebrow.

Reluctant to stir up trouble, I choose my words carefully. "He was—concerned. He mentioned a problem with women in your past."

With a thump, Nick drops onto the couch beside me. The worn cushions sag under his weight, sending me sliding up against him. He pinches the bridge of his nose. "I can't believe he told you about—"

I lay my hand on his knee. "He didn't give me any details. He just asked if I was trifling with your, um, affections."

"Shit." He slumps against the seat back, sighs up at the ceiling, then tilts his head toward me, his smooth confidence replaced by crumpled resignation. "Clara, I'm sorry. He has no business grilling you."

"Hey, it's okay. He obviously cares about you. It was weird, though."

"Well, he helped me through a hard time a while ago. He means well, but he can be overprotective."

I can relate. The few friends who stuck around after Jared's death sometimes treat me like I'm made of thin porcelain. Until lately, that is, when Harry and Margot started pushing me to date again.

"Think nothing of it." I raise my glass. "Here's to overprotective friends."

We clink and sip, then Nick raises his glass again, "To anthropology. Without it, I wouldn't have come to your shop, and I wouldn't have met you."

"Okay. To anthropology." Another clink, another sip. At this rate, I'll need a rideshare home.

"I almost did archeology, you know." Nick grins. "As a kid, I read about King Tut. I used to dig up stuff in my backyard: old bones, rocks. I set up a 'museum' in the potting shed."

"What changed your mind?"

"A trip to Pompeii my freshman year. Have you seen those frescoes? Boom. Horny history nerd changes his major."

As he leans across my lap to grab a book from the coffee table, his shoulder brushes against my breast, a little whisper of stolen pleasure.

Nick opens the book, *The Erotic Art of Pompeii and Herculaneum*.

"I think this is the one Leo was bellowing about. Most of these are frescoes from brothels discovered when Pompeii was excavated in the eighteenth century. See?"

The images are cracked and faded, but still remarkably well-preserved, considering they survived centuries of burial in volcanic ash.

"Here's Priapus, god of sex and fertility." The Roman god wears a serious expression and an impossibly enormous erection.

"And these are from the walls of a brothel." He points to a short-haired man reclining against cushions while a wide-hipped woman with elegantly upswept hair straddles him.

Nick's hand brushes against mine as he turns another page. "This one's from the public baths." A naked woman with a serene expression sprawls on a bed while a toga-clad man crouches before her, his face against her shaved crotch.

They shaved back then?

"They're, um, lovely." I take another sip of wine to cool my parched mouth.

Nick closes the book. "Am I making you uncomfortable, Clara?"

"Not at all," I lie. Maybe it's the alcohol, or maybe it's his solid, warm body pressed against mine, but despite my embarrassment, I'm eager to see more. "I'd love to visit Pompeii someday."

"You should." His dark eyes sparkle with enthusiasm. "It's eerie, walking those streets. Any minute, you expect someone in a toga to emerge from a doorway and beckon you inside."

I point to the page. "Into a brothel like this?"

He chuckles. "We have this silly idea that people long ago were stuffier about sex, but in many cases, they were much more relaxed about it than we are today. Like here. This is one of my favorites."

Nick opens the next book across his lap and reveals engravings of white-wigged ladies and gentlemen cavorting half-dressed, their flushed, swollen genitals on display.

"Paul-Émile Bécat. Early twentieth century. His drawings pay homage to an era devoted to pleasure."

Nick's long forefinger traces the drawing, a young woman wearing only her wig, white silk stockings, and a dreamy expression, impaled on the rigid cock of a dark-haired young man wearing only a poufy shirt. The two of them balance on an ornate chair, while the man glances over his shoulder to a male visitor standing primly in the doorway.

"His specialty was illustrated playing cards, like these. He was quite prolific."

As I flip through page after mesmerizing page, a tingling warmth builds between my thighs. When I lean closer to examine the drawings, the slippery, sloped leather cushion slides me against his leg. He keeps his gaze on the artwork, but the book trembles slightly in his hands, and his breath fans my cheek.

"This one is extraordinary." He flips to a rosy fantasy of ancient Greece. A dark-haired couple reclines on the ground beneath a tree, captured in mid-coitus. Both are naked but for Greek-style sandals. The male figure has white-feathered wings, and a quiver of arrows lie on the ground beside the lovers. Their bodies are beautifully rendered, smooth and ideal, their genitals exquisitely detailed. The girl lies on her back, the youth on his side, affording a complete view of his engorged cock parting her furry folds. The artist perfectly captures their slow, languorous movement, the luscious union of their bodies.

Nick softly closes the book and lays it across his lap. He leans back on the sofa and sighs.

So do I.

"How does he do it?" I ask when my galloping pulse finally slows to a trot. "Those drawings are so, so…"

Nick flashes a bashful grin. "I think it has to do with really enjoying sex and loving the human body. He drew every possible combination—men with men, men with women, women with women, mixed groups. He just enjoyed the gift of sensual pleasure."

"Doesn't everyone?"

"I'm not so sure. Most of us wrap our sexual urges in so many other agendas, we lose our connection to our bodies, to the joy of…"

I giggle. "*The Joy of Sex*? You have that book too?"

"Of course, it's a classic. The artwork is kind of charming, in a hairy hippie sort of way."

Our laughter eases the tension between us.

I stretch and yawn. "Sorry, long day. So, you collect all this erotic artwork, and then you write about it?"

"Basically, yes. My book will explain shifting notions of sexual attractiveness throughout history."

"And will this be a book we'd stock in our store?"

"If I do my job right." He gazes at me over the rim of his glass as he takes a languorous sip. A scarlet drop clings to the corner of his mouth.

I stare, transfixed. Should I dab at the drop with my napkin? With my tongue?

I force my eyes away from the tempting sight. Though I haven't finished my second glass of wine, the room is spinning. The explicit drawings, the sensual rumble of Nick's voice, the warmth of his thigh pressed against mine—it all combines to create a powerful intoxication. I clench my hands in my lap, crumbling my paper napkin.

Nick flicks the drop away with the tip of his tongue, and I release a noisy sigh of relief. He arches an eyebrow, then reaches across my body again and grasps another book. His muscles flex beneath his thin sweater, and my gaze caresses the tapered line from his broad shoulders to his trim waist.

I'm faced with a choice—cut this off now or jump his bones. Because I can't resist much longer.

Caution prevails, and I lay my hand lightly against his back. "Nick, I think I've seen enough sexy artwork for one night." My voice quivers. I gulp the rest of my wine, then set my glass down on the coffee table with too much force, chipping the base. Heat flushes my whole face. Hell, I'm probably strawberry-red from hairline to toes. "Damn. I'm sorry."

Nick reassures me in a soothing voice, "I'm the one who should apologize. I'm making you uncomfortable." He sweeps up the shard with his napkin and flashes me a boyish smile. "I work with images like this every day, so I sometimes forget others aren't used to this stuff. Please know I had no intention of upsetting you."

He takes my hands, and I try hard to force a calm expression, even though my pulse is racing. The amber flecks in his eyes dance in the candlelight, their glow drawing the truth out of me like a magnet tugging metal.

Deep breath. Just ask. He won't bite.

"Nick, how did you know when it was time?"

"Time?"

"To move on. To let someone in."

He shifts away, but the saggy sofa cushion slides him back against my thigh.

"Can't fight gravity." Chuckling, he drapes his arm across my shoulders. "Honestly, my body was ready before my heart was. Even if the heart is withered, the body goes on breathing, eating, feeling, wanting." He fingers a strand of my hair, his gaze far away. "A friend saw how closed off I'd become, and she...helped me."

"How?"

"By seducing me. There was wine involved, and music. She was—persuasive." He cups my shoulder. "And I'm grateful to her for nudging me across that threshold."

Avoiding his penetrating gaze, I focus on the flickering candles. "Did you love her?"

"Yes and no."

"Huh?"

He shifts again, his expression solemn. "You see, I'll never love anyone the way I loved Diana. She was unique in all the world. But she wouldn't want me to spend the rest of my days pining for her, miserably alone. My friend helped me realize it's okay to enjoy my life, and that one day I might even love again." The corners of his lips twitch upward. "It's not something you can rush, but it will come in time if you relax and open your heart." He lays his hand on my knee and squeezes gently. "And I'll always love her for that."

"You don't feel disloyal to Diana?"

"No, I don't. Diana is always with me, in here." He taps his breastbone. "I haven't forgotten her."

"Wow." I sink against the back of the sofa. "I need a friend like that."

There's a change in Nick's gaze—a brightness that flares in his dark irises. With exquisite slowness, he traces my jawline with his forefinger.

"You'll find that friend when the time is right." He glances at his watch. "In any case, it's late. I'm afraid I've had too much wine to drive you home. Shall I call you a ride?"

I stifle a groan of disappointment. If he'd let his hand drop from my face to somewhere below, would I have resisted? Or would I have clutched his warm, beautiful body like a lifeline?

I'm torn between regret and relief. Soon I'll decide if I'm ready to take this step, and if Nick is the man to help me through it.

Soon, but not yet.

I pull out my phone and open the rideshare app. "Thanks, I've got it. I'm parked a few blocks away. I'll come fetch my car in the morning."

He stands in one smooth motion, grasps my hand, and pulls me to my feet, treating me to a view of his bulging biceps. Knocked off-center by the sudden movement, the wine, and Nick's nearness, I land with my palm against his chest. His warm, broad, solid chest.

With a low, sexy laugh, he grasps my arms to steady me. "If you leave me your keys, I'll drop off your car tomorrow morning. What's better for you, the bookshop or your place?"

The thought of Nick on my doorstep triggers a shiver of panic. "The shop, please. I can walk to work. It's not far."

We wait together on his front stoop while stars wink in the inky sky. The cottage's patchy lawn already sparkles with dew, and the sounds of campus life have faded to late-night quiet. When I shiver beneath my thin wrap, Nick steps behind me and wraps his arms around my shoulders. His hair tickles my temple as he murmurs in my ear, "I'm so glad you came, Clara. Thank you for trusting me."

I nestle into his arms, relishing the warmth. As long as I don't turn to face him, I'm safe.

His voice rumbles through his chest. "I understand what you're going through because I've been there, Clara. I promise not to ask for anything you're not ready to give, but I'd love to see you again."

A smile stretches my lips. "I'd like that."

"How about Friday?"

I stiffen in his arms. Damn, I'd nearly forgotten about my date with Dalton.

His lips brush my ear. "Ah, you're busy. Saturday, then?"

The driver pulls up, the idling of his engine almost loud enough to cover the thundering of my heart.

"Saturday." Gathering my courage, I pivot to face him. His tawny skin gleams softly in the golden light of the porch lamp, like some ancient deity lit from within. Longing pierces me to the marrow. I brush my fingers along his jaw and wait, barely breathing.

The moment unfolds in slow motion. Nick's lids lower and his plump lips part as he slowly closes the distance and presses his mouth to mine. That first soft contact is like a pebble tumbling into a pond, sending ripples of pleasure out and down in ever-expanding waves until my whole body tingles. One slow, shared breath, and then he kisses me again, oh so softly, the tip of his tongue gently probing, searching for mine. One small taste, and then he releases me.

Drunk pleasure, I sway on my high heels, nearly tumbling backward down the stairs.

"Whoa, let me help you."

I cling to the hard curve of his biceps until I'm safely inside the car.

Nick presses a soft kiss to my fingertips before letting go. "Good night, Clara."

I open my mouth, but I've forgotten how to speak, how to breathe. The driver pulls away, and I watch Nick fade into the summer night.

Nick

I watch Clara's rideshare retreat until it disappears around the corner. Most of the surrounding houses are dark, the empty street silent except for the crickets' song and the distant hum of traffic. But the night air seems to vibrate with promise. Even though the chilly breeze raises goosebumps on my skin, a thrum of energy warms my body.

That kiss—

If I grin any wider, my cheeks will crack.

I've kissed a dozen women in the two years since Diana's death, but never in that time has a kiss affected me like Clara's. The soft warmth of her thigh against mine, her heavy, silky hair brushing my shoulder, the whisper of her breath against my lips... It cost every last atom of strength to keep from deepening our kiss, pressing against her, pulling her back inside the cottage. Would she have come? Or would she have bolted?

Eleven more days. Not much time to earn the trust of a woman whose loss is so fresh, whose heart is so barricaded. Despite the aching tension in my groin, I'm glad I held back. If I'm careful, eleven days might be enough to start something real.

And then what? I've committed to a two-week seminar for graduate students. Afterward, maybe a visit to my sister in Corvallis, only an hour away from Eugene, and our mother's house in Portland. Now that Leo is single again, he might welcome my company.

My laugh echoes in the empty street. Who'd have thought I'd be so eagerly planning a summer of couch-surfing instead of enjoying my spacious apartment in Berkeley? I seldom have time to explore the city I've called home for five years, the city that will become my permanent home if I make tenure.

When I took the job, I figured Berkeley was close enough to my family, but if I fall for Clara... I glance at my little Karmann Ghia parked in the driveway. I'm going to need a sturdier car for all those trips up to Oregon.

If I fall? Hell, I'm so gone for this woman, it's ridiculous.

My phone buzzes in my pocket: a late-night text from Enid Barthlesmann, my department chair.

Enjoying your visit to the Ducks?

Why would she contact me at this hour? I picture Enid's round face, her cloud of white hair, her colorful jewelry clinking and jangling as she zips through the hallways. I'm damn lucky to have such a powerful ally, especially after last year's blunder. Without her support, I'd have been toast.

I text back:

> Always fun up here. Leo sends his regards. How's George?

> No better, no worse. Having a hard night. Everything on track for your July class?

> Yes, Ma'am.

> Good. Tenure committee meeting soon. Make your class sparkle, kiddo.

I tuck my phone away. Tomorrow is soon enough to worry about sparkle. Tonight, I'm basking in the glow of new possibilities, maybe even new love. I cast one more glance at the stars, sparkling like diamonds scattered on velvet.

Tonight I spoke brave words to Clara about fresh starts and opening her heart, but words are one thing, actions another. I'll have to navigate some big obstacles—like geographical distance and that bald guy she's dating—but she's worth the effort. A bone-deep certainty tells me our connection was meant to be.

Chapter Sixteen

♥

Clara

"I should sleep with him. Just get it over with. Right?"

"Mew."

My lips still tingling from last night's kiss, I pace up and down the empty aisle, muttering to myself. Lulu trails after me, adding her wisdom to the debate.

"I mean, I've gotta take the first step sometime. Why not now?"

"Mowrr."

"Nick's here. He's willing. He's gorgeous."

"Meow."

"And he'll be gone in, what, two weeks?"

"Mrrowrp."

"After I cross the threshold, I can forget about him."

"Prrrupp."

"I was this close, Lulu." I hold my forefinger and thumb a millimeter apart. "I could've just taken his hand, gone back inside, and..."

Images flash in my mind's eye: my hands sliding under his shirt, over his tawny skin, tugging at his belt, his breath hot on my throat...

"God, listen to me!" I plop into the armchair at the head of the history aisle. "I can't just use Nick. And if I did, which would be despicable, I couldn't just snap my fingers and forget him, not after how kind and compassionate he's been."

Lulu springs into my lap. I stroke her fur absently.

"That's the problem. I like him too much. He's too..." My vision slides into dreamy soft focus, and my head lolls, offering my throat to his imaginary kiss. Then I jolt upright. "I should call him and cancel our date for Saturday. I really should."

Lulu offers no comment beyond a swish of her floofy tail.

I slump back in my chair. "Maybe Dalton's the better choice?"

"Mrrrrrrr." Lulu lays back her ears.

"What? He's cute, he's nice, he's here. And he's Harry's cousin." I giggle. "And he has a huge..."

The cat hops down and stalks toward her basket behind the counter, her tail held high.

"You're right. I don't have to have sex with anyone."

"Of course you don't have to. But do you want to?"

I squeak and jump to my feet.

Margot must've let herself in through the back door, the one with no warning bell overhead. Sneaky little ninja.

She plants her fists on her hips and peers down the aisles on either side of me. "Sorry, didn't mean to interrupt. Who are you talking to?" She clutches her Doctor Bacon T-shirt, eyes wide. "Oh. Were you talking to Jared?"

"No, just myself."

As if I weren't already suffering enough, now guilt stabs me at the thought of being unfaithful to Jared, the love of my life, the one I still turn to for guidance. How can I ask him whether to have sex with another man?

"This is impossible," I mutter under my breath and stride to the front door, where the UPS guy waits with a carton of books.

"Morning, Clara. I've got two more for you in the van." He's wearing shorts today. Bobby's too young for me, but those legs! Strong, tan, covered with golden fuzz. I bet they'd tickle against my skin.

Great, now I'm ogling the delivery dude. Clearly, I need to get laid and clear up all this distracting sexual tension. I should be focused on my business, not my libido.

And Dalton is definitely the safest candidate, because if just one kiss from Nick sets my head spinning like this, imagine what a night in his bed would do.

A shiver shimmies down my spine as I imagine just that.

"This one's heavy. Where do you want it?" The UPS guy's biceps bulge under the weight of the huge carton.

"On the counter, please."

A second man trails in, half-hidden by the oversized box he carries. This guy's wearing long pants, but the rear view is very nice indeed: a firm, round butt, narrow waist, broad shoulders, curly dark hair...

"Thanks, man," Bobby tells his helper.

"Don't mention it." Nick sets his load down on the counter and flashes a killer grin.

I gape at him like a goldfish fallen from its bowl.

The UPS guy has to ask me a second time to sign for my packages, which I quickly do, then scoot around the counter, putting distance between myself and the man who makes my heart pound like a conga drum. No, make that the whole rhythm section.

Lulu saves the day. She trots over from her favorite basking spot in the front window and, purring loudly, makes passionate love to Nick's ankles, twining round and round.

Margot and I exchange a puzzled glance. Lulu usually waits for strangers to approach her. Not satisfied with a scritch behind the ears, she vaults into Nick's arms. Our shop cat is smitten.

He murmurs sweet nothings to the cat, a fond smile lighting up his chiseled Greek god face.

Margot wiggles her fingers. "Good morning, Professor. Good to see you again."

Nick carries Lulu to the window and points with his cleft chin. "All the parking spaces on this side were filled, so I left your car over there, in front of the donut shop."

"How about donuts and books?" Margot calls from behind the counter, where she's loading new volumes onto the rolling cart.

"We're still working on the beer idea." I incline my head toward the back of the shop.

"I'll put this invoice on your desk." Taking the hint, Margot disappears behind the screen, no doubt to eavesdrop.

Nick dangles my car keys from his forefinger. Apparently satisfied with the arrangement of orange hairs she's left on his dark shirt, Lulu leaps down, butts her head against my ankles, and trots off.

Nick moves closer and lowers his voice. "I hope you're as happy to see me as your cat is."

"Shall I rub my head against your ankles?" I bite my lip. I shouldn't be flirting with him, especially since I'm so conflicted about how to handle the whole Nick-or-Dalton, sex-or-no-sex situation, but with Nick so near, his dark eyes sparkling, my resolve melts like ice cream in the Sahara.

This would all be so much easier if I hadn't kissed him.

He leans on the counter, bringing his face level with mine. With one finger, he toys with my scarf—actually, Jared's, an antique silk aviator's scarf he wore on our first New Year's Eve together. Its coolness soothes my overheated skin.

"So, are we still on for Saturday?"

Say no, say no, say no.

But the voice of reason has no power over my stupid mouth. "Sure. I'm looking forward to it."

A slow smile spreads across Nick's lips. "Good. My friend Carmen is performing at a wine bar near the campus, The Amphora. Do you know it?"

I shake my head.

His eyes flick toward the wooden screen, and he slides closer, lowering his voice to a near-whisper. "Clara, I'm so glad we've met on this trip. I didn't come here looking for..."

He pauses as if searching for the right words. "For romance. But I want you to know, I feel a very special connection with you."

Romance? Oh my.

I clear my throat. "But Nick, you live so far away."

"I wish I didn't." He fingers my scarf, his hand hovering dangerously close to my breast. "But my family is here. I have friends here." He raises his eyes to mine. "I'll be back as often as I can manage."

"Oh." The sound escapes on a whoosh of breath. The promise of his return changes things. A lot.

The shop phone shrills from my desk. A moment later, Margot pops out from behind the screen, her face solemn. "Clara, I'm sorry. You're going to want to take this."

"I'll let you go, then." Nick runs his hand down my arm, his touch light. "See you Saturday at seven-thirty?"

"Yes."

"Here?"

"My place." With effort, I step backward, breaking his magnetic hold on me. "Twenty-seven thirty-nine Elm. Upper flat. Gotta go." I dart behind the screen before I do something foolish, like kissing him again.

At my desk, Margot covers the receiver with her palm. "It's Lonnie."

Lonnie Davenport owns the building housing Book Nirvana, along with Coffee Dreams next door. A jovial fellow of about seventy, he's been very kind since Jared's death. But now he's retiring and handing the management of the building over to his son, a forty-something, self-styled business shark with beady eyes. Between gossip from Arnie's café and cryptic comments from Lonnie, I know big changes are coming.

"Clara." His voice is rough today, phlegmy and ragged. "Kid-do, I need to set up a meeting. How about this afternoon?"

"Oh, um..." I tap the keyboard, checking my schedule. "Sure. What time?"

"Let's say two at Arnie's place."

"Okay..." But he hangs up before I can ask any questions.

"Can you stay until two, Margot?"

"Sorry, I have a class. Big graphics presentation. Harry should be here, though."

I'd hoped Harry might attend the meeting with me, but I have no one else to man the shop during my absence. I'll have to face this alone. I hunch over my desk, my fingers snarled in my hair.

Margot's hand falls lightly onto my shoulder. "Think he's going to raise the rent?"

"At least."

"End the lease?"

"Maybe." I've been keeping that possibility on the back shelf, carefully hidden behind daily business. The thought of losing Book Nirvana twists my gut into knots. Surely Lonnie won't do that to us. He loves the bookshop. He toasted our success when we cut the ribbon on opening day. He stood by my side at Jared's funeral.

"Don't worry, Clara." Margot's pixie face is grave. "We'll figure something out."

I pat her hand. "I know we will."

The doorway bell tinkles, and Margot leaves to greet the customers. I stay behind the cover of the wooden screen, my busy brain spinning dire possibilities. I cradle my throbbing head and whisper, "Help me, Jared."

A loud thunk springs me upright again.

"Lulu, what's got into you today?" Margot calls.

I go out to investigate. Tail twitching, Lulu perches at eye level on the shelf nearest my desk and stares at the paperback she's knocked to the floor: *Coffee: Our Favorite Addiction.* While I watch, she bats another volume off the shelf: *Coffee: A Love Story.*

"Shoo, Puss." I pick up the two books and lift the cat down. She orbits my ankles a few times, then strolls away.

This is Jared's answer? Get a coffee? Must be a coincidence. I'm already too jazzed up on worry and lust. Coffee would only make things worse.

"I'm sorry, Clara, but it's the best I can do." Lonnie clasps his big, callused hands on the table, his baggy eyes downcast.

Beside him, his son Darryl smirks over a pile of papers.

"Pops has a big heart, but he doesn't have a head for business. Me, I see things more clearly. It's nothing personal, Mrs. Martelli. We're in business to turn a profit, not to support charity cases."

My guts roil, and my fingers itch to smack that oily smile right off his smug face.

Beside me, Arnie narrows his eyes. "I call bullshit. We've both paid our rent on time for years. You won't find better tenants than us."

"Remodeling the building will cost you a fortune," I add. "Keep us and you don't incur any new expenses."

Darryl sneers. "A brew pub will bring in more customers in a week than you do in a month. I already have an excellent offer on this property. My market research shows..."

"Whoever did your market research is an idiot." Arnie's face glows an alarming shade of magenta. "Look out the window. There are already two brew pubs on this block."

"And there's a big coffee shop right over there." Darryl leans in and grins, showing his veneered teeth. "And a huge bookstore six blocks from here. Face it, you two can't compete."

My heart pounds in my throat, but I take a deep breath, force my voice into a calm, soothing register, and lay my hand atop Lonnie's, ignoring his son. "Lonnie, please don't sign the building over yet. Give us two months. If we can pay this higher rent, you'll save yourself a lot of hassle."

Arnie and Darryl squawk at once. "There's no way we can—"

"Dad's not in charge here. I am—"

Lonnie smacks the table, rattling the coffee cups. "Darryl, I still own the building. Clara's made a good point. I want some time to think about it." He stands and nods to Arnie and me. "I'll call you tomorrow." He moves toward the door. "C'mon, son."

Glowering, Darryl snatches up his paperwork and stalks after his father, but not before whispering, "Start packing."

I clasp Arnie's clammy hand and squeeze, desperate for human warmth and support because my head's buzzing, and my vision's blurry around the edges as if I might faint.

Arnie's forehead rumples. "Shit, Clara. How are we gonna pay that much rent? It's nearly doubled. I'm barely making payroll as it is."

"Me too. We've got to figure something out, though. What can we offer that those corporate stores can't?"

He snorts. "Well, we've got charm, but you can't eat that."

"We've got personality."

"History."

"Connection with the community."

Arnie barks a hollow laugh. "We've got bupkis, dear lady. Absolute bupkis."

I smack the table. "Damn it, I'm not giving up yet. Don't you give up either."

"Don't worry," he grumbles, smoothing his gleaming, gelled hair. "I'll hang in there until the axe falls."

Chapter Seventeen

♥

Clara

Back at the bookshop, Harry is chatting amiably with a couple of college students at the register. One look at me and his smile fades. "You have a good day, now," he tells them. "Let me know how you like this author."

The customers leave, each clutching a slim volume of anime.

I wince. To keep the place open, we'll need lots more customers, each leaving with an armful of books—that is, *if* Lonnie grants us a reprieve.

Harry scoots around the counter and seizes my hands. "What did he say?" He leads me to an armchair nestled beneath a potted ficus. "Is he renewing the lease?"

My shoulders are almost too heavy to shrug. "He'll let us know tomorrow. His son..." My voice quavers. "He said, 'Start packing.'"

"That greasy little rat!" Harry bolts to his feet and pulls out his phone. "I'm calling Lonnie right now."

"Harry, no. Our best chance is to appeal to Lonnie's loyalty, and I've done that." I push myself up on wobbly legs. "Meanwhile, let's assume we're staying put and think about how we can afford the new rent."

When I share the sum Darryl demanded, Harry runs a hand over his forehead and whistles. "It's going to take a lot more than one beer night to pay for that."

"Anything we can do to increase sales will help."

A little past four, the doorbell tinkles, and Dalton strides in, waving a check. He grins at his cousin, then at me. "Our school librarian hunted up some extra funds. Got any more ancient history books?"

His wide smile eases a bit of the tension off my shoulders. He looks so cute in his red North Eugene H.S. Highlanders polo shirt, jeans, and gigantic Nikes. Though a few silver strands glisten in his short, golden beard, Dalton beams happy, youthful energy—something I desperately need right now.

"Let's see what we can find."

He follows me to the history aisle and reaches above my head to pull a volume from the top shelf. "*African Mythology Illustrated*. Perfect."

"Glad to help." I try to match his cheerful tone, but my reply comes out flat.

Dalton's pale brows scrunch together. "Clara, what's wrong?"

"Business troubles," I grumble, avoiding his eyes. He's so nice, so open and easy-going, and last night I kissed Nick. Hell, "kiss" isn't a strong enough word for what we shared. Nick's mouth on mine melted my bones and filled my mind with stars.

Dalton sets the book down and gently grasps my shoulders, turning me to face him. "Is that all?" I'll bet his students confess to all kinds of mischief under that patient, steady stare.

"Well, no." Reluctantly, I gaze up into his pale blue eyes. They radiate kind concern, which makes me feel even more guilty. "Dalton, I have to tell you, I'm sort of seeing someone else."

He flinches backward. "Sort of?"

I flap my hand. "We have a date on Saturday. I don't know if anything will come of it, but it's only fair to let you know."

Scowling, he drops his grip on my shoulders and strides away, pivots, and paces back toward me. Then away, then back again. He opens his mouth as if to speak, then snaps it shut.

My chest constricts at the thought of hurting this sweet man who's been nothing but kind to me. Should I have kept my date with Nick a secret? No, telling Dalton was the honorable thing to do.

Finally, he plants himself in front of me, folds his arms, and leans his rangy body against the bookshelf. "So, you've decided on him?"

"Well, no, I haven't decided anything."

He passes his hand over his face, covering his wide mouth. His forehead rumples, and his gaze lands somewhere far away. When he drops his hand, his expression is relaxed, almost unconcerned.

"Okay. Thanks for telling me. So, we're still on for tomorrow?"

I blink in surprise. "You still want to?"

His crooked smile reappears. He steps closer and studies me for a long moment.

"Clara, you're lovely. And funny. And kind. I'm not surprised I have competition." He raises his hand and lets it hover over my cheek before brushing a strand of hair behind my ear. "But I think we could be really good together. Will you give us a chance?"

A flush of tenderness for this sweet, unpretentious man washes over me. "Of course I will. I really like you, Dalton."

"Well, that's a start." He picks up the book, slings his free arm over my shoulders, and we walk back to the register, where we find Harry pacing, glowering and muttering to himself.

He glances up at our approach, his blue eyes full of fire. "Did she tell you?"

Confusion twists Dalton's features. "Well, she..."

"It's criminal! After all these years of lining his pockets, now he wants to give us the boot."

"Oh." Dalton turns to me. "Business troubles, right?"

"Yeah." I sigh, suddenly wrung out. If I have to explain this again, might as well do it from a comfortable seat. I sink into a cushy armchair. "The landlord is either going to raise our rent crazy high or end our lease. We find out tomorrow."

"But this is the best bookstore in town." Dalton sits across from me and pulls his chair up so our knees press together. He clasps my hands, his touch gentle. "And I'm not just saying that because it's yours."

I flash a smile of gratitude. "He's passing on the management to his son. He wants to replace us and the coffee shop next door with a brew pub."

Dalton grimaces. "Another one? This street's already full of them."

Hopefully, Lonnie will see things that way too.

Harry rings up the next customer—again, just one book—then pulls up a stool beside his cousin and sits. "I remember when this place was bigger, before the coffee shop went in. It was always crowded."

I perk up. "When was that, Harry?"

"Oh, about twenty years ago."

"I remember too," Dalton says. "I used to come here with my dad. He'd buy stamp magazines, and I'd buy comics. Why don't you carry magazines, Clara?"

"We dropped them a while ago. Didn't sell many, and when that big corporate store opened, it didn't seem worth the trouble."

"They don't carry the really interesting ones, though."

"That's a thought." I glance around. The bookshelves and tables already fill every available space. "Where would we put them?"

"Let's see, weren't they over there?" He points to the wall we share with the coffee shop. "You're right, Harry, the shop was bigger. When did that wall go in?"

"Not sure. Maybe Arnie knows."

Dalton moves to the wall and raps it with his knuckles. He shifts a few steps to his left and knocks again.

Harry's mouth hangs open, then slowly spreads into a wide grin. "Right, we could…"

"We'd need the landlord's approval, and the coffee shop guy's…"

I shake my head. "What are you two talking about?"

Harry beams. "We could knock down the wall and combine the two businesses. Make it a book café, where people can wander back and forth from one to the other, like they do in the big chain store."

I scratch my head. "But my appeal to Lonnie was how letting us stay avoids the costs of renovation. Now we're gonna ask him to renovate?"

"Yeah, that is a puzzler." Harry scrunches his mouth to one side and eyes Dalton. "Could we do it ourselves?"

"I don't think we'd need a permit." He taps on the wall again. "We only have to open a wide doorway here."

"What's your schedule like?" Harry asks.

"Mostly free after this week. It wouldn't take long." Meeting my eye at last, he grins and raises one shoulder. "My dad's a contractor, so I've done this kind of work before."

My heart thuds. It's a far-fetched idea, but combining the bookshop with the coffee shop might give both me and Arnie a fighting chance against our corporate competition. Customers like sipping coffee while they browse books. Hell, the big chain stores make millions off that model. And together, we could plan more special events to draw in thirsty readers.

"I'll talk to Arnie. If we can put something together by tonight, I'll send it to Lonnie." I'm talking too fast and grinning like a giddy teenager.

Dalton lopes to my side. "I'll talk to my dad. There's not much he doesn't know about construction."

I throw my arms around him and squeeze him tight. "Thank you, Dalton."

He chuckles, unable to return my embrace since I've pinned his arms. "I'm glad to help if I can." He plants a soft kiss on the top of my head. "I'll call you later, Harry."

"You bet, kiddo." Harry moves off, giving us a moment alone.

Dalton scuffs his big running shoes on the carpet. "So, I'll see you tomorrow?"

"Absolutely." I stroke his cheek, scratchy with pale scruff, then stand on tiptoe and peck his lips. They're scratchy too, probably chapped from running, but warm and pliant.

"Wow." Flushed and grinning, he retrieves his new book and ambles away, graceful as a giraffe.

I stare after him, kneading the back of my neck. If this works out, I'll be in Dalton's debt, which will complicate things with Nick. But there's no time to think about that now. If I'm going to get a proposal to Lonnie, I'll have to scramble.

Chapter Eighteen

♥

Nick

"Move your ass, Nick! Faint heart never won fair lady." Leo guns the engine of his '71 Mercury Cougar while I lock up the cottage. I swear, once he gets behind the wheel of that boxy beast, he loses half his common sense—maybe more.

"You haven't told me where we're going."

"To defend your woman's honor." He flashes a pirate grin and peels out before I even close the passenger door.

I peer over my shoulder. "What's with all the signs in the back seat? You running for office?"

"A bit of political activism. We're resisting gentrification, protesting corporate homogenization..." He waggles his bushy ginger eyebrows. "We're stickin' it to the man."

"Which man?"

Leo's comical theatrics are amusing, but it took me weeks to get this afternoon's appointment in the university library's rare books collection.

I quickly forget about my appointment once we zoom onto Willamette Street and I spot Clara's bookshop, its entrance obscured by a crowd, mostly college-age people with a sprinkling of gray and white heads among them. The protesters mill about in front of the one-story brick building, waving signs and chanting, "Save Book Nirvana! Save Book Nirvana!"

Leo sandwiches his Mercury into a not-quite-legal parking space and hops out.

"Take your pick, Nicko-me-boy." He extends three poster boards in neon colors: *Books, not Beer*; *Save Our Indie Bookshops*; and a quote from Cicero: *A room without books is like a body without a soul.*

Jaw tight, I push away the proffered signs and grab my friend's collar. "Leo, why are they picketing Clara's shop?"

"Haven't you heard? Landlord's selling it out from under her. Gonna turn the place into a bar."

"But that's—she didn't—I just talked to her yesterday!" I snatch up the Cicero sign and stride across the street, nearly colliding with a local news van. As I push my way through the crowd, a familiar swath of glossy black hair catches my eye. "Darcy?"

The sign she's waving overhead reads *Resist corporate piracy!*

"Hey, Nick! Isn't this great?" She elbows me with her free arm. "The things we do for love, right?" She hollers in a high, piercing voice. "Buy a book, people! Buy a book!"

I force my way to the shop door and inside, where I face an even thicker throng of customers. Behind the counter, the old guy and Margot ring up books while Clara, wide-eyed and pale, fields questions from a TV reporter while clutching the shop cat to her chest like a furry shield.

"Mrs. Martelli, what do you say to all these loyal customers who've gathered to support you?"

"Um, thank you?"

Poor beauty looks like she's about to topple. I drop my sign and rush to her side.

A flash of relief lights her face. "Nick, I..."

Her chin wobbles, sending a bolt of emotion right to my core. I plant myself between the camera and Clara. "Could we have a moment, please?"

With a shrug, the reporter motions her camera operator over to the long line of customers waiting at the counter.

I gently take Clara's elbow and lead her behind the wooden screen, out of view of the crowd. "Clara, what is going on? Leo says your shop's in trouble. Why didn't you tell me?"

She collapses into her desk chair and claws her fingers into her hair. "It was Margot. She didn't talk to me first. She just summoned them!"

"All these people?"

She nods. "She blasted the news all over social media. It seems our Margot is a wizard with hashtags." A fat tear rolls down her cheek as she raises her glassy eyes to mine. "She meant well, but she may have ruined everything."

Moving on irresistible instinct, I gather her into my arms, stroke her soft, wavy hair, and croon, "It'll be okay. We'll figure it out." I yearn to say something, do something more helpful, but what? All I know is the woman I love is in distress and—

The woman I love.

The weight of that thought hits me like a warm, fuzzy bomb, right in the gut.

Examined with a rational mind, this makes no sense. I met Clara less than two weeks ago, and the amount I know about her could fill a thimble—yet my head is filled with technicolor visions of a future shared with her.

I'm bewitched.

But right now, I need to focus on getting these media hounds off her tail and out of her shop.

I cup Clara's face in both hands. "Sweetheart, tell me. What's going on?" She wipes her eyes with the back of her hand. "Yesterday, after you left, I met with the landlord. His son wants to end our lease, the coffee shop's too, and put in a bar."

"Another one?"

"That's what everyone says." She flashes a wobbly smile. "There are three on this block. Anyway, Lonnie, the old land-lord, was going to give us his decision today. But this—" She waves toward the chaos beyond the screen. "How's he going to react when he hears about this?"

I cradle her face and wipe her tears with my thumbs. "Okay, I agree. Margot didn't think this through. In fact—" I glare over my shoulder. "I'll bet Darcy helped her dream up this scheme. Sounds like her style: damn the consequences, full speed ahead. But now all these people are here, so let's make our case."

Clara's distress touches me more deeply than anything has in a long, long time, and I've got to find a way to turn this mess to our advantage.

"Make our case how?" she asks with a sniffle.

"Let's go tell the reporter your story." I gently grip her shoulders. "It would take a damn stupid landlord to evict a pretty widow and her adorable cat when half of Eugene shows up to support her. On live TV, no less."

When we step out from behind the screen, a second news crew has joined the fray. Both teams close in like eager kids attacking a pile of cookies.

"Mrs. Martelli!" A young male reporter with shellacked hair thrusts his mic into her face.

I push it away. "Just a moment, please."

"Who are you?"

"Doctor Nick Papadopoulos. I came up from the University of California at Berkeley to shop here, because Mrs. Martelli maintains one of the finest collections of—"

Clara squeezes my arm hard. Message received.

I continue. "Of books about the social sciences. Independent bookshops like hers offer something that larger corporate bookstores can't. To see this focal point of our community replaced by yet another brew pub would be a tragedy."

I give the camera what my sister calls my "puppy-dog face," the one I used as a kid to get my way. Eyebrows scrunched together, eyes wide, lower lip protruding just a tad, and...bingo. The second reporter holds her mic to my face and blinks, her mouth hanging slack.

"Right, so, Mrs. Martelli—" The male reporter sidesteps me and pokes his mic toward Clara.

She clears her throat, squeezes my hand, and steps forward. "Please, call me Clara."

I step aside and let her take the spotlight, but I watch closely in case these bozos get out of line and upset her further.

Margot taps my shoulder. "You were really great, Professor. Thank you."

I glare at the spiky-haired sprite. "You summoned all these people? Without telling Clara?"

The girl gulps audibly. "I posted something about the landlord's threat, yeah, and tagged a few friends from the U of O. I guess that photo of Lulu on the book table grabbed a lot of attention..." She trails off, looking sheepish.

"You did good, kiddo." A wiry, white-haired guy claps his hand on Margot's shoulder, then narrows his sharp blue eyes. "And who are you?"

I offer my hand. "Nick Papadopoulos. I'm Clara's—friend."

"Is that right?" The old man's grip is like a vise, and his scowl is a warning—I'm not the only one feeling protective of Clara.

The reason for his enmity soon becomes clear. A tall, lanky, bearded guy about my age pushes his way through the crowd still milling at the shop's entrance. The news cameras' lights gleam off his shiny shaved head as he lifts his chin to the older man, then makes a beeline for Clara, who's leaning against the counter clutching her necklace.

When she spots the newcomer, her worried expression relaxes into a weary smile. Without a word, the newcomer enfolds Clara in his long, gangly arms and rocks her slowly.

And she lets him, snuggling into his embrace with a sigh.

Waves of heat and cold race up and down my spine. Clearly, I'm up against serious competition, but there's no way I'm backing off now. If I have to fight for Clara's time and affection, so be it.

Clara

I gently extricate myself from Dalton's arms. The look on his face is one I won't soon forget: sharp concern and anger mixed with warm affection. I squint up at him. "Aren't you supposed to be in school?"

"One of my students saw the social media ruckus. Apparently, she buys her manga comics here. She wanted to stage a walk-out to come support your store." He cracks a crooked smile. "And to skip math class."

He surveys the crowd filling Book Nirvana from wall to wall. "I have planning period after lunch, so I came right over. Tell me what you need me to do."

"Introduce me to your friend, Clara?" Nick steps up behind Dalton and glares like a guard dog on high alert, dark eyes narrowed, nostrils flared, jaw tight.

Oh, crap.

I'm not ready for this confrontation. I'd hoped to keep Nick and Dalton separate until I decide which is a better fit. Too late. What an idiot I am, thinking I could juggle dating two guys at once. Perhaps Margot's right and younger people wouldn't be bothered, but we're not college kids, and this isn't a story in *Cosmo*—it's my life, and I'm botching it.

Alerted by the tightness in Nick's voice, Dalton straightens to his full height and faces his rival.

The contrast between them is striking. Dalton stands a good three inches taller than Nick, his long body a sculpture of sharp planes and angles—a lanky, blue-eyed Viking standing between me and danger. Nick, on the other hand, is muscular and powerful, dark and elegant, and undeniably beautiful. And his fists are clenched at his sides.

Oh Lord, so are Dalton's.

I step between them. "Dalton, this is Nick Papadopoulos. He's a professor from Berkeley."

Nick's eyes slide toward the red door.

"Just visiting, then?" Dalton's voice rasps, tense and low.

Nick nods, his lips clamped and bloodless.

Each man silently takes the measure of the other.

My stomach knots, but damn it, I've played fair. I told each of them I was seeing someone else. So why do I feel so guilty?

Dalton breaks the silence. "You have anything to do with all this?"

Nick redirects his scowl to the protestors outside. "No, you?"

"I didn't see any of my students out there."

I interject, "Dalton teaches social studies at North Eugene High School."

Nick raises an eyebrow but says nothing.

Just then, shouting draws our attention to the doorway. The landlord and his son are pushing their way through the mob. Red faced and scowling, Darryl lowers his head like a charging bull and plows toward me.

Nick and Dalton close ranks in front of me, shoulder to shoulder, arms crossed. When Darryl darts to the right, Nick's hand shoots out and grasps his arm. Wincing, Darryl heads left. Dalton plants his big, bony hand on the weasel's chest.

Lonnie grasps his son's jacket and yanks him backward. "Cool it, Darryl."

"But, Pops, this is...this is..." He splutters and gasps as if he's been dunked in a swimming pool.

"I said hush."

Pouting like a scolded toddler, Darryl steps back and lets his father have his say.

Lonnie's jowly face is flushed, but a hint of amusement twinkles in his gray eyes. "Clara, care to explain this?"

"I swear, it wasn't my doing. One of my employees made a social media post about our possible closure, and the news spread."

He crosses his arms and glances at Margot and Harry, still bustling behind the counter. "I can guess which one. Anyway, I want you to know this doesn't affect my decision."

My stomach drops. "So, you've decided."

He nods, his face solemn. "Two months."

"Dad, you—"

Lonnie raises his hand. "Drop it, Darryl."

Relief floods me, weakening my knees. I've been granted a reprieve.

"I'll extend your lease for two months, and then the rent goes up. Take it or leave it." He glances at my scowling body-guards and softens his tone.

"It's a fair market price, Clara. Other merchants on this street pay at least that much per square foot. I'm fond of you, but I've got a family to support." He rolls his eyes toward his red-faced son.

I nod. "Okay. Fair is fair. And thank you, Lonnie."

From behind his father, Darryl huffs. "Now will you call off the dogs?"

I straighten my posture and smile sweetly. "If you're referring to my customers, they'll leave when they're done buying books. Lonnie, does Arnie get the same deal?"

"Same deal."

"Good. Do you have time for a coffee now?"

He shrugs. "I guess."

"I'd like to talk to you about that doorway. Dalton, can you stay a few more minutes?"

Dalton's gaze slides toward Nick. "Sure. Let's go next door."

"I'll be right with you." I wave him on.

While Dalton and Lonnie move toward the exit, I turn to Nick, who's watching them go, his dark eyes narrowed, his jaw tight.

"Nick, thank you. You don't know how much your help means to me."

"And Dalton? How is he helping you?" His tone softens, but his posture is rigid.

"He's going to open up the wall between the coffee shop and our place if the landlord allows it."

Nick cups my elbows and pulls me closer. "I want to help too, Clara."

"But you won't be here."

"Not as often as I'd like, but I can spread the word about your business. Especially about the red room." Something flashes behind his eyes. "Have you taken Dalton back there?"

I flush hot enough to fry eggs on my skin. "No."

"Good." His phone pings in his pocket. He pulls it out and taps the screen. "Damn. Sorry, I have an appointment with some rare books. I wish I could stay."

I pat his arm. "Go. I'll see you tomorrow." Standing on tiptoe, I brush a kiss across his cheek. His freshly shaved skin is smooth and scented with a subtle, mossy cologne. "Should I dress up?"

He presses his soft, warm lips to my temple. "Where whatever makes you feel comfortable. See you tomorrow."

Grinning like a giddy schoolgirl, I watch him slide through the crowd. Comfortable is not how Nick makes me feel. Stirred up, aflutter, warm and soft and languid and tingly—but not comfortable.

Chapter Nineteen

♥

Clara

With my stomach still roiling from this morning's ruckus, the last thing I want is a fancy pasta feast. But after all he's done to help me, how can I postpone my date with Dalton?

Earlier, in Arnie's café, Dalton sketched out his plans for opening a wide doorway between Coffee Dreams and Book Nirvana. Despite Darryl's grumbling, his father agreed to the plan. After all, if the building ends up as a pub, he'll demolish that wall anyway.

Arnie and I agreed on the rest: some of my bookshelves will be transferred to Arnie's place, and some café tables will be moved to my shop. Honestly, it's such a natural, mutually beneficial plan, I'm kicking myself for not having thought of this before.

Harry said it best: "Dalton's idea might just save our bacon."

Even Margot's social media blunder has a silver lining: the protesters bought a lot of books. In fact, it's the first time in years I can recall seeing this much empty space on the shelves.

Shortly before closing, Harry grips my shoulders in his big, gnarled hands. His blue eyes radiate concern. "Clara, I know this is a hard time for you, and having those two guys panting at your heels isn't making it easier, right?"

"You noticed, eh?"

"Kind of a comical sight, really. I'm hoping you'll end up choosing Dalton, of course. That fancy professor makes me nervous."

"Why, Harry?"

His forehead rumples. "I don't like the hungry way he looks at you. And he won't be here for you when you need him."

It's a good thing Harry doesn't know how his younger cousin tried to suck my face off last week.

"Anyway, for what it's worth, I hope you won't let either of those young bucks rush you into something you're not ready for. A man who's worth your time will wait."

"Oh, Harry—" My eyes mist over as I hug him. "Thank you."

Back at home, I frown at my reflection and toss another garment onto the growing pile on the bed. This dress is too sexy; that top is too low cut. Those pants are too loose; these are too ragged. Since Jared's death, I've fallen into the habit of wearing a silky blouse with comfortable jeans: businesslike on top, practical underneath. But Pomodoro is a fancy place, deserving of something special. My only date-worthy outfit is the one I wore to Nick's place, and it's got a wine stain.

Besides, that outfit arouses memories of Nick's tantalizing kiss—not what I want on my mind while dining with Dalton.

The tension between my two admirers this morning hit me hard. I didn't seek either of them out, but that doesn't change the situation: two good men care for me. I'm fond of them both, each for different reasons, and soon, I'll have to choose. It's the honorable thing to do.

My libido casts its vote for Nick, but letting lust take the wheel would be stupid, even if that's how Jared and I...

I set down my hairbrush and stare at my reflection. Huh. It's true—strong chemistry tumbled Jared and me into bed, and afterward, we just sort of...clicked.

But how often does a woman get that lucky?

My practical nature leans strongly toward Dalton. He's sweet and helpful, smart and funny, and *here*. He doesn't stir up uncomfortable feelings the way Nick does. One more date with each guy, I promise myself, and then I'll decide.

This trusty gray wool skirt will do for tonight. But which top? Nothing strikes the perfect note between friendly and a tiny bit flirtatious. I strip off yet another blouse and slump on the bed, my head in my hands. A breeze whispers through the open window.

"What am I doing, Jared? This is crazy. I'm not ready for a new boyfriend. I can't even get dressed for a date."

A sudden flash of memory lights up my senses: my husband stands behind me, gazing at my reflection in this very mirror. He lifts my hair, lets it fall over my shoulders, and presses his cheek against mine. "There, babe. See how beautiful you are?"

Tears ambush me again, crumpling me like paper.

"How can I do this?" I scrub at my streaming eyes, smudging my carefully applied eyeliner. "I can't even pick a damned blouse! How'm I supposed to choose a new guy and..."

Wind stirs the curtains. On the sill, a black-capped chickadee perches, cocking his head from side to side.

"Hey there." I wipe my runny nose and smile at my tiny visitor. "Want to help me pick a blouse?"

The bird fluffs its feathers, then shimmies them back into place.

Why not? This is no crazier than the rest of my day. I grab two tops at random from the bed. "Which one?"

My visitor tilts its head and hops to the left. "Chick-a-dee-dee-dee," it trills and then flies off.

"Thanks, buddy. Peach blouse it is."

A message from beyond? A crazy woman talking to birds? Either way, at least I've made a choice.

I'm meeting Dalton at the shop. Beyond contrite over today's social media debacle, Margot insisted on closing up, freeing me to deal with bills while I wait. Oh joy.

"Hey Clara, check this out." She pops around the screen and waves her phone under my nose. "Look, it's you!"

Ugh. In this clip from KVAL News, I'm as pale and grim as a prisoner facing the firing squad, clutching poor Lulu to my chest while I answer a barrage of questions. The video cuts to a photo from nearly ten years ago: Jared and me in front of the shop, his arm around my shoulders. We're grinning as if we have our whole lives ahead of us.

My breath catches, and my vision blurs.

Margot's soft hand falls on my shoulder. "You look so happy together."

"We were." I smooth my skirt. "Well, how do I look?"

"Snazzy. Nick will love it."

"No, I'm going out with Dalton tonight."

"Oh, the bald guy?" Her grin falters for a split-second. "He seems nice."

"He is nice."

So I've got one employee on Team Nick and one on Team Dalton. Lulu loves everyone, so she's no help.

The doorway bell's tinkle cuts off further discussion. "I'll get it." Margot trots toward the counter.

I suck in a breath, shake myself like a wet dog, plaster on a smile, and follow her.

Dalton's examining a rack of local comics. In repose, his bony face seems older than his years. But when he smiles at my approach, he lights up with warm, playful energy. Dalton's beauty manifests in motion, whereas Nick is beautiful in repose, in motion, whenever, always.

Tonight, Dalton's cobalt dress shirt brings out the blue in his eyes, and his tailored slacks hug his powerful thighs. Instead of his usual running shoes, he's wearing stylish brogues polished to a high gloss.

"Wow, Clara. You look—" His gaze rakes my body. "Amazing." A wash of pink colors his cheekbones. "I hope you're hungry."

"Very," I lie.

His sly smile makes me wonder if he's referring to more than just pasta, but he's a complete gentleman as we stroll side by side toward the restaurant—no groping, no drooling, not even the tiniest ogle.

"I talked to my dad today," he says when we pause at an art gallery's window. "He'll lend me the tools I'll need to make the doorway. I can start work as soon as school lets out."

"Is that really how you want to begin your summer break? I mean, I'm grateful, but..."

He plants himself in front of me, his expression solemn. "Clara, let's get this out of the way. I'd do this for Harry's sake, even if I wasn't interested in you." His wide mouth softens. "To be clear, I am. Very. And I know about Professor Tzatziki, but..."

I bite back a giggle.

His crooked grin is adorable. "Sorry, that was immature. Anyway, if nothing else, I'm glad to help a new friend. Besides, Arnie offered me free coffee for life. I'd start this weekend, but—"

"You have a race up in Washington, right?"

"Yeah, in Tacoma. We've been training for a while."

"I wish Harry could go with you."

He shrugs. "Harry's not so good on hills anymore. He'll run the Eugene half-marathon with us in the fall, nice and flat, along the river." We resume walking, and he nudges me with his arm. "I hope you'll join us."

"A half marathon? Holy cow."

"Piece of cake if you train all summer."

I smell the restaurant before we reach it. Pomodoro opened a few months ago in what used to be a shoe shop, now redecorated with fake stone and plaster statuary—a kitschy, garlic-scented grotto.

The hostess leads us to a table near the window. Dalton pulls out my seat, a throne-like chair in padded red velvet.

"I feel like the queen of Pasta Land."

"Yeah, it's over the top, but I hear the food's great."

"Aaaay, Paisano!" A server rushes over and claps Dalton's shoulder. The cartoon Italian accent comes from a plump Asian guy about our age who executes a theatrical bow. "You must be la bella Clara."

Dalton rolls his eyes and mutters, "Tone it down, Vinny."

The server ignores him. "My name is Vincente, and I'll be serving you tonight. Would you like to hear our specials?"

"Um, sure." I fight to restrain a giggle.

With the eager enthusiasm of an amateur opera singer, Vincente sing-songs a long list of pasta specials, the daily fish, and a beefsteak alla Florentina.

"So many choices." I scan the menu. "What do you recommend, Vincente?"

He leans in and stage-whispers, "I recommend this guy here. He's-a good-a fella."

"Vinny!" Dalton swats him with his menu.

"Scusami." He drops the accent and grins broadly. "I went to school with Dalton. Can't resist teasing him. So, I'll let you two talk. Wave at me when you're ready to order." He bustles toward the bar.

Dalton swipes a hand down his face. "Sorry, Vinny's a character. He majored in theater, and this is how he puts his talents to use."

"Oh, hey, haven't I seen him in that dinner theater place by the freeway?"

He chuckles. "Don't mention that, or we'll never get rid of him."

Vinnie swoops by and deposits two highball glasses. "Il aperitivo della casa. On the house. Enjoy." And just as quickly, he dashes away.

I sniff the orange liquid. Dalton takes a sip. "A Negroni, I think."

It's delicious—a little sweet, a hint of bitterness, and very potent. We each choose a pasta dish, then wait until Vinny is safely out of range before continuing our conversation.

"So." I clasp my hands around my drink.

"So." He stares at his glass, his long, golden lashes gleaming in the candlelight. "I, uh...want to thank you..."

"For what?"

This time, his blush reaches the tips of his ears. Nice ears, I decide, set close to his shaved head, with plump lobes that would be fun to kiss.

Yikes, this drink is strong!

"For giving me another chance after I groped you. I'm sort of...out of practice." His bashful smile tugs on my heart.

"Well, you seem like a pretty nice guy, and Harry vouches for your character."

He gently grasps my fingertips. "I am a pretty nice guy, except when the full moon turns me into a werewolf."

"Oh, is that what happened?"

He shrugs, grins, then releases me. "Oops. Promised to keep my hands to myself, didn't I?"

I pull his hands back to the center of the table and hold them lightly. "The moonlight won't reach us in here, so I'm safe for now."

"For now." His eyebrows flick upward. "So, what shall we talk about?"

"Um, family?"

"I have one."

"Me too." I take another sip and realize I'd better pace myself or I'll be soused by the time our food arrives. "Are you youngest, oldest, only?"

"Middle," he says. "Older sister, younger brother. She's an artist; he's an addict."

"Wow. That must be hard."

"It's hardest on Mom, especially when he stole her engagement ring. We haven't seen him in..." He counts on his fingers, "Six years now. So, your turn."

"Okay, I have a younger sister in Texas, a stepbrother here in Oregon, and a stepsister in Hawaii. I like the girls a lot. Him, not so much."

He nods and drums his fingers, his gaze bouncing from table to table.

Am I boring him?

"You all right, Dalton?"

He flashes a tight grin. "Yeah, just avoiding the elephant."

"I beg your pardon?"

"This is where you ask about my divorce, right? Harry told you about Tiffany."

I snort a laugh. "Sorry. He said she was kind of a gold digger, so that's the perfect name for her."

His tense expression relaxes. "She'd call it ambition. And I was an idiot not to see it. But you know how it goes—we ignore those red flags while they're waving in our faces. Afterward, we remember all the warning signs." He gulps his drink, then shakes his head. "Wow, that's strong. I think Vinnie's trying to loosen my tongue."

Apparently, Vinnie's plan is working. The flush on Dalton's face probably isn't just from the alcohol, though. He's obviously still pissed at his ex. With good reason, it seems.

"Well, some things are hard to talk about."

"Yup." His sigh sets the candle to flickering. "If you don't mind, I'd rather save this topic for another time."

"Sure. Yeah. Of course." I look around at the other couples chatting easily over their enormous plates. This date is turning out to be more work than I expected. "So, what are your summer plans, besides tearing out our wall?"

The tension between us lightens as he regales me with stories from last summer's tour of Canada, involving several 10K races and a marathon. "I swear, the mosquitoes were this big." He spreads his long fingers. "But the mountains are magnificent. Have you been up there?"

While Vinnie delivers our entrees and uncorks a bottle of Pinot Grigio, I tell him about the trip Jared and I made to Victoria. Then we share destinations on our bucket lists, falling into a pleasant give-and-take.

All right, then. He's easy to talk to, as long as I avoid sensitive topics. We dig into our mountains of pasta, going through the crisp, cold wine much too fast.

"Clara, you're a great listener. I'll bet you'd be a great traveling companion, too." He twirls up the last of his fettuccine al salmone, then pauses with his fork in mid-air. "Maybe I can talk you into coming on our Labor Day trip to Baja?"

"Whose trip?"

"The running club. We're doing a 10K race and some snorkeling." Noodles dangle like seaweed as he gestures with his fork. "Crystal-clear waters, colorful fish, warm sun on your back." He pops the pasta into his mouth and waggles his eyebrows flirtatiously.

"Here, you've got some sauce on your chin."

He thrusts his jaw out and lets me wipe the spot, then grasps my hand and kisses it. "You're delicious," he declares.

Definitely too much wine, but so what? This is fun.

"More delicious than smoked salmon in cream sauce?" I parry with a teasing grin.

He kisses my knuckles again, then smacks his lips. "At least as delicious." His blue eyes crinkle at the corners. "I haven't had a proper taste yet."

Feigning shock, I hide my giggle behind my napkin. I'd better slow our roll before this gets out of hand.

Dalton pulls back. "Oh crap, there I go again. Sorry, Clara. I just—" Slumping back in his chair, he heaves a frustrated sigh.

"I find it hard to keep my cool around you. You're very lovely and very kind." He folds his hands like a schoolboy trying to be good. "You're the first lady who's had this effect on me in a long time."

"Really? Well, I'm flattered." Dalton's flustered reaction is disarming. We're both in a similar place, dipping our toes into the dating pool after a loss. His awkward uncertainty eases my own tightly wound nerves.

By the time we finish the wine and our shared dessert, a decadent panna cotta topped with raspberries and limoncello, we've slid from talkative to giggly. After paying the bill, Dalton offers his arm and pulls me to my feet. Between the alcohol and my high heels, I lose my balance and totter right into his chest. His long arms close around me to keep me upright.

Is that applause I hear? I glance over my shoulder and spot Vinnie the waiter, beaming at us. The couple he's serving joins in, and soon half the restaurant is clapping. In a gorgeous tenor voice, Vinnie warbles, "That's amore!"

I duck my head to hide my flushed cheeks as I tug on Dalton's sleeve. "Let's get out of here."

Arm in arm, we trot outside, giggling like teenagers, the awkward beginning of our date long forgotten. He wobbles a bit as he peers up and down the street. "Right. Your shop is...this way." He lunges in exactly the wrong direction.

"Nope. The other way."

"You sure?"

"Absolutely."

He pivots, and we set off down the sidewalk, my arm cozy around his waist. The night air has cooled, so I snuggle closer to enjoy his warmth. All along the street, couples and groups of friends stroll and talk and laugh. It feels so good to be part of it all again.

Soon, too soon, really, we reach Book Nirvana.

I release my grip on his middle. "Here we are. I'd ask you in for a nightcap, but all I have is instant coffee."

Leaning against the glass door, he lowers his voice to a sexy rumble. "I love instant coffee."

Oh dear. Time to stall. "So, no running club tomorrow morning?"

"Right. We're driving up to...to..." He twirls his wrist, searching for the right word.

"Tacoma? For a race?"

He holds up his forefinger. "That's it. Man, getting up at five is going to be rough."

His crooked smile is so appealing, I almost ask him in. After all, what trouble can we get into? Unless, of course, he asks about the red door.

He clears his throat. "So, I'd better call for a ride. Mind if I wait inside?"

There's no way to deny him without being a jerk.

"Sure." I fish my keys out of my bag and open the door. The shop is dark except for the glow from the streetlamps out front. "Shall I turn on the lights?"

"No need." He pulls out his phone and taps the screen. "Okay, driver's on his way."

He must have heard my sigh of relief because he drops his gaze and shoves his hands into his pockets.

Damn, this is awkward. He might be a horny goofball and not the best at small talk, but Dalton Garvey is a man who keeps his promises.

"Dalton, I had a really fun time tonight. Dinner was superb."

He inches closer. "It was fun. Thanks for giving me another chance, Clara."

I scoot toward him, almost close enough to rest my chin on his chest.

His voice lowers to a husky whisper. "I hope I convinced you I can keep my hands to myself."

I smile up at him, mesmerized by the glimmer in his sky-blue eyes. "Is it really so difficult?"

"Excruciating." Hands still in his pockets, he leans down to kiss me goodnight. He lands a bit off-center, so I take his jaw in both hands and redirect him. His short beard tickles my palms. His lips are warm and dry. A pleasant kiss, without the rush of heat ignited when Nick's lips touched mine.

Maybe that's a good thing. Perhaps love lasts longer if it grows slowly.

Love? Hell, that's not what I'm looking for—just a friend to help me take this first step back into the land of the living.

I open my eyes and see desire simmering in his gaze.

"Clara." His big hands slide up my arms, his voice a raw whisper. "You are so beautiful."

He lowers his head, his lips a hair's breadth from mine, and waits for me to make the next move. Why not? I like this man, and he's just as vulnerable as I am.

I brush my lips over his, and his rush of breath heats my cheeks. This time, Dalton restrains himself more than he did on our first date, but when his long fingers splay across my back, pulling me tight against him, I flutter between excitement and panic. Do I want this? Just one whispered "Yes" and I can put this milestone behind me.

Headlights flash in the big plate-glass window, throwing our shadows onto the floor. Flinching, I shield my eyes.

Breathing heavily, Dalton releases me. "Damn, I'm sorry, Clara."

"Don't apologize." I pat his arm, grateful for the interruption—and also a little frustrated. "We've both had too much to drink."

He raises my hand to his lips and tenderly kisses my palm. "Good night, lovely Clara. Can I call you when I get back from Tacoma?"

"Please do."

He leaves the shop, flashing a boyish grin over his shoulder.

Once he's gone, I let out a long whoosh of breath and check my reflection in the mirror over my desk. Flushed cheeks, hair mussed by Dalton's fingers, lipstick smeared by his urgent kiss. And how do I feel? Shaky, but not exactly melting with desire. His kisses don't leave me cold, but they don't heat me like Nick's. I can still taste Dalton's garlicky, winey tongue, still feel the soft scrape of his beard, the pressure of his hands on my hips, but...it just isn't the same.

Maybe it's better to go into a new relationship with a clear head, with more control, with reasonable expectations. Hoping for mind-blowing chemistry right off the bat is like hunting for unicorns.

Anyway, tomorrow I'll repeat this dance with Nick, and then I'll make my decision—or just shelve the whole question and concentrate on saving my business.

Before locking up the shop, I check the red door. Safely locked, no lights glowing from within. For now, that's exactly how I want it.

Chapter Twenty

Nick

I pace the floor of my borrowed office on the University of Oregon campus, trying to talk sense to my inner caveman. I have no right to be this worked up. Clara's been fair. She told me she was dating another guy. I should be too mature for jealousy, but the sight of her embracing that bald beanpole stabbed me with a sharp blade of primitive emotion. The other guy's probably been sniffing around her for a while now, and he's a local. All I can offer Clara is a long-distance courtship. She deserves more.

But that doesn't stop the throbbing behind my eyes, doesn't keep my shoulder muscles from clenching like fists. Keeping my cool tonight will be difficult but crucial.

In my pocket, my phone trills. It's my department chair.

"Enid, what's up?"

"Nick, dear boy, I have news." All the usual warmth has drained from her voice, leaving it shaky and thin. "George is in the hospital. That bastard cancer is back, and it's spread to his liver. I was hoping to delay my retirement until next June, but I may not have that option now."

In a moment, my petty jealousy is forgotten. Poor Enid, facing a battle for her husband's life. I know all too well how hard that will be. And in the end, she'll lose.

"I'm so sorry. Is there anything I can do?"

"Thank you, dear. There's nothing to do but wait." She clears her throat. "Listen, you have a publisher lined up for your book project, right?"

"Barston Press has accepted my proposal, but..."

"You should finish sooner rather than later. Your students adore you, Nick, and so do I. I wish all our instructors were as lively as you." Her sigh whooshes into the receiver. "The next department chair may not look so favorably on your work."

"Won't it be Carlos?"

Dr. Carlos Hernandez, a respected and well-connected anthropology professor, has expressed admiration for my research.

"He's my recommendation, but Nancy has a lot of clout with the administration."

"Oh." The drummer pounding behind my eyeballs turns up the volume.

Nancy Lewington is a tight-lipped, stick-spined specialist in dead languages, and no fan of my work, or me, for that matter. She's complained at department meetings about the "pornographic slides" I show in class. Even worse, the way she curls her lip when we pass in the halls tells me she believes the rumors.

"Anyway, I wanted to let you know. If I retire, I won't be able to protect you, Nick. Your best chance is to publish your book."

"Okay. Thank you. And please give my best to George."

I disconnect the call and slump into a chair. So much for spending most of my summer in Oregon courting Clara. To save my job, I'll have to devote all my free time to this project.

A rap on the door snaps my head up. Leo stands there, a steaming mug of coffee in each hand and a rakish grin on his fuzzy face.

"What's wrong? All those sexy pictures depressing you?"

I accept the proffered mug and sip gratefully. "Just got bad news." I quickly relate the gist of Enid's call.

"So, the race is on, eh? Nick versus the tenure committee. Why does this Nancy woman hate you, anyway?"

I haven't shared all the details of the scandal that nearly took me down the previous year. In fact, keeping it quiet is my only chance of hanging onto my job. "Just a bitter person who hates sex, I guess."

"In Berkeley? Too bad." Leo leans his wide ass on the edge of my desk and slurps his coffee. "You wouldn't have that problem here, you know."

"Yeah." I sigh. "Clara says Oregon's a sexy state."

"Ah, the fair Clara. Any developments?"

The mention of her name brings a smile to my lips. "We're going out tonight. The Amphora. Brazilian jazz."

Leo whistles. "Very sexy. And then, back to your place for a little...research?"

"If the gods are kind. I'm not pushing it, though. This one's worth waiting for."

"If you say so." He drums his fingers on the desk. "I don't know why you put up with this Berkeley bullshit. Take the job up here. Just imagine." He drops his big hand onto my shoulder. "You and me, teaching side by side, rowing after work, lighting up the town at night..."

"Leo, it's just a part-time gig, and I'd be starting the tenure race all over again."

"You'll find something else to fill your empty hours. Working in a bookstore, perhaps?" He claps me on the back. "Anyway, I'll leave you to your dirty pictures. Text me after your date. I want details, man. I'm living vicariously through you now."

With a grunt, I turn back to my notes. I found some excellent material in the U of O library and now have to piece it into my outline. But my thoughts keep drifting to Leo's suggestion. If I apply for the job opening up here in Oregon...

"Don't be ridiculous," I mutter aloud. "I have to think long term. I can't uproot my life based on a crush."

I sip my scalding coffee and bend to my task. The clock is ticking.

But if I stay away from Clara all summer, that bald guy will make his move—and that thought ties my stomach into knots.

I've got to find a way to balance this book project and wooing the woman I want more than...tenure?

Shaking my head, I try to focus on sexy Pompeian frescoes, but it's Clara I see, heavy-lidded, her upswept hair in sensual disarray as she lounges on a sofa, awaiting her lover...

Let it be me, Clara.

Clara

For the umpteenth time, I peer through the window by my apartment door, then recheck my watch. Ten minutes until Nick arrives.

I pace to the entry hall mirror and inspect my makeup. Too much? Not enough?

"It's just a date," I mutter as I pull my make-up pouch from my purse and dust a little more sparkle across my cheekbones.

"Just a few hours." I fluff my hair, which kind of defeats the point of the half-hour I spent taming my unruly curls.

I slick on another layer of dusky rose lipstick, wondering whether I'll smear it off before the night is through—and how. On a wineglass? On Nick's cheek? His neck? Will I leave rosy prints on his firm belly, following a trail of silky dark hairs?

"Nothing to get worked up about." I force myself to sit on the sofa and pick up a magazine.

I'm being ridiculous. The outcome of tonight's date with Nick rests entirely in my hands—though it's his strong, smooth hands I'm obsessing over—and his mesmerizing dark eyes, and his smile, simmering with the promise of pleasure.

If indulging in a tumble with the visiting professor feels right, I'll indulge. If it doesn't, we'll have spent a pleasant evening together. I'm a grown-up woman who can handle my decisions...even if I have the heart of an indecisive chicken.

Nick's soft knock startles me into ripping the page. I whoosh out a shaky breath, count silently to five, then stride to the door like the confident lady I'm pretending to be. When I open the door, my breath seizes.

He is so pretty.

"Nick. Hi. Um, come in," I splutter.

His dark curls are neatly combed back, which leads to thoughts of how I might mess them up. His espresso-brown eyes shine beneath lush lashes, and a seductive half-smile plays across his full lips. His cashmere sweater hugs his chest and shoulders just enough to hint at the firm expanse of muscle beneath. Before my gaze slides further south, he whips out what he's holding behind his back: a huge bouquet of coral-hued lilies interspersed with roses in shades from palest blush to deep orange. In the center, one perfect wine-red rose.

"I was hoping to find something to match the color of your hair." His gaze drinks me in from head to toe, and for a moment I consider scattering the floor with petals and pulling him down on top of me.

Get a grip, woman!

"Nick, they're glorious. Thank you."

His soft kiss against each cheek warms my skin. "You're lovely, Clara."

"So are you." I clear my throat. "I mean, you look nice."

"Thank you." He glances around. "Cute place you have."

"It's comfortable. I don't spend as much time here as I'd like, though." Nervous chatter tumbles from my lips as I search the dining room for a vase. "I practically live at the shop these days." I pull a cut-glass vase from the sideboard, then nearly drop it. "I'll just get some water."

"Let me help you." He follows me into the kitchen and unwraps the flowers while I fill the vase. "Scissors?"

I hand him a pair of kitchen shears.

"Nice tools." He inclines his head toward my collection of Wüsthof knives, mounted on a magnetic rack beside the sink.

"I told you I like to cook."

He deftly snips the ends of each stem. It's odd having a man beside me at the kitchen counter—cozy, familiar, something I haven't felt in a long time.

He places the filled vase on the dining table. "Shall we?"

I paste on a smile I hope passes for calm and collected. "Let's go."

He holds the door of his little green Karmann Ghia while I do my best to lower myself gracefully into the seat. When he switches on the ignition, the sound system blinks to life, and a husky alto voice croons Brazilian jazz.

"That's Carmen. She teaches vocal music at the university. We'll hear her tonight, at the bar."

I try to relax as the lights of Agate Street flash past. Nick is a smooth, fast driver, and his car hugs the curves, pushing me back into my seat.

"So, how's your project coming?" I ask.

"It's time-consuming, pulling together all those pictures and notes. I'll need to make a second pass through your red room before I go back to Berkeley. My deadline's been bumped up."

Behind the red door with Nick—what a thrilling, scary thought. I clear my throat. "Sure, any time."

At a stoplight, he turns to face me. "I was serious about helping you, Clara. I know some people who could set you up with a much better website and attract a lot more online business."

"And are these people in Berkeley?"

"Yeah. Damn." He brightens. "But I could photograph the books on my next trip up."

"When will you be back?"

"Mid-July. I'll probably camp out on Leo's couch or stay with my sister in Corvallis. Of course, it'll be hard to work with my little niece climbing all over me." He grins. "Besides her dad, I'm her favorite jungle gym." His chest rises on a deep sigh. "Some changes at work mean I'll have to devote most of my summer to finishing this book project, but I'll do my best to carve out time for us."

Us. I like the sound of that a little too much for such a short acquaintance.

"Well, your work has to come first, of course."

He pulls into the driveway of the cottage where we shared our tantalizing first kiss. Still gripping the wheel, he gifts me a dazzling smile. "Work will be rough for a while, but my dad taught me the importance of a well-balanced life." His hand drops onto my knee. "Spending time with you will help me weather this storm, if you're willing."

I gulp down the spiky lump in my throat, recalling Harry's comment that Nick looks like he'd like to eat me up. Harry nailed it.

So much for taking things one day at a time. "Aren't we going to the wine bar?"

"It's right over there." He points toward the campus. "Do you mind walking? Parking is nearly impossible there, and it's a beautiful night."

I wiggle my toes in my strappy, high-heeled sandals. "Sure."

But Nick doesn't reach for the door. Instead, he squeezes my hand.

"Before we go, Clara, can we talk about the elephant in the car?"

"Sorry, what?"

He brushes a finger against my cheek, his whispery touch setting off fireworks that dance across my skin.

"I guess you can tell I'm very attracted to you. But I recall how hard it was to take my first steps toward dating again." He smiles sheepishly. "My friends kept trying to set me up with nice women, but I backed out of half a dozen dates before I finally worked up the nerve." He weaves his fingers through mine. "I remember how, whenever I hesitated to do something I really wanted, Diana said, 'I double-dog dare you.' I can hear her saying that now."

His thumb strokes the back of my hand. "I really want to know you, Clara. It won't be easy with me down in Berkeley and you up here, but I'll be back as often as I can. I hope you'll give me a chance."

I can't hold back a shiver as his words strike deep. This is no mere fling he's offering. I suspect the word "mere" could never be used to describe an intimate encounter with Nick Papadopoulos.

"Anyway," he continues. "I understand how hard it is because I've been there. And I won't pressure you to do anything you aren't ready to do. But maybe it's time to dip your toes back into the water. Because life is for the living."

Reaching deep within myself, I find the strength to meet his probing gaze. His eyes, nearly black in the low light, are gentle, but something flickers in those dark pools. Something dangerous? I'll never know unless I work up the courage to dive in.

"Thank you, Nick. You're a fascinating man, and I think there may be something between us. And yeah, it scares me to admit that." The words slip out so easily. "I'll look forward to your next visit."

A broad smile crinkles the corners of his eyes, and he lifts my hand to his lips. "Shall we?"

Chapter Twenty-One

♥

Clara

The balmy night air lifts my hair as we stroll the three blocks to the wine bar, a long, narrow building with a high stamped-tin ceiling. Inside, jazz fans from twenty-one to eighty are crammed around tiny tables. I follow Nick to a low stage holding a keyboard, an upright bass, and a microphone.

"This is us." He pulls out my chair. "We're lucky tonight. Carmen doesn't perform very often."

The waitress brings us a bottle of Malbec, very rich and complex, and a wooden board with crusty bread, a crock of creamy cheese, and a fan of thinly sliced salami and prosciutto. I swirl my glass and sniff the wine's intoxicating perfume while I check out our fellow music lovers. I've never been to this place, never even heard of it. Really, I've gotta get out more often. So many pleasures to taste, and I've been holed up in my bookshop, ignoring them.

I take another sip and set the glass down, promising myself to be more cautious after last night's overindulgence.

Nick and I make easy small talk about our favorite non-sexy books while we wait for the show to begin. "I love corny 1950s space operas," he confesses. "And those classic British mysteries."

I smear a slice of bread with cheese spread, then top it with a sliver of prosciutto. "I never get tired of Miss Marple. Have you tried Wilkie Collins?"

Before he can answer, the stage lights come up, and a fiftyish woman in a slinky velvet sheath sashays to the microphone. Her dark hair is arranged in a loose knot, and a large tropical blossom flames behind her ear. Her accompanists are clad in black, which makes her stand out all the more in her ruby-red dress. Leaning into the mic, she breathes a sultry "Boa noite" and nods at Nick before beginning.

Carmen's singing is like her dress: velvety, liquid, sultry. My store of Portuguese words doesn't extend much beyond "Good evening," but the song's meaning is clear, a celebration of love and life's pleasures, a story of heartache and joy. Her hips shift smoothly from side to side as she sings, her flashing dark gaze focused on the back of the room, as if her lover stands there watching.

Eyes closed, I cradle my chin on my interlaced fingers and sway to the music. Nick's fingertips trace lazy circles on my back, leaving a trail of delicious tingles.

Carmen's next song is a sultry bossa nova. Nick's hand drifts upward, brushing the hairs at my nape. He lingers there, gently kneading, and I lean into his caress until I'm melting like butter.

Nick's touch has me so relaxed, my hand slides off the table, my fingers brushing his leg. His flesh is warm beneath the cool cloth. Carmen croons of Brazilian love—on the beach, I imagine, at sunset...a couple alone, their skin caressed by the sea breeze.

Caught up in the seductive mood, I lean closer to Nick and skate my fingertips over his thigh. His sharp intake of breath draws my attention from the music. *Oh my.* I bite my lip to temper a wanton smile. The firmness beneath my fingers is not a fold in the cloth, but rather something much more substantial. I quickly retreat, but a shiver of anticipation runs from my fingertips right to my core.

"Obrigado," Carmen breathes into the mic. "Thank you. We're going to take a little break now."

Nick's dark eyes glitter in the candlelight. "Obrigado, Clara."

His nearness, his husky voice, the music, the wine—it's all so intoxicating. He twines a lock of my hair around his fingertip, and something gives way deep inside me, like a dam overflowing. Heat curls down my spine and sizzles over my skin.

To hell with waiting. I want this man. Right now.

I lean my head on his shoulder, brush my lips against his ear, and whisper, "Let's go."

His irises darken as he captures my hand and kisses my fingers. "You're sure?"

"Very."

A glow of clarity warms me from top to toe. Tonight might be just a passing encounter leading nowhere, but I'm ready to surrender my fears.

He drains his glass and raises the bottle, still half-full, eyebrows raised in a silent question. When I shake my head, he sets it on the table of a young couple beside us. "Cheers."

"Um, thanks?" the skinny young man says. His date giggles.

Nick nods to the singer, then clasps my hand and leads me through the crowd, the muscles of his broad back shifting beneath his sweater as we weave between the tables. Mere minutes from now, I'll slide my hands over the bare skin I've fantasized about. Will he be a gentle lover, or quick and urgent? Will I see him again after tonight? I push away any thoughts of the future and consequences. All that matters is taking this first step back toward life, toward passion, toward joy.

Our dance begins long before we reach his temporary home. Nick kisses me beneath the first tree we pass, his hands sliding up my back and over my satin blouse. His silken tongue parts my lips, and I taste the wine he gulped a moment ago.

"You are so delicious, Clara," he murmurs as his lips trail over my jaw and down my throat. Purring, I thrust my fingers into his dark curls and surrender to the sweet ache of desire.

A hoot of laughter from a passing car yanks us back to earth, and Nick releases me.

"Right." He chuckles. "Shall we take this somewhere more private?"

I slide my arm through his, and we continue up the tree-lined street, stopping to kiss beneath the next tree, and the next, each kiss more passionate. I can only keep my hands off his warm, strong body for a few moments before I'm compelled to touch him again, to reassure myself he's real and here and wants me as much as I want him.

Two blocks from Nick's place, he moans into my hair and slides his hands up my sides to cup my breasts. It's a cliché, but I swear I see fireworks behind my closed lids as I arch into his touch.

"Get a room!" someone calls from across the street.

I giggle like a horny teen on prom night as, hand in hand, we continue our path toward privacy.

One block away, Nick growls, scoops me into his arms again and presses me against a tree trunk, his erection prodding my belly. My sex throbs with sweet fire.

"God, Clara," he rumbles, his lips on my temple. "You feel so good, I could just..."

I plant my palms on his chest and push him back. "Don't keep me waiting any longer, Nick."

As he pulls me up the stairs to his door, I half expect a movie scene: the hero and heroine stumbling backward, tearing at each other's clothing, unable to restrain themselves as he takes her hard against the wall.

But it's not like that.

Nick pauses on the stoop and holds both my hands tenderly. "Clara, I don't even have words for how much I want you. But are you sure?" His dark eyes gleam in the low light, and his broad chest rises and falls.

Beneath my flaming need, a glow of tenderness suffuses my body. Knowing the gravity of this moment, Nick won't let me be swept away by passion. If I cross this threshold, it must be my clearheaded choice.

I caress his strong jaw, skim my fingers over his cheekbones, trace the full curve of his lower lip with my thumb. His hot breath grazes my hand.

Funny—after all that emotional turmoil, all that dithering, when the moment arrives, I have no doubts, no regrets. I clasp the small of his back and snug his hips to mine. "I'm sure."

He opens the door, and our dance continues. Chest to chest, hip to hip, we sway to the remembered beat of smoky jazz as we drift across the living room and toward the bedroom, kissing languorously, hands roaming, sliding, grasping. Nick hums against my temple and strokes the length of my back. On a moan, I arch my throat and press my breasts against his chest, propelling him backward. When we reach his bedroom door, he grasps my shoulders gently.

"Wait here." He slips inside and closes the door.

Breathless, I lean against the door frame.

From within comes the sound of shuffling, drawers closing, then the soft wail of a saxophone.

The door opens, and Nick stands before me, barefoot but otherwise fully dressed, a present for me to unwrap. Behind him, votive candles flicker in cut glass tumblers, and a slow bossa nova pulses from a little speaker on the dresser.

Taking my hand again, Nick draws me into the room. "You deserve beautiful surroundings. If I were at home, I'd create a scene worthy of you."

"This is lovely," I reassure him, touched that he would pause in such a heated moment to set the mood.

"You're lovely." He pulls me against him. The throbbing between his legs calls forth an answering pulse from my body. He sways me in time to the music until we bump against the mattress. And then he dips me like a tango maestro, easing me onto his bed.

Nick kneels and unfastens the straps of my sandals, tosses them aside, and slides his warm hands over my feet and up my legs.

"So beautiful." He buries his face between my breasts as he tugs my blouse loose from my jeans and slides his hands up my sides, his palms cool against my burning skin.

Planting one knee on the bed, he slides me backward until I'm stretched fully across the mattress. Hovering over me, he coaxes my blouse buttons open as he rains kisses down my throat, between my breasts, over my trembling belly. His hot breath warms my skin through my jeans, and then his fingers slide the zipper down and tug the rough cloth over my hips. The brush of his lips leaves a smoky trail of pleasure, grazing my inner thighs, the inside of my knees, each ankle. He peels my jeans off my feet before stroking and kissing his way back up my legs. I gasp when he nibbles the sensitive flesh of my inner thighs, the sensation like feathery lightning.

Sighing, I undulate beneath his caress, lulled by his gentle, probing touch. No hurry, no force—just silken seduction, slow and sweet and patient.

He licks me, trailing the tip of his tongue to the apex of my quivering thighs. He pauses a moment to skim a fingertip over my lacy panties, ever so softly, sending cascades of shivers through my body. His hot breath is delicious between my legs, and I ache for more.

But he continues to slide his hands and mouth up my body, slipping my blouse off as he rises, until I lie beneath him in only my lace bra and panties.

His lips caress my nipple through the fabric. Groaning, I grasp his soft curls, but he pulls back and smiles devilishly.

"Not so fast, lovely lady. We have all night."

He straddles me and pulls his sweater over his head, tossing it aside. His chest is bare underneath, and the candlelight gleams on his tawny skin, his muscular pecs, his tight belly. While I glide one hand over the sprinkling of dark hairs that arrow toward his belt, he softly sucks the fingers of my other hand, one at a time. The sensation is heavenly, but that's not where I want his hot, wet mouth.

With a groan, I buck my hips and roll him beneath me. "My turn."

I grasp his wrists, straddle him, and press my throbbing sex against his hard shaft. I kiss his arched throat, and his pulse leaps beneath my tongue. Down I slide, pressing my cheek against his chest to feel his pounding heartbeat beneath the crisp hair that tickles my skin. He inhales on a hiss as I circle each smooth nipple with my tongue.

"So good..." he moans.

I kiss my way down his firm belly and circle his navel, dipping the tip of my tongue inside before reaching for his belt buckle. His fingers fumble to help me, but I bat them away.

This may be my only time with Nick, and I intend to wring every last drop of pleasure from tonight.

"We have all night," I breathe against his warm flesh. He answers with a groan.

Slowly I tug his slacks down, revealing his long, fat shaft straining the silky fabric of his boxer briefs. I exhale over the length of him, barely brushing his beautiful cock with my lips. A shudder runs through him.

When his pants are off, I slide up his strong legs, raking him lightly with my fingernails, my gaze locked onto his. He's burning as hot as I am, and I feel a surge of sensual power, knowing I'm giving him as much pleasure as he's giving me.

Nick writhes on the bed when I brush the swelling of his balls, then slide back up to kiss him deeply and press my slick core against his hardness.

"I surrender," he growls and rolls atop me again. He slowly bucks his hips, sending shivers of pleasure and aching anticipation deep into my core. With a groan, I clasp my legs around him.

He fumbles with the back of my bra, which fastens in the front, then gives up and peels it over my head. His warm, wet tongue bathes each breast in turn, making me gasp and arch into his caress. He claims my mouth again, probing deeply while he tugs off my panties. His fingers part my swollen folds, sliding over my clit and deep inside me, igniting electric shocks of bliss that steal my breath.

His undershorts catch on his erection as I try to tug them down. He helps me, and my eager hand closes around his hard, hot, silky shaft while he strokes and teases me until I'm trembling on the edge of climax.

"Now, Nick. Please."

He buries his face in the crook of my neck while his free hand fumbles in the nightstand drawer. I hear the crackle of the condom wrapper and reach down to help unroll the thin sheath over his throbbing cock. As soon as it's snugly seated, he rolls atop me, lifts my thigh, and fills me with his hard heat. I gasp, relishing the sensation of being touched so deeply. I've missed this, needed this, after so long without a man's touch.

I clutch his smooth ass and pull him tighter to me as he strokes in and out, slowly and smoothly, his eyes locked onto mine. After a few heavenly moments, his gaze softens and his lids half-close. "God, Clara, so good..."

He's moving faster now, his cock impossibly hard as he presses deeper and deeper inside me. The music and candle-light and smooth flesh and slick wetness all swirl into a vortex of unbearable pleasure as ecstasy crashes through my body and mind. There is no him, no me, only a blinding flash of glory.

The first wave past, I catch my breath just as Nick loses control. His strong fingers dig into my flesh, his hips pistoning fast until his body goes rigid and he shouts my name, eyes shut tight as he rides his own wave of delight. The pressure of his hard body against my clit sets off delicious aftershocks, and I rock beneath him, squeezing him hard with my thighs.

Minutes later, we lie in each other's arms, my head resting in the hollow between his shoulder and chest as his fingers thread through my hair. Gradually, my pulse slows, my breath finds its rhythm again, and my body melts into Nick's.

Unwilling to let the moment end, I reach down to caress his cock, still pulsing wetly against my thigh. He hisses and flinches away.

"Too sensitive." He kisses my hair and strokes my arm with a feather-light touch. "I haven't come so hard in years."

Neither have I. Not since...

I brace myself for a flood of emotion that doesn't come.

Breathing deeply, I nestle my cheek against his chest and take inventory of my body and mind and heart. My muscles are pleasantly tired and heavy, as if I've run a few miles. The slick, swollen flesh between my thighs still tingles. Like a well-stroked cat, I'm draped comfortably over Nick's almost-slumbering body.

And inside? Inside, I feel warm, relaxed, strong. There's a tinge of sadness, but no regret. I'm okay. More than okay, I'm refreshed and happy. I've lain with this wonderful man and, come what may, this moment is a new beginning.

Chapter Twenty-Two

♥

Clara

I wake to find a folded note on the pillow beside me. The scent of fresh coffee drifts through the open bedroom door, but the cottage is silent, and the sheets where Nick slept are cool.

I unfold the paper.

Lovely C,

Alas, I've got an early appointment. You were sleeping so soundly; I didn't want to wake you. There's breakfast in the kitchen. I'll stop by your shop later today.

Thank you for trusting me. I know what a big decision this was, and I'm honored you chose me. You are truly one of a kind.

—N

Is this goodbye? An elegant kiss-off? That can't be right, not after what he said about wanting to know me, about returning often and helping me promote our erotica collection. But there's no mention of a repeat encounter, and men will utter all sorts of lies to bed a woman they want.

No, damn it, I won't let myself spiral into self-doubt. I made my choice, and I don't regret it. Whatever the outcome, Nick's given me a glimpse of the life I could rebuild.

Closing my eyes, I lift the sheet to my face and inhale his rich, woodsy scent. A few glossy dark hairs cling to his pillow. I wind one around my finger and sigh, letting the memories unroll like a movie highlights reel: whispers and moans, silken skin, powerful muscle, delirious pleasure that lifts me out of myself. How long has it been since I experienced truly living in the moment? Too damn long, that's for sure.

I chuckle. Who'd have thought this dumpy little cottage could deliver such a life-changing experience? Hell, I expect that anywhere I couple with Nick would become a magical place.

Eventually, I trail into the bathroom, tiled in avocado green. I shower in the chipped tub, sudsing myself with Nick's herbal-scented shower gel. If he were here with me, I'd slide my slippery hands all over his muscular chest, watch bubbles trail down his firm belly, water dripping off his...

A familiar ring tone sounds from the bedroom. I rinse and towel off. There's a voice mail notice waiting for me.

"Hey, Clara," Margot giggles into the phone. "Sorry, I'm, ah, going to be late today. I'll get there as soon as I can."

Behind her, another woman laughs, and I recognize the sultry voice of Nick's assistant, Darcy.

Well, well, it seems I wasn't the only member of my staff to get lucky last night. Good for her, though I don't trust that raven-haired tease.

Time to get back to work. Whether this connection with Nick blossoms or remains just a sweet, brief memory, I have responsibilities to tend to.

I help myself to coffee as well as a croissant and a ripe peach. Before leaving, I pause in the doorway for a wistful glance at the cottage, the site of my re-entry into the world of the living, then softly close the door behind me.

I wait on the stoop for my driver to arrive. Blinking in the bright morning sunlight, I reach deep inside for a bit more of last night's courage.

Deep breath. I'm okay. In fact, I'm just grand. I can have some fun with a handsome man. It doesn't have to mean anything.

But my brave words don't erase the nervous tickle in my belly, and the memory of Nick's touch haunts me all the way home.

On the surface, today feels like any other day. I shelve books, greet customers, answer calls from vendors, and wrap packages for shipment. But while I work, I notice things I haven't really seen in months, maybe longer—dust motes dancing in the morning sunlight, the silky slide of Lulu's fur against my bare ankles, the rumble of music and conversation from Coffee Dreams next door, the merry notes of the brass bell greeting each customer.

During a pee break, I flash a grin at my reflection. I'm fine. I've done a brave thing. Good for me.

But as the hours tick past, my certainty falters. Here I am in familiar surroundings, doing what I do every day. Nothing has changed—except I miss Nick. I search for his face around every corner, and my gaze keeps straying to the red door.

Harry finishes ringing up a customer's stack of mystery novels and joins me at the front table display, where I keep trying different arrangements and color combinations, but nothing looks right.

"You okay, Clara?"

I shrug and glance over my shoulder. The shop is empty but for the two of us.

Harry rests one big-knuckled hand on my shoulder and, with the other, moves a stack of slim yellow volumes to the topmost position on the table. "There. Better."

Coarse white hairs tickle my palm when I give his hand a fond squeeze. Will I ever have a partner to grow old alongside, someone faithful and strong like Harry?

"I'm okay," I reassure him, "just a little distracted."

He quirks a wiry eyebrow. "You sure you don't want to take next Saturday off?"

Until that moment, I'd almost forgotten that looming milestone, the first anniversary of Jared's death. The realization steals my breath.

"I'll decide later." I smile at my old friend. "Hey, are you all right? You're pale today."

The circles beneath Harry's eyes are more pronounced than usual, the lines around his mouth more deeply etched.

He waves off my concern. "Just a little under the weather. One of those summer colds. I'll have a hot toddy and a nap when I go home. By the way, we're almost out of business cards. Should I order more of the same?" He pulls one from his pocket. It features an old shot of Jared and me in front of a bookcase, his arm slung over my shoulder as we grin at the camera. Behind us, the red door gleams.

My eyes mist over, but I smile through it. "No, let's get a new picture taken, you and me and Margot."

Harry's grin etches deep parentheses in his cheeks. "That's my girl. Don't forget Lulu."

At the mention of her name, our shop cat trots over and meows loudly, hoping for a kitty treat.

"Right. Lulu too."

Harry squeezes my shoulder. "I know it's hard, kiddo, but I'm glad to see you moving on."

When I evade his gaze, he squeezes again. "Hey, moving on doesn't mean we love our lost darlings any less. It means we don't live the rest of our lives in sorrow."

How lucky am I to have such a wise, compassionate friend?

"You're right. Thank you, Harry. By the way, weren't you supposed to work the afternoon shift today?"

He grins. "I was. Had a barber appointment. Until I got a call from a giggly young lady this morning. I think our Margot hooked a live one last night."

"That was nice of you."

He chuckles. "Love trumps haircuts any day."

Love trumps a lot of things, but I can hardly call what Nick and I shared love, can I?

Later, on my way to Arnie's place for coffee and a sandwich, my phone pings, and my heartbeat kicks into overdrive. It's a text from...

Oh. Dalton. My shoulders relax. Just a few words and a photo. Damp and bedraggled, he grins at the camera and clutches the medal hanging around his neck. His long legs are mud-spattered, and wet running shorts cling to his superhero thighs.

Came in second in my age group.

Congrats!

His reply comes right away:

Can't wait to see you. Back late tonight.

Yikes! Is he asking to see me tonight? I stand rooted to the sidewalk, finger poised above the screen, until a passing teen bumps my shoulder.

"Sorry, ma'am."

"Watch where you're going, dork!" his companion scolds.

"What? I said sorry."

They move off, and I make my decision.

Call tomorrow?

Three dots, and then

With pleasure

I let out a whoosh of breath and run my fingers through my hair. This is getting dangerous. But really, why should I sever my connection to Dalton just because I had one hot night with a man who's leaving in a few days, possibly forever? Hell, it's midday, and still not a peep from Nick. And we haven't spoken about being exclusive. And it's not like I'm planning to jump Dalton's bones anytime soon.

And I'm making excuses.

The thought of committing to a long-distance relationship with Nick is slightly terrifying.

What the hell, Clara? You're getting miles ahead of yourself.

For the moment, I'll keep my options open.

A little after two, I'm rearranging the glass case of antique children's books when a familiar baritone voice spins me around.

"I have a complaint."

I whirl to find Nick so close, I can feel his warmth and smell his woodsy cologne. My fingers itch to touch him, and I nearly do, until I sense Harry's watchful eyes. Instead, I tuck my hands into my pockets to avoid temptation.

"A complaint about a book?"

"About your shop." His eyes are hooded, but the corners of his full lips twitch.

"What about it?"

"It's too far from Berkeley."

"Ah." My restraint crumbles. Blocking Harry's view with my back, I run a fingertip along the top edge of Nick's belt.

He inhales sharply, inches closer, and murmurs into my ear, "I want you now." His hot breath tickles my neck. "I can't concentrate, can't remember what I wanted to say. Today's meeting was a joke. All I could think about was your skin, your scent, your voice..."

My whole body flushes. So much for my notions about easy, casual sex.

He reaches for my waist, but I push softly against his chest. "Nick, not here."

"Where, then? When?" He nuzzles my neck, and for a moment I forget how to form words, hypnotized by memories—the way he moved inside me, the heat and heaviness of his body.

"Seven?" I ask.

He grimaces. "Shit."

"Huh?"

He grasps my shoulders, neither quenching my thirst nor freeing me to catch my breath.

"I have a dinner meeting tonight with Leo's department chair. I'd ask you to join us, but then all I'd do is grope you under the table and babble nonsense."

"I see. Guess it's not so easy to mesh our schedules."

I didn't mean it as a rebuke, but he steps back and drops his hands to his sides, his gaze downcast.

"Clara, I—" His chest rises and falls on a deep sigh. "I won't force this. If last night was all you wanted, I'll let you go. But please know, I want more." He pierces me with those dark, hypnotic eyes.

I yearn to release the words burning in my throat: *Yes, Nick, I want you too. We'll make this work, somehow.* But indecision grips me. It's frightening to feel so much so soon.

"May I call you tonight?" he asks.

That gave me a few hours to ponder my answer and my future—with Nick, or without him.

I nod. "I'll be waiting."

Chapter Twenty-Three

♥

Clara

While Margot rings up the last few customers, I give the bookshelves a final inspection. "It's just infatuation," I whisper, shaking my head as if shooing a fly. "Just sex. Nothing to lose my mind over." My phone shrills, making me jump and drop a heavy book right onto my toe. Hissing a string of curses, I hop on one foot as I fish the noisy pest from my pocket.

Missed call. Nick.

While I massage my sore toe, a red dot appears beside the voice mail icon. Margot is at the counter ringing up a pile of graphic novels. I catch her eye, hold up my phone, and duck behind the screen by my desk.

"Clara, it's Nick. Turns out the department chair's a fast eater. We're almost done. Can I meet you at eight?" A few heavy breaths, and then, "Please."

I play his message again. And again. "What do I do, Jared?" I whisper.

An answer comes, maybe from my own inner wisdom, or maybe from my lost love, watching over my shoulder as I squirm in uncertainty. Either way, the message is clear.

Listen to your heart.

"That doesn't help," I moan. My heart isn't speaking up at the moment. And anyway, my heart belongs to Jared. But the rest of my body votes to return Nick's call.

With a wince, I push the Call Back button. It rings once, twice...

"Clara."

"Hi."

Again, I hear his whispery breath. My skin prickles into goosebumps at the memory of his breath fanning my neck. I shift in my seat, suddenly aware of the pressure of my jeans against my most sensitive skin.

"Can I come by?" he asks. "Will you see me?"

Just breathe. In, out. "Of course, Nick."

"I'll be there in a few minutes."

Wait a minute, what happened to eight o'clock? But he's already hung up. It's six forty-five, and the college is only a short drive away. There's no time to go home and straighten up, so I grab the cosmetics bag from my desk and head for the restroom.

A moment later, Lulu mews and makes a beeline for the front door.

"Hello, Puss. Yes, yes, I love you too." Nick's deep voice rumbles like a contented tiger's.

"Oh, hey, Professor." I hear muffled conversation between Margot and Nick, but my feet refuse to move. Finally, Margot calls my name.

Deep breath. Okay, go.

He's sitting in the big armchair by the door with Lulu sprawled on his lap. I might have a hard time choosing between my two suitors, but the cat's preference is clear.

Nick rises at my approach. Offended at losing her seat, Lulu stalks away.

We stand toe to toe, gazing at each other. Something's off tonight. He seems less composed, more—anxious? Sad? He reaches for my hands. His palms are damp.

"How was your dinner?"

"It was—weird." He takes a deep breath. "Clara, I've been offered a job."

"Oh? Where?"

"Here."

I blink up at him. "But you already have a job. You can't just quit. Can you?"

"It would be difficult. And the U of O position is only part-time for now, so..." He brushes stray hair from my cheek. "What do you think?" His voice trembles. "I don't have long to decide."

"You're seriously considering a move up here?"

He nods. "In some ways, it's a good career decision for me. But that's not the only reason."

My heartbeat revs like a Harley Davidson. "Me?"

Lips clamped tight, he nods.

"Wow." I stumble backward.

He clings to my hands, dancing me down the cookbook aisle. "Is that a good wow or a bad wow?"

"I'm just surprised. Last night was amazing—"

He pulls me closer. "Please don't say 'But.'" Crooking a finger under my chin, he tilts my face up and kisses me deeply, his lips soft and tender. My body responds enthusiastically, but my head spins like a carnival ride.

Finally, he releases me. "Tell me I haven't scared you off."

His eyes are misty. So are mine.

A book tumbles to the floor. "Sorry!" Margot's voice floats from behind the bookshelf. "Tried to squeeze in too many books."

Nick picks up the fallen volume, a florid romance. "Love's Gamble," he reads. "See? Someone's sending you a message."

"I'm pretty sure that someone is Margot." I trail my fingertips across his chest, relishing his solid warmth. "Okay then. Yes, Nick, I'd like to have you closer. It would give us time to find out whether this is just a fling or maybe…"

"Something real." He gathers me in for a long, slow, sweet kiss that almost quiets my nagging doubts.

Almost.

His hands cup my face, then slowly slide downward. His right hand lands on my hip, pulling me tight against him. His left thumb brushes the side of my breast. An observer wouldn't notice this stolen caress, but the feelings he stirs in me are too incendiary for such a public place. I moan against his neck and snug him tighter, loving the delicious thrill of his hard shaft against my belly.

My gaze flicks to the red door. Do I dare to pull him back there for a quick roll on the settee? The doorway bell's tinkle banishes that wicked thought. A group of white-haired ladies enters, chatting merrily. From wherever she's been hiding, Margot bustles to the counter to greet them, throwing a glance over her shoulder as she passes. Nick's dark complexion helps hide his flush of arousal, but my flaming cheeks and mussed hair are a dead giveaway—and the swelling in his wool trousers is hard to miss.

"Go!" Margot whispers. "I've got this."

Nick wraps his arm around me, clutches his jacket to hide the insistent bulge, and propels me toward the door.

"Excuse me a moment," Margot says to the customers. My brilliant assistant scoots behind the screen and emerges with my purse. "I'll close. See you tomorrow."

Nick chuckles into my hair as we quick-step to his car. "You should give her a raise."

·❤·❤·❤·❤·❤·

This time, we don't even make it to the bedroom. We stumble backward into Nick's cottage, shedding clothing as we go. My blouse is already off and my jeans halfway down when we land on the lumpy couch. Nick kneels to tug off my shoes, then grasps my jeans and pulls, lifting my hips off the cushion. The juxtaposition of his boyish eagerness and his elegant appearance makes me laugh aloud—and he joins in, clasping me tightly. He licks away a tear of mirth trailing down my cheek, and I return the gesture, enjoying the salty taste of his skin, the rich scent of his moss and cedar cologne.

With my fingers twined in his soft curls, I pull him in for another kiss. His powerful back muscles tense as he rocks his hips, slowly grinding his cock against me. Shooting stars of pleasure zing from my clit, electrifying my skin. Every inch of me cries out for more.

My fumbling with his belt is interrupted by a buzz from his pocket, followed by a merry marimba tune.

"Shit. Darcy." He pulls out the offending phone, taps the screen, and grins. "She says don't wait up."

"Good!" I wrap my legs around his waist.

Nick gazes deep into my eyes, golden glimmers dancing in his espresso-brown irises, and I swear in that moment he can see inside me—every swirling thought, every flicker of desire, every fear and hope. His lips curve in a devilish smile as he lowers his weight onto me and rocks me in a slow rhythm that pushes me deeper into the already-sagging couch.

I giggle. "Do you suppose this is how the couch got its character?"

"Let's put another dent in it." His mouth closes over my nipple, and he releases a moan that buzzes against the tender skin.

Arching my back, I give myself to his kiss, all my nerves singing.

"Wait." He grabs his phone, taps it, and the room fills with the soft strains of Brazilian jazz. "They're playing our song."

"The horizontal mambo?" I giggle again, and my laughter turns to gasps of pleasure when Nick slides down between my parted thighs and presses his humming lips over my damp panties. I sway to the beat beneath his caressing mouth and hands, the sweet ache building until I can't bear to wait another second.

"Please, now," I gasp.

He hooks his fingers through the elastic and tugs my panties off. But instead of rolling his strong body atop mine, he kneels between my thighs, lifts my legs, and drapes them over his shoulders. Teasing me mercilessly, he nibbles the tender flesh at the top of each thigh. Eyes half-closed, I roll my head to the side and gasp again when I spy our reflection in the mirror above the dining room cabinet.

Fascinated and furiously aroused, I watch Nick's tongue trace torturous circles, round and round, closing in on my pulsing center. He parts my swollen folds with the tip, oh so softly, just one taste, achingly sweet.

"God, you are so delicious, like a ripe peach." He rests his cheek against my thigh, and the scruff on his jaw scrapes divinely against my skin. With a fingertip, he traces each swollen lip of my pussy, then slides slowly inside me. He keeps his finger there, gently undulating as his tongue resumes its exploration.

The pressure building in my core is agonizing, exquisite, driving away all awareness of the world outside. There is only this place, this moment, this man.

At last, his circling tongue finds my clit, stroking up one side and down the other, at first with feathery lightness, then more firmly. I growl filthy words and grasp his soft, curly hair.

"Ah, ah, ah. Patience," he chides and pulls back to kiss my inner thighs and stroke me from hips to knees. "Relax. I want to explore every luscious inch of you."

Once again, he nibbles and licks and hums his delight, and I really do try to give him the patience he asked for, but my need is too strong. Just a few more exquisite flicks of his tongue and I scream, my voice raw, my thighs clamped around his head as wave after wave of climax rips through me.

"Yes, yes, give it to me," he growls. I squirm away from his probing tongue, the sensation so strong it steals my breath. But he persists, clasping my hips firmly as his caresses spin me away on an even stronger surge of bliss. My blood courses like river rapids. I laugh and cry out and sob until, completely spent, I collapse onto the sofa, happy, helpless, and exhausted.

Nick nibbles his way up my stomach, pausing to suckle on each breast before kissing my mouth, his lips swollen and slick.

With great effort, I push myself upright and propel him backward until he stands before me.

"Look to your left," I murmur against his flat belly.

He chuckles. "You clever girl. Were you watching us the whole time?"

"Not the whole time, since you made my eyes roll up in my head." A wicked grin stretches my lips. "Speaking of head..."

Amused by my own raunchiness, I slide my hands up his strong thighs, savoring the heat of his skin, the fuzzy softness of hair beneath my palms. I hook my fingertips through the waistband of his shorts and tug them down. His swollen shaft springs free and bops my nose.

"I've missed you," I coo and wrap my hands around his hot, silky cock.

Nick's breath comes out in a hiss when I kiss the velvety plum head of his cock.

"Oh, you like that, do you?"

"Yes, ma'am. Very much. More, please." He rakes his fingers into my hair but lets me control the pace. I feather kisses over the pulsing length of him, then take him in as deeply as I can, stroking my way back to his fat crown with my lips and tongue. His flesh throbs beneath my touch.

It's so exhilarating, this feeling of feminine power, and I want to torture and tease until Nick loses control. I want to see his animal side.

"So good," he moans, his words blurring into a guttural growl.

I stroke his shaft with one hand and, with the other, gently cup his balls, which snug tightly against his body at my touch.

His breath catches. "Do that again."

I glance up, only to find him watching the mirror, hypnotized. The sight ignites a glow deep inside my core, and I'm going to enjoy giving him a good show. On and on I tease him, alternating long licks with whispery nibbles, then swooping low to tongue his balls.

"God, yes, more." His hips buck, and his head falls back, eyes closed. His rhythm increases, and I grip his thigh to control the tempo.

"Clara, I want to come inside you." He tries to pull back, but I hold him firmly.

"Next time." I speed my motions, stroking him with both hands. My tongue flicks the luscious, plummy head of his cock until he cries out, calling my name over and over in a frantic prayer. I take him in deep, loving his throbbing heat, the salty taste of him as he surrenders to ecstasy.

Gulping air, he collapses forward and clutches the back of the sofa for support. When I release him, he drops down beside me, his warm, heavy body relaxed and yielding—until I try to caress his still-pulsing shaft.

"No, please. Too much." He grasps my hand and laughs, his head thrown back. "Oh, what a mess. Let me..."

He snatches a linen handkerchief from his pants pocket and tenderly wipes my chin. "Thank you, my angel."

And then he stretches out on the sofa, snugs me to his side, and lazily strokes my back. My head fits perfectly in the hollow between his shoulder and chest. The strong, steady rhythm of his heart, the weight of his arm around me, safe and warm, lulls me toward sleep. There's no need to move, no need for words, just peace and comfort in our quiet connection.

We're together now, and together we'll figure out the rest.

Chapter
Twenty-Four

❤

Nick

I'm swimming up from a warm, hazy, soothing place. I want to linger there, but insistent pins and needles in my arm pull me to the surface. I blink to clear my sleep-blurred vision and find Clara half-atop me, pinning me against the back of the couch, her hair cool and silky against my jaw and throat. Grinning, I inhale its floral scent, stroke the curve of her hip, and trace her ribs, so prominent beneath her moonlight-pale skin.

Peace and contentment envelope me. I almost can't believe she's trusting me to be her first lover since losing her husband, but the evidence is strewn all over the living room—my underwear on the coffee table, her bra flung over a lamp, another crumpled linen handkerchief on the sofa pillow. Grandma P would flip her wig if she knew I've been using her annual Christmas gift to clean up Clara's beautiful, cum-smeared face.

It's still dark out, so we haven't been asleep long. I slide out from beneath her and gaze down at my sleeping beauty. Her closed lids flutter. Is she dreaming of me, of us? She rolls onto her back, and I hear a distinct rumble from her midsection. With a pang of guilt, I remember she came straight from work to my place, and I ravished her without feeding her. I unfold the fleece U of O blanket from the back of the couch and, after one last look at her nude body, so soft and unguarded in sleep, gently cover her.

Her lids flutter open. "Don't go."

Her plea yanks on my insides, flushing me head to toe with the primitive, compelling need to take care of her, protect her.

She draws her forearm across her eyes, and her lush breasts peep out from beneath the blanket. "What time is it?"

"Almost nine. Are you hungry?"

She gifts me a dreamy smile. "Yes, actually. Starving."

"Do you like Thai food? There's a place just up the street."

"Ohhh..." She stretches like a sleek cat. "I'm so comfortable here." Reaching out, she trails her fingers over my bare arm.

"Then stay." I kiss her forehead. "I'll go get us something."

She's asleep again before I finish dressing. As I close the door softly behind me, my phone signals an incoming message.

Enid's number.

If it's not too late, call me. Bad news.

And, just like that, my rosy haze evaporates.

I wait to place my order at the Thai restaurant's takeout counter before returning her call.

"Twenty minutes," the tiny grandmother behind the counter tells me.

Pacing on the sidewalk, I return Enid's call.

"Nick, dear boy." My mentor's voice shakes, paper-thin. "It's all gone to shit."

My shoulders tense. It's unlike her to curse.

"Tell me."

"George is not responding to radiation. They're going to try a new treatment on him."

Damn. I'm fond of Enid's husband, a retired chemistry professor with a dry sense of humor and a raspy voice. Theirs is a late-in-life romance, and their playful, flirtatious banter gives me hope. If Enid and George can be so happy together, maybe I'll find someone too, someone to share my later years, build a home, perhaps even a family of our own.

And now, just as I'm reveling in hope for a new start with Clara, Enid's facing the loss of her great love.

"The thing is," she continues, "this treatment's only available at the Mayo Clinic."

"In Minnesota?"

"Yes. We leave tomorrow. I know you're visiting friends up there, hon, but I need you here. I can postpone the meeting until Tuesday, but no later."

"Meeting?"

"I'm retiring, effective immediately. The whole department will reshuffle. It'll go better for you if you're present, Nick."

A deep weariness slumps my shoulders. "Okay. I'll be there."

I end the call, blow out a long breath, and resume my pacing. I could call her back, tell her I'm taking the job at the University of Oregon.

"Order for Nick."

No, I can afford to wait. Leo's boss gave me a week to decide. Better to see how things fall out in Berkeley first. I've learned the hard way that hasty decisions lead to regret.

Clenching the paper bag, I hurry back to Clara. I'd hoped for another week together. Will what we shared tonight persuade her to wait for me?

· ❤ · ❤ · ❤ · ❤ · ❤ ·

Clara

I doze on the saggy couch, my bare skin warmed by the fuzzy blanket and sweet, steamy memories. Sex with Nick has relaxed all the tension from my body and mind—and revived my appetite.

The doorbell rings. Odd, did he forget his key? I comb my fingers through my matted hair and wrapped the blanket around my naked body. What fun to greet Nick by flashing him! I'll bet that'll ignite another round of ferocious sex.

I fling open the door and am about to fling open the blanket too, but I freeze at the unexpected sight of Nick's assistant Darcy holding a bottle of Chianti and a pizza box. Her eyes narrow. Clearly, me wrapped up like a burrito is not the menu she had in mind.

She juts her hip and shakes back her long, jet-black hair. "Where's Nick?"

"He, um, went to get some dinner."

"Uh-huh." With a bored expression, she slithers around me and into the cottage.

What had happened to 'Don't wait up'?

Darcy deposits the pizza and wine on the coffee table and kicks my crumpled jeans and panties away with the toe of her motorcycle boot. She plops onto the couch, then rakes me with an up and down gaze. She cocks her pierced eyebrow.

"Had a good time, did ya'?" From the pocket of her slashed jeans, she pulls a baggie of cannabis. From the lace bra peeping through her low-cut T-shirt, she extracts a packet of rolling papers, opens the pizza box, and deftly fashions a fat, tight joint. Firing it with an engraved silver lighter, she takes a deep drag, then extends it toward me. "Have some. Makes the crappy pizza taste better." When I just gape at her, she adds, "Makes bad news easier to take, too."

I wave her offer away and bend to retrieve my clothes. "Nick didn't mention you'd be joining us."

"Oh, I'm always around." She takes another drag, holds her breath for an impressively long time, then blows a stream of skunky-smelling smoke. "Now, where's that corkscrew?"

While she rummages through the kitchen drawers, I retreat to the bedroom to get dressed, unsnarl my hair, and repair my smudged mascara. A bit more composed and confident, I return to the living room and find Darcy stretched out on the couch, one hand behind her head, devouring a slice of greasy pepperoni pizza.

She waves her snack. "Sure you don't want some?"

"No thanks." I step toward the end of the couch, but Darcy doesn't withdraw her booted feet, so I perch instead on the rickety chair beside the fireplace, feeling very much like an intruder.

"Have some wine, at least. 7-11's finest." Without waiting for my reply, she pours some into a plastic tumbler.

Why not? It might steady my nerves. Nick called her an excellent assistant, but right now, my inner alarm is blaring. Whatever game she's playing, Darcy's intentions are far from benign.

I gulp down the flat, fruity wine.

"Good girl. Take your medicine." Darcy nods. "So, what are your plans once Nick leaves?"

"What do you mean?" Her condescending tone scrapes my nerves like sandpaper.

"We're outta here tomorrow. Can't keep all those hot little grad students waiting." She looks me up and down, smirks, then chugs her wine.

Flushing hotly, I fiddle with my glass. Nick didn't mention when his job offer here would start. Of course, he has classes to teach in Berkeley. Still, Darcy's smarmy tone stings my pride. "Maybe Nick's not ready to leave."

Her cool gaze bores into me, making me want to squirm.

"Oh, honey, you didn't fall for slick Nick, did you?" She takes another bite of pizza and continues talking while she chews. On most people, that would look disgusting. On Darcy, it's earthy and sultry. Damn it.

"Listen, you seem like a nice lady. But Nick got what he wanted from you, a big pile of books and a quick lay. He's already gone. Might as well face it." She gulps more wine, burps, and giggles.

I straighten my spine. How dare she?

"That's not what Nick told me," I assert in my haughtiest grown-up voice.

She waves dismissively. "I mean, you're cute and all. I wouldn't kick you out of bed." She relights her joint and props her boots beside the pizza box. "But do you seriously think you can compete with all those twenty-two-year-olds throwing themselves at Nick?"

I open my mouth, but no quick, witty retort leaps out. Embarrassment and resentment glue me to my chair, along with growing dread. Nick is about my age, with just a sprinkling of gray at his temples. Would he really engage in flings with his students? Couldn't that get him fired? Or maybe it's Darcy who wants him, and she's trying to scare me off.

I suck in a deep breath and straighten my spine. "What about Margot? Don't you want to see her again?"

Darcy snorts. "What for? I'm not sentimental. I got what I wanted from her."

Poor, sweet Margot. She deserves better than this bitch's scorn. I've never resorted to violence, but I'd like to smack that smug expression right off her sharp, pointy face.

Darcy crosses her arms, inflating her cleavage. "Besides, Berkeley is my home. It's cruel to build up false hopes, like Nick is doing with you."

Darcy's back is to the door, and she's so intent on tearing me down, she doesn't seem to notice when Nick quietly enters and stands glowering in the doorway. She waves her wine glass. "Why would he hang onto an old widow like you when he could have any young chick he wants? He does it all the time."

He slams the door. Darcy jumps with a squeak and sloshes wine down her cleavage.

"Darcy." His face is set in grim lines, lips tight, eyes narrowed. His fist strangles a takeout bag.

"Nick! I, uh...shit." She slumps on the couch and clutches her forehead.

"Get out." His voice is tightly reined thunder as he gestures at her dinner mess. "Take your things with you."

"But I—"

"Just go."

Her face contracts into a fierce scowl bordering on tears. She slams the pizza box shut, jams the cork back into the wine, and stomps to the door. Passing me, she hisses, "It's true, you know."

Nick shuts the door firmly behind her, then leans against it, his face wan, his eyes flat and staring. I want to go to him, stroke his shoulder, ease the tense moment, but my butt is rooted to this uncomfortable chair.

Finally, he steps forward, his movements halting. "Clara, I'm so sorry."

Pressure burns behind my eyes. A tear slides down my cheek and drips off my jaw.

He strides across the room, kneels, and folds me in his arms, but I'm rigid in his embrace. Even his soft lips kissing away my tears can't release me. I cross my arms, protecting my heart, and rasp out, "Explain this to me."

"Please, sit with me." He tugs me to the couch where, a few hours before, he made me see stars. The thought makes me want to vomit. I huddle where I am.

"Is it true, then? You're going back to Berkeley tomorrow?"

He spreads his palms in an appeasing gesture. "I have to go back for an emergency staff meeting."

I glare, my vision blurred by a fresh wash of tears. "You said we had another week together. You said you might take a job up here. And now you're leaving?"

He folds forward, his elbows on his splayed knees. "My department chair just called. Her husband is ill, and she's resigning. I don't know when I'll be back, exactly, but it won't be long, I promise."

"And the girls, Nick?"

He hesitates, no doubt trying to compose an answer that won't send me out the door.

Too late.

I snatch up my bag and bolt.

But Nick's right behind me. On the stoop, he catches my arms and spins me to face him.

"Look, Clara, I don't know why Darcy wants to poison what's growing between us. Please—" He releases my arm and caresses my jawline with his fingertip. "Please listen to me. I'll answer all your questions."

My stomach aches. My head buzzes. The urge to flee is unbearable. But the vulnerability in his dark eyes holds me fast, even though I'm a thousand percent sure this is goodbye, and I've been played for a fool.

"Will you come inside?"

"No. Tell me here." I cross my arms and shiver in the cold night air.

He drops his gaze and massages his temples for a moment, then nods. He slips off his leather jacket and drapes it, warm and heavy, around my shoulders.

"There was a girl. One. A year after Diana died. She sort of...anyway, it doesn't matter what she did. She was my grad assistant, and it was wrong."

"Did you love her?"

He shakes his head slowly. "I was lonely and flattered. At the time, it seemed—we had a special connection, and we took it too far, you know?"

I stare straight ahead, trying hard not to crumple into tears.

"She was twenty-three. It only lasted a few weeks. We both realized how stupid it was, how stupid we were." He scrubs both hands through his curly hair. "But someone saw us together. Word got around, and it nearly cost me my job."

"It should have."

Nick reels backward under my harsh words, but I'm too caught up in the grip of a nauseating memory to care.

Doctor Sanchez, my academic advisor, a handsome, distinguished man in his forties who promised me a much-needed scholarship. In the midst of my parents' divorce and struggling to carry a heavy course load, I'd leaned on him as a safe, supportive mentor. But he wasn't safe.

"You're so lovely, Clara, so much more mature than the other girls. Think about the work we could do together..."

I remember the sickening feel of his clammy hand on my knee, the stink of stale cigarette smoke on his breath. I recall my panicked, stumbling steps as I backed out of his office. I should have reported him, should have told someone.

And now, fists clenched at my sides, I glare at Nick, another man who's not what he seems. Darcy was cruel, but she was right.

His beautiful brows rumple. He reaches for me. "Clara, please. I'm being straight with you. I made a huge mistake. I've never repeated it, and I never will. I don't want some young girl. I want a grown woman." He takes my clammy hands in his. "I want *you*."

My breath coming in shallow pants, I stand transfixed as a silent battle wages inside me. Nick is not Dr. Sanchez, but he did take advantage of a young woman as naïve and vulnerable as I was back then.

His voice cracks with emotion—or is he that good an actor? "You're the first woman I've had feelings for since Diana died. God, do you know how hard it is to say those words? It feels like I'm betraying her. But there it is—I care for you, Clara. Please, give me a chance."

My heart vibrates in sympathy, but I can't get past Darcy's warning.

"Feelings? Is that what you call it, Nick?"

A sexy growl emerges from his clenched jaws. "Clara, I'm not talking about my dick. I'm talking about my heart."

We face off for a long, silent moment. I don't step closer, but I don't walk away. Goosebumps prickle every inch of my skin, except where Nick's warm hands enfold mine.

Finally, I croak out a question. "What about Darcy?"

"Shit. Darcy." Releasing me, he pulls his phone from his pocket, types a message, then shows me the screen.

You're fired. Go back to Berkeley.

He hits Send, and it whooshes away.

"Why would she lie to me, Nick? What does she have to gain?"

He scrubs his hand down his face. "I told her I might take a job here. That was stupid of me. Her job as my grad assistant pays her tuition."

"But Nick, she said there were girls. Lots of girls."

He clasps my shoulders and squeezes gently. "There was *a* girl. One. It's a mistake I won't repeat." He reaches for my waist, trying to tug me closer. "Haven't you made a mistake before, Clara?"

My heart thunders. "Maybe I have. Tonight."

I turn away.

"I'm not leaving here until you talk to me, Clara," he calls after me, his voice ragged with desperation.

But I have no more words to give him. Once again, panic compels me to flee.

Chapter Twenty-Five

♥

Clara

As soon as I reach the safety of home, I peel off my clothes, including Nick's leather jacket which I unwittingly ran off with. A long, hot shower erases every trace of our ill-advised passion, but Nick's stricken expression is burned into my retinas.

I crawl beneath the covers, but sleep eludes me. For hours, I lie awake, listening to the trees whisper outside my window. I want to believe Nick, to excuse his horrible violation of student-teacher trust as a fleeting mistake. But having lived through it, I can't.

Restless and achy, I roll out of bed and slide the pane wide open. The night wind lifts my hair and caresses my bare shoulders.

"What should I do?" I ask the velvet darkness.

The leaves' whispered reply offers no comfort.

I pace in the darkened bedroom, the wooden floor cool under my feet.

On the one hand, I know from recent experience how hard it is to face dating again after losing a beloved spouse. How can I hold it against Nick if, in a vulnerable moment, he gave in to a seductive invitation, when I've done the exact same thing? I went to Nick expecting nothing more than a short-lived fling. What right do I have to be hurt because he had sex with a grown, willing woman? Okay, a very young woman, but still old enough to know what she was getting into.

I sink onto the bed and curl up beneath the covers, questions dive-bombing my brain like a swarm of agitated hornets.

Can I ever trust him again? True, he admitted his affair with a student, but his explanation is too conveniently perfect to believe. On the other hand, why would he leave his job in Berkeley and move to Oregon if all he wants from me is a fling? Heart-meltingly gorgeous, smart, seductive, Nick could have any woman he wants, and he wants me.

For now.

"Arrrggh!" I growl into the pillow. "What should I do?"

Just be patient.

I jolt upright, uncertain whether that voice came from inside me or from somewhere beyond. Either way, it's true—I don't have to decide today. After a shock like last night's, I deserve some time to breathe.

Good thing I set my phone to silent, because Nick calls seventeen times during the night and sends a dozen texts, all pleading for my response.

In the morning, I send one reply.

> **You need time to sort this out, and so do I. Let's give it a week. You shouldn't make a career decision based on a few nights of**

What word best describes what we shared? Passion? Attraction? Self-delusion?

I erase the last line and hit the Send button. And for the next few days, even though I flinch every time my phone buzzes, I resolutely ignore all further communication from Nick.

But I don't block him.

At work, Margot sulks around the shop with downcast eyes and slumped shoulders.

"What's wrong with her?" Harry asks. "She acts like she's in mourning."

"Have you asked her?"

"Of course. She says it's nothing, but clearly, it's something pretty big."

"I'll talk to her." No doubt, we're suffering from the same malady.

I wait until a quiet moment near the end of Margot's shift when the late afternoon sun paints the shop in mellow, golden light. I find her rearranging the front table display, her gaze distant. She's abandoned her usual dramatic eye makeup and left her blonde hair unspiked. Even her eyebrows are unadorned—no twinkling rings or crystal beads.

"Hey, kiddo. You don't seem like yourself today. You okay?"

She shrugs and continues stacking books.

"Harry's worried about you, and so am I."

She turns with a sigh and leans one hip against the table, knocking an avalanche of books onto the floor. "For fuck's sake," she snarls and stoops to pick up the mess.

I kneel beside her.

"Damn it!" She sits down hard and wraps her skinny arms around her knees.

Silently, I rub her back and wait for the storm to pass.

Finally, she gives a mighty sniff and looks up, a wry grin on her tear-stained face. "I feel so stupid. It was just a little adventure. Nothing serious. I knew that going in." Fresh tears spill down her cheeks. "She said, 'Now don't be stupid and expect to see me again.' Why did she have to be so cruel about it?"

I pull her close and rock her. "Oh Margot, I'm sorry."

Her body quakes with sobs, but she continues, talking it all out, and I envy her the ability to pour out the hurt and be done with it.

"I mean, I get it. She lives there, and I live here. But to brush me off like that, after all the sweet things she said when we were, you know, together..." She sniffles against my shoulder. "We stayed up all night talking and touching and...I thought she really got me, you know? Really saw me for who I am. Was. Whatever."

I wince. It seems Nick and his assistant are two of a kind. Twenty-four hours ago, I was so sure we shared a special connection, and now...

An ugly thought twists my stomach. Did Nick dispatch Darcy to deliver the bad news? No, I can't allow myself to think that. Maybe I'm a gullible fool, but I need to believe the pain in Nick's eyes was real.

I send Margot home early and close the shop on my own, checking each aisle for misplaced books. My echoing footsteps remind me how alone I really am.

I almost forget to retrieve my phone from my desk, having kept it hidden away all day to avoid temptation. Before opening my messages, I take a long, steadying breath. Nothing new from Nick, but there's one from Dalton.

> **Back home. Sore from the race, busy during last week of school, but can't wait to see you again. Dinner tomorrow night?**

My clenched jaw relaxes into an easy smile. In all my obsessing over Nick, I forgot about Dalton—funny, kind, undemanding. Just what I need.

I quickly text back:

> Sounds great. Looking forward to hearing about the race.

His answer comes just as fast:

> Call?

So much for undemanding. Oh well, it'll get my mind off Nick.

"Clara. Hey. It's good to hear your voice."

I laugh. "I haven't said anything yet."

"Okay, it's good to hear your ring." A moment of silence, then, "I missed you."

Guilt needles me when I realize I haven't missed him. I've been too wrapped up in Nick to think of anything else.

"Last week of school, eh? Must feel good."

"You know it. The teachers are just as excited as the kids. So, you're free tomorrow night?"

"Sure. This time I'm taking you out, though."

"Hey, that's not necessary."

"I insist. Do you like Thai food?"

There's a long, awkward pause. "Clara, we went out for Thai food. Before the musical, remember?"

"Oh, shoot. Of course we did. Sorry." I kick myself mentally. "How about Indian?"

"As long as you're there, I don't care where we eat. Pick you up at seven?"

"Make it seven-thirty. At my place." I give him the address. "I'm looking forward to it."

His warm, rumbly chuckle vibrates against my ear. "Not as much as I am."

I end the call and tick off our dates on my fingers—that first after-work beer, the high school musical, the wine-soaked Italian dinner... Not long ago, Margot explained that young people consider a third date the gateway to sex. Have I unwittingly invited Dalton into my bed?

I ponder that possibility as I drive home. My too-hot reaction to Nick's touch clouded my judgment, leaving me vulnerable to deceit. Maybe sex with Dalton would help clear my head of the muddled mess Nick left behind.

Or maybe I should just give up on sex entirely. Ugh—what a depressing thought.

Nick

I pace the hallway outside the anthropology department's conference room, my footsteps thudding on the worn green carpet. For the past five years, I've spent more time in this building than in my apartment in the Berkeley hills. Now, with my mentor gone, my workplace feels strangely empty, like an abandoned movie set. It seems that with the slightest push, the wood-paneled walls would collapse around me.

And they will if the new department chair has her way.

I check my phone for the tenth time. Still nothing. Clara hasn't changed her mind. She wants a week to think about it, but I don't have a week. I need to choose today.

Leo will know what to do. I jog to my office and lock the door behind me.

My friend's voice booms through the phone. "Nicolas! I was damned sorry to hear about Enid. Good woman. So, who sits on the throne now?"

"Nancy Lewington." Even saying her name turns my stomach.

"Huh. I take it that's bad?"

"Yup." I resume my pacing, much less satisfying in my overstuffed little office. Back and forth, I stalk like a wild animal in a very small cage. "She knows, Leo."

"About your job offer? Good. Let her see that other universities want you. You're a hot commodity, Nick."

"Not here, I'm not." I sink onto the cracked vinyl loveseat and run my hand over my sweaty face. I've been avoiding this painful moment of reckoning, but if I want Leo's perspective, I'll have to come clean about the whole ugly business.

"You remember that Christmas, when I didn't come up to Oregon?"

"Right..."

"I said it was because I had too much work."

"Right..."

"I lied." I slump in my seat.

"No shit." Leo chuckles. "Academia is a fishbowl, my friend. I've heard the rumors. Figured you tell me when you're good and ready. Or never. Up to you."

I groan. "God, Leo, I thought we'd covered it up. How could I be so stupid?"

My stomach in knots, I confess the mistake that's come back to bite a big, bloody chunk out of my ass.

When I finish, Leo gives a low whistle. "So, you haven't heard from her since?"

"Lydia? No. She was just as glad to be out of it as I was. She graduated with well-earned honors, but if they knew about us, people would always say..."

"She slept her way to the top of her class?" Leo chuckles. "People can be stupid." His pencil taps like a woodpecker, an old habit that shows up whenever he's deep in thought.

"Anyway, Nancy saw us kissing in my car." Admitting my reckless stupidity flushes me with embarrassment. "Turns out she's been holding onto that information, waiting for her chance to cut me with it."

"Well, what you did wasn't illegal. I mean, you weren't her instructor when it happened, right?"

"No, but I had been, the semester before." I gaze at the gnarled oak tree outside my office window. A half-dozen students lounge in its shade, reading, dozing, talking, kissing. I remember sitting there with Lydia, comforting her after an ugly breakup with her boyfriend. The last few autumn leaves shivered above us—two broken-hearted people, both very fond of each other, both aching for a lost love. I remember Lydia's soft hand grasping mine, her liquid blue eyes brimming with tears. It was so easy to fall into her arms. So easy, and so stupid.

Leo's voice yanks me back to my present shit storm. "So get a lawyer, defend yourself."

"If I do, the scandal will spread beyond Berkeley. For the rest of my career, I'll be dogged by rumors, even if I'm exonerated." I sigh into the phone. "Enid's gone, Nancy's in, and she wants me out."

"Well, hers isn't the only vote, right?"

"No, but she's got a lot of allies here. Unless I can publish my book before the tenure committee meets, I don't have much of a chance." I massage my aching forehead. "Enid got me an interview for a full-time, tenure-track position."

"Where?"

"Nebraska."

"Good God, man, are you daft?" he splutters. "Your family's here. Your friends are here. The woman you want is here. Come to Oregon!"

Ah, but the woman I want doesn't want me—or so it seems.

Leo softens his tone. "I know you, old friend. What's stopping you?"

"Darcy told Clara."

"About your little peccadillo?"

"Yes."

"I take it she wasn't pleased."

"That's an understatement."

Tap, tap, tap. Finally, "Do you want her, Nick?"

"God, yes." The agonizing truth slips out before I can stop it.

What I feel for Clara is so much more than mere lust. When she stormed out, my heart withered to a cold lump of regret and self-loathing because I'd found love again, only to lose it to the consequences of my past stupidity.

Leo scoffs, "Then come fight for her!"

I chew on my pencil.

"As I recall, Diana wasn't convinced right away either," he adds, "but you didn't give up on her."

He's right. Back in my undergrad days, my well-earned player reputation made Diana wary. Convincing her I wanted more than a quick tumble took a lot of time and gentle courtship.

And imagine what I'd have missed if I'd given up on her.

Like a hit of strong whiskey, a flush of energy rushes through my body, driving me to my feet. "You're right, my friend. Thank you."

I dial Leo's department head, accept the position, and then make one last call. For this one, I leave my stuffy office, walk out into the brilliant sunshine, and sit on the bench where I made the blunder that set all this in motion.

So far, I've been able to protect her, but if Nancy has her way, my ill-chosen lover could get burned.

The phone rings and rings. Finally, she picks up.

"Lydia, it's Nick."

Chapter Twenty-Six

♥

Clara

I usually enjoy shelving new romance novels, but today, Nick's dark eyes flash from every cover, along with his seductive smile, his broad shoulders and muscular chest... Every handsome cover model is a piercing reminder of his voice, his scent, his touch. But Margot's busy with a gaggle of kids in the picture books section, so I grit my teeth and power through.

When the last hulky hero is safely tucked away, I carry another new arrival to the self-help aisle: *Finding Your Purpose at Midlife*. Do I have a purpose beyond running this bookshop? It's a question worth considering, and one that might keep my mind off Nick.

Next up: the sports aisle, where hunky dudes grin smugly from their book covers. Naturally, my mind flashes to Nick in his Spandex rowing gear. I don't have any more books about that sport. I've checked. Twice. But I do have a whole shelf of books on running. One cover photo features a lanky runner with a friendly smile and a shaved head, just like Dalton's.

With a loud meow, Lulu demands my attention. She spirals around my ankles before trotting toward the back of the shop. I follow and find her batting a paw on the red door.

"What's up, Lulu-girl?"

She head-butts the door.

"Mouse in there?"

Once I fetch the key and let her in, she darts inside and sniffs the baseboards, then crouches and stares at the wall, her tail whipping.

"Oh dear." I squat to examine a hole in the baseboard. "Just what we need, mice nibbling our most expensive books." I stroke Lulu's silky ginger fur. "Good job, Puss."

Harry pokes his head through the door. "Afternoon, Clara. Got the weekly orders ready for your signature."

I point to the hole.

He grins widely. "Well done, Kitty Cat! Same exterminator as last time?"

I nod and push myself up, calculating how big a bite this will take from our bottom line. Might as well shelve the new erotica books while I'm here.

Before leaving, Margot pops into the red room. "You okay back here? Want me to take care of this?"

"I'm fine." I hold up a heavy volume of erotic poetry. "Got several new ones."

She crosses her tattooed arms. "You sure?"

"It doesn't bother me." In fact, I hadn't given it a second thought until Margot's reminder. Guess I've finally conquered my fear of this room.

Margot throws a glance over her shoulder. "Harry's with the customers. Can I see the new stuff?"

I point to the stack on the floor. "More ancient Greeks chasing each other across vases, and some art deco nudes."

"Pretty." She picks up a coffee-table book with a Freddy Mercury lookalike dressed in leather chaps, a leather cap, and nothing else, astride a gleaming motorcycle. "Hot stuff. Ever done it on a motorcycle, Clara?"

"Is that even possible? Wouldn't you fall off?"

"Maybe not—if you're limber."

We giggle as Margot leafs through the photos, various combinations of leather-clad models, all pouty and sultry and a bit intimidating. Margot sighs when she reaches a photo of two women. One, short-haired and wraithlike, grips the handlebars of a big Harley, her head thrown back while, behind her, a raven-haired Amazon clutches the driver's breasts, her mouth on the smaller woman's throat.

Well, that's just cruel. I give Margot's skinny shoulder a squeeze.

She shrugs. "Yeah, Darcy called yesterday. Lost her job with Professor Adonis, but she's already got a new position."

Deep down, I'm not surprised.

"Older woman, this time. Music professor." Margot closes the book. "She wants me to come visit her in Berkeley."

"I thought she told you to forget her."

Another shrug. "People change."

"Will you go?"

"I might. I think I could have some fun without falling in love with her. I mean, now that I know who she really is." A grim edge tempers her smile. "Sometimes, good sex is worth it."

She hops up from the floor as only the very young can. "Well, better get going. And hey, thanks for listening yesterday. I really needed to get that out of my system."

Amen, kiddo. If only I could figure out how to get Nick out of mine.

She pauses in the doorway. "You know you can always talk to me too, right?"

I'm touched by Margot's concern—and by her philosophy. Maybe some meaningless sex would clear my head and give me perspective. Dalton's made it plain he's interested. Should I just go for it?

After I finish dressing for my date, I check my phone one last time. Still no message from Nick. My stomach sinks at the sight of that blank screen.

Well, I asked for a week to think, so he's honoring my wishes—a good sign. Or perhaps he's written me off as too much trouble. I put away my phone and push aside thoughts of burning bridges and slamming doors.

Asking Dalton to pick me up at home was a bold move, but I figure he won't try to jump my bones before dinner. He shows up promptly at seven-thirty, clutching a bouquet of supermarket daisies. His broad, friendly smile melts the tension from my neck and shoulders.

Standing on tiptoe, I smooch his cheek. "So pretty."

I carry the flowers into the kitchen to find a vase. When I return, I realize the coffee table already holds Nick's huge bouquet. Dalton's gaze is riveted to the spot. Beside that lush arrangement, his daisies look scrawny and pathetic.

"I love daisies," I reassure him. "So fresh and honest."

He doesn't ask about the roses, so I don't offer an explanation.

"Shall we?" I grab my jacket and purse from the coat tree. It's nice not to worry about dressing up for a date. Dalton's wearing jeans and a cotton sweater over a T-shirt—and his running shoes, of course. My jeans are snugger than his, and my V-neck sweater shows a hint of cleavage. I chose flats tonight to prevent me from losing my balance and tottering into his arms again.

"I hope you'll like this place. It's one of my favorites," I say as Dalton pulls his VW station wagon into the parking lot. "It's not fancy, but they have the best lamb vindaloo. Can you handle some heat?"

A flush tints his prominent cheekbones.

Oops. Better choose my words more carefully.

He takes my arm, his bashful grin sliding into something darker. "I like it hot, Clara."

The scent of butter and spices wafts out when he opens the restaurant's glass door. From her elaborately carved podium, Mama Banerjee greets us warmly. "Ah, Miss Clara. How are you this evening? Introduce me to your young man?"

Mama B isn't much older than me, but she envelopes her customers in grandmotherly warmth.

My date extends his big, bony hand. "Dalton Garvey. Pleased to meet you."

Mama B tests his grip, nods her approval, and leads us to a table in the corner, beneath a brass lantern inlaid with colorful glass tiles. "You want menus?"

I cock an eyebrow at Dalton. "Do you trust me?"

His smile blossoms like an unfurling flower. "Completely."

"We'll have lamb vindaloo, butter chicken, and chana dal." Something hot, something rich, something soothing.

"Garlic naan?"

Dalton nods.

Garlic kisses, then. Because I'm pretty sure we'll go at least that far.

Mama Banerjee brings frosty beers and a basket of fragrant naan, plus cool cucumber raita for dipping. We dig in while we wait for the rest of our food.

"So, school year's almost over, eh? Must be nice."

"Still have to finish my grades and pack up my classroom. How about you, Clara? Do you take time off in the summer?"

"Not often. The bookshop keeps me busy."

He leans onto his elbows and reaches for my hands. "I hope you'll consider taking a day or two after we're done with the work on your shop. Maybe a trip out to the coast?"

"I could probably arrange that." It's a bit too early to plan a weekend getaway with a guy I barely know, but I suspect Dalton will be a fun travel companion. A vision flashes in my mind: sitting beside him in his battered VW station wagon, laughing as we cruise a scenic coastal highway, the wind whipping through my hair and his...not hair.

Mama B arrives with the food. "Enjoy, dear heart. You too, sir."

"She takes good care of you, eh?" He holds the platter while I take a big scoop of basmati rice and top it with spicy curried lamb.

"She's a born mother."

Would I have been?

I scold myself for opening that mental door. My chance at motherhood has passed, and there are lots of ways I can build a satisfying, meaningful life without kids of my own. Besides, nobody gets through life without some regrets, and this is mine. It could be far worse—for example, I could have never known real love.

Dalton's smile quirks to the side. "It's funny. I love working with my students, but I've never actually wanted kids of my own." He chews thoughtfully, and then his eyes open wide. He grabs his beer and chugs half the bottle.

I can't resist batting my lashes. "Thought you liked it hot. Try a little yogurt with it to calm the heat."

We laugh and talk our way through all three dishes, avoiding touchy subjects like his ex-wife and my late husband. When he finishes his beer, I raise my hand to get Mama B's attention.

He grips my fingers gently. "None for me. Considering how our last date turned out, I'll take it easy this time."

Our bellies full, we leave the restaurant about nine. Dalton starts his car and turns to me with a twinkle in his blue eyes. "Can you spare another hour? I'd like to show you a favorite spot of mine."

I remember Margot's words. "Sometimes, good sex is worth it." Though I'm still not sure I'm ready for sex with Dalton, a little making out might be fun.

"Sure, just for a little while."

"Great." His smile lights up with so much adorable, youthful energy, I can see why his students love him.

He drives east toward the Willamette River and past a sign that declares the park closed at sunset.

"Don't worry," he says, "there'll be lots of people here."

He pulls into a parking lot near the riverbank, and indeed, there are a half-dozen cars, probably full of teenagers making out. I wonder if any of them are his students. In any case, he parks far enough from the other cars to give us some privacy.

Dalton pulls the key from the ignition. "The river's pretty at night. Want to go take a look?"

"Sure."

He leads me down a weedy path to a picnic table a stone's throw from the riverbank. We sit side by side on the tabletop, like a couple of kids.

It's colder here, and when I shiver, Dalton drapes his arm loosely around my shoulders. I scoot closer to enjoy his warmth, and we rest in comfortable silence for several minutes, listening to the soft whoosh of the water and watching the bats swoop and zig-zag over its gleaming surface.

His gaze is unfocused, distant. With the moonlight shining off his shaved head and throwing his deep-set eyes into shadow, he looks like some warrior from a science fiction story, weathered, stoic, and wise.

"This is a good place to think," he says at last.

"It is." I lean my head on his shoulder. "What do you come here to think about?"

"Work stuff, decisions, relationships, the meaning of life." He nudges me. "You know, trivial matters."

"Well, if you figure that last one out, let me know."

Dalton holds my gaze, his smile slowly fading. Moving in for a kiss? No, he turns back to stare at the dark water. I marvel at the length of his legs, his long bony fingers, wondering how they'd feel against my bare skin.

That thought doesn't leave me hot and tingly, though, just curious.

He leans his elbows on his knees and stares out at the slowly gliding river. "I used to come here with Tiffany."

"Ah." This is a big deal, when a very private person like Dalton opens up about such a painful subject. Unlike my foolish self, pouring out my angst to the nearest attractive stranger.

"Is it hard to go places you went together?"

His lips compress. "Yes and no. But I've lost enough to her. I won't let her take this place away from me." He straightens and flashes a crooked grin. "Hey, sorry. Nothing more boring than a guy who drones on about his ex, right?"

"You're not boring, Dalton." And I mean it. Though he's taciturn on some topics, he's otherwise a good companion, easy to talk to, funny and sweet. I really like him and hope our friendship will grow.

He gives his head a little shake. "Anyway, that's over and done. We're here now, and it's a beautiful night."

"Right." But will the fence he erects around his divorce mean he won't want to hear about Jared either? Because what I need most is a friend to talk to about that very subject.

I take his hand and lace my fingers through his. "We can't change the past; we can only live in the present."

Up goes one golden eyebrow. "You're pretty wise. Must be all those books you read."

"Yup. Smartness seeps into my pores."

He bumps my shoulder with his. "You know, if I ever gave up teaching, it would be for something like what you do."

Now there's an interesting thought: Dalton and me running the bookshop together? I shake my head and rein my focus back to the present.

"Getting cold?" he asks.

"A little. It's so pretty, though."

"How about we watch the clouds from inside the car? We could listen to music and, you know, enjoy the moment." His playful grin flattens as he scans my face. "Unless, of course, that other guy?"

My head, heart, and lady parts wage a silent battle. And though the war is far from over, my head wins this skirmish.

"Don't worry about him. He's—it's nothing." That's a big fat lie, but between Nick's past and mine, I'd be smart to shelve our attraction under M for mistake.

Dalton's long forefinger trails down my arm, raising goosebumps. "Well then, what do you say?"

Sitting in Dalton's car at Make-Out Point will certainly lead to kissing, possibly more. Why not see whether we click physically?

I fill my lungs with cool, river-mud scented air. The earthy scent grounds me in the present moment and helps me focus on the kind, funny, honest man beside me. "Let's go."

Chapter Twenty-Seven

Clara

Dalton holds the car door for me, then switches on the engine for some heat and cues up music from his phone. In a breathy alto voice, a singer croons about love and regret.

"I don't recognize this one." I remark.

"A benefit of working with teenagers. They introduce me to artists I'd never hear otherwise."

I nod along to the beat. "I like it. Good music, beautiful view."

Shadowy clouds sail swiftly across the moon. The silvery skyscape matches the melody somehow, melancholy and lovely.

"I like the view in here even more." Dalton brushes a lock of hair from my forehead. His blue eyes are darker in this dim light, searching mine, but he waits for me to make the next move.

Touched by his gentleness, I lean my cheek into his palm. For a long moment, he holds my gaze, then lowers his head and presses his mouth to mine, softly this time, unhurried, even a bit tentative. He lets out a long, garlic-scented breath and slides his arm around my shoulders, pulling me closer.

The gear shift pokes my ribs. ""Ouch. I miss bench seats. How do young kids make out in cars these days?"

He has the cutest laugh-crinkles at the corners of his eyes. "I don't know. I'll have to ask them." Twisting to reach for me, he slams his knee into the dashboard, hisses in pain, then glances over his shoulder. "Would it be creepy of me to suggest..."

Holy cats, I haven't made out in the back seat of a car since high school. I hesitate, but not for long. As tall as Dalton is, we can't really stretch out back there, so there's no question of going "all the way."

Giggling, we clamber into the back seat, and Dalton wraps me in his long arms. "Clara, you're a special lady," he murmurs into my hair. "I'm so glad I met you. I owe Harry big-time."

He kisses me again, twisting to press himself against me as much as the space allows. Snorting with laughter, we wriggle and squirm in a vain effort to get comfortable. Finally, he scoops my legs over his lap.

I try to focus on the sensation of his lips on mine, his broad hands stroking my back, my hair, my arms, but I'm distracted by the sheer silliness of a grown woman and a very tall grown man squished into the back seat of a car.

"Hold on." Dalton fiddles with a knob beside the headrest, grunting and scrunching his face comically, which makes me giggle even more. Finally, the seat back drops with a thunk, and I fall onto my back with Dalton propped above me on one elbow. Oops. Station wagons have lots of room. Maybe this wasn't so smart.

"Right. Where were we?" He brushes his lips across my forehead, my cheek, my neck, then seals his mouth to mine and probes my lips apart with his garlicky tongue. I stifle another giggle, trying to disguise it as a moan of pleasure, but I end up sounding more like a wounded moose.

He pulls back, his brows furrowed. "You okay?"

"Fine. Great. Come here." I pull him down, and he recommences his exploration, his hand sliding up my side toward my chest.

I arch into his caress, and he cups my breast, his touch warm and pleasant, but not thrilling, not electric like Nick's.

"You're so beautiful," he murmurs, sliding his hand beneath my sweater. "May I?"

I bite my lip and nod.

He tugs my top over my head, skillfully pops open my bra, then makes his own moose-moan when my breasts spill free of the satin and lace. Goosebumps prickle my skin at his touch—passion or just cold air? Honestly, I'm not sure, but Dalton's arousal is so intense, so flattering, that tingling sensation deep in my belly must be desire.

He engulfs my nipple in a deep, suckling kiss, and I struggle to suppress a giggle as his warm tongue, not so much velvety as tickly, teases my sensitive skin. But when he nips me with his teeth, a little zing of pleasure brings a smile of relief. Maybe this will work after all.

I indulge my curiosity and caress Dalton's shaved head, now making its way down my belly one kiss at a time. His scalp is softer than I expected and very smooth. How does that work? Does he just shave his whole head every morning? Well, not the beard, obviously.

And why am I thinking about my partner's grooming routine instead of enjoying the moment?

A new song begins, a male voice mumbling to a driving techno beat. Dalton's laugh vibrates against my bare stomach. "Sorry. Gotta work on my make-out playlist."

"Oh, you have a playlist?"

"Actually, no. Haven't needed one for a long time." He rises as far as the cramped space allows and with one swift motion tugs his T-shirt and sweater over his head, rolling them into a pillow for me. His muscles are tight and well-defined, his pale chest and flat belly covered with fuzzy blond hair. I explore this new terrain and giggle again at the tickly sensation on my palm.

Dalton's watching me, his gaze uncomfortably sharp. His lips twist to the side, then he sighs and reclines beside me, his head cradled on his bent arm.

"What is it?"

He traces spirals over my goose-bumpy skin. I wiggle closer, and his erection prods my thigh, but he shifts away.

"You know, as a teacher, I have a lot of experience with trying to keep someone's attention when their mind is elsewhere." His hand flattens on my stomach, rising and falling with my nervous breath. "This feels a lot like that."

My breath stops. He's right—and I'm as wrong as a person can be. Dalton is a good man, dealing with his own deep pain, and I'm using him to chase mine away.

Neither of us is ready for this.

Our gazes catch and hold. Dalton's fingertips make one last whispery circuit of my breasts as if memorizing their shape. He cups my cheek. "As much as I want you, tonight's not the night, and this old bucket of bolts is definitely not the place. You deserve better, Clara."

"I'm sorry, Dalton," I whisper, my voice shaky.

"Don't be sorry," he reassures me with a lopsided smile. "You've opened my eyes to a hard truth. I'm not ready for this kind of intimacy." Reaching across me, he retrieves my top, then pulls his sweater over his head.

"Here, you've got..." I pluck one of my hairs from his short blond beard.

"A souvenir." Laughing, he pulls me backward into a tight hug. We lie there for a long time, my head cradled on his firm chest, our breath fogging the windows and blurring the moonlight.

Dalton's long fingers feel good in my hair. His steady heartbeat feels good against my cheek. Maybe, in time, we'll find our way to something hotter than this feeling of comfort, but for the moment, I'm happy in his arms.

"How long have you been divorced?" I finally ask.

He huffs. "We've been separated for a while, but it's not final until next month."

Holy crap. I'm sure Harry told me Dalton is divorced. Well, that explains a lot.

"Do you still love her?"

He shakes his head. "My love for Tiffany died the death of a thousand cuts." His chest rises and falls on a deep sigh. "But it hurts, knowing how hard I tried and still failed. I wish I could go back in time and ..." He chuckles. "Yeah, useless pondering. Time travel's impossible, right?"

We lie entwined for hours, talking like old friends, honest and unguarded. It seems our clumsy attempt at sex has dissolved all the awkwardness between us. Dalton pours out his heart, and I vow to punch his hateful bully of an ex-wife right in her weasel face the first chance I get—not that I know what she looks like, but she sounds weasely to me. And Dalton listens sympathetically to my struggles with uncoupling sex from my love for Jared.

"It feels like I'm betraying him, you know?"

"You're not." He kneads the back of my neck with his long, strong fingers. "If he loved you the way you deserve to be loved, he'd want you to be happy."

My reaction to his empathy and kindness dampens his sweater a little, but he gracefully ignores my tears until the wave of grief passes.

Eventually, my bladder calls an end to our heart-to-heart cuddle. After a quick pee in the bushes, we drive home in companionable silence, Dalton's left hand on the wheel and his right hand in mine. It's nice, lovely even. Though we may never share the fiery chemistry I found with Nick, I've made a new friend.

And though we haven't talked about Nick at all, tonight's catharsis has cleared away the worst of my shock and pain, leaving me with a clearer view of the situation. Nick is not Professor Sanchez, and he's been nothing but kind to me. As far as I can tell, he's been honest too, and he deserves the chance to explain.

As the streetlights of Eugene slide by, I resolve to text him as soon as I'm home. I won't let the echoes of my trauma steal away what could be... No, I won't call it love. That's ridiculous. I barely know the man. But there is something between us, something undeniable.

When Dalton drops me off in my driveway, I lean through his open window and plant a kiss on his forehead. "I had fun tonight. You're a good guy, Dalton, and I'm enjoying getting to know you."

His bashful grin is adorable. "I'll be by soon to move those bookcases and measure the doorway."

"Oh, right." The night's events completely wiped the renovation project from my mind. "You're sure?"

"A promise is a promise. Besides, this isn't goodbye, Clara. It's just an awkward hello." He seizes my hand, gives it a loud smack, and drives off.

Before I can overthink that statement, another set of headlights flares to life, attached to a little green Karmann Ghia. Nick rolls past slowly, his fiery eyes boring into mine, his face contorted in a scowl. Anger or pain? He doesn't linger long enough for me to find out.

"Nick, wait!" I bolt after him but quickly realize the stupidity of chasing him on foot. His taillights have already disappeared around the corner, and I have no idea where he's going. Should I call him now or give him time to calm down? Or will tomorrow be too late?

My first impulse is to implore Jared's help and wait for another sign, but Nick is speeding away, and I've relied too long on help from a ghost. This is my life. Only I can decide what I truly want.

Fists clenched, I glare in the direction Nick fled. "Damn you," I growl. "You didn't come all this way just to chicken out now."

Okay, I'm talking to myself as much as to him.

With my jaw set, I jump into my car and peel out of the driveway, my tires squealing on the pavement.

Chapter Twenty-Eight

♥

Nick

I lift my head from the lumpy pillow on Leo's saggy sofa bed. "Go away." My voice sounds like I've been gargling gravel.

"Nick, for Christ's sake. Get out here and drink a beer with me."

"I'm not thirsty."

"Of course you are. You just drove straight through from California. What's it take, seven hours?"

"Nine."

"So, come have a drink with me."

I roll over, my back to the door.

"Don't make me drag you out by your ankles."

I bury my face in the pillow and roar, even though I know resistance is futile. Leo will persist until I emerge from self-imposed solitary confinement. I heave myself upright, punch the pillow for good measure, then stalk to the door.

Leo stands on the other side, holding two frosty mugs. "God, you look like hell."

"Blasphemer." I follow my sadistic friend to the balcony, where he's set a table with his finest gourmet goodies: neon cheese puffs, salted peanuts, and a pouch of beef jerky, plus a mini cooler of craft beers.

I sink into a creaky wicker chair and gaze glumly into the night. In the distance, campus lights twinkle.

"You've aged ten years, my friend," Leo observes and wipes foam from his bushy ginger beard.

I rake a hand through my hair, which sticks up every which way, then over my jaw, scratchy with stubble. My eyes still burn from hours of headlight glare, and my head throbs like an epic hangover.

"So, IPA or red ale?"

"Whatever."

"In my experience, IPA goes best with heartache."

"What goes best with wounded pride?" I grab a handful of cheese puffs.

"Whiskey. Got some of that too. Shall I?"

I wave him off.

"So, the lady was not alone." Leo sips his beer and strokes his beard.

"Nope." I upend my bottle and chug half its contents.

"I don't suppose you let her know you were coming."

"Nope." I prickle under Leo's incredulous stare. "She told me not to call."

"You thought you'd surprise her?"

"Yup." And that turned out to be my stupidest idea since Lydia. Disgusted, I gulp the rest of my beer.

"Jeez, man, are you auditioning for a spaghetti western? Talk to me!"

I let fly a magnificent belch. "What is there to say? She chose the other guy."

"Don't be daft. You've been gone three days. How serious could it be?" Leo stands, stretches, and scratches his hairy paunch.

"You should come rowing with me, work off that gut."

"Don't change the subject." Leo plants his fists on the arms of my chair, boxing me in. "Since when have you become such a quitter?"

I roll my eyes.

"My God, you're actually pouting like a fuckin' toddler." He paces the length of his third-floor balcony. "I'll tell you what. Tomorrow evening, I'm going to pay a visit to the fair Clara. Say, around five. And I'm going to ask her if she's talked to you." He flashes a wolfish grin. "If she says no, I'm going to tell her you're here, sulking on my balcony. And then, my fine Greek friend, I'm going to ask her out. I'm more charming than any bald, skinny high school teacher."

I clench my fists so hard, I fear the skin on my knuckles will crack. "You wouldn't."

"I would. You'd better get to work on your campaign speech, old friend." Leo claps my shoulder and then leaves me alone on the balcony.

With a groan, I pull my phone from my pocket and tap the screen: Another message from Clara.

Nick, please. Talk to me.

I consider pitching the phone off the balcony, watching it spin, end over end, as it sails into the night sky.

Leo's right: I am being childish. And anyway, Eugene is my home now. There's no going back to Berkeley. I've burned that bridge. But the thought of facing Clara after seeing her kiss that bald guy tears my gut to shreds.

What an idiot I've been, taking this job without talking to her first. I'm much too old to be blinded by romantic notions of the rosy reunion I visualized all the way up the I-5. I'd knock on her door, present her with the ridiculous armload of red roses I bought from a farm stand, and tell her the whole story. Then she'd throw her arms around my neck and forgive me my trespasses.

What a pathetic moron.

Still, what's done is done. My condo sold within twelve hours of listing, and my stuff is scheduled to arrive Friday. Besides, Leo will make good on his promise to rat me out.

The traitor steps up behind me and proffers a crystal tumbler full of amber liquid. When I take it, he gently squeezes my shoulders. "Fight for her, Nick."

"What's the point?" The whiskey's burn slides down my throat, loosening the fist clenched around my stomach. "She thinks I'm a despicable playboy."

"And you're going to let her keep thinking that? You're here for the next academic year, at least, so get to work on winning her back."

Caught in my misery, I don't reply and just take another long draw of whiskey.

Leo resumes his pacing, as if delivering a classroom lecture, hands clasped behind his back. "Here's the crucial question: What does that guy have that she wants?"

"I don't know." I drain my glass, hoping the liquor will hasten sleep, or at least make Leo's patronizing tone less grating.

"Think, man! Stability? Local connections? 'Cause it sure ain't looks."

"You've seen him?"

"At the protest. Saw the two of you through the window. Pretty cool the way you bounced that asshole landlord off your chests like a couple of cartoon superheroes."

Leo scoots his chair closer and sits facing me, elbows on knees. "Show that woman you're a man she can count on."

"Why would she care at this point? She's got a boyfriend."

He claps his big, ruddy hand onto my knee. "I saw the way she looked at you. You still have a chance. Call her."

I release a long, rasping sigh and massage my aching forehead. "Okay, okay. I will. Tomorrow."

There's one painful call I need to make first. God knows I don't deserve her help, but she may be my last hope.

Chapter Twenty-Nine

♥

Clara

After driving all over the U of O campus searching for Nick's car, after texting again and again and leaving a half-dozen voice mails, I finally collapse into bed just before dawn, still clutching my phone.

And this morning, still nothing.

There's no way I imagined him. Nick is here in Eugene. But after seeing me kissing Dalton, will he ever speak to me again? Has one chaste kiss cost me so dearly?

Then again, given what I've learned about his past, maybe it's for the best.

After a fast, scalding shower, I get to work a few minutes before ten-thirty. This is the first time in years I've arrived late. When I let myself in through the back door. I hear voices up front, including Harry's raspy baritone. Too exhausted to fake a cheerful countenance, I slip behind the screen and attack the ever-growing pile of bills.

I open a spreadsheet which shows a sharp upward blip in sales the day the picketers descended on the shop. But since then, the numbers remain stubbornly, depressingly low. No matter how many times I add up the figures, there's no escaping the painful conclusion: we're operating in the red. If this renovation doesn't draw more customers, I'll have to close Book Nirvana's doors for good. That possibility, on top of my simmering anxiety over Nick, snarls my belly into a pulsing knot of nerves.

Coffee would help me focus, but getting it means leaving the safety of my office. I wait until I hear the doorway bell's tinkle and the merry chatter of a mother with small children, then slip sunglasses over my tear-swollen eyes and quick-step toward the door like a celebrity avoiding the paparazzi.

"Good morning, Clara," Harry calls out.

I can't face him yet. He knows me too well and will immediately recognize my distress.

"Just getting a coffee," I sing out, sailing past. "One for you, Harry?"

"Sure, thanks."

Most of the seats in Arnie's place sit empty. He sets down the towel he's polishing the counter with and greets me with a weary smile.

"Like a ghost town in here, isn't it?" He picks up a to-go cup. "The usual?"

"Please."

Tilting his head, he regards me for a moment. "Actually, no. That's not what you need."

Surprised, I peer at him over the top of my sunglasses.

"Uh huh. Just as I thought. Desperate times call for cappuccino with extra chocolate." He dumps beans into his grinder and pulls out a fresh filter for the espresso machine. "So, what's eating you, gorgeous, besides the usual money shit?"

"How can you..."

"Those puffy red eyes of yours. Unless you're stoned." He squints at me. "Is that how you're coping?"

I pull off my sunglasses with a sigh. "You're right. It's money and men."

"A deadly combination, for sure." He sets a large cup beneath the spigot. "So, which man?"

"The Greek one."

Arnie grins. "Oh, yes indeed. He is a delightful morsel. Done you wrong, did he?"

"Sort of."

"Well, that bald fella seems mighty fond of you."

I sigh again. "He's lovely, but somehow we just don't...we don't click physically, you know?"

He nods. "Chemistry is a fickle bitch, isn't she?" He tops my milk foam with a liberal dusting of cocoa powder. His eyes flick toward his front window. "Uh-oh."

I follow his gaze and freeze.

Nick stands on the sidewalk, his hand splayed on the window, looking—nauseated?

His dark eyes are hooded, his full lips slack, his broad chest rising and falling as if he's been running, but his gaze pins me where I stand. I've never seen him look so disheveled, so uncertain.

My muscles tense, ready to run to him—until I spot the petite blonde at his elbow. She tilts her young, shiny face up toward Nick, then to me, then back to Nick. She blinks her enormous blue eyes, points in my direction, and says something to him. He nods, his gaze never leaving my face.

The doorbell tinkles as she enters the shop. Nick brings his fist to his mouth and strides away.

My heart, and my breakfast, climb up my throat. The young woman walking toward me is in her early twenties, pretty, rosy-cheeked—and heavily pregnant.

She extends her hand. Too stunned to think, I take it.

"Hi, Clara. I'm Lydia, Nick's, um…" She throws a wide-eyed glance over her shoulder, but he's gone. "I'm the one who got him in trouble."

I drop her hand and stumble backward, my gaze riveted on her baby bump.

Her eyes widen even more. "Oh, no! No, no, no. He's not the father." She raises her left hand to display a diamond twinkling on her ring finger.

Behind the counter, Arnie stifles a giggle.

Lydia twists her floaty top. "Nick asked me to come talk to you."

"You came all the way from Berkeley?"

"I live in Portland now. Do you mind?" She glances over her shoulder at the cushy armchairs near the front window. "I'm eight months along, and my feet get tired."

Wordlessly, I follow her and plop into a chair. Arnie bustles over with my coffee. "A decaf for you, hon?" he asks.

"A mint tea would be great, thanks." The smile she tilts up at him is sweet—angelic, even. She turns back to me with a sigh. "So I guess the secret's out."

My mouth is so dry I have to force the words out. "Nick—he—seduced you?"

Lydia's half-smile is wistful. "No, it was very mutual."

"But he was your teacher?"

"He had been." She pauses while Arnie sets a steaming teapot and cup before her. "I was his graduate assistant when we—got together." She fills her cup and dumps in a stream of sugar.

"Like Darcy?"

A grimace flickers over her pretty face. "You met her?"

"She's the one who told me about you."

Lydia's laughter bursts forth like a gunshot. "She's a fine one to talk after cutting a swath through the anthro department."

She sips her tea, and when she fixes me with her luminous eyes, I can see why Nick fell for her. She's stunning, disarming, and her gaze brims with sympathy. "Look, I could tell you all about how Nick and I ended up in bed. What it boils down to is we were both brokenhearted, and we sort of fell together. It was stupid, and we quickly realized that."

"Were you in love with him?"

She shifts in her chair, her gaze drifting back toward the window. "I wanted to think so, but pretty soon I had to admit it was just a rebound thing. I mean, he made it easy to pretend. He was so sweet, and so good in bed..."

A hot flush climbs my cheeks.

"But he was almost twice my age. And if people found out, we'd both be tainted forever. You know how it is. If you're female and cute, they'll say your achievements are due to that." She tilts her chin defiantly. "I earned my grades. Nick had nothing to do with it."

Her glare softens. "Anyway, I've forgiven him, and I've forgiven myself. We both made a mistake. I'm not going to spend the rest of my life paying for it."

She lays her hand over mine. "Neither should he." She squeezes. "And if anyone else asks me about our affair, I'll deny it. Just so you know."

"Why tell me, then?"

"Because Nick's hurting, and I still care about him. Not the way I did back then, but—he's a good man."

I sit in silence until a movement outside catches my eye. Nick stands at the window watching us, his hands hanging slack at his sides. He seems so—defeated.

"Well, go on." Lydia pokes my arm with her spoon. "He's going to stand there like a sad puppy until you talk to him."

Slowly, I rise from my chair and approach the door, my heart fluttering like a ticking bomb.

He leans beneath one of the sycamore trees lining the street. My traitorous memory flashes back to the night when we first came together, when he pressed me up against a tree just like this one, half-mad with desire. I remember his strong hands clutching my hips, his thumbs grazing my breasts as he pulled me tight against him. Now, his arms are crossed, his shoulders rounded, his gaze downcast.

This would be so much easier if I just hugged him tight, pressed my cheek to his chest, and forgot this whole mess ever happened. But no, we have to wade through this part. I take a deep breath, forcing my shoulders down and my chin up.

"So, you're back."

"Yes." He doesn't meet my eye. In fact, he seems much more interested in my shoes.

"For how long?"

"That has a lot to do with you."

Finally, he raises his eyes to mine. Longing and hurt swim in their dark depths. My reserve wobbles, tugged off center by his powerful gravity.

But I stand my ground, arms crossed over my foolish heart. "I'm confused, Nick. I stay up all night, trying to reach you. I drive all over town, looking for you. First you ignore my texts and calls, and then you send your ex-girlfriend to plead your case?"

His eyes narrow, and his lips clamp into a tight line. "Are you in love with him?"

"No." It's easy to say because it's the truth. "But he's my friend, and I care about him."

His sharp exhalation lifts my hair. "Okay. I don't like it, but I respect your feelings."

"So, how long, Nick?"

"A year, at least." He inches closer.

"What about your summer class in Berkeley?"

"I quit."

"You can do that?"

"I kind of had to." His gaze flicks toward the café where Lydia stands in the doorway. "Excuse me."

He goes to her, takes both her hands, and speaks too softly for me to hear. The tenderness in his eyes stirs prickly feelings deep inside me, making me suddenly understand his point of view.

This woman holds a piece of his heart, and I want all of it.

I blink in surprise at the sudden intensity of my emotions.

He's not mine. I have no right.

But there it is—it hurts to watch him embrace Lydia.

"Nice to meet you, Clara." She gives me a cheery wave before waddling down the street and around the corner.

Nick watches her go, then turns back to me and closes the distance between us. Taking my hand, he gently tugs me to the wooden bench outside my shop. I sit beside him and let him lace his fingers through mine, noting the thrill of warmth that shoots up my arm from where we touch.

Determined to keep control, I fix him with a tight stare. "So, where did you run off to last night?"

"Leo's place." He shifts to face me. "Clara, I'm sorry. That was childish of me. I should've called you first, should've let you know I was coming. But when I saw you kissing that guy..."

"His name is Dalton."

He shrugs. "My pride was hurt. And my heart. Seeing you look at him with love in your eyes, I kind of—lost my mind."

"And is it coming back to you now?"

"Slowly, I guess." He chuckles. "Leo helped. He hides some wisdom under his scruffy exterior."

"Hmm. How did he convince you?"

"He said, 'Ask yourself: what does the other guy have that she wants?'"

I run my thumb over the back of his hand. "Dalton is here, and you were far away. He really likes me. He's kind, he's funny, and he doesn't have a scandal in his past."

"That you know of."

"Touché." I lean onto his shoulder, enjoying his solid warmth. "So, where do we go from here?"

His long dark lashes lower, and his voice drops to a seductive rumble. "Your place? I don't think you'd like Leo's guest room. The sofa bed squeaks."

A flash of irritation pushes me to my feet. "Nick, for God's sake. Do you think you can just show up here with your bedroom eyes and—"

He stands and raises his palms in surrender. "Sorry, sorry. That was inappropriate. I'll be good, I'll be patient. I promise." He raises two fingers together. "Or is it three fingers for scout's honor?"

The face and body of a Greek god, and funny too. Yikes. I try not to smile and almost succeed.

"Come on, Clara. Don't be so hard on me. On yourself too." He steps close enough to feel his warmth, the whisper of his breath against my cheek.

But thinking with my libido got me into this mess. I clench my fists.

Nick points to his chest, then to mine, his finger an inch from my cleavage. "This thing between us, it's powerful. You know it, Clara. We fit together, you and I."

"How many other women have you fit together with lately?"

Nick raises both hands, his fingers splayed.

Oh my God, ten?

"None, Clara. There is no other woman for me now." He grips my shoulders and gently squeezes. "You're it."

"I'm it? Are we playing tag?"

He releases me and rolls his eyes skyward, no doubt pleading with his father Zeus for intervention.

"Clara, you. Are. It. My mate. The one. You." He pokes my sternum, and warmth radiates from his touch like ripples in a pond.

I grasp his hand and try to push it away, but he holds my fingers, gentle but firm.

"Why should I believe you, Nick? We've only been together..."

"Only twice. But that's enough to know." He lowers his head until we're nose to nose and envelopes my hand in both of his—warm, soft, seductive. My resolve melts like butter on a hot stack of pancakes.

"Why are you afraid, Clara?"

"Why are you pushing so hard? You've been through this. Starting over with someone new, it's..."

He squeezes my hand. "I do know. It's incredibly difficult, opening that door, finding the courage to step through. But I also know how much better my life is since I stopped clinging to grief." He strokes my cheek with his fingertips. "Your heart is clenched like a fist, Clara. I remember that feeling so well."

My vision blurs, and I curse the tears spilling down my cheeks.

He wipes them away with his thumb. "You'll never stop missing Jared, never stop loving him, but you can love again."

"How can you be sure?" I whisper.

His gaze reaches deep inside me, a gentle, insistent push.

"Because I loved Diana. And now I love you."

Heat flashes through me. My heart batters my ribs. Panicked and barely breathing, I decide I must be furious because there's only one other emotion that could trigger this inner tumult, and that can't be real. I can't be in love with Nick after such a short time.

Rage is the safer choice.

I push his hands away and hiss through clenched teeth, "How fucking dare you?"

Eyes wide, he stumbles backward.

"Sex is not love, Nick. You don't even *know* me. Claiming you love me to get more sex, that's just, just...cruel!"

"Clara, I'm not..."

"If you want to take a job here, I can't stop you, but don't you dare mess with my heart just to get what you want from me. Go find one of your—your adoring students." I stalk to the shop door, then turn to spit over my shoulder, "I'm sure they'll be lining up for a taste of Professor Horny-pants."

"Clara, please!" He follows, hot on my heels. "I have to see you again. Let me come back tonight. We can..."

"I have a date."

It's a lie, but I don't care. I need distance, time to think and talk this out with someone who isn't trying to seduce me.

I need Jared. And the anniversary of his death is just two days away.

Chapter Thirty

❤

Clara

"Clara, wait!"

I ignore Nick's ragged plea and flee into my shop. Choked with sobs, I dart into the restroom and slam the door behind me. The cold water I splash on my blotchy face removes what's left of my mascara. Just as well. Most of it has melted into vertical stripes on my cheeks. I plant my hands on the sink's rim and stare into the mirror, willing my brow to uncrumple, my chin to stop trembling, my nose to stop running. Eventually, they do.

When I emerged, Margot,Harry, several customers, and even the cat are staring at me.

Great.

I glance at the front window, grateful to see Nick has moved on, then wave to the assembly. "I'm okay."

Before their attention brings on another flood of tears, I dart to the shelter of the screen, drop into my chair, and rest my throbbing head in my hands.

It's Harry who finally joins me and oh-so-softly lays his hand on my shoulder, silently waiting.

"I wish you were thirty years younger, Harry." I sniffle into a tissue.

Chuckling, he rubs my back. "Why, darlin'?"

"Because you're sweet, and understanding, and patient." I give him a watery smile. "And handsome too."

"Well, I thank you for the compliment, but I'm seeing someone."

"Of course you are." I sigh. "Women must be pounding on your door day and night."

"Not exactly." He pulls up a folding chair and sits beside me, stretching out his long, bony legs. "Besides, I don't need women, just one special woman."

"And have you found her, Harry?"

He raises a wiry white eyebrow. "I think so. Time will tell. So, your professor is back."

I push myself upright and wipe my nose. "Did you hear our conversation?"

"Not much. But your face went bright red. I figure he either proposed or said something to piss you off."

I marvel at Harry's powers of perception.

He crosses his arms. "So, you this mad at Dalton, too?"

"No. No. Dalton is sweet."

"But horny, right?"

Is there any part of my private business Harry isn't privy to?

"I ran into him at Bluebeard Coffee this morning before work. When I asked him how your date went, he blushed beet-red, just like my favorite boss."

My laughter tastes bitter on my tongue. "Curse of the fair skinned, I guess."

Harry gives my hand another squeeze. "He's a good guy. It's none of my business, of course, but I think he's a much better match for you than Professor Hot-Pants out there."

"How so?"

Harry purses his lips for a moment. "Well, first of all, I know him. He's warm-hearted and kind. He hasn't been out catting around since his wife left him. Plenty of women in the running club would jump at the chance to date him, but he's been taking his time."

Guilt twinges behind my forehead. I actually had a hand in rushing Dalton, though I didn't mean to. "You know, Harry, Dalton told me his divorce isn't final yet."

"Oh? I thought..." He rubs his chin.

I'm not sure whether he's prevaricating or confused, but I let it slide. "Dalton's going to need more time before he's ready for anything serious."

"And you too, eh?"

"Yeah. Something like that."

"Well then, don't you let those young men rush you." He slaps his broad hands on his thighs. "Now, I want to talk to you about something else."

Harry's blue eyes are solemn, the dark circles beneath more pronounced than I've ever seen them.

"Maybe it's time to think about hiring more help, Clara? After all, Jared used to take care of the administrative duties, right? Now it's all on you."

I flinch at the mention of his name.

Harry's brows draw together. "Hey, I'm sorry, kiddo. That was insensitive of me."

"Don't be sorry. You're right. I've been trying to do the work of two people, and it's wearing me out. It's hard on you too." I swipe at my eyes with my sleeve. "I still miss Jared every day. I guess I will for the rest of my life. And I've been clinging to my routine to keep him close." A fresh tear slides down my cheek. "That's not working so well."

"Oh, hey now." He pulls me into a hug. I'm so damn lucky to have a friend like Harry. I've come to depend on him, and on Margot. But maybe it's time to branch out. After all, Margot will graduate in another year, and Harry has mentioned how his bucket list includes travel to far-flung places.

"It's okay. As soon as we finish the renovation, I'll put up a *Help wanted* sign. We could use a few more part-timers."

But how will I pay them?

He pats my back. "Then you can take some time for yourself. I worry about you, Clara. Lately, you seem so preoccupied."

I give him a tight-lipped smile.

"I hope I haven't made things harder for you by introducing you to Dalton. You know, it's okay if you tell me to butt out of your love life. Only you will know when you're ready."

"Oh, no, don't apologize. Dalton's a sweet guy. And if you hear of any likely candidates for the shop, please let me know." I squeeze his wiry arm. "You're a good judge of character, Harry. And thank you for putting in so many hours lately. You're my rock, you know."

That night, I awake in blackness, my heart thudding, the sweat-clammy sheets snarled around my legs as if I've been running in my dreams. A nightmare? I can't remember.

I lie there, listening to the chanting of the crickets and the far-off hum of traffic. Finally, my breathing slows, and I slide into a half-dozing state. An image swims up: Jared's sitting on a stone wall, wearing cut-offs, flip-flops, and his favorite Portland Triathlon T-shirt. A light wind ruffles his chocolate-brown hair. His surroundings remain hazy.

He cocks his head, smiles, and reaches out his hand. Rough stones scrape my legs as I boost myself up beside him and gaze into his eyes. Their familiar deep blue twinkles in the sunlight. I stroke his messy hair, then lean onto his shoulder, solid and warm.

He clasps my hand, the feeling of his palm against mine as familiar as my own heartbeat.

"Hard decision, eh?"

I nod and close my eyes. The sunlight warms my back. Somewhere nearby, the surf whispers in, out, in, out.

"Wish I could help you decide."

My chest tightens. "Please help me, Jared. It's too hard without you."

He strokes the hair away from my forehead, his touch whisper-soft. "I can't, babe. But you'll make the right choice."

When I open my eyes again, I'm alone on the wall by the sea. The view comes into focus: the little cottage near Cannon Beach where we spent our last wedding anniversary. I recognize the flagstone patio where we drank cold IPA and dined on fresh crab. Jared's paperback novel lies on the wooden picnic table. But where has he gone? Twisting, I peer over my shoulder. Far up the beach, a lone figure retreats, fading like a shadow.

I leap down and bolt after him, sand puffing beneath my feet, slowing my steps. "Wait! Talk to me!"

The shadow turns. "I'm always with you, Clara. Nothing can change that. Be happy."

The wind picks up, blowing stinging sand into my eyes. I rub them...

And find myself in our bed, curled up on Jared's side, hugging his pillow. Sunlight streams through the window, blinding me. I wince and check the alarm clock: past eight already. Clutching the sheets to my chest, I brace myself. Jared's nighttime visits usually leave me shaken, but no tears come, the sharp ache of grief replaced by a sense of comfort.

Whatever my choice, I'll be okay.

· ♥ · ♥ · ♥ · ♥ · ♥ ·

Nick

"Over there. No, not the—yeah. Dining room."

I've never seen such an industrious crew. Four men with limited English bustle into the house and back to their truck, toting heavy cartons and furniture like worker ants carrying grasshopper parts. At this rate, they'll be unloaded and gone by the afternoon. Good. I have plans for this place tonight.

"Can I help?" I ask Ivan, the crew boss.

"No, sir. You sit." The burly, red-faced man points to the sofa they just deposited opposite the flagstone fireplace. "Is better we do."

Ivan hands me a clipboard holding the bill of lading. "You check number, okay? Is faster this way."

"Twenty-seven!" Tran calls out, only his legs visible beneath a huge carton.

"Office, please."

The wiry little man chugs up the stairs.

Damn, I'm pretty fit, but I've got nothing on these guys.

Might as well relax now. There'll be lots of lifting to do later. In the interest of time, I elected to do the unpacking myself.

Will Clara like this place? Will she even cross the threshold? Shaking my head, I run a hand through my messy hair and pray, for the umpteenth time, that I haven't scared her off for good.

I've been stupid, rash, carried away by strong emotion like a love-struck teenager, but yesterday, I told Clara the truth. And I've stayed away from her shop and apartment, though I nearly had to nail my shoes to the floor to do it.

All the explaining and cajoling in the world won't help right now. I can only hope, after twenty-four hours to cool down, she'll be more receptive to my next approach.

"Thirty-six."

"Um, garage."

My phone pings in my pocket: a text from Lydia:

It wasn't easy, calling her after over a year of separation, and I'm surprised how readily she agreed to drive up from Portland. Despite the mess our brief liaison caused, I'm still fond of Lydia, still protective of her. And seeing her pregnant touched something in me, a nagging sense of loss.

This house would be perfect for kids once I clean up the tangle of blackberry vines swallowing the yard. There's room for a child's bedroom—two, even, and plenty of space for indoor play in the generous living room. The kitchen is big enough for homework and messy baking projects, and the porch would be perfect for decorating at Halloween. I picture a pair of kids thundering up and sliding down the wide wooden banister.

With a sigh, I close the door on those pointless fantasies. I've missed my shot at being a father, but I'm not giving up on Clara, not without a fight.

"Forty-two!"

"Kitchen."

Chapter Thirty-One

♥

Clara

Harry's out for a medical appointment, and Margot hasn't yet arrived for her afternoon shift when Darryl, the new landlord, strolls through the front door, his thumbs looped through his belt. Like a movie sheriff come to clean up a lawless town, he plants himself in the entrance and surveys his domain, a smirk on his florid face.

"Well, well, Mrs. Martelli, you still haven't started on the new doorway? Thought that was the key to your salvation."

My hackles rise, and it takes all my self-control to keep from snarling. "We start work on Monday."

He purses his lips. "Place is pretty empty."

"Lunch break is over." I glower at him. "Most people are at work."

"Whatever." He strolls past the counter and down the first aisle: self-help, inspirational books, educational resources.

He could use all three of those.

But he doesn't pull any books off the shelves. Probably not the reader type. He stops at the red door, runs his hand over the slick scarlet lacquer, then tries the doorknob.

"It's locked." He quirks an eyebrow.

"Yes."

"What's back here?"

The thought of letting Darryl through that door makes my skin crawl, but how can I refuse? I swallow a bubble of bile. "That's our erotica collection."

An oily smile oozes across his face. "Well, well. Miss Clara's hiding some dirty secrets."

Heat creeps up my throat. "I'm not hiding anything, Darryl. We keep it locked to protect minors."

He saunters toward me, his voice syrupy. "I'm not a minor. Why don't you show me what you've got back there?"

I glance at the front door, praying for an interruption. A group of college students pause, point at the window display, and move on.

Shit, shit, shit.

Face scrunched, I reach for the key, dangling on its velvet cord behind the counter. As my fingers close around it, the front doorbell tinkles, and a half-dozen people burst in, laughing. They all wear matching red polo shirts with *North Eugene High School* embroidered on the breast, along with a wee Scots Highlander playing the bagpipes. Leading the way, his shiny head gleaming in the sunlight and a huge grin on his face, is Dalton.

"And this is the lovely Clara," he announces with a sweeping gesture, like a circus ringmaster introducing the next act. He slings his arm over my shoulder and smooches my cheek. "I told them about your ten percent educator discount," he adds with a wink.

I paste on a broad grin. "Of course! We always support our local educators. Are these your colleagues?"

Dalton makes introductions, ignoring Darryl, who lingers at the counter, scowling and tapping his foot.

"We're on our way to Marco's Pizza to celebrate the end of the school year. Care to join us?"

Two of the men chant, "Beer, beer, beer."

"Afraid I can't. I'm alone in the shop at the moment." I roll my eyes and tilt my head toward Darryl.

The two men face off like a pair of bucks about to lock horns. With his gaze locked on Darryl's, Dalton plants a kiss on my temple. "You're so conscientious," he says in a voice that lands somewhere between a purr and a growl. "Always taking care of business."

"Move over, lover boy." One of the teachers, a wide-hipped woman with a brilliant smile and a cloud of salt-and-pepper hair, dumps an armful of paperbacks on the counter. "Pizza and beer are well and good, but this is my idea of summer fun." She holds up a book emblazoned with a bare-chested hunk.

Another woman follows, holding three mystery novels. "I hear you. I want me some sex and dead bodies."

"Kinky!" her friend squeals.

"Not sex with dead bodies, you perv."

Standing on tiptoe, I kiss Dalton's cheek and whisper, "Thank you."

He mutters, "Teachers read a lot," then raises his voice for Darryl's benefit. "I'll be by about eight on Monday to start the doorway."

"Oh, sorry sir," a third teacher says to Darryl, who's still glowering from his corner of the counter. "Were you ahead of us in line?"

Darryl harrumphs and stalks out the door, throwing a final comment over his shoulder. "We'll do this later, Clara."

"Do what?" Dalton asks.

"He wanted a tour of the erotica collection," I whisper as I ring up the teachers' purchases.

A slender man with a silky voice clutches the edge of the counter. "Did you say erotica collection?" He exchanges a wide-eyed look with the plump fellow behind him. "We'll be back."

After I ring up their purchases, more than I'd usually sell in a whole afternoon, Dalton sends his teacher friends ahead.

I clutch his forearm and exhale a rush of nervous laughter. "You turned up just in time."

"Thought I'd send some business your way. Then I recognized that sleazeball from the other day. He looked like he wanted to eat you up." His fingertips stroke lightly up and down my arm. "That's my job."

What happened to "just friends?"

"So, you have an erotica collection?" His pale gaze flicks toward the red door.

"Yesss..."

So much for putting our sexual involvement on hold. The seductive rumble of his voice suggests he's ready for another go right now. "So, are you free tonight?"

"I, uh..."

The doorbell tinkles, and Harry's voice booms into the shop. "Dalton!" Grinning broadly, he strides over and claps his young cousin's shoulder, clearly pleased to see us together.

"Everything okay, Harry?"

"Doc says I should eat more protein; can you believe it? So I'm taking Evie out for steak tonight."

Dalton nudges me and murmurs, "Sounds like fun."

"I'm sorry, Dalton, I really can't tonight. But I'll see you tomorrow morning for the running club, okay?"

Harry wrinkles his brow. "Are you sure that's a good idea, Clara?"

"Absolutely." I've decided, despite Nick's advice, the best way through the anniversary of Jared's death is to keep busy, keep to my routine, keep myself surrounded with dear friends and my beloved shop, leaving me no time to think about Nick's disturbing declaration of love, about Dalton's sweet, awkward kisses, about how much I ache to have Jared beside me.

Harry raises an eyebrow but doesn't argue further. He slides behind the counter and ties on his Book Nirvana apron.

"Everything okay, Clara?" Dalton has picked up on the tension, but I hope he doesn't know about Saturday's significance. Our friendship is refreshingly normal, an anchor amid all this emotional chaos.

"I'm just a little overwhelmed with all this." I gesture toward the bookshelves.

"And I'm not helping, eh?"

"You are, actually. Thank you, Dalton." I peck his cheek. "I'll see you tomorrow."

"All righty then." A blush colors his bony face as he lopes off after his friends.

When he's gone, Harry comes around the counter and takes my hands. "Are you sure you want to run tomorrow?"

I smile into his kind blue eyes. "I am. A good run will clear my head. And I plan to work, too."

He gives me a dubious half-smile. "I'll be here if you change your mind."

I hug him tight. "Thanks, Harry. You're a wonderful friend."

At closing time, I'm halfway out the door when I realize I've left my phone in my desk drawer. I'm tempted to leave it there but remind myself that's not how responsible adults behave. Though bone-weary from a long day on my feet, I trudge back to fetch it. Text messages from Nick crowd the screen. The first arrived at three:

> **I want to show you something. Spare me half an hour?**

Another at four-thirty:

> **I know you don't like surprises, but please, just a few minutes.**

And at six:

> **Please, Clara. I need to talk to you.**

My laugh crackles dry as old bones. Gotta hand it to Nick Papadopoulos. The man does not give up easily. Yesterday's emotional ambush has left me as wrung out as a smelly string mop—and haunted by my rabid reaction. Because honestly, I want him just as desperately as he seems to want me.

Ever since I chased him off, his declaration of love has played on loop in my head. From the glow in his eyes to the trembling in his voice, everything about him seemed sincere. But rather than taking a moment to breathe through it, I sliced his head right off.

Yet here he comes for another try.

I hug the phone to my chest. "Jared, babe, what should I do about this guy?"

Silence. No books with apt titles slide from the shelves, no voices whisper on the wind, no little birds land on the windowsill. Not even a meow from Lulu—nothing.

Damn. I'm on my own.

Someone raps softly on the window behind me. I shriek and drop my phone, which skitters underneath the counter. A muffled voice calls my name.

It's Nick, of course, his hand cupped against the glass. He steps back and raises both palms—a gesture of surrender? Of befuddlement? His expression is solemn, his full lips parted.

My heart aches to fling the door open and throw my arms around him, but my feet stay rooted to the floor.

Lulu, however, has no such scruples. Meowing loudly, she trots from her hiding place, her tail aloft, straight to the front door where she sits, twists to look at me, and pats the door with her paw.

Well, I asked for a sign.

"Okay, okay. I'll let him in. But it's on your head if this goes badly."

I flip the lights back on because facing Nick in the dark is much too dangerous, too tempting. When I turn the key, Lulu darts onto the sidewalk. With a cry of alarm, I lunge after her.

But she isn't heading for the street; she wants Nick. In one graceful motion, he scoops her up and deposits her on his shoulder, where she drapes herself like a furry shawl, rubbing her head against his neck.

I step back to let them enter. Warmth and energy roll off his body as he passes, just inches away.

"Thanks. She's never darted out before."

"She likes me." He scritches behind her ears, drawing her deep thrumming purr. "I wish her mistress felt the same way."

"Well, cats don't care who else has been rubbing on their favorite person, or who will rub there next. They only care about what they want right now."

He furrows his brows. "No one's been rubbing on me, Clara. Not even a cat." He moves closer but, mercifully, doesn't touch me. "After what we shared, I don't want anyone else."

I drink in the sight of him and, with great effort, restrain the urge to reach out and brush a stray curl from his forehead.

Tonight, he'd traded his usual elegance for a disarmingly shabby look: jeans faded across the knees, battered tennies, and a faded flannel shirt with sleeves rolled up to reveal a long scrape on his muscular forearm. Even in this mussed state, he projects the same easy confidence that first drew me in. Dress a panther in old jeans, he's still a panther. Strong, sexy, dangerous.

I pluck a scrap of paper from his shirt. From her perch on his shoulder, Lulu bats playfully at my hand.

Nick murmurs sweet nothings—to the cat. "Lovely Puss. I've missed you, sweet girl. So soft..."

Satisfied, she hops down and trots away.

I keep my gaze on Nick's feet. Tension crackles between us.

"I, uh—" he starts.

"You, uh—" I overlap, then laugh. "This is difficult."

Nick takes my hand, and a flush radiates up my arm and down my spine, like a buzz of electricity. I've missed that feeling. I want more.

"It doesn't have to be difficult, Clara." He shuffles close enough to smell his woodsy cologne, with a faint whiff of sweat beneath. "When I'm with you, everything feels easy. It's being apart from you that's difficult."

I close my eyes to shut out his probing gaze. Every molecule of my body wants to surrender to his magnetism, but I hold my ground, though I don't let go of his hand.

"Taking a job here is a big gamble, isn't it?"

"The prize is worth the risk." He laces his fingers through mine. "Anyway, I want to show you something. Will you come with me, just for a few minutes?"

"Um, I..." Inside my head, an obnoxious siren wails.

Irritated, I mash the mental Mute button. It's about damn time I stop being so skittish and defensive. Why shouldn't I go with Nick? I have no plans for the evening, and he's come all the way to Oregon to pursue me. That's not the behavior of a man looking for a quick lay.

I blow out a shaky breath and straighten my shoulders. "All right. Half an hour."

His beaming reaction gives me a glimpse of the happy little boy he once was, with a dimpled smile, unruly dark curls, and enormous, sparkling eyes. "Great. I'm parked over there. I could drive you, or..."

"I'll follow you." Skittish or not, sharing a tight space with Nick is too dangerous, too tempting. If I'm going to make a smart choice, I need to think with my head, not my lady bits.

Chapter Thirty-Two

♥

Clara

I climb into my Subaru and follow him through two traffic lights, around the corner, and a few blocks north. He pulls up in front of a Craftsman bungalow covered in dark-red shingles, with columns of river rock supporting the porch roof. The front yard is a jungle of blackberry vines, weeds, and leggy climbing roses.

He hops out of his car and trots over to hold my door. "Bienvenue chez moi."

"You live here? Since when?"

"Since today." He grins like a kid opening a Christmas present. "Come see. It's a mess, but it's going to be great."

I follow him up the overgrown flagstone path. I could have walked here from the shop, or from home, maybe a dozen blocks away. He's practically my neighbor.

Is that tickle in my belly excitement or a warning?

He opens the heavy wooden door, and I stand beside him in the foyer, clutching his hand and gaping like a landed fish. To the left, square columns frame the entry to a cozy parlor, perfect for reading, complete with bookshelves and stained-glass windows. To the right, a larger living room with a padded bench in the bay window, a river-stone fireplace, and built-in cabinets. The art deco ceiling lamps must be original to the house. Moving cartons litter both rooms, and scraps of packing paper lie balled up in the corners.

"The kitchen's back there." He tugs at my hand. "Come see."

I scoop my lower jaw off the floor and follow him. I'm admiring the floor-to-ceiling cabinets and the black-and-white tiled floor when the doorbell rings.

Frowning, he glances at his watch. "Excuse me." He jogs to the door.

"Tío!" a child's voice squeals.

"Bella!" More voices and footsteps follow. "We're in the kitchen. Come."

"We? Who's we?" a woman asks.

They all appear in the doorway. A dark-haired girl of about six clings to Nick, her arms around his neck and her skinny legs circling his waist. A short, muscular man grins and punches Nick's arm. "You didn't tell us the house came with a pretty lady."

The woman has to be Nick's sister. Tall and slender, with his high cheekbones, her skin is a shade darker. Long, curly hair cascades over her broad shoulders.

With her brother's panther-like grace, she slides silently into the kitchen and glances from Nick to me, then back to Nick, one eyebrow raised.

The sight of Nick holding a beautiful child makes my breath catch. His niece clearly adores him, and they seem so natural together, so comfortable.

The little girl squirms out of his arms and wipes her button nose on her forearm. "Are you my uncle's girlfriend?"

Nick shrugs a sheepish apology.

His brother-in-law laughs. "Bella, here. Take a tissue."

She blows her nose with a mighty honk, then trots toward the stairs. "Can I pick my room?"

"What do you mean, your room?" Nick asks.

"For when I visit, silly." She thunders up the stairs like a baby elephant.

"I'll get her," her father says. "Nice to meet you, Miss..."

"Clara."

"I'm Jaime." He flashes a friendly smile, then hurries after his daughter.

The woman sashays to Nick's side and cocks her head, lips pursed in an unspoken question.

Nick smooches her cheek. "You're early."

"Yeah, sorry. Traffic's usually much worse." She lifts her chin in my direction and waits.

"Clara runs the bookshop I told you about, over on Willamette Street."

"Book Nirvana? I've been there. I don't remember you, though. I talked to a man."

I smile. "White hair? Devilishly handsome? That's Harry."

"No, this was a young guy. Very handsome, though."

Her comment lands like a punch to the solar plexus.

Nick winces. "Cali, she's..."

I take a deep breath. "That was my late husband."

His sister's fingers fly to her throat, clutching a delicate gold crucifix. "I'm so sorry. I haven't been back here in a while. I didn't know." All her sternness melts away as she reaches for my hands. Her touch is gentle, her eyes misty. "It's hard, eh? We lost our father last summer. And, well...you know about Diana?"

I nod. "He told me. She sounds like a very special person."

Nick's smile of gratitude is so sweet, I want to hug him, but I refrain, unsure how to behave in front of his family.

He clears his throat. "Clara Martelli, meet my sister, Calista Peña."

"I noticed the resemblance."

The two siblings frown at each other.

"We don't look alike," Nick insists with a shrug.

Calista's husband chuckles from the doorway. "You do so." He turns to me, his face alight with mischief. "Put a dress on Nick, he looks just like Cali, am I right?"

"I'd like to see you try," Nick grumbles.

Cali ignores the joke. "Where's Bella?"

"Unpacking Nick's towels. So, we gonna eat or what?"

"I'll get it," Cali says. "Clara will help me." She slides her arm through mine, giving me no choice but to follow her to an SUV parked at the base of the driveway, blocking my car.

Guess I'm staying for dinner.

Calista beeps open the hatchback. "So, how long have you and Nick been together?"

"Oh. Um, not long."

Her elegant eyebrows wing up. "Really? I got the impression you were getting serious. It's not like him to just quit his job."

My cheeks flush under Cali's scrutiny.

Maybe she notices, but she busies herself pulling grocery bags from the hatchback. She sets them on the ground, then faces me, hands on hips. "Listen, I'm gonna be nosy, because he's my little brother, and I've gotta look out for him, you know?"

I nod and brace myself.

Cali slams the hatch, making me jump. "Nick's been alone for a long time. I haven't seen him this excited since, well, since Diana."

"Oh." I avert my eyes from her penetrating stare.

She frowns. "You don't feel the same way?"

"I, er—" My throat tightens.

"Great." She rolls her enormous dark eyes heavenward. "My brother's in love with a woman who doesn't care."

I grab her arm. "No, that's not what I meant."

Cali narrows her eyes, waiting.

"I mean, he told you he was in love with me?"

"No, but it's written all over his face. In his voice too. I know my brother. He likes to play Mr. Suave Professor, but he's too soft-hearted for his own good."

"Listen, I really like Nick." That's putting it mildly, but I can hardly tell his sister about how his mere presence melts me into a puddle of desire. "But we've only been together a few times, and..."

"Been together?" She shakes her head. "Thinking with his dick again." She hefts two grocery bags and nods toward the third. "Get that one, would you?"

I scoop up the bag and hurry after her. "Calista, wait."

She halts, but her expression is skeptical.

"Nick's assistant, she told me something that made me wonder if..."

Cali sets the bags on the front stoop and plants her fists on her hips. "Darcy, right?"

I nod.

"Nasty little bitch. I told Nick she was no good." Her Greek-goddess face scrunches into a bitter scowl, and for a minute I think she's about to spit on the sidewalk. "What did she tell you?"

"She said he slept with lots of students at the college."

This time, she does spit. I jolt back, slightly horrified.

"Look, Nick had a little fling with a grad student. It was stupid, but he was a lonely widower, and she was all 'Boo hoo. Comfort me, Nick.'"

"You met her?"

She nods. "Cute kid, but she was just looking for attention. My brother was too horny and heartsick to see it. Nearly got himself fired."

I must look unconvinced because Cali grips my shoulders hard.

"But he learned his lesson. When that Darcy chick came on to Nick, he turned her down. Miss Sexy-Pants couldn't believe he'd say no, right?" Calista releases me and rakes me with an appraising glance. "Pretty lady like you hanging around Nick, I can see how that would piss her off."

I sink onto the front steps, befuddled.

Calista sits beside me and takes my hand. "I guess it all boils down to this, Clara—who do you trust? Because Nick's got his heart set on you, and he doesn't give up easily."

Tears prickle my eyes. I want to trust Nick, to trust his straight-talking sister, his kind, funny brother-in-law, his adorable niece. I want to visit this beautiful house often, to help Nick tame this jungly garden, to drink wine with him on this porch, watch the sunset, make love in front of the big stone fireplace...

A shudder runs through me. "I'm scared, Calista."

She nods solemnly. "Moving too fast, eh?"

"Warp speed."

We sit there for a moment, side by side, watching the sparrows hop among the scraggly blackberry vines in the gathering dusk. Finally, Calista slaps her knees and pushes herself up. "Good enough for me."

"What do you mean?"

"You wouldn't be all torn up like this if you didn't care for Nick." She opens the front door. "Come on, let's eat."

What a feast! We assemble monster sandwiches of pastrami, turkey, hummus, cheese, olives, marinated mushrooms—pretty much every tasty possibility from the deli case.

"This is good," Bella declares. "Look, I can't even get my mouth around my sandwich." She tries, and a glob of hummus squirts onto her lap.

"Ay ay ay," her father says. "We didn't bring a change of clothes, mija. Don't make such a mess."

"We aren't sleeping here tonight?" Bella sticks out her lower lip.

"How we gonna do that? Tío Nick still has to unpack everything."

"I can sleep on the couch." She crosses her arms and points her chin at me. "How come she gets to sleep over?"

I splutter, nearly spraying iced tea onto the table. "I'm going to sleep at my house." I glance at Nick, who makes an apologetic face.

Bella hops down from her chair and lays her soft, mayonnaise-smeared hand on my arm. "You can sleep at our house if you want."

"What a nice offer. Do you live far away?"

"We live this many." She holds up six fingers, then seven, then shrugs.

Calista interjects, "We live in Corvallis. I went to school out there, met this guy, and stayed."

Jaime grins and wipes mayo from his chin. "She couldn't resist me."

"Or maybe I couldn't resist the greenery. It's a pretty town. Right, Nick?"

"Right." Nick's gaze holds mine. "Lovely."

Something warm flutters in my belly, as if my sandwich were full of butterflies instead of pastrami.

"So," Jaime asks, "when we gonna see that project you're working on?"

His wife shushes him and tilts her head toward their daughter.

Bella declares loudly, "Tío makes sexy books. I'm not allowed to see them. Only grown-ups." She makes loud kissing noises.

Nick rolls his eyes, and everyone laughs. After we finish our dinner, Calista rises and tugs her husband's sleeve. "Let's clean up."

"I'll help." I start to rise.

"No." Her tone is firm. "You stay. We got this. Come, Bella."

Bella collects our paper plates, and giggling, follows her parents into the kitchen.

I fold my greasy hands on the table. "So, Nick, you brought me here to meet your family?"

Eyes downcast, he picks at his napkin.

"Did I pass inspection?"

"Oh, Clara, it's not like that. They weren't supposed to arrive until later. I just wanted you to see the house. I was so excited to find such a beautiful place, and I wanted to share it with you."

"Relax." I take his hand. "I like them. This place, too."

"I hope you'll visit often." With his thumb, he gently massages the back of my hand. Even that simple touch sends my thoughts zooming straight to his bedroom. Is it unpacked, I wonder?

The golden flecks in his irises sparkle in the mellow light of the chandelier. Then the light flickers, and something buzzes.

"That's the second lightbulb gone out since I arrived this morning. This place is going to need a lot of work."

"Will you have time?"

He smiles wistfully. "Between work and yearning for you, I'll be pretty busy."

"Nick, I—"

"Well, we gotta go." Calista bustles into the room, propelling Bella before her. "I put the leftovers in your fridge. That ought to keep you alive for a few days." Her eyes flick to our clasped hands, and she smiles. "Come on, Jaime. The recital starts in twenty minutes. Your sister will be pissed if we're late."

"Coming." He trots after them. "Nice to meet you, Clara. Hope to see you again soon."

Bella runs to me and throws her arms around my middle. "Goodbye, Tío's girlfriend." She gives me a noisy cheek smooch, does the same to Nick, then hurries after her parents.

We follow them to the door and wave as they drive away.

Nick shakes his head and chuckles. "Family, right?"

I hope he doesn't notice the way I flinch. Meeting Nick's family is a keen reminder of what I've missed.

"They're great, Nick. Thank you for letting me meet them."

He takes my hand, his broad palm warm against mine. "This wasn't how I planned it, but I'm glad it worked out this way."

"You're a wonderful uncle." I squeeze his hand. "You never wanted kids of your own?"

"I did." His gaze slides away. "We did. It just didn't work out, and then she got sick…"

His dark eyes soften the same way mine do when I think of Jared.

I open my arms, and he steps into my embrace, easy this time, light, his hands clasped behind my hips. He brushes his lips over my hair and whispers into my ear, "I'm glad you stayed for dinner, but you deserve better than pastrami."

"I happen to love pastrami." I kiss him, long and soft and sweet.

His breath comes out in a whoosh, and he pulls me in tight. His hands roam over my back, into my hair, down to my waist and up again to my breasts. When his thumb strokes my nipple through the thin fabric of my blouse, a lightning bolt of pleasure sizzles right to my core. I moan and slide my hands beneath his shirt, relishing the silky warmth of his skin.

A soft inner voice cautions me to slow down, but with Nick, there's only speed, heat, urgency.

It takes every bit of my strength to stop touching him.

"Nick, tomorrow is—"

"June twentieth. The anniversary of Jared's death."

My breath catches. "You remembered."

"It's an important date." He strokes my cheek with his forefinger. "I'm here for you, Clara. If you want me."

I do want him, more than I'm willing to admit. I want to stay right here, help him unpack, talking and laughing into the night, and then make slow, sweet love in his bed. But I can't, not tonight.

"I can come help at your shop tomorrow if you need some time alone."

I chuckle. "A professor ringing up books?"

"Hey, I'm all about the books." Hooking his fingers through the waistband of my jeans, he snugs me closer. "Especially the ones behind your red door."

"And I look forward to sharing them with you, but not this weekend."

He releases me. "I understand." His eyes shine with compassion. "I love you, Clara."

When I open my mouth to respond, he touches his forefinger to my lips. "Don't answer. Just sit with it, see how it feels. Okay?"

Eyes swimming, I nod.

He walks me to my car and waits while I start the engine and roll down the window. A soft evening breeze whispers around and between us.

"You'll call me if you need me? Promise?"

"I promise." With great reluctance, I back down his driveway and drive toward home, alone.

Chapter Thirty-Three

♥

Clara

One year. I've been alone for one year.

I expected a ragged night, dreams slashed by horrible images—Jared's swollen, bruised face, his battered body on the hospital gurney, and the blood. So much blood.

Instead, I awake to birdsong and gentle sunshine streaming through my bedroom curtains. I've slept well, untroubled by dreams.

How can this be?

That's exactly what I said that awful day when, quaking with fear and grief, I stumbled out of the hospital and into the bright, sunny parking lot. How could something so horrible happen on such a beautiful day?

Slowly, cautiously, I extend one leg from the bed, and then the other. I push myself up, and they hold my weight. Last night, I laid out my running things: silky blue shorts, a sunny yellow tank top, and an emerald-green zippered shell, along with Jared's faded headband. In the past few weeks, I've been easing away from my habit of wearing something of his, but today, I need him close.

My strategy is to let the day unfold, to let whatever feelings might come wash through me without clinging to them or fighting them. I have the rest of my life to mourn my husband, so there's no need to rip open that wound today, just to honor his memory. Jared definitely wouldn't want me to do that. In fact, he would be proud of me for running again. Pushing my body hard the way he pushed his makes me feel connected to him.

I open the door to Blackbeard Coffee and pause a moment to let it wash over me: the scent of dark roast, the happy din of conversation and laughter, the lively runners wearing every color of the rainbow. Feeling oddly detached, as if a thick but invisible wall separates me from the scene, I take a deep breath and plunge in.

Mona, the woman who accompanied me on my first run, hollers, "There she is! Welcome back, Clara!" Her high-volume greeting alerts Dalton, who comes loping through the crowd. He moves like a greyhound, light and springy on his big feet, broad hands swinging in smooth arcs at the ends of his long, long arms. He closes on me, enfolds me, presses me tight against his chest.

Oh no. Harry told him.

"Clara," he murmurs into my hair. "I didn't know it was today. Are you sure you want to run?"

Tears press hard behind my eyes, but I blink them back. "Yes. I'm sure. And Dalton, I don't want to talk about it, okay?"

He nods solemnly. "Sure. Just know I'm here if you need me."

"Thanks." I squeeze his waist before releasing him. "Where's Harry?"

"Over there, next to the redhead."

Using the fellow's ginger man bun as a homing beacon, I find Harry leaning one elbow on the counter, yawning. He straightens at my approach.

"Clara." He opens his arms wide. I snuggle into his embrace and let him rock me. "You sure you're up for this, kiddo?"

"I'm sure. A run will do me good." I glance over my shoulder to where Dalton stands watching us with sharp attention. "You told him."

Harry cups my face in his palm. "He knew something was wrong, and he cares about you, Clara."

"I know. And I'm glad he does. But I really don't want anyone else to know, okay? Today will be easier if everyone's not tiptoeing around me."

"So noted. Say, you want this muffin? My stomach's not so hot."

Weird. It's not like Harry to turn down sweets. "Are you coming down with something?"

"Pish-tosh." He waves as if shooing a fly. "I just had a big dinner last night."

"Wagons, ho!" someone calls from the doorway, and we all file onto the sidewalk. A tall man in his fifties whistles for the group's attention. "There's construction on Coburg Road, so today we're heading toward Skinner Butte Park. Ready?"

He breaks into an easy gait, with Dalton beside him and Harry close behind. I'm in the rear of the pack again, between talkative Mona and Raoul, a heavy-set teenager with a determined scowl and a plodding gait. As before, Mona peppers me with questions.

"So, you and Dalton are an item now?"

"We're friends."

"Niiice. He's a good guy. Cute, in a skinny sort of way. Me, I prefer guys with more meat on their bones."

Raoul, twenty years her junior at least, shoots Mona a wide-eyed glance of alarm.

"Don't worry, hon," she reassures him, "I don't go for younger guys. You're going to be a fine-looking man, though."

With great effort, the hefty kid pulls ahead, leaving Mona and me to chat as we run.

"Gorgeous day, right?" She says between gasps and huffs. "I love summer. Makes me feel like a kid again. Remember the first week of summer break? How it just..."

I tune her out, my attention caught by a crowd of runners ahead, gathered roughly in a circle.

"Call nine one one!" someone shouts.

A cold finger of dread pokes my stomach as I trot up to join them. So many are taller than me that all I can see is Dalton kneeling over someone, his face rigid with grim determination as he presses rhythmically on the man's chest.

Heart drumming, I scan the fallen man's knobby knees, his wiry legs covered with pale hair, his purple and silver running shoes...

Hot panic rises in my throat and erupts in a ragged scream. "Harry!"

Nick

Book Nirvana should be open by now, but the lights are off. I rattle the handle—shut tight. The noise brings the orange tabby trotting toward the glass door. She mews silently from the other side.

Backing up, I notice a hastily scrawled sign affixed to the window:

Closed for a family emergency.

Something is very wrong if Clara and her two assistants are all gone. Is Clara sick? Hurt? Did that bastard landlord do something to harm her? There are a hundred possible non-dire explanations, but my caveman heart screams "Danger."

When I call Clara's number, it goes to a notice that her voicemail is full. My scalp prickles and tightens as I search my memory for any mention of her family—a stepsister in one place, a sister somewhere else, and a stepbrother here in Oregon. What about her parents?

Damn it to the depths of Hades, I should know these details about the woman I love.

Then again, maybe Clara just couldn't face the shop on the anniversary of her husband's death. That makes sense.

Except, where are Margot and the old guy who's so protective of her?

I swallow around a prickly knot of worry and type another text message before pocketing my phone.

She promised she'd call if she needs me.

Please call, Clara.

Clara, Two Hours Later

The same hospital, the same day. Only Jared never made it to the ICU.

Harry lies in a narrow bed, one of six in the Intensive Care Unit, monitor wires and IV lines trailing from his chest and arms. The antiseptic smell of cleanser and rubbing alcohol, the piercing beep, beep, beep of the machine monitoring his damaged heart, the squeaky sound of shoes on the buffed linoleum—razor-sharp memories of that horrible afternoon, one year ago, when doctors and nurses clustered around Jared's bed, trying in vain to stop the bleeding, to save his life.

Pushing away from the glass divider, I bark out a sob. The sound brings Dalton running from Harry's bedside. His face is nearly as gray as Harry's, but his arms are warm, strong, comforting. He rocks me silently and presses his lips to my forehead. Finally, he snuffles, wipes his reddened eyes, and tilts my chin up.

"You should go. There's nothing you can do here. I'll stay until Evie arrives."

"But what if he...if he..." I can't choke out the word.

"I'll call if anything changes. The doctor says he has a good chance. All those years of running kept him strong, except for the blockage in his heart." He kisses my temple. "Go, Clara. This is too hard on you."

"I want to see him first."

Dalton releases me and goes to the ICU desk. I watch his whispered conversation with the head nurse. She nods, and he beckons.

"She says five minutes. I'll be here." He folds his lanky frame into a vinyl chair and rests his head in his hands.

I tiptoe to Harry's bedside. Lying there so still and pale, he seems to have aged ten years, his ashen skin paper-thin, his arms blotched with purple from needle jabs. His eyes move rapidly behind their dark, bruised lids. They flutter open.

"Clara?" His voice creaks like a rusted hinge.

"I'm here, Harry." I grasp his hand, so cool and waxy. Just hours ago, he was warm and strong and safe. And now I might lose him.

"Hurts like hell," he murmurs and coughs out a laugh. "Never thought I'd go like this."

"You're not going anywhere, Harry," I whisper fiercely, squeezing his hand. His grip flutters, or perhaps I imagine it, before his head lolls to the side and he snores softly. I kiss his clammy forehead, then back away, clattering into an IV stand.

"Ma'am, you should go."

The nurse doesn't have to tell me twice.

"I've gotta get out of here," I inform Dalton, my voice wire-tight. When I hit the hallway, I break into a trot. By the time I reach the exit, I'm running, my sides gripping hard as I gulp air. With the hot sun heavy on my back, I sprint to my car, slam the door, and peel out of the parking lot.

Nick, Three Hours Later

Three hours later, and still no answer from Clara. I've checked her apartment twice and quizzed her neighbors. I've searched the phone listings for other Martellis in the area. None of them know Clara. Of course, Martelli is Jared's name. I slam my fist onto my desk, still surrounded by packing boxes. How can I feel this strongly about a woman and not even know her family name? No wonder she doesn't trust me.

But I want to know her, her whole history, everything that's made her the fascinating woman she is today, the woman I want by my side now and always. I've got to find her.

The park. Maybe she followed my advice and went there to be alone with Jared's memory. I shed my loafers and tie on my saggy old tennis shoes. I'll scour those trails until I find where she's holed up, nursing her grief.

I fire up my Karmann Ghia and drive past her shop one more time, just to be sure. Still no lights, no sign of life, so I steer toward Alton Baker Park. Heavy traffic slows me on the Ferry Street Bridge. Drumming my fingers on the leather-wrapped steering wheel, I watch the Willamette River crawling below, shining bright blue-green in the summer sunshine.

Diana died on a crystal summer day like this one. Trapped on the bridge, I remember the stab of sunlight when I emerged from the hospice building, how I shielded my streaming eyes in pain and disbelief. How could the sky be so blue? How could the world just go on while my beloved lay dead and my heart labored to keep beating without her?

And now Clara's all alone, facing that same merciless sunshine. I have to find her.

The park rises before me, a welcoming oasis of green. I feel it in my bones—she's nearby. No luck in the first big parking lot, near the rock garden. No sign of her Subaru near the amphitheater. I climb out of my car and consult a park map beside the path. Four more parking lots. My finger hovers over the map. Where would she go to find peace?

There. A small lot near the river. I spot her Subaru half-hidden beneath the overhanging branches of a gnarled live oak. The space beside her isn't strictly legal, but I'll take my chances with the park police.

The riverside trail is crowded with runners and bikers, families pushing strollers, kids on scooters and skateboards...but no Clara.

Cool your jets, Loverboy. Sending her here was your idea. Let the woman breathe.

Trudging under the weight of my own foolish panic, I return to the lot, lean against her car's bumper, and try hard to quiet my racing mind.

I'm here, Clara. Come to me when you're ready.

Clara, on the Run

My sides ache and my shins are screaming, but I can't stop running. On and on I pound through the park dodging happy families, sweet old couples strolling hand in hand, galumphing dogs and their laughing masters, and the bicyclists who whizz by with a muttered "On your left." As long as I keep moving, sucking in long, sharp breaths, my feet slapping the pavement in a steady rhythm, everything else blurs. Jared, Harry, my shop, Nick, Dalton—it all recedes like the fading memory of a nightmare.

Just keep running.

But my burning throat demands a pause. When I recognize the trailhead where I began, I turn toward the parking lot and the water bottle I forgot in my car, too distracted by my frantic need for flight. I'll give myself two minutes to stretch my aching back and rehydrate before hitting the trail for another round. No matter how bloodied my feet will be, how sore my muscles tomorrow, I have to keep moving. It's the only way to stop grief and terror from swallowing me whole.

I slow to a walk and fish my phone from my pocket. I must've missed the ping signaling Dalton's text:

> **No change. Doc says he's resting comfortably.**

I hunch over my phone and type a quick response:

> **Thanks. For everything.**

> **You okay?**

> **No, but I'll get through it.**

I tuck my phone away, look up, and freeze. Legs and arms crossed, eyes closed, Nick is leaning on my car. He seems to be asleep.

Drawing nearer, I drink in the beauty of his face in repose, his long lashes against his perfect cheekbones, his strong, straight nose with its flaring nostrils, his full lips relaxed and slightly open, his shiny dark curls tumbled by the wind. A Greek god slumbering in a parking lot.

He came for me. How did he know where to find me?

I lay my hand on his arm. He inhales and blinks, then jolts forward and grips my arms.

"Clara."

"Hi." I try to smile, but my chin wobbles.

"Are you all right?"

I pinch my lips together and shake my head.

Without another word, he enfolds me.

In his arms, I surrender my tightly clenched self-control. Nick holds me tenderly while ragged, gulping sobs wrack my body.

"Mommy, what's wrong with that lady?" a child's voice pipes from behind us. A van door rolls open. A seatbelt clicks.

"Hush, Peanut. The lady is sad. Leave her be."

"The man is sad too."

The door slides shut with a thunk, and the van pulls away. I turn to see a pair of bright eyes peering at me as the minivan rolls past. The child presses her hand to the glass.

A hiccup of laughter bubbles through my tears. I gaze up into Nick's face, dark and tight with worry.

I cup his cheek. "We're quite a spectacle."

"The kid's right." He fishes in his pocket. "Damn. No handkerchief today."

"I have Kleenex in the car." I unlock the Outback and mop up my wet, snotty face. "How did you find me?"

"When I saw the sign on your shop door, I imagined all kinds of calamity." He wipes a tendril of damp hair from my forehead. "Then I remembered our conversation about spending today in the park. I figured this anniversary qualifies as a family emergency."

I shake my head as fresh tears course down my face. "It's not that. It's Harry."

"The old guy in your shop?"

"We were running. He had a heart attack."

Nick steps back as if bracing himself. "Is he..."

"In the ICU. I couldn't stay." My voice tightens. "It's the same hospital where Jared, where he..."

"Oh God." He pulls me snug against him. His arms hold me safe and warm, but no embrace can shut out icy-cold reality. Any minute now, I might lose my dear friend. My whole body aches with dread.

"Do you want me to take you there?"

I shake my head. "Dalton's there. He'll call me if anything changes." I sniffle against his tear-damp shirt. "I don't trust myself to drive. Can you take me home, Nick?"

He takes my keys and helps me into the passenger seat. When we pull into my driveway, I try to reach for the door handle, but my arms won't move, and my feet feel welded to the floor.

I turn to him, my voice tight with panic. "I don't think I can be alone here today."

"Then don't. Stay with me as long as you want. You'll know when you're ready."

He follows me upstairs, helps me pack an overnight bag, then drives the dozen blocks to his new home. Inside, he holds my elbow to steady me as we climb up to his bedroom, now free of moving cartons. He eases me onto his bed and kneels to unlace my shoes.

"Nick, I can—"

"Hush. Let me do this." He tucks my shoes under the bed, then goes into the bathroom. I hear water gushing in the tub.

"You'll feel better after a bath. I'll bring you some tea." He closes the bedroom door behind him.

I strip off my clammy running clothes and ease into the steaming water, wincing at the irony. Yesterday, it took every bit of my self-control not to end up in Nick's bedroom. Today, the second worst day of my life, here I am. Naked, too.

There's a soft knock on the door, and Nick's hand appears, holding a steaming mug.

"I'll put it by the sink. I plugged in your phone. It's on the dresser."

"Nick."

He opens the door wide enough to see how carefully he's averting his gaze.

"You can come in, you know. There's nothing here you haven't seen before."

He chuckles. "I'd better not. It'll just—complicate things. You rest, Clara. I'll be downstairs if you need anything."

"Thank you. And Nick?"

"Yes?"

"You're a good man."

His laughter rumbles low. "Well, that's a start." He closes the door behind him.

Chapter Thirty-Four

♥

Clara

Sunlight slants through the curtainless windows and straight into my eyes, stinging like sand. I rub them and sit up, for a moment, completely lost. The ceiling is much higher than the one in my bedroom, and this comfortable bed with its heavy walnut bedposts? Definitely not mine. Then it hits me. I curl into a ball, cradling my aching center. Nick's scent clings to the pillows: woodsy and mossy and comforting.

Nick's room. Nick's bed. He left me here to rest. I need to thank him. Facing whatever comes next will be easier with him beside me.

Already, I'm paying for that long, punishing race through the park. My muscles shriek when I push myself out of bed. The pain helps, somehow. It seems fitting that my body hurts the way my heart is hurting—for Jared, for Harry. I rummage through my duffle bag and find an old pair of jeans and one of Jared's triathlon T-shirts. After splashing water on my face and pulling my hair into a ponytail, I pad downstairs barefoot.

He's not in the kitchen, though he's left a pot on the stove with a bowl and spoon beside it. I lift the lid. It's chicken noodle soup—a sweet thought, but my stomach rebels at the sight.

"Nick?"

"Hmmm." His voice sounds raspier than usual. Must have fallen asleep on the couch. I tiptoe through the dining room. The long, lean figure on the sofa shifts, and one lanky arm stretches toward the ceiling.

"Dalton?" I blink in astonishment as he rolls upright. Still wearing his running clothes, now rumpled and twisted, he bounds to his feet and rushes to me, wrapping me in a tight hug. The sharp odor of his sweat-soaked T-shirt stings my nose, but the familiar planes and angles of his body comfort me.

"You're up." He presses his lips to my hair.

"What are you doing here?"

"Nick went to get his car and asked me to stay with you."

"But, how?"

"Margot. She came to the hospital looking for you. Called someone in Berkeley, got Nick's number. I guess she figured if you weren't at the shop and you weren't at home, you'd be with him."

His hangdog expression twists my heart. "I wasn't with him. I went to the park, tried to run it off, you know?"

He nods glumly. "That's what I'd do."

"Nick drove around until—"

"He told me." He sinks onto the couch, pulls me down beside him, and clasps my hand for a long, silent moment. "Guess I lost out to Professor Zorba."

I lean against his bony shoulder. "Papadopoulos."

"Whatever. Still hurts."

Really? I'm grieving one loss, fearing another—who happens to be his relative, and he's focusing on who gets into my pants?

I fold over, bury my face in a sofa pillow, and scream.

"Hey, hey now." He rubs my back in slow circles. "I'm sorry, Clara. You don't need to deal with my ego, not today of all days."

Eyes closed, I mutter into the pillow—easier than meeting his wounded gaze. "I care about you, Dalton. Hurting you is the last thing I want to do. But I don't know how all this will fall out."

He gently pulls me upright, then lifts my chin. "Look, Clara. I know our first time together was kind of a disaster, but that doesn't mean I don't want you. I do."

And here it is. Door A or Door B? I can only walk through one, and right now, I wish I could go back in time and turn down both Nick and Dalton. Meeting someone new was supposed to lift me out of misery, not dig me in deeper. And no matter what I do next, I'll hurt a good man.

Lowering my gaze, I whisper, "Nick says he's in love with me."

"Do you believe him?"

I nod.

He claps a hand over his eyes and slouches against the back of the couch. "Well, shit. He's bringing out the big guns."

"Dalton, I—" I lay my hand on his shoulder. "Can we talk about this later? I just can't deal with this today."

He flashes a gentle smile. "Of course. I'm being selfish when I should be supporting you. I'm sorry."

The doorknob rattles, and Nick steps into the room. His dark gaze locks on mine and then shifts to Dalton. The two men stare silently at each other, the tension between them as palpable as the floor under my feet. Finally, Nick steps forward. "Dalton, thanks for staying."

"Don't mention it." He slides toward the end of the couch, making room for Nick on my other side, a peace offering. Nick sits, leaving me sandwiched between two broad shoulders, two strong thighs.

"I stopped by your shop on the way back," Nick says. "Margot gave me a new sign for the door. Arnie let me in."

"New sign?"

"Said you'd reopen tomorrow. She'll bring a few friends to help out until you're ready to come back."

"Oh, Margot." My voice wobbles.

Both men reach for me at once. I clasp Nick's right hand and Dalton's left.

Finally, Nick breaks the tense silence. "What do you want to do, Clara?"

"I guess I'd rather just stay closed for the weekend until we know more about Harry's condition."

Dalton speaks up. "The doctor said they'll do an angioplasty tomorrow morning."

Nick squeezes my hand. "That's good news. If they can wait until tomorrow, the damage to his heart isn't as bad as we thought. But there's another reason you might want to open tomorrow. That asshat landlord of yours came in while I was talking to Arnie. Made disparaging comments about your ability to keep the shop open."

"Lonnie said that? Older man, red face, gray hair?"

"No, the greasy guy who bothered you the day of the pickets."

"Crap. Darryl."

Dalton scowls. "He was bothering Clara yesterday."

The two men exchange a meaningful glance.

Nick bobs his head. "We open tomorrow."

"What do you mean, we?"

"It's been a long time, but I can run a cash register."

"Me too," Dalton adds. "Margot can tell us what to do. You and I will take turns going to the hospital."

I take a deep breath. "Okay, then. We open tomorrow."

Upstairs, my phone trills. I bolt to my feet, but Nick pushes me back onto the sofa. "I'll get it."

Dalton takes the opportunity to slide his arm around my shoulders. I let him but keep my eyes on the stairway. Nick trots down, hands over my phone, and stands with his arms crossed, staring daggers at Dalton.

"For God's sake." I shrug off Dalton's arm and stalk into the kitchen, leaving the guys to their pissing contest.

Margot's left a voice message: "Harry's awake. He wants to see you."

I go upstairs for my purse and return to find both men still glaring.

"Harry asked for me. Nick, you have my key?"

"I'll drive you." Dalton heads toward the door.

"The hell you will," Nick growls, hot on his heels.

Dalton's chin juts like a cartoon superhero's. "Harry's my family."

"Clara's my—"

"Cut it out!" I snap. "I do not need this now." My sharp tone slices through their bickering. I thrust out my hand. "Key."

Chastened, Nick drops it into my palm.

I blow out a breath. "Thank you both. Nick, I'll be back later for my stuff. Dalton, if you still want to help tomorrow, I'd be grateful."

I climb into my car, slam the door, and drive off, alone.

At the last traffic light before the hospital, I catch sight of Nick's little green sports car in my rear-view mirror. Heat climbs from my chest to my face. "I cannot effin' believe this."

I zoom into the first available spot and jog to the entrance.

"Clara, wait."

I don't care how pretty the man is, how sweet and considerate, he's got some nerve following me after I specifically told him not to. "Now is not the time, Nick," I snarl.

"I know. I'm sorry. I just—"

I whirl on him. "I'm not here to talk about your feelings, Nick. I'm here to see Harry."

He raises his palms in a sheepish gesture. "He asked for me too."

"Huh?"

"Margot called, right after you left."

This makes no sense. Harry doesn't even know Nick.

I force my shoulders down. "Let's go, then."

In silence, we ride the elevator to the fourth floor. At least a dozen people in running clothes crowd the ICU waiting room, talking in hushed tones, *Get well soon* balloons bobbing above their heads. In the corner, Mona clasps the hands of a pretty, white-haired woman with gentle eyes and a brow pleated with worry.

"Hey, Clara." Mona looks Nick up and down, her expression somewhere between suspicion and naked lust. "This is Evie, Harry's sweetheart."

Evie blushes becomingly and takes my hand. "Pleased to meet you, Clara. Harry's so fond of you."

I pull her into a hug. "How's he doing?"

"He was awake a few minutes ago. They've got him on some strong pain meds, so he's pretty loopy. His son is flying in from New Mexico. He should be here soon." She pats my hand. "Let's get you in there before the nurse sends us all away. I think she's getting tired of all this ruckus."

Evie tugs me toward the nurses' station and beckons to Nick. "Come on, dear. Harry wants to talk to Clara's young man too."

Nick hesitates in the doorway. "Are you sure he meant me?"

"He said to bring the professor."

The nurse in charge of the ICU drills us with a stern stare. "Five minutes. Keep it calm and quiet, please. Harry needs his rest."

This time, Harry's cheeks hold a little more color, but my heart squeezes at the sight of my dear friend so still under the thin blankets, surrounded by beeping medical equipment. I reach for Nick's hand.

Harry's eyes flutter open. "There she is. How's my girl?"

I chuckle, touched by his concern. "I'm okay. How are you, Harry?"

"Pretty stoned." He rolls his eyes toward Nick, and his focus sharpens. "Introduce me to your friend."

"Nick Papadopoulos." He extends his hand. His eyes widen at the strength of Harry's grip.

Yup. It's a day for pissing contests.

Harry coughs. "Look, I don't have a lot of time. Tomorrow they're sticking some wires into my heart. It'll either cure me or kill me."

"Harry," I squeak.

"Hush, kiddo. Doc says my chances are good. But I don't want to leave things unsaid. Nick, do you love her?"

Nick meets Harry's steely gaze. "I do, sir."

"Will you take care of her when I'm gone?"

He nods. "If she'll let me."

My heart wobbles.

Harry turns his pale gaze on me. "Well, you know I'd rather see you with Dalton, and you know why. But if this guy is what you want, so be it. Just promise me you'll take your time." He squeezes my hand, his fingers warm and rough. "I love you like a daughter, Clara."

"Oh, Harry," I sob and press his hand to my heart.

Harry's lids drift closed. "Gonna sleep now. Be well, Clara-bell."

We linger at his bedside, Nick's arm around my shoulders, watching the steady rise and fall of Harry's chest until the nurse chases us away.

Afterward, I sit beside Nick on a bench in the hospital courtyard, beneath the rustling leaves of slender birch trees. Exhausted inside and out, I cling to his hand.

"I just can't imagine a future without him. I mean, he's seventy-four. I know he can't keep working at the shop forever, but...he's always been there, you know? He really is like a father to me."

"What about your own father?" he asks softly.

"We don't get along. After his breakup with Mom..." I don't have the energy to explain further, and besides, what's the point? Dad left us in every way it's possible to leave someone, and for my own sake, I've made my peace with his betrayal. Some people just don't know how to love.

"Since Jared's death, Harry's been my rock."

Nick squeezes my hand. "Well, you've got a couple of guys lined up to audition for that role."

"Yeah." I sniffle. "But to embrace one, I have to hurt the other."

"Look." He pivots to face me. "I'm here. Dalton's here. And Harry's right, you should take your time with this decision. But eventually, you're going to have to choose—one of us, or neither of us. Someone's going to be hurt. That's just how it is."

Eyes downcast, I nod. I wish this could play out like one of those reverse harem romance books where the heroine ends up with both men, but I'm not built like that, and neither are Nick and Dalton.

Nick's thumb rubs soothing arcs over my knuckles. "It boils down to this: What do you really want, Clara? Do you want a business partner? A husband? A casual boyfriend?"

"Right now, I just don't know."

He sighs and weaves his fingers through mine. "Fair enough. But for the record, I know exactly what I want: a life here, with you. A home, with you. A family, with you."

"A family?" My voice rises to a squeak.

"Yeah." Smiling tenderly, he strokes my cheek. "You, me, a baby. More than one, if we have time. Imagine it, Clara—that big fireplace crackling, a couple kids in pajamas thundering down those stairs to open their Christmas presents. We've been up all night, putting together some damned Barbie thing..."

"Stop!" I bolt to my feet, knotting both hands in my hair. "Nick, I..." Too agitated to wrap words around this inner turmoil, I tilt my face to the sky and howl, all the pain and loss pouring out in a ragged, animal cry.

Nick tries to pull my rigid body against him. "Clara, what is it?"

"No!" I plant both hands on his chest and shove hard enough to send him stumbling backward, his mouth agape.

"You don't want children? Is that it?" His gilded dark eyes swim with pain and confusion.

"Nick, I'm thirty-nine. I'm a widow."

"I'm forty-two. I'm a widower. So?"

The words pour out between wracking sobs. "Jared and I, we were trying. To have kids. But we never got the chance. And then you come along, and we just fall together, and I meet your family, and you tell me you love me when you hardly know me, and you say you want babies, and it's all..." My throat constricts, cutting off my garbled rant.

Nick's expression dulls and hardens. "The house, the kids, Christmas—you wanted all those things with Jared."

I swipe at my streaming eyes. "It's so damn unfair."

He grips my shoulders hard, his fingers digging into my flesh. "Of course it's unfair. And I wanted all those things with Diana." His eyes blaze. "I watched her *die*, Clara. It took a long time, and she suffered horribly. You think that doesn't hurt me every day?"

He sinks onto the bench and folds over, his head in his hands. "You're not the only one who's scared by this."

Stunned, I sit beside him. Nick has seemed so sure of his feelings, but he's still struggling as much as I am.

I stroke his back, my fingers skimming over iron-hard muscle. "I thought sleeping with you would be this brave, fun thing. Just a lark, you know? The first step toward reclaiming my life. But you were so kind, and so seductive—body and soul. I didn't expect to feel this much for you. And now, I feel..." Heaving a huge sigh, I dredge up the truth he deserves. "Foolish. Like I'm setting myself up for another heartbreak. And then Harry..." I gesture toward the hospital building. "I care for you, Nick, but I don't have the strength to face this now."

He doesn't answer, but he doesn't move away.

I slide my arm around his waist. "I wish I could tell you what you want to hear. But today, I just can't."

His voice is a harsh croak. "I understand. It's not fair of me to ask that of you. I'll see you around, Clara." He rises and walks slowly away from me, back toward the parking lot.

I watch him go, praying I haven't closed the door between us forever.

Chapter Thirty-Five

♥

Clara

Time, as they say, has a way of healing all wounds, or at least helping a wounded person catch her breath.

Harry's out of the ICU now but will have to remain in the hospital for another week or more while they monitor his new cardiac stent. When I enter his room two days after his collapse, he looks so much better, I tear up with relief.

"Now, now, no more boo-hoos," my old friend chides as the nurse fiddles with a monitor attached to his chest. "You've been spending far too much time fussing over me when you should be taking care of Book Nirvana."

"The shop will be fine. Margot and I have things handled, and Dalton starts work on the doorway tomorrow." I pull a chair up to his bedside. "What's the doctor say?"

He takes my quaking hand in his broad, veiny one, his grip as warm and strong as ever. "So far, so good. I'm due for some cardiac rehab, but they expect me to make a full recovery."

My voice breaks. "Thank God."

Without a word, the nurse hands me a slim box of tissues and gives my shoulder a pat before leaving us alone.

Harry scoots higher on his pillows. "Evie and I have been talking, kiddo. In fact, she managed to sneak back in after visiting hours. The night nurse wasn't pleased about that." He chuckles, then strokes his stubbled chin. "An experience like this opens a man's eyes. I've been given a second chance—a rare and wonderful gift. That bucket list of mine? It's time to start emptying it. As soon as the doctor gives her okay, we're going to Australia and New Zealand." He gives me a look brimming with concern. "You gonna be okay without me?"

"Absolutely." I bob my head and hope the worry gnawing at my gut doesn't show. "In fact, I've posted two part-time positions on a job-search site."

"Replacing me already?" Harry claps a hand to his repaired heart.

"My friend, no one could ever replace you." I pluck a handful of tissues from the box and mop up my leaky face.

Harry wiggles his fingers in a "Gimme" gesture, so I hand over the tissue box.

"I'd give you a big hug, kiddo, but there's too many wires."

I squeeze his hand. "Consider yourself hugged. You're the best man I know, Harry."

And if I don't stop this love fest now, I'm going to be a blubbering mess—the last thing Harry needs.

"So many flowers," I chirp, scanning the room. Every horizontal surface holds bouquets, potted plants, those mini balloons on sticks, get-well cards, and stuffed toys, including a teddy bear in running shoes.

"Your professor friend sent that one." Harry points to a ceramic pot brimming with succulents. "The card is interesting."

He tilts his chin, inviting me to take a look.

Wishing you speedy healing, Harry. You mean the world to Clara, and I'm grateful she has a friend like you in her life.
— Nick Papadopoulos

I clasp the card to my heart and fight back another wave of tears.

Harry raises one wiry eyebrow. "So, how's it going on the boyfriend front?"

I haven't seen or spoken to Nick since our last tearful parting. He's texted only once:

> **Thinking of you, Clara. I'm here if you need me.**

And that's all.

Well, what did I expect after screaming like a rabid beast—not the reaction a man's looking for when he says, "I love you." But that harsh cry was completely, nakedly honest, and the best I could do under the circumstances.

Whatever comes next hangs on how I handle the hurt I've inflicted on two good men.

"Honestly, I don't know, Harry."

"Have you made up your mind?"

I nod solemnly. But before I can elaborate, there's a sharp rap on the door, and Dalton's shiny head pokes inside. "Got room for one more?"

The melancholy, crooked smile he gives me is quickly replaced by a wide grin aimed at his cousin. "Looking good, Harry. You've got your color back." He sets his gift, a pair of fleece-lined slippers, on the foot of Harry's bed and folds his long frame into the other bedside chair.

While Harry relates his test results to Dalton, I rise and ease toward the door. I'd hoped to meet Dalton on neutral ground, perhaps the park or a coffee shop, but here he is, and I need to say my piece before he starts tomorrow's renovations—that is, if he doesn't back out.

I clear my throat. "Dalton, when you're finished visiting with Harry, could you meet me in the cafeteria?"

Dalton's blue eyes laser onto mine. His Adam's apple bobs.

Harry's sharp gaze misses none of the unspoken tension between us. With an exaggerated yawn, he nestles into his pillows. "Actually, I'm feeling sleepy. Why don't you two grab a coffee? We can catch up later, Dalton. And thanks for the slippers."

Wordlessly, side by side, we ride the elevator down to the first floor. As the door opens, Dalton's knuckles brush mine. "You really want a coffee? You look like you're about to vibrate right out of your shoes."

"That obvious, eh?" I nudge him with my shoulder, grateful to him for breaking the awkward silence. "How about if we go outside?"

I lead him to the same peaceful courtyard where Nick and I spilled our hearts out two days ago. Except for an elderly woman dozing in her wheelchair and some hopeful pigeons, we have the space to ourselves.

I sit on a cement bench and pat the spot beside me. This'll be easier if I don't have to worry about my knees giving out.

Dalton sits, stretches out his long legs, and takes my hand, his long thumb rubbing arcs over my knuckles.

"So." He gazes at our reflection in the wall of windows.

"So." I lean onto his shoulder and promptly forget the speech I rehearsed late into the night. "Dalton, you're a wonderful guy."

"But I'm not the guy for you."

I give a wry laugh. "You're better at this than I am."

"I'm not." His gaze drops to his shoes as he sucks in a deep breath. "But it's a two-yeses, one-no situation, right? Like naming a baby." He releases my hand and gives me a sorrowful look that pierces my heart.

"Yeah, like that. And I want one."

"A baby?" His eyebrows climb skyward.

"Maybe two, if it's not too late."

Eyes narrowed, he rubs his shaved head. "Well, I guess I could consider..."

"Dalton, that's not the only reason." I lay my hand on his forearm. "You're wise and funny and caring, everything I could want in a friend, but you and I just don't have the kind of chemistry I share with Nick."

His brows contract. "Who says we don't? I want you, Clara. Meeting you turned the lights back on in my heart. I'm feeling things I thought I never would again."

God, this hurts so much! I'd do anything to spare him this pain.

"I'm truly sorry, Dalton, but I'm not in love with you."

He places his enormous hand over mine and lets it rest there, still and silent, while the pigeons close in, hoping for snacks. A particularly bold one puffs out its iridescent breast and pecks at Dalton's shoe.

Finally, he squeezes my hand and huffs a laugh. "You know, of all the break-ups I've endured, yours was the kindest." He releases me and straightens. "This isn't the first time I've had a crush on someone who didn't crush back. I'll get over it eventually. And I really do wish you the best, Clara. You're a good person. You deserve happiness."

Weak with relief, I slump in my seat. I did not expect this to be so easy, but Dalton is a deeply compassionate person. The woman who ends up with him will be lucky indeed.

Once again, he nudges me with his arm. "Just please know, if it doesn't work out with Nick, I'm still here. Now." He claps his hands and rubs them together. "What time can I start tomorrow?"

Chapter Thirty-Six

♥

Nick

"That should do it." Dalton snaps his toolbox shut with a bang.

I clap him on the shoulder. "Well done, man. I'm impressed." It takes tremendous self-control, but I manage to unclench my teeth before saying it.

Dalton raises one pale eyebrow, but his half-smile has lost its barbs.

The tension of working alongside my rival for ten hours has worn my nerves to a frayed, frazzled mess. Even though today is her only day off, Clara stays the whole time, only leaving us to pick up lunch. My pride smarts from being relegated to apprentice status beside Dalton's easy mastery of tools, especially the wicked-looking reciprocating saw he uses to cut through the drywall. More than once, it occurs to me how easily he could "slip" and eliminate me from the competition for Clara's hand.

But we manage the renovation, speaking as little as possible. The heavy physical labor of demolishing drywall almost takes my mind off the tension nibbling at my gut.

All the while, Clara's sea-green gaze follows me, testing my patience. That's what this is, a test of my loyalty, my emotional maturity. And I'm handling it well.

So is Dalton, damn it.

No insults, no squabbles, no shoving, just hours of near-silent, begrudging cooperation.

And now, a wide doorway stands open between Arnie's coffee shop and Clara's place, lined with pale wooden trim. Tomorrow, Dalton will install the glass doors. Were it not for the sheets of heavy plastic protecting the two shops from construction debris, you'd never know the opening hadn't been there all along.

Clara steps between us, winds her arm through my elbow and her other arm through Dalton's. Her soft, warm touch is reward enough for now, until I can get her alone. But since our last private moment at the hospital, she hasn't given me the chance. Of course, she hasn't been alone with Dalton either, as far as I know. He wasn't here on Sunday when I reported for cashier duty. When Margot arrived with two college friends to help, Clara sent me on my way with a kiss on the cheek. Nice, but not nearly enough to satisfy my relentless impatience.

And now, the job is done. On the other side of the plastic barrier, Arnie taps his foot. "Are we ready for the grand unveiling? Closing up all day cost me a bundle, you know. Let's rip this shit down."

I catch Dalton's eye and sigh. Arnie's contribution to the construction project has been limited to coffee refills and admiration of our muscles.

Clara steps forward and grasps the plastic sheeting. Arnie grabs a handful from his end and counts, "Three, two, one." They both yank, and the barrier flutters down around their feet.

Beaming beautifully, Clara wades through, hugs Arnie tight, and the two of them dance in a circle like giddy teens.

"Oh, my Gawd," Arnie crows, "this is gonna be awesome." He tugs her to an empty bookshelf waiting to be filled. "Let's put some really juicy romances here, and maybe some thrillers, and..." On and on he natters.

Dalton mutters, "We do the work, and he gets the hugs."

"Right?" I stoop to gather the plastic.

"Hey, Nick."

The little hairs on my nape rise as I stand to face my adversary.

Dalton crooks a wry smile. "Look, this has been hard on both of us. I just want to say, however things turn out with Clara, you're all right." He extends his hand.

I take it. There's no macho squeeze between us, no more testing our strength. It isn't up to us, anyway. It's up to her.

"You're a good guy, Dalton. If she chooses you, she'll have chosen well."

He arches one eyebrow but says nothing further. Instead, he follows Clara into the coffee shop and wraps his long, gangly arms around her. Wincing, I look away. No point in torturing myself.

Finally making himself useful, Arnie grabs a broom and shoos Clara and Dalton out of the café. "I'll get this. Y'all have earned a rest. Go on now, scoot."

I help load the last of Dalton's tools into his station wagon and watch with gritted teeth as he kisses Clara good night—just a chaste smooch on her forehead, but anyone with eyes can see the heat behind the gesture.

"We'll visit Harry tomorrow, okay?" He murmurs into her hair.

She nods, her arms around him, her chin on his chest. They fit well together, I realize with a pang, their easy manner like a long-married couple's. Even though Dalton hasn't been on the scene any longer than I have, I feel like an intruder.

"Good night." She waves from the sidewalk until Dalton's taillights disappear around the corner.

"Well, I guess I should get going too." If I'm lucky, she'll give me an even warmer goodnight kiss.

Clara pushes her hair back from her eyes, a mysterious half-smile on her lips. She moves closer and opens her arms. I step into her embrace, and she nuzzles my neck, shooting a shiver of pleasure down my spine.

"What's your hurry?" she purrs.

With a thump of surprise, my heart kicks into overdrive. I cup her face in both hands. "Believe me, Clara, I'm in no hurry to leave you."

"Then stay." She steps backward into her shop, towing me with her. "I'm hungry. Are you hungry, Nick?"

By the mischievous sparkle in her eyes, I suspect she's not talking about food.

"Starving." I tug my T-shirt away from my sticky neck. "I'm a mess, though."

She inclines her head toward the restroom. "Go clean up, then. I'll meet you in back."

She's stocked her shop's cramped restroom with a fluffy cotton towel and herbal-scented hand soap. I wash my face and run a comb through my hair. From outside the door, I hear the familiar pop of a wine cork.

Hot damn, Clara saved her celebration wine for me? I hurriedly strip off my T-shirt and unbuckle my belt. My impromptu bath leaves the floor soaked, so I mop up with paper towels, say a silent prayer for luck, then open the door.

Clara

When the restroom door closes behind Nick, Lulu emerges from her hiding place beneath the cookbooks, stretches, and trots to me.

I rub behind her silky ears. "This is it, Lulu-puss. Make or break, do or die—what did Dad always say? Shit or get off the pot." I wrinkle my nose. "Not a very apt metaphor, in this case."

I make a final check of the scene I've been surreptitiously setting up all day.

Plush blankets atop cushy yoga mats—check.

Picnic basket filled with cheese, bread, grapes, prosciutto, olives—check.

Wine chilling in a dented ice bucket—check.

Extra towels, in case things get messy—check.

Battery-powered candles scattered among the bookshelves—check.

Brazilian jazz on the speaker—check.

And a pile of books I pulled from the special collection: erotic images to inspire us, not that Nick will need much inspiration. All day, he's been shooting me heated glances, but he showed admirable restraint, never jostling Dalton or firing off snarky comments.

In his shoes, I don't think I could've remained so calm.

The restroom door clicks open, and Lulu trots toward it with a plaintive mew. My furry friend is head-over-tails gaga for Nick.

"Hello, Puss. Where's Clara, hmm?"

Soft footsteps approach. Nervous to the point of vibrating, I fluff my hair and perch on the edge of the velvet settee. Slowly, the red door opens.

And there he stands, his dark curls damp, his eyes sparkling in the ersatz candlelight, his lips soft and open.

"Wow." His gaze roams the room, then lasers in on me. In three swift steps, he closes the distance between us, pulls me to my feet, and clasps me hard against his strong, delicious body. His lips press to my throat, my closed eyelids, and then he takes my mouth and kisses me breathless.

After a thorough, sensual plundering, he breaks the kiss and cups my jaw with both hands, his thumbs stroking my temples. The amber fire in his irises dances as he searches my face. "Clara, is this real? You chose me?"

Nodding, I slide my fingers where they've longed to go for the past two days: through his hair, along his jaw, over the firm curve of his shoulders, his chest, around his neck to pull him closer and taste him again. I moan softly, all the things I want to say forgotten in this rush of lust and relief and—yes, I can say it now—love for this amazing man.

It doesn't make sense to fall so hard so fast, but my heart thrums with certainty, with a bone-deep sense of rightness. We fit, Nick and I.

He nuzzles my throat, his fingers working the buttons of my blouse until it falls to the floor. With a panty-melting growl, he grasps my bra strap in his teeth and tugs it over my shoulder.

While he feathers kisses over my collarbone and between my breasts, I pull his T-shirt free from his belt and stroke the smooth planes of his back. His muscles soften like butter beneath my hands. When he pulls his shirt off and tosses it away, I trail my fingertips and the tip of my tongue around each dark nipple. Growling deep in his throat, he pulls me toward the settee. "Your turn." He eases me into the seat and kneels before me.

His soft curls brush beneath my chin as he whisks my bra off. Weak-kneed with desire, I grasp his shoulders as he gently squeezes each breast, his lips satiny-soft, sliding across and around and between. He swirls his silky tongue over each sensitive peak and sucks gently at first, then more urgently, until I cry out with pleasure and just a whisper of pain.

He kisses his way down my belly, unfastens my jeans, and slides his tongue down, down, down as he pulls my jeans over my hips. He teases me, sliding just one fingertip inside my panties while his thumb strokes my sopping seam through the fabric. A hot, sweet ache is building there, and I'm afraid I'll come before I even finish undressing him.

"Stop." I grasp his wrists and pull him to his feet. "My turn."

I take his mouth in another searing kiss, then sit before him to unfasten his belt. Pressing my lips to the bulge in his jeans, I heat the fabric with my breath, then nibble the hard length of him. His groan is a raw, animal sound, his head thrown back as he strokes my hair.

"Clara."

The way he whispers my name with so much longing fires my blood. I need to taste him. Now.

I tug his jeans over his hips to reveal thin black briefs that barely contain his straining erection. With lips and teeth and tongue, I tease him through the fabric, pausing only to dig my fingers into the smooth muscle of his ass.

"So good," I murmur against his warm, flat belly. "So hard, so ready." Impatient for my prize, I hook my finger beneath the elastic and strip his shorts off. He kicks them away and widens his stance, allowing me to caress his silky balls, which tighten at my touch. And then, just to tease him, I trail the tip of my tongue up his long, swollen shaft.

His ragged cry will haunt my erotic dreams.

I wrap both hands around his length and stroke upward, swirling my tongue over the plump, purple head of his cock, drawing a salty tear of pleasure.

With a groan, he lifts me beneath my arms and lowers me onto the improvised bed I've arranged on the floor. He crouches over me, straddles my body, strokes his fingertips through my hair. His sigh heats my skin. "You are so beautiful."

Words are beyond me now, so I give him a lust-drunk smile, caress him with my eyes, run my fingertips over his temples, his throat, his broad chest, his tightly muscled belly, then grasp his hips and pull him down to where I'm aching for him.

His pulse thrums beneath the silky skin of his cock as I grasp him, urging him toward my throbbing center. His eyes half-closed on a groan, Nick slides oh so slowly between my tingling folds, deep, deep inside, then slowly withdraws until he's barely touching me. My senses swim with delirious pleasure, every nerve singing.

He withdraws on a hiss. "Damn. Condom." He reaches for his jeans, crumpled on the floor.

My whole body quivers, craving his return, and something inside me slides into place, something I've been struggling against ever since I first laid eyes on this beautiful, kind man.

This is my second chance at happiness, at finally having what fate stole from Jared and me—a family of our own. God only knows whether Nick and I will get the chance, but hard experience has shown me how fragile life is. Nick loves me, and he wants what I want. In his arms, by his side, I'll rebuild my life and give him—and hopefully, our child—all the love in my still-beating heart.

I grasp his wrist and kiss his palm. "No condom, Nick."

His face contracts in a question. "You're on birth control?"

I shake my head. "I'm not a young woman. If we're going to start a family, there's no time to waste."

His breath comes out in a rush, and he presses his body against mine from chest to toe. His cock throbs with need, but his eyes soften with emotion as he slides his hand around my nape and gently squeezes. "Clara, do you mean it? Are you sure?"

The answer wells up from deep inside, from a place I've kept carefully guarded for too long.

"I'm sure, Nick."

With a cry somewhere between a sob and a laugh, he seals his lips to mine, nudges my thighs wider with his knee, and slides home.

The sensation of his bare skin so deep inside licks me with sweet flame. I arch my back and clutch his tight, hard ass to pull him in deeper. He captures my wrists and grasps them above my head as he drives his heated flesh into me. With perfect, aching slowness, he slides out, his breath ragged, his eyes never leaving mine. And then he surges into me again, each delicious thrust tugging hard on my clit, igniting sharp sparks of ecstasy.

The rosy room around us fades. Driven by our shared hunger, his tempo increases. My whole world becomes his heat, his magical touch, his breath on my cheek, the fire in his dark eyes. My pleasure coils tighter with each feral thrust until a ecstasy rockets through me, lifting me above doubt and fear. I cry out and gasp for air, dimly aware of Nick's fingers digging into my hips, his hoarse voice moaning my name again and again as he fills me in a hot, wet rush.

I clasp him tight, cradling him while he shudders into me. I whisper into his shoulder, my fingertips stroking his back, too bliss-drunk to say anything but "Yes, Nick. Yes, love. Yes."

Gradually, our breathing slows, and we relax on our bed of blankets, Nick's body heavy and soft atop mine. After several minutes, I squirm to escape his weight.

"Sorry." He chuckles and rolls off, landing beside me. He presses his forehead to mine. "There you are."

"Here we are." And somehow, that strikes me as funny, staring into his dark eyes from so close he seems to have three or four of them. Giggling, I smooch his lips.

He's laughing too. "That was...astounding."

"Phenomenal."

"Ferocious."

"Luscious."

He rakes his fingers into my hair and peppers my face with kisses.

I giggle and squirm. "That tickles."

"You're delicious. I want you again."

"Already?"

"Okay, maybe a quick nap, but then again, first thing." He eases my head onto his chest.

Nestling into the lovely spot where his shoulder meets the swelling of his pectoral muscle, I watch his chest's gentle rise and fall. My hand seems so pale against his burnished bronze skin. I trace spirals with my fingertips and stroke the soft hairs dusting his pecs.

He's fading fast, his breathing becoming deeper, his words blurring into a sleepy mutter.

"Mmmuhh mmm?"

"What's that?"

But he's out, flat on his back, snoring softly. With a wide, contented smile, I cuddle against him and surrender to sleep.

Lulu wakes us, her rumbling purr loud in my ear. I open one eye and find myself face to furry face with the cat, who head-butts my cheek before resuming her kneading dance on Nick's bare chest.

"Huh?" He blinks, stretches, and grins. "Hello, Puss."

Lulu stretches luxuriously under his caress, then hops off to sniff our picnic basket. With dainty precision, she helps herself to a cube of smoked Gouda and trots away.

Nick chuckles into my hair. "Hello, my love."

"Hey there..." I hesitate, relishing the words on my tongue before releasing them. "My love."

"Wow." He wraps his arms around me and kisses me tenderly. "It feels so good to hear you say those words."

Joy bubbles and fizzes through my veins like champagne, leaving me so giddy and light I could float away if not for Nick's anchoring embrace.

"I thought it would be hard to do. But it's so easy." I kiss his eyelids, his nose. "It feels right."

With a firm hand between my shoulder blades, he presses my heart to his. His hairy chest tickles my nipples. "More?" he murmurs into my hair.

"Food first. Aren't you starving after all that work?"

"When you're naked, I forget petty concerns like hunger." Sitting up, he reaches for the picnic basket. "But if my lady is hungry, she shall be fed. If the cat's left us anything."

While I set out our delayed picnic, he pours us each a glass of wine. "Let's see," he says, raising his glass, "what shall we drink to?"

"To…a fruitful partnership."

We clink, and he whispers his fingertips over my belly. "Fruitful?"

I dissolve into laughter. "I was actually thinking of the bookshop, but that too."

Nick holds my gaze for a long, loaded moment, then sets down his glass, rises to his knees, and cups my face in both his hands. "Clara, had I known, I would have planned something worthy of the occasion." Grinning, he cocks an eyebrow. "Though it's hard to beat a naked candlelit picnic in a room full of sexy books."

A shiver seizes me as I realize what's happening. I can barely hear his tender words over my thundering pulse.

"I love you, Clara. You make me happier than I ever thought possible. I want to share the rest of my life with you. Will you marry me?"

I hold my breath and close my eyes as Jared's words ring in my memory:

Follow your heart.

Home, family, partnership, love. We've both been through the hell of loss, and now we get a second chance.

Joyful tears spill down my cheeks. This is crazy fast, impossibly deep, and potentially the most foolish decision I've ever made—or the wisest. But the tingling warmth filling my chest leaves no room for doubt.

Sliding my fingers into Nick's rumpled curls, I pull him to me and brush a whisper-soft kiss across his lips.

"Yes, Nick. I will."

Epilogue

Clara

Three months later

The brass bell above the bookshop door tinkles as Nick rushes in, dripping wet from the heavy autumn rain. He shakes his head, sending drops flying. As always, Lulu dashes to greet him.

"Hey, Puss-Face." He sheds his drenched coat and scoops her up with one hand while holding out a wrapped package with the other. His dark eyes sparkle, and a wide smile stretches across his luscious mouth. "It's here, my love. Your advance reader copy."

"Really? This is it?" I take the parcel, squeeze him tight with my free arm, then rip the wrapping paper away. "The cover's magnificent!" I squeal.

Gleaming bronze surrounds a helmeted Greek warrior sporting a proud erection. He reaches for a nude maiden, demurely clutching a cloak to her breast. The title is perfect.

Eternal Erotic Dreams: from Ancient Temples to Modern Fantasy.

Margot's lightning-rod earrings tinkle as she peers over our shoulders. "Looks like you two. Congratulations, Professor." She pushes the cart of new books down the aisle and calls out, "Oh yeah! Got an email from Harry. He'll be back from Australia in time for the wedding."

Nick squeezes my arm. "Check out the inscription."

The dedication page bears a single line: *To Clara, bringer of light, and keeper of the red door.*

Flushed with pride and pleasure, I kiss his cheek, then flip through the pages. Nick's book features erotic art from earliest Phoenicia all the way to 1940s pin-ups and modern black and white photos, with scholarly commentary on changing ideals of sexual attractiveness. Behind our red door, Nick found just what he needed to complete his research. News of his project has spread on campus, too, boosting enrollment in his classes at the U of O.

Enid, his former boss, was right—this sexy book has been a real career boost for Nick.

I spent hours helping him with "editorial feedback," which is what we called it when his page mock-ups inspired us to try the depicted poses—with delicious results.

Nick pats my still-flat belly. "Are you sure your wedding dress will fit by the time Harry gets back?"

I smooch his bearded cheek. He's let his scruff grow fuller at my request, and Nick in a beard is indescribably sexy. "Absolutely. I picked a flowy design, and I'm only two months along. Is Bella ready to be our flower girl?"

"Calista says she carries her practice basket everywhere, scattering bits of toilet paper all over the house."

We hired a team to tame the jungle surrounding Nick's place, revealing a lovely, rose-lined garden complete with an arbor where we'll exchange vows.

We would have married sooner, but there's been no time to plan a wedding, what with selling my apartment, moving into Nick's house, and planning the bookshop/café's grand re-opening. Fortunately, the increased customer traffic and updated website are generating enough income to hire more part-time help.

I slide my arm through my fiancé's. "You sure you're okay with Dalton attending the wedding?"

"I'm sure." He quirks a half-smile. "As long as he doesn't try to kiss the bride."

"No worries. His new girlfriend has all his attention these days." Laurel's arrival in Eugene has soothed the tension between Nick and Dalton, as well as providing me with a valuable new employee.

"So," Nick asks with a flirtatious eyebrow waggle, "how many copies should we order for the red room?"

"I've cleared a whole shelf. It'll be our top seller, I'm sure. In fact, we should plan a launch party." I goose his muscular behind. "This book will make so many couples happy, Eugene will probably name a street after you."

Nick presses a sweet kiss to my forehead. "Thank you, love."

"For what?"

"For taking a chance on me. For listening to your heart instead of your fear."

I lace my fingers at the small of his back and rest my chin against his chest. "Want to hear something weird?"

"Absolutely."

"I think Jared and Diana steered us together."

With Nick's help, I've finally reached the point where I can talk about Jared without sadness. In a way I can't quite explain, I know he's still with me, happy to see me basking in the warmth of my new family.

Watching over the bookshop we built, Jared's photo smiles at me from the desk Nick and I now share. Beside him sits a framed picture of Nick's Diana, a sturdy blonde with a mischievous grin, leaning on her rowing oar. I like to think she and Jared are friends in the great whatever-comes-next, watching over Nick and me as we grow Book Nirvana together.

And a third, more recent photo shares space with our lost loves: a candid shot of us embracing at our housewarming party, surrounded by friends and family as we toast our new life together.

Squeezing me tighter, Nick rests his chin atop my head. "Tell me again why you picked me."

He never gets tired of hearing this.

Chuckling, I pat his chest. "Because you're so pretty, my Greek god. Because you stood by my side when I needed you, and you're kind to my friends, even to Dalton. Because you're brilliant, and funny, and your touch takes my breath away. Because you pulled me out of darkness and into a bright, happy new life." I wind my arms around his neck. "S'agapó, Nick."

Happiness sparkles in his dark eyes. "And I love you for learning Greek, for having our baby, for opening your heart to a horny old pest, for making a home with me." And he kisses me, right in the middle of the shop. Customers swirl around us, ignoring our giggling embrace.

Until a little boy with huge brown eyes tugs on my skirt.

"Book Lady, read me a story?"

His mother flashes an apologetic smile. "Jared, the book lady has to work."

"And this is my favorite part of the job." With a pat on Nick's butt, I send him on his way. "Come on." I take the little one's hand. "You pick out a book."

Thanks for reading Nick and Clara's story! Don't worry—Dalton finds his HEA in ***Runaway Love Story: Book Nirvana 2,*** coming March, 2025, and Margot's turn comes in ***Love, Art, and Other Obstacles: Book Nirvana 3*** coming April, 2025.

Want to spend a little more time in Book Nirvana? For my newsletter subscribers, I've compiled the story behind the story: the real-life inspiration that sparked ***Through the Red Door,*** research on Clara's naughty books (for adults only), and one very spicy deleted scene. To claim your copy, visit sadirastone.com and look for the Newsletter Subscriber Bonuses page.

Read on for more books by Sadira Stone. But first...

Reviews are the lifeblood of hard-working authors like me, so if you enjoyed ***Through the Red Door***, I'd be so thrilled and grateful if you'd leave a review—even a line or two about what you enjoyed helps so much! Just find the book's retail page on your favorite online bookseller's site and find "Leave/Write a Customer Review" – usually located near the stars or book title. Thank you from the bottom of my heart! Extra virtual smooches for reviews on Goodreads and Bookbub.

Book by Sadira Stone

♥

Next in the **Book Nirvana** series: ***Runaway Love Story,*** coming March 2025.

Wrong time, wrong place, perfect guy.

Laurel

Fired again, and now darling Maxie needs my help. That San Francisco art gallery job will have to wait. I'm stuck in Eugene, Oregon, rescuing the auntie who rescued me.

Running into Dalton ignites a sweet flirtation that quickly turns spicy. He's almost perfect: a beloved teacher and coach, wise and funny, and so compassionate with Maxie.

But he wants lasting love, and I'm only passing through. No matter how much I crave him, I can't let him derail my dreams.

Dalton

Between my scheming ex and Mom's dementia, this is the worst summer break ever—until Laurel.

Though she stubbornly denies her artistic gift, she's brilliant, stunning, forthright, and the spark between us grows hotter each time we meet. But she's clinging to big-city dreams, and I can't leave my hometown.

When a social media post about our budding love goes viral, Laurel's insecurities flare. To keep her from running away, I'll have to convince her how brightly she can shine right here.

Come to Book Nirvana for a spicy, funny, heart-wrenching tale of true love and second chances.

Runaway Love Story was previously published and has been revised and updated with new chapters.

And don't miss Book Nirvana 3: ***Love, Art, and Other Obstacles*, coming April 2025**
I can't help craving my rival.
Margot
Who needs family? On the cusp of launching my graphic arts career, I'm all about freedom—no fences, no limits, and no more bigoted family weighing me down. Between college, work at Book Nirvana, and a high-stakes art competition, I barely have time for my part-time girlfriend, much less a flirtation with my competitor, even if his cocky, ginger-bearded hotness makes me question my "no strings" rule.

Elmer
Family is everything, and I've found my family of the heart in the Eugene, Oregon art scene. But something is missing ...until Margot, my rival for an art grant we both desperately need. That prickly little sprite lights me up body and soul, but she fears I'm out to clip her wings. I'm not made to share my heart with more than one, and falling for Margot could wreck me.

Come to Book Nirvana for a red-hot love triangle that forces two young artists to redefine success, family, and freedom.

Love, Art, and Other Obstacles was previously published and has been revised and updated with new chapters.

Bangers Tavern Romance Series

Come to BangersTavern for super-steamy rom-coms featuring chosen family, diverse characters, creative cocktails, and the best tater tots in Tacoma. Four full-length novels and one novella each deliver a satisfying HEA and an unforgettable holiday bash in the neighborhood bar that feels like home. One night in Bangers, and you'll want to return again and again!

Trappers Cove Romance Series

Welcome to Trappers Cove, a quirky Washington State beach town nestled among the pines. Here you'll find steamy, small-town, grownup romance , laughter and tears, heart-warming chosen family, Madame Zora's Psychic Emporium, and all the best beachy fun!

For bookish news, reader exclusives, and romance freebies, visit sadirastone.com and sign up for Sadira's bi-monthly reader newsletter.

About the author

Award-winning contemporary romance author Sadira Stone spins steamy, smoochy tales set in small businesses—a quirky bookstore, a neighborhood bar, a vintage boutique. Set in the U.S. Pacific Northwest, her stories highlight found family, friendship, and the sizzling chemistry that pulls unlikely partners together. When she emerges from her writing cave in Las Vegas, Nevada (which she seldom does), she can be found shaking her hips in dance class, playing her guitar (badly, but getting better), exploring the Western U.S. with her charming husband, cooking up a storm, and gobbling all the romance books. For a guaranteed HEA (and no cliffhangers!) visit Sadira at **sadirastone.com**